T0110129

CHRISTOPH RANSMAYR

THE DOG KING

Christoph Ransmayr was born in 1954 in Austria. He is the author of two previous novels, *The Terrors of Ice and Darkness* and *The Last World,* which was a best-seller in Germany and winner of the Elias Canetti Fellowship and the Franz Kafka Literary Prize. For *The Dog King,* Ransmayr shared with Salman Rushdie Europe's Aristeion Prize in 1996. He currently lives and works in a village outside Dublin, Ireland.

INTERNATIONAL

THE DOG KING

THE DOG KING

CHRISTOPH RANSMAYR

TRANSLATED BY JOHN E. WOODS

VINTAGE INTERNATIONAL

VINTAGE BOOKS

A DIVISION OF RANDOM HOUSE, INC.   NEW YORK

The Library of Congress has cataloged the Knopf edition as follows:
Ransmayr, Christoph. [date]
[Morbus Kitahara. English]
The dog king / Christoph Ransmayr; translated by John E. Woods.

p. cm.
ISBN 0-679-45057-2.—ISBN 978-0-679-76860-9 (pbk.)
I. Woods, John E. (John Edwin) II. Title.
PT2678.A65M6713   1997
833'.914—dc21   96-39160
CIP

Book design by Cassandra Pappas

www.randomhouse.com

BVG 001
146712470

For Fred Rotblatt
and in memory of my father,
Karl Richard Ransmayr

CONTENTS

THE DOG KING

CHAPTER I

A FIRE IN THE OCEAN

T WO BODIES LAY BLACKENED IN THE
Brazilian January. A fire that for days now had leapt
through an island's wilderness, leaving charred corridors
behind, had freed the corpses from a tangle of blossoming lianas
and also burned the clothes from their wounds—two men in the
shade of an overhanging rock. They lay a few yards apart
wrenched to inhuman poses among stumps of ferns. A red rope
that bound them together guttered in the embers.

The blaze swept across the dead men, erased eyes and facial
features, moved on crackling, returned once more in the draft of
its own heat and danced on the decaying shapes—until a cloudburst drove the flames into the iron-gray ashes of toppled
quaresma trees, finally forcing all the heat into the moist heart of
their trunks. There the fire burned out.

And so a third corpse was spared incineration. A good distance
from the remains of the men, a woman lay under dangling roots
and swaying fronds. Her small body had been minced by hacking
beaks, the fare of beautiful birds; had been gnawed until it was a
labyrinth for beetles, larvae, and flies that crept and buzzed about

3

this grand repast, battled over it—a panoply of silky, lustrous wings and armor, a festival.

At the same time, an airplane was tracing rumbling loops above the Bahia de São Marcos, although gathering storm clouds repeatedly forced it to turn back toward Cabo do Bom Jesus. Scarcely ten nautical miles from the Atlantic coast, the pilot, a surveyor, spotted that rocky, surfbound island across which the brushfire's ribbons strayed now here, now there—a crazy, smoky path through the wilderness. The surveyor flew over the devastation twice and concluded his radio message, amid hisses of atmospheric interference, with the same word written beneath the island's name on his map: *Deserto*. Uninhabited.

CHAPTER 2

THE CRIER FROM MOOR

B ERING WAS A CHILD OF WAR AND KNEW
only peace. Whenever talk turned to the hour of his
birth, he was told to remember that he had cried his first
cry during Moor's only night of bombs. It was a rainy night in
April, shortly before the signing of the armistice that in postwar
schoolrooms was still just called the Peace of Oranienburg.

A bomber squadron heading toward the Adriatic coast that
night had dropped the rest of its fiery burden into the darkness
above Moor's lake. Bering's mother, her legs swollen from preg-
nancy, was carrying a sack of horsemeat home from the black-
market slaughterhouse. The soft meat, barely drained of its
blood, lay heavy in her arms, which made her think of her husband's belly—when she saw a huge fist of fire rise into the sky
above the plane trees along the lakeshore, then another . . . and
left her sack behind in the lane and began to run madly toward
the burning town.

The heat from the biggest fire she had ever seen had already
singed her eyebrows and hair, when suddenly from out of a black
house two arms grabbed hold and dragged her into the depths of

a cellar. There she wept until a contraction took her breath away.

Among mildewed barrels, then, and several weeks too soon, she brought her second son into a world that seemed to have reverted to the age of volcanoes—nights when the earth flickered beneath a red sky. By day, clouds of phosphorus obscured the sun, and in wastelands of rubble the inhabitants of caves hunted pigeons, lizards, and rats. Rains of ash fell. And Bering's father, the blacksmith of Moor, was far away.

Years later that same father, deaf to the terrors of the night his son was born, would frighten his family by describing what he, *he* had suffered during the war. Bering's throat would go dry and his eyes burned each time, each of the many times, he heard how as a soldier his father had been so thirsty that on the twelfth day of battle he had drunk his own blood. It was in the Libyan desert. It was at Halfayah Pass. The shock wave from a tank grenade had hurled his father to the hot gravel. And there in the blazing desert, a red, strangely cool trickle had suddenly run down his father's face, and jutting his chin like a monkey and puckering his lips, he had begun to slurp, distraught and disgusted at first, but then with growing greed—this spring would save him. He returned from the desert with a wide scar on his forehead.

Bering's mother prayed a lot. Even when the war and its dead sank deeper into the earth with each passing year and finally vanished under fields of beets and lupines, she still heard the booming of artillery in summer thunderstorms. And on many nights the Virgin appeared to her, just as She had back then, whispering prophecies to her and news of Paradise. When Mary had faded and Bering's mother stepped to the window to ease the fever of the visitation, she saw the lake's unlighted shores and fallow hills that rolled in black waves toward even blacker mountain ranges.

Bering lost both his brothers: the younger one dead, drowned in a bay of Moor's lake, where he had been diving in the icy water for "teeth," for a disbanded army's scuttled ammunition overgrown with red algae and freshwater mussels, for copper projectiles that he would pound with stones to remove the casings and, after drilling a hole into each, would wear like a string of fangs around his neck. The oldest brother was lost as well, had emigrated to somewhere in the forests of upstate New York. The last news they had of him, years ago, was a picture postcard of the Hudson River, whose gray flood always reawakened sorrow for the drowned boy, too.

On the anniversary of her son's drowning, when Bering's mother would set a garland of blue anemones and wooden bowls filled with wax adrift on the lake, there was always one such floating candle for Celina as well, the Polish woman who had stood beside her during that night of bombs.

Celina, who had been deported from Podolia and conscripted for forced labor, had fled that night into the dirt cellar of a burning vineyard and dragged Bering's mother with her to safety. When the blacksmith's wife screamed at the sudden onset of labor, Celina had prepared her a bed of gunnysacks and damp cardboard between oaken barrels, then had cut the newborn's umbilical cord with an apron string and her teeth, had washed him in wine.

While from the world above only the crash and tremor of impact found its way into depths barely lit by suet candles, the Polish woman held mother and child in her arms, prayed loudly to the Black Madonna of Częstochowa, and drank more and more of the half-fermented wine, until along with her fervent prayers and litanies she began to pass judgment on the past few years:

This night's firestorm was the Madonna's punishment for Moor having flung its men into war, for letting them march in terrible armies to Szonowice, and even to the Black Sea and to Egypt. It was retribution for the order that sent Jerzy, her fiancé in the cavalry, to storm tanks beside the river Bug—and then had come the barrage . . . his beautiful hands . . . his beautiful face . . . ,

Queen of Heaven!

Punishment for the charred ruins of Warsaw and for stonemason Bugaj, who together with his family and neighbors had been herded into the woodyard where Szonowice's charcoal was burned, then made to shovel their own graves,

Madonna, Comforter of the Afflicted!

Revenge for her ravished sister-in-law Krystyna,

Refuge of Sinners!

And for Silberschatz, the sexton from Ozenna . . . The poor man had hidden in a lime pit for two years, until someone betrayed him and he was found and thrown into the lime pit at Treblinka for all eternity,

Queen of Mercy!

Atonement! for the ashes on Polish soil and for the meadows of Podolia trodden to mud . . .

And Celina the Pole was still weeping and lamenting long after the world above had turned as silent as death and Bering's mother had fallen asleep exhausted.

The men of Moor, Celina whispered into the baby's tiny fists, pressing them again and again to her mouth to kiss them, the men of Moor had risen up against the whole world—and in its fury the world with all its living and dead would come storming across the fields in a Last Judgment: angels with flaming swords, Kalmyks from the steppes of Russia, hordes of troubled souls deprived of their mortal remains without consolation of the Church, ghosts! . . . And fierce Polish uhlans on charging steeds, and Jews from the Holy Land, their munition belts and bayonets jangling, and all those who had nothing more to lose and no other faith to embrace than faith in revenge,

Amen.

In the end, Celina Kobro from Szonowice in Podolia, shipped to Moor to do forced labor, became its first casualty, when four days later she died beneath the bullets of a victorious battalion sweeping down over the town. It was a misunderstanding. A frightened infantryman mistook the bundled-up figure of the Polish woman, who was leading a horse through the darkness, for a sniper, for an escaping foe, shouted "Stop!" and "Don't move!" twice to no avail in an unintelligible language—and shot.

The very first burst of fire hit Celina in the chest and neck and wounded the horse. Celina had wrapped the old nag's muzzle and hooves in rags and was quietly leading the unclaimed animal out of the occupied town in order to hide it in a stand of firs, thus saving it from requisition or slaughter—the horse was *her* booty. Lamed, it hobbled off into the night, while Celina lay there on mossy stones and heard the approaching infantryman's rapid strides only as the distant, strangely solemn sound of her death: the rustling of leaves, breaking twigs, a deep, profoundly deep breath—and finally that suppressed cry, the private's curse, after which every sound died away and fell back forever into silence.

Celina was buried the next morning near the train station, beneath charred acacias and next to a miner from Moor Quarry, a Georgian prisoner of war who had starved to death a few hours after the victors marched into town.

In Moor, citizens were driven from their homes. The farmsteads of defeated partisans of the war burned. In Moor, once-feared quarry overseers had to endure every humiliation in silence: seven days after liberation—it was a cold Friday—two of them were dangling from wire rope.

In Moor, chickens and scrawny pigs were chased across sooty fields and Heroes' Square as moving targets for rifle practice, and their carcasses were left for the dogs—in starving Moor. . . . And all the suddenly outmoded medals, decorations, and heroic busts, wrapped now in flags and discarded uniforms, went up in flames or were sunk to the bottom of cesspits, vanished into attics, cellar hideaways, and hastily dug holes. In Moor, the victors ruled. And whatever complaints about their rule might be lodged at their headquarters, the answers and decisions of the occupying forces were generally just an ugly reminder of the cruelty of the army in which Moor's men had served and obeyed.

True, these were not the riders of the Last Judgment who moved through the town on mud-caked packhorses and stared down out of tank hatches and from open-roofed troop transporters, not the avenging angels and ghosts of Celina's

prophecies—all the same, the first in a series of foreign commandants who moved into the community hall, converted now to
headquarters, was a colonel from the district of Krasnoyarsk, a
flaxen-haired Siberian with watery eyes, who could not forget the
dead in his own family, moaned in his troubled dreams, and gave
orders to shoot on sight anything that moved in Moor's alleys
and yards during what seemed like randomly imposed curfews.

The war was over. But during just that first year of peace,
Moor, so remote from battlefields, would see more soldiers than
in all the drab centuries of its previous history. So that at times it
seemed as if Moor's hilly landscape encircled by mountains was
not simply the site for a strategic deployment of forces, but as if
the world's concentrated power had chosen, of all places, this
remote spot for some equally monstrous and chaotic maneuver.
During that first year, the occupation zones of six different
armies overlapped and crisscrossed in Moor's battered fields and
vineyards, in its deserted farmyard lanes and boggy meadows that
swallowed a man's every step.

On the wall map at headquarters, Moor's hilly region resembled nothing so much as a sample page of capitulation.
Negotiations among competing victors were forever defining and
distorting lines of demarcation, transferring valleys and streets
from the mercy of one general to the despotism of another,
dividing up cratered landscapes, moving mountains. . . . And
next month's conference would then come to entirely new and
different decisions. For two weeks at one point, Moor suddenly
ended up a gaping no-man's-land between armies, was evacu-
ated—and reoccupied. Bering's farmstead likewise remained tied
in a knot of transient borders—and yet was never anything more
than a wretched bit of booty: a sooty forge, an empty stall, a
sheep meadow, fallow fields.

And if for the first two weeks of the armistice it had been only
the Siberians of the colonel from Krasnoyarsk who held Moor
under their control, after they departed a Moroccan battery
under French command marched into the town. May arrived,

but the year remained cold. The Moroccans butchered two milch cows hidden in the ruins of Moor's sawmill, unrolled their prayer rugs on the pavement outside headquarters, and to the incredulous horror of Bering's mother no bolt struck from out of the blue when an *African* shot the cemetery chapel's Madonna off her gilded wooden cloud.

The battery stayed on into summer. It was followed by a regiment of Scottish Highlanders, Gaelic sharpshooters, who at least once a week celebrated the anniversary of yet another unforgotten battle with a trooping of the colors, bagpipe music, and black beer. Finally, when the few cultivated fields had already been harvested and again lay as dark and barren in the frost as the rest of the land, an American company relieved the Highlanders—and the regime of a major from Oklahoma began.

Major Elliot was a willful man. He ordered a full-length mirror screwed to the front door at headquarters, and he would ask everyone from the occupied zone who arrived with a petition or a complaint what or who he had seen in the mirror before entering. If he was in a rage or bad mood, he kept asking the same sequence of questions, bored away until the petitioner finally described what the commandant wanted to hear: a pig's head, a sow's bristles and hooves.

With Major Elliot, however, Moor would not only be subjected to strange punishments—humiliations that the defeated population finally came to accept as incomprehensible lunacies—but it would also see a noticeable improvement. In place of the savage and random revenge of passing troops or prisoners freed from the labor camp, there was now the martial law of a victorious army. During the first winter of peace, hardly a day passed without at least one new decree issued to deal with the threatening chaos—laws against plundering, sabotage, or pilfering coal. A skinny sergeant, a fan of baseball and nineteenth-century German poets, translated paragraph after paragraph of the new penal code into a strange bureaucratese and then posted his work on the bulletin board at headquarters.

While the town of his birth grew poorer each day, Bering, swaddled in shredded flags, lay in a swaying clothes basket suspended from a beam, lay there and cried—a gaunt baby plagued by scabies, lay helpless, reeking of milk and spittle—and grew. And even if Moor should perish, the son of the blacksmith lost somewhere in the desert grew tougher with each new day. He cried and was nursed, cried and was carried, cried and was kissed and cradled in the arms of the blacksmith's wife, who passed many nights keeping his basket in motion and imploring the Madonna to let her husband return. As if contact with the earth terrified him, the baby could not bear any fixed spot and raged wide-eyed if his exhausted mother took him from the basket and brought him with her to bed. Try as she might to soothe and reassure him, he cried.

It was dark during Bering's first year. Well into the Peace of Oranienburg, both windows of his chamber stayed boarded shut—at least this room, the only one in the blacksmith's house whose walls bore no cracks or traces of fire from Moor's night of bombs, was going to remain safe from plunderers and whizzing shrapnel. There were still mines out in the fields. And so Bering rocked, floated, sailed away through his darkness and listened sometimes to the cracked voices of three hens rising from the depths below him—they had been rescued from the forge's burning stall on the night of bombs and finally locked up along with all other valuables inside this one undamaged room.

In Bering's darkness, the clucking and scrabbling of these hens in their wire cage was always louder than the din of the locked-out world. Even the rumble of tanks maneuvering in the meadow—once the sound found its way through the nailed-down planks—seemed muffled and very remote. Bering, a flier among caged birds, seemed to love these chickens—and sometimes he would even cease his desperate cries when, with a sudden jerk and blink, one of the birds would raise its voice.

Whenever his mother set out to go from farm to farm—and sometimes to other villages, for days on end—to trade screws, horseshoe nails, and even the blacksmith's welding tools hidden in the cellar, for bread, meat, or a glass of moldy jam, Bering was watched over by his brother, a jealous, foul-tempered teenager, who hated this screeching bundle. His brother frightened moths and cockroaches out from behind the wallboards and in helpless rage tore the insects to pieces; he plucked threadlike legs, one after the other, from the plates of beetles and tossed their maimed bodies to the chickens beneath the baby's basket—and having fed the birds, would then set them in panic with a candle flame. Never stirring, Bering listened to these voices of fear.

Even years later, it took only a single cry of a cock to awaken in him the most puzzling feelings. Often it was a melancholy, helpless anger directed at nothing in particular, and yet it bound him to his hometown better than any other human or animal sound could.

When, one snowy February morning, after a quiet hour of spellbound listening, her baby began to cry again, Bering's mother took it as a sign from heaven and, horrified, she bore the hens' cage from the room—for the voice was like a chicken's squawk. The crier was clucking like a laying hen! The crier rowed with his arms, and from his basket were stretched little white fingers cramped into claws. And hadn't he raised his head with a jerk, too?

The crier wanted to be a bird.

CHAPTER 3

A TRAIN STATION
BY THE LAKE

WHEN MOOR'S BLACKSMITH, NO LONGER a prisoner of war, returned home from Africa that stark autumn, Bering could say about three dozen words, but with greater enthusiasm he could cry recognizable imitations of several birdcalls—he *was* a chicken, was a collared dove, was a screech-owl. This was in the second year of peace.

The news, scribbled on an army postcard, that his father would soon be arriving had brought changes to the forge: in return for a loaf of bread, a Moravian refugee plastered cracks and whitewashed walls, and the windows of Bering's room were open again at last, the nails removed. The noise of the world now found its way to him undiminished. He cried in pain. It was his hearing, the Moravian said as he covered traces of the fire, his broom dripping lime—the boy's ears were too sensitive. His hearing was too delicate.

As always, Bering cried inconsolably—and indeed it was as if he were *fleeing* into his own voice, as if his voice were his defense . . . yes, as if his own cries were more bearable and less shrill and piercing than the clamor of the world outside those open windows. But long before he had taken his first step into that world, the crier seemed to have sensed that for someone with delicate hearing the voice of a bird offered a much better refuge than the crude bellowing of a human being. Between the lows and highs of animal song lay all the peace and security you could yearn for in a ramshackle house.

The whitewashed rooms were scarcely dry when the Moravian refugee departed, leaving behind an odor of foul water—and a quieted child. Bering's mother had taken the Moravian's advice, had paid him two glasses of schnapps for wax plugs that he claimed were formed from tears shed by candles at Meteora—the healing candles of the rockbound monasteries of Meteora! And now whenever her son cried, she stopped his ears.

Moor's blacksmith arrived on the day of harvest home, on a transport train infected with dysentery. In the ruins of the train station by the lake, a great press of people waited for the released prisoners. A sullen uneasiness spread along the platforms. Rumors from the countryside around the lake claimed this transport would be the last train to arrive in Moor before the railroad line was shut down.

It was a day hung with clouds, the first frost was on the fields, and the chill stank of burnt stubble. In the stillness of October, the thud of the approaching steam engine was audible long before the pennant of smoke they longed to see appeared above the poplars lining the carp pond—now it crept toward the lake.

Deep in the crowd was Bering, a scrawny child barely eighteen months old, holding his mother's hand, invisible among legs, coats, and shoulders merging and parting again above him, but he heard the gasps of the engine long before all the others and listened spellbound. Coming ever nearer was a puzzling breathing he had never heard before.

The train that finally pulled into the bombed-out shell of the station at a crawl consisted of four closed cattle cars and at first glance looked like those trains of misery that had rolled into

Moor Quarry during the war years—usually at dawn and crammed with captured *enemies* and conscripts for forced labor. The same groans came from inside this train's cars when it was shunted onto the sidetrack by the shore and came to a screeching metallic stop at the bumping-post. The stench was the same, too, when the sliding doors stood open at last. Except this time there were no heavily armed, uniformed overseers and no bellowing military police positioned along the embankments, but only a few bored infantrymen from Major Elliot's company, who were watching the spectacle of arrival, but with no orders to interfere.

As the train stopped, the crowd suddenly came, burst to life. Hundreds of people, released now from years of waiting, pressed around the train as if it were a monstrous animal they had hunted down. A murmur grew to a loud jumble of voices, an uproar. Most of these people were no less emaciated and ragged than the freed prisoners, stumbling now with no baggage from the cars, holding up their hands to shield their eyes from the light. A thicket of arms rolled toward them—a uniform blur of faces barely recognizable in the blinding light. Tattered flowers and photographs, pictures of missing men were held out like trumps in a card game with death. Names were called out, pleas and entreaties:

Have you seen this man, my husband!
Seen my brother, do you know him
Is he with you
He has to be with you
But you've just come from Africa

. . . they shove and push, until those who have now found each other share caresses as they stammer or embrace without speaking and at last take their first steps together away from war—and are suddenly scuffling again to be the first to the waiting room, which has no roof. It is said there is bread there.

Under the waiting room's open sky stands Major Elliot, arms dangling, the town secretary at his side, behind them a brass band without uniforms, which, when the secretary gives the sign, first plays an old, slow tune, and only then a march. It is obvious the band is missing a lot of instruments. Just one clarinet. And no bugle.

Then it grows still. No one out on the platform can recognize whoever that is giving a speech there under those two flags. A pair of loudspeakers on wooden poles carry the words over tracks and heads and far out on the lake.

Welcome ... homeland in ruins ... future ... and take courage!

Who still has ears for words now! Bering feels only the pain of layered shrill tones coming from the loudspeakers, which he takes to be the sound of a single ugly voice.

Once the speaker falls silent, more music, the thin song of a zither, backed by an accordion, the sort of thing heard in taverns before the war; then a woman sings, but has to break off twice, because she's sobbing or sneezing, it isn't clear which.

Musicians, singers, speakers, even Major Elliot himself are finally swallowed up in the crowd. The welcoming ceremony is over. Now bread and powdered milk are doled out to these wretches, a week's ration. The secretary keeps the lists and signs forms. Some of the recipients can no longer stay on their feet; they buckle, sink to their knees. At last each of them may go wherever he pleases, for the first time in years, wherever he pleases. But where?

As if lost in the tumult, the blacksmith's wife stands with Bering on one hand, and his brother on the other—who is angry as always, but keeps quiet for fear of his mother's threats. There is no sound from Bering either. The engine's breathing still roars in his ears.

The blacksmith's wife has not held up a photo. She and her sons were pushed and shoved by the crowd, here and there—any direction would do for her. She knew, wanted to believe more than anything in the world, that this time she would not wait in vain among the blackened walls of Moor's station. She has brought flowers; Bering's brother holds them clenched in his fist. They are cyclamens from the overgrown banks of the millpool.

With her sons on both hands, the blacksmith's wife cannot fight her way through the crowd as the others do. She and he have never raced toward each other, but have always approached each other hesitantly, often in shame and embarrassment. Then the war blew the sand dunes of North Africa—and even dammed up a whole sea—between them. They hardly know each other.

But as in the past, the blacksmith's wife must wait for him this time, too. Deep in the crowd, she has to wait and stand on tiptoe and keep looking until her eyes sting from the cold wind off the lake and tears run down her face.

She is not aware that she is weeping, doesn't hear herself speaking the blacksmith's name, over and over, a charm, a magic formula. Bering is at her side, dazed by this first crowd of his life and by the racing pulse he feels in the hand holding his.

Once the bread is doled out, the skirmish for returnees grows easier, almost festive; little groups separate from the throng, hugging and even laughing now; horse-drawn wagons pull up—a truck, too. Elliot's soldiers wrest a forbidden flag from a grumbling driver, rip it up, shove the man into their jeep. Hardly anyone seems to notice. Only the arrested man's mud-caked, scraggly dog circles the vehicle, barking and jumping and snapping at his master's foes, and stops only after one of the soldiers whacks its skull with his rifle butt.

Immeasurable,

immeasurable the time that must pass until the shoulders and heads in the sky above Bering fly away and the crowd thins out. As if that gasped breathing, which has ceased now, has cleared them a path, Bering suddenly feels his mother's hand tug him away, and his brother with him.

At last the blacksmith's wife can move forward to where several figures are still standing, gray against gray, not mingling with the waiting crowd. Twice she thinks she has discovered that lost face, that familiar face, which is then twice transformed into the face of a stranger, until after an eternity, not ten feet away, there the blacksmith stands before her. Only now does her heartbeat rob her of all her strength, and she realizes that she was already prepared for failure.

The blacksmith is a thin man, who has stopped in his tracks so suddenly that the man behind him bumps into him hard. He holds against the blow and looks at her. He has a beard. His face has black spots. She has remembered him just like this and yet so different. She knows about the scar on his forehead from a letter sent from the field. But it terrifies her now. What kind of war was it that he had been lost inside it for so long and has come back to her now like *this*? She no longer knows. Half the world has perished with Moor, that she knows, and also that, along with Celina the Pole and the four cows from their stall, half of humanity has vanished into the earth or gone up in flames— Holy Mary! But he is the only one of all those who vanished who has ever held her in his arms. And he has returned.

His sons are afraid. The brother claims no longer to remember that man there, and Bering has never seen him before now. His sons clutch tightly to their mother's hands, who has no free arms like the others, those happy women in the ruins of the station.

So they stare at one another, the sons at the terrible stranger, the stranger at the mother, at the brother, at Bering. Each is silent. And then the stranger does something that makes Bering gape his mouth wide for a cry of terror. The thin man points at *him*, is beside him in two long strides, reaches for him with both hands, lifts him away from his mother, lifts him up to himself.

Bering senses that the breathing he heard in the distance must come from this man. And before him now he sees the scar on the blacksmith's forehead, the wound that has surely made that man there so thin and makes him gasp for breath; and at eye level now with his father he cries for help, cries words that are meant to tell his mother there behind him what is terrible about this man, he cries,

Bleeds!

he cries,

Stinks!

and squirms in the arms of the thin man and knows that no words can help him. His mother is a mere shadow far behind him. He floats there like that, catches three breaths, four, and suddenly feels a tug that rips his cry in two, feels a hammering that hurls the tatters of his voice high up into his head, and from his own mouth he hears again at last that other, protective voice that bore him through the darkness of his first year. And in his father's arms he begins to cackle! to cackle like a crazed, panicked chicken, waving its arms, its wings, a bird that is frightened to death, so that the thin man finally can hold on to it no longer. He drops fluttering toward the earth.

CHAPTER 4

THE STONY SEA

THREE WEEKS AFTER THE BLACKSMITH returned home, the Freedom Train was still standing at the bumping-post. The stench of urine and shit drifted from the open sliding doors of the cattle cars, and pigeons cooed in the fetid straw; refugees lying in wait along the embankment hunted them with slingshots and nets. These were days when the first ice sparkled in the deep ruts of the road to the lake, when peddlers banged on shutters and doors, yet behind the rolled-down grille of Moor's grocery only withered bunches of lavender swayed in the draft—and when Major Elliot approved the blacksmith's petition and, until further notice, assigned the freed prisoner welding apparatus from army stocks.

The first glimmers and sparks from the reopened forge were followed by ear-splitting hammer blows on axles, stall gratings, and weathervanes; and an iron oak branch, the first item ordered by a newly founded veterans' organization, glowed red as it writhed on the anvil. The blacksmith talked to himself, yammered in his sleep, but sometimes amid the din of work he would abruptly begin to sing, stanzas of army songs and *lalala*, whereas

Bering still bore injuries from being dropped from his father's arms. A turban of hospital bandages now made his face look tiny and truly like a bird's.

For the blacksmith, however, this stained dressing on his son's head was merely a reminder of his days in the desert, and he told stories about wandering dunes that buried demolished convoys beneath them, sat at the kitchen table and conjured up drifting fields of sand spouts that rose up and fell away again within a single second, heralding a storm, and sounded like needles dropping on an earth made of glass. . . . And he described oases where a caravan might find refuge before the murky sun was put out by clouds of sand.

But try as he would to explain the desert to his family, even attempting to imitate a dromedary's grimace or the laugh of hyenas, the thin man in Bering's mother's bed remained so terrifying to the boy that for weeks Bering spoke not a word, could not even manage the sound of a bird.

The train on which the thin man had arrived, nine cars and a tank locomotive, stood week after week in the ruins of Moor's train station like some crazy misrouted stray forgotten by all offices and headquarters—and in the end, it was never again to leave its last stop.

It was a cloudless frosty day, when a column of American sappers who had moved up from the lowlands began dismantling the tracks. As if to signal some special punishment, the first hammer blows fell on a switch-tower infamous among quarry laborers as *The Cross of Moor*. From this tower—its switch hidden among nettles, peppermint, and brambleberries—all trains rolling along the shores of Moor's lake during the war had been divided into *white* and *blind*.

In war and in peace, white trains had brought the same passengers to the lake: spa guests whose breathing whistled, fat sufferers from the gout, fish vendors every Tuesday, and commuters from the lowlands. As the faraway battles went on, there arrived more and more soldiers on leave from the front and severely wounded officers, who spent the final days of their lives on striped lounge chairs under the sunshades of the Grand Hotel. For white trains, the switch was always pulled to the right—anything white rolled down a gentle grade to Moor Station, the last stop.

Blind trains never reached the station. Blind, that meant no windows, meant a train with no markings, no hint of origin or goal. Blind—those were trains of closed freight and cattle cars with prisoners. Only on boarding platforms, in the cabooses, and sometimes on the sooty roofs were people ever visible—overseers, soldiers. For those trains, the switch always clanked to the left. They then rolled downhill, too, toward a dusty shore in the hazy distance—to the quarry's shore.

There was a lovely view of the lake from the railings of the bullet-riddled watchtower beside the switch. Even decades later, as a prisoner of Brazil, Bering would recall that view as the image of his origins: a green fjord seemed to lie there far below, an arm of the sea spraying reflected light. Or was it a river that over the course of eons had burrowed into the rock beneath it and, tamed now, crept through ravines of its own persistence? Between wooded slopes and bare bluffs, this lake wound deep into the mountains, until it battered against the sheer cliffs of an inaccessible wasteland.

Viewed by clear weather from across the expanse of water, the quarry's terraces looked simply like bright, monstrous steps leading from the clouds down to the shore. And up there, somewhere high above the top of this giant granite stairway, high above dust clouds from the blasting, sagging roofs of the barracks by the gravel works, and any traces of all the agonies that had been suffered on the Blind Shore of the lake—high above it all, the wilderness began.

Rising above the quarry, mightier than all else that could be seen of the world from Moor, were the mountains. Every rockslide that poured down out of those icy regions to be lost in its own dust, every gorge, every opening on a ravine with its swarm of jackdaws, led deeper into a labyrinth of stone where all light transformed itself into ash-gray shadows and blue shadows and polychrome shadows of inorganic nature. On the wall map at headquarters the name of these mountains, written across its peaks and meandering contour lines, was edged in red: *The Stony Sea.* Forbidden, inaccessible, all its passes mined, this sea lay between zones of occupation, a bleak no-man's-land buried under glaciers.

When rain showers moved in off the Atlantic, obscuring the view across the lake, the mountains and their snow fields that lasted well into summer could sometimes hardly be distinguished from the advancing bad weather. On days like that, the Stony Sea fused into a two-dimensional barrier of rocks, clouds, and ice—and on that barrier were words indelibly written in Bering's memory:

HERE

ELEVEN THOUSAND NINE HUNDRED

SEVENTY-THREE PEOPLE LIE DEAD

SLAIN BY THE INHABITANTS OF THIS LAND

WELCOME TO MOOR

Major Elliot had conscripted stonemasons and bricklayers to write, to *erect,* this inscription in five monstrous, irregular lines across five terraces no longer worked for their granite—each letter as tall as a man, each letter a freestanding masonry sculpture made from the rubble of the barracks by the gravel works, from the foundations of the watchtowers, from the reinforced concrete fragments of a demolished bunker. . . . Thus, Elliot had transformed not just an abandoned hillside of the quarry, but indeed the whole mountain range into a monument.

Naturally the residents of Moor, Leys, and Haag—of the whole shoreline—tried to obstruct this inscription at the quarry: with letters of protest, declarations of innocence, and a sparsely attended protest march along the lake promenade, even with sabotage. The scaffolding around the letters collapsed twice—the supports had been sawed through, and one night that unbearable number of dead, stretching over 120 feet, was bludgeoned to illegibility.

But Elliot was the commandant. And Elliot was angry and strong enough to carry out his threat that for every additional act of sabotage, new and even worse indictments would be inscribed on cliffs and hillsides, across a line of buildings. And so in the end, there the masonry letters at the quarry stood: huge, rough, whitewashed, and visible from a great distance; stood in closed ranks like Moor's vanished soldiers, stood like columns of slave laborers at roll call, like the victors beneath the hoisted banners of their triumph. And whatever horrible number the inscription recorded, there was no doubt that beneath it, in rubble and in soil matted with the roots of firs and pines, lay the dead from those barracks by the gravel works.

Eleven thousand nine hundred seventy-three—Elliot kept the camp's confiscated death registers, those endless lists of names written in a hand that looked like ornamented knife blades, locked in his safe at headquarters; during his regime, he had them brought out only once a year, on the anniversary of the signing of the Peace of Oranienburg—the first occasion, however, was when the letters at the quarry were being erected. Guarded by military police, the death registers were displayed inside a glass showcase set out on the steamer dock for a whole week, and black flags on the crookneck lamps lining the shore promenade snapped in the wind.

When on the last day they were displayed and the column of sappers moved in to dismantle the Cross of Moor and began transforming the railroad embankment back into a vacant, useless mound, Bering's mother stopped her son's delicate ears with wax—the sound of chains and tracks being ripped from their spikes resounded across the backwater town and far beyond its shores.

Alarmed by this jangling and the sounds of hammer blows,

hundreds of people had gathered on the embankment within an hour. And they kept coming. As far away as in the remote villages of Leys and Haag, people could see columns of smoke from the bonfires of burning creosoted ties torn from Moor's most important link to the lowlands and to the world.

The enraged crowd threatened the soldiers with fists, shouted questions and curses at them. Now, with winter so close, the worst rumors about the railroad being shut down were coming true. Shut down! Moor reduced to a mud road. Moor cut off from the world.

Unmoved, the sappers ripped one piece of track after the other from the embankment and heaved the old iron up onto railroad cars, which were then pulled back one more short distance from the lake. And so a freight train crept back to the lowlands, taking its tracks with it.

Moor's outrage and helplessness appeared only to amuse the detachment. Despite the cold some soldiers cast aside their uniform jackets and shirts as if this were heavy summer work—and revealed tattoos: inky-blue eagle's heads and wings on their biceps and shoulders, blue mermaids, blue skulls, and crossed flaming swords.

One of the tattooed men responded to the crowd's shouts and curses by crossing two crowbars like scissors and then, inside the steadily shrinking space between his detachment and the locals, began to dance. He stamped in a circle, set up a wailing chant, and in a grotesque pantomime pretended the scissors were cutting his throat. With his gaze fixed on his audience, he heightened his wail to a rhythmic scream, in which the people of Moor recognized a broken phrase in their own language: *Off-with-his-head-Off-with-his-head!*

Ith-is-ed! Ith-is-ed! three or four of the dancer's comrades chanted along, banging out the rhythm with pickaxes, shovels, and hammers.

Suddenly a stone flew through the air. And another. In the next few seconds their rage at these tattooed, half-naked men became a hail of whirring embankment gravel that pelted the soldiers. But at the very moment the first stones struck, a sergeant standing guard fired warning shots from his machine gun over the heads of the crowd.

In the abrupt silence that followed the echoes of this burst of fire could be heard the footsteps of the commandant—Major Elliot had sprung down from the boarding platform of a railroad car and pushed the sergeant aside; now he strode out between the hushed crowd and the tattooed men poised for counterattack and began to bellow. Screamed—screamed something about a beginning, about a first step . . . and repeated one strange-sounding word over and over. It was a name never heard before: *Stellamour*.

CHAPTER 5

STELLAMOUR, OR,

THE PEACE OF ORANIENBURG

B ERING WAS SEVEN WHEN HE LOST HIS
bird voices. It happened during a dusty spectacle that
Major Elliot called Stellamour's Party and ordered held
at the quarry four times a year. Among blocks of granite and in
the ruins of the barracks by the gravel works, Moor was supposed
to learn what the heat of a late summer day or the icy cold of a
January morning means for a prisoner who has to endure the seasons in the open air.

In the course of such a *party*, on an August day much like one
of those in the desert, Bering's father collapsed under a massive
load and lay there on his back, trying in vain to get to his feet.

The sight of his father's struggles made the seven-year-old
laugh so hard that it ended in a kind of hysterical game, and he
wriggled alongside this big beetle at the edge of a pond, flung his
arms about, and shrieked until a soldier on guard stopped his
mouth with an apple.

And after this laughing fit, whenever the blacksmith's son
sought refuge in chicken coops or in the shadow of a flock of

ascending birds, he could only whistle, coo, and squawk like a
person merely attempting to imitate a chicken, a thrush, or a
dove—and was never again the bird voice itself. What he did
retain after this loss, however, was the ability to recognize the
rarest birds, even accidental visitors to the lake country, by a
single call: alpine swift, kingfisher, ivory gull, and hen harrier;
little egret, whistling swan, pied wagtail, Leach's petrel, little
bunting . . . During his school days, Bering filled empty columns
in one of the forge's old order-books with their names.

In those days Stellamour's image, a portrait of a smiling bald
man, was available in all sizes; it adorned posters, was hung on
gates, sometimes took the form of a huge mural covering the
entire firewall of some burned-out factory or barracks.

The judge and scholar Lyndon Porter Stellamour, in an easy
chair before a wall of gaily colored books . . .

Stellamour in a white tux, between two columns of the
Capitol in Washington . . .

and Stellamour in a sport shirt, waving with both arms from
the rayed crown of the Statue of Liberty . . .

> *Stella-*
>> *Stella-*
>>> *Stellamour*
>>> *High-court Justice Stellamour*
>> *From Poughkeepsie in the thriving Empire State*
>>> *Empire State New York . . .*

was the refrain back then of a strange hymn—half pop tune, half
nursery rhyme—sung by mixed choruses at the trooping of the
colors and at festive assemblies. Stellamour's name—carefully
spelled out in unheated, drafty schoolrooms, to be scratched then
on slates with chalk, and finally more engraved than written on
wood-pulp paper with fountain pens—had long since become
indelibly preserved in the memories of a new generation. Even
above the entrance gates to rebuilt water mills and newly

founded sugar-beet factories were banners on which the judge's words had been sewn:

Our fields grow the future

But also:

Thou shalt not kill

Since the days when Major Elliot's sappers had torn up the rail line to the lowlands and Moor had vanished from train schedules, the inhabitants of the occupied zones had gradually come to realize, had been *forced* to realize, during a long process of demolition and devastation that Lyndon Porter Stellamour was not simply some new name in the army and regime of the victors, but the sole and true name of retribution.

Moor still remembered quite well, and even after all these years with some outrage, the day on which Elliot had first ordered the villages along the shore to appear at the quarry in closed ranks, for not only was that damned inscription (whose exact wording had long since gone full circle round the lake) to be unveiled that day, but above all—at least that was how the flyers and posters for this first party read—so, too, was Stellamour's peace plan. (It was also said that attendance would be kept and anyone staying away from this festival without a valid excuse was subject to punishment under martial law.)

And so at the prescribed hour a great procession of people, all as filled with hate as they were intimidated, crept toward the quarry. Led by secretaries installed by the army to replace the old mayors and council members who had disappeared into re-education camps, people from around the lake arrived—some walking the abandoned embankment, some bumping in horse-drawn wagons or oxcarts along the narrow gravel road at the foot of the embankment, some rowing skiffs or leaky boats across the lake. It was a muttering, humiliated company, in which even the bravest barely dared to whisper behind his hand that the commandant had gone crazy for good and all.

No doubt about it—only a crazy man governed like this. The blackened walls of the barracks by the gravel works, the ragged spirals of barbed wire, and the rusty antitank barriers were all decorated as if for a garden party. Lanterns dangled from conveyor belts and elbow pipes, mossy blocks of granite wore bouquets of metal flowers and oak-leaf wreaths that the blacksmith had been ordered days before to cut from a roll of tin, and a crane towering up out of the pond was hung with garlands.

"Let him croak," the blacksmith said, tying his boat to the quarry pier, and spat in the water.

"Protect us from him," Bering's mother whispered, and kissed a medallion of the Black Madonna.

Wherever Elliot appeared that day, in his jeep or at the bow of a patrol boat, vulgar gestures were made behind his back. But as twilight set the lanterns aglow and the five inscribed terraces of the quarry were lit with torches as tall as men, the villagers did indeed stand in long, silent rows and stared at the veiled message, stared at the panels of fabric in the garish colors of war. Sewn together from hundreds of cloths and rags, uniform shirts, grimy camouflage canvas, and Moor's old flags, these banners billowed in the wind like waves leaping and plunging across the masonry letters.

Here eleven thousand nine hundred seventy-three people lie dead. For Bering, who stood among the people of Moor that night and was thrilled by each element of the unveiling ceremony but knew nothing about the meaning of the inscription, it looked as if crazy people were running about under these tossing cloth banners with arms held high, trying to find some open path, some way back into the world.

But then it was only just the commandant who stepped out into the bright cone of a spotlight in front of the veiled monument and mutely gave the sign. Now the panels dropped into damp sand and puddles and fluttered awhile until they were sopping wet and finally lay still.

The columns were silent. More than three thousand people were assembled, but the only sounds came from the lake, gusts of wind, crackling torches. Monstrous, whitewashed, and visible at

a great distance, the inscription floated above their heads and cast
a tangle of lurching shadows in the quarry basin.

The commandant strolled up and down in front of the
masonry letters of WELCOME from the L to the C to the O and M
and back again, and the cone of light followed him. Suddenly he
turned toward the columns, waved a funnel-shaped roll of papers
in his fist, as if he were trying to shoo flies, and shouted: "Back!
Back, all of you! Back to the Stone Age!"

Uncomprehending, weary from the long journey and from
standing so long, the columns of people gazed up at the gesticulating figure and did not grasp that what Elliot's voice was
bawling at them from a dozen loudspeakers tied to branches and
poles, was Stellamour's message.

Now Elliot smoothed out the pages, which kept rolling back
up again the moment he let go, held them up close to his eyes,
and began to read aloud the paragraphs of a peace plan at such
great speed that the rows of people could make out only scraps of
sentences, foreign words—but above all the curses and commen-
tary with which Elliot constantly interrupted the formal tone:

Riffraff! . . . work the fields . . . haystacks, not bunkers—
it crackled and hissed from the loudspeakers—*no more factories,
no turbines, no railroads, no steelworks . . . armies of shepherds
and farmers . . . re-education and conversion: of warmongers into
swineherds and asparagus diggers! And of generals into carters of
manure . . . back to the fields! . . . with oats and barley among the
ruins of industry . . . cabbage heads, dunghills . . . and steaming
cow-pies in the lanes of your autobahn, where potatoes will grow
next spring! . . .*

With a harangue that followed paragraph 22, Elliot broke off
his speech as suddenly and angrily as he had begun it, crumpled
the pages of the peace plan into a ball, and threw it at the feet of
the man next to him—it was his adjutant.

That evening the assembly concluded with neither band music
nor hymns. The columns were made to stand and stand there in
the silence, until the last torch had burnt out and the white-

washed letters loomed pale in the darkness. Only then did the commandant send the villagers out into the night.

The following week the power station on the river was shut down; the turbines, even transformers at the relay stations, were carted off on Russian army trucks—as per paragraph 9 of the peace plan. But the heavily armed soldiers guarding the demolition had an easy job this time: there was no protest from Moor.

Whoever did not run a diesel generator in his shed or cellar once again lit kerosene lamps and candles of an evening. The roads and streets were pitch-dark at night. Only the parade grounds and the bulletin board at headquarters were lit by erratically flickering circles of bulbs.

One morning two soldiers plodded through the snow up the hill to the forge and in the name of Stellamour demanded their welding apparatus back. Not even Bering's mother could learn how the blacksmith had bribed them so that in the end they retreated with just a piece of scrap metal, leaving the apparatus behind hidden in the cellar.

In those days the blacksmith would often sit across from his speechless son, who was so crazy about birds, and teach him the names of tools. But the blacksmith grew increasingly monosyllabic with his wife, who prayed one rosary after the other, and he finally had no friends left, either, in the tavern down by the dock.

Moor slid inexorably back through the years. The display windows of the grocery and drugstore were shuttered. It grew quiet around the lake; motors that had not been confiscated and shipped off grew dusty. Fuel was as expensive as cinnamon and oranges.

Only in warm proximity to the army, in the vicinity of the barracks and officers' private quarters, was there always enough light, with bands playing on Saturday nights and jukeboxes all the time—was there no lack of anything. And yet in the course of a single year, time's backward slide left its noticeable mark even on these reservations of a vanishing present. The number of troops was reduced. Bit by bit they were ordered back to the lowlands. Left behind were cold buildings and soldiers who had lost their vigilance: they tolerated the petty smuggling that supplied a meager black market; they sometimes overlooked faked stamps on passes and safe-conduct papers and watched impassively as the first emigrants left these backwater villages. But whatever happened, Stellamour's countenance was always smiling down from office walls, from posters and advertising pillars—the image of a bald and just man.

Major Elliot, however, remained implacable. The letters of the Grand Inscription had to be freshly whitewashed with each thaw, and four times a year—every October, January, April, and August—the villages on the lake were ordered to the quarry for Stellamour's Party and stood in long rows between the ponds and towering walls of green granite. Instead of letting things take their course, letting the horrors of the war years gradually grow pale and indistinct, Elliot constantly invented new rituals of remembrance for these parties. Moreover, the commandant himself seemed to be addicted to the very past that he ordered be stirred up again and again.

During office hours, Elliot sat like an assessor of fire damage among stacks of singed or lightly charred files and logbooks, and not only everyone who came to petition or complain, but by now all of Moor as well, knew that these were the confiscated records of forced labor salvaged from the flames: lists of names, columns of numbers, cubic measurements, records of punishment— blackened paper that contained just one thing: the history of the barracks by the gravel works.

In January of the same year in which Bering was to lose his bird voices, Elliot discovered among these records a portfolio of photographs. These were water-stained snapshots of the torture of camp life: prisoners in striped fatigues, prisoners in the quarry, prisoners standing at attention outside their barracks. . . . And staring at this album, Elliot invented a duty that would make him unforgettable far beyond the borders of the region under his command.

He began to use these pictures as the basis for ghostly mass scenes to be reconstructed during the course of each party by the residents from along the lake—then captured by a regimental photographer. The pictures had to look alike. Using the classification of prisoners he found in the salvaged records, Elliot insisted on realistic costumes and ordered the supernumeraries from Moor to dress up as *Jews*, as *POWs, Gypsies, Communists*, or *race defilers*.

Costumed as the victims of a defeated power that had dragged the men of Moor to their doom, the locals had to appear at the very next party wearing striped fatigues to which were sewn badges of nationality, identifying triangles, and stars of David; had to stand in line outside imaginary delousing stations; had to pose in front of an immense block of granite as Polish foreign laborers or Hungarian Jews holding hammers, wedges, and crowbars; and had to fall in beside the foundations of the demolished barracks for roll calls exactly like those Elliot had seen pictured in his album.

But Elliot was not cruel. He did not insist that his supernumeraries stand half-naked in the snow like the figures in his mildewed snapshots, but provided them blankets and discarded military coats for as long as they had to pose; children and old people were allowed to wait in tents during the set-up. Except, that is, for the hours of roll call, those horrible, icy, unbearable hours that passed amid the bawling of commands, of numbers and names—that eternity was also spared no one standing in line there now. The parties of January and April were spent reconstructing these scenes.

For the summer festival, the day on which Bering's father ended up lying on his back kicking like a beetle, the commandant ordered them to recall a picture that along its jagged white lower border bore the penciled-in title, *The Stairway*.

In this photograph could be seen hundreds upon hundreds of bent backs, a long procession of prisoners, each bearing a wooden barrow on his back, and in each barrow was a large square-hewn stone.

The prisoners hauled their loads in formation up a wide set of stairs carved into the rock, which led from the pit of the quarry up four working levels to a rim vanishing into the fog. The stairway, which had survived undamaged through war, the camp's liberation and demolition, and the first years of freedom, was so steep and irregular that it was very hard to climb even with no burden.

Moor knew these stairs well. For although it was one of the facts most fiercely denied during the early interrogations under Elliot's command, by now everyone around the lake really did know that most of the dead in the mass grave at the foot of the Grand Inscription had died on these stairs—slain by their burden, dying of exhaustion, blows, kicks, and shots fired by overseers. Woe to anyone who stumbled on this stairway and lay there for even a heartbeat.

But Elliot was not cruel. Elliot demanded only an external illusion this time as well, and forced none of his supernumeraries to heave onto his barrow one of the genuine ponderous hewn stones still lying scattered at the foot of the stairs like monuments to the agonies of death endured there. Elliot simply wanted the pictures to look alike and did not insist on the unbearable weight of reality.

Whoever wished to do so, then, had the commandant's approval to carry a dummy stone, an imitation made of papier-mâché, cardboard, or rags glued together; in fact, Elliot permitted even lighter, featherweight materials—newspapers folded into stones, stone-gray pillows. . . .

The stairway, however, was as steep, as wide and long as in the picture. And the heat was intense.

On that summer day, it was Moor's blacksmith and two other men who were too proud and too stubborn to accept easier conditions and merely sham their burden.

When Elliot gave the command to begin, the blacksmith rolled one of the large square-hewn stones onto his barrow, strapped it on tight, eased the weight onto his back, stood up with a stagger, and, joining his column, climbed some thirty or more steps. And then went slower and slower, until the dreadful weight pulled at him from behind, forced him back on his heels, and sent him falling into an empty space already cleared by those who followed him.

Rotating and tumbling head over heels in a backward somersault, he plunged down the stairs and landed on his back, but could not get up again, while his column climbed higher and higher without looking back at him—and Bering broke away from the crowd of old people and children who had been excused from any burdens and ran toward his funny father. As he skipped along, he began to shriek with delight at this game he had never seen before.

CHAPTER 6

TWO SHOTS

B ERING WAS TWELVE WHEN HIS YOUNGER
brother drowned in the lake . . . and nineteen when his
older brother also disappeared from his life, first making
his way with an army pass to the harbor in Hamburg, then
moving on to the forests of North America to find a better
life. . . . In that same year, a swarm of iron filings unleashed by a
lathe injured his father's eyes so badly that from that day on the
blacksmith saw the world only as if through a tiny window overgrown with flowery patterns of frost.

As a result of that accident and his promotion to only son and
sole heir by the disappearance of his brothers, Bering took the
workshop out of his father's fumbling hands, calmed his mother
at night—who was being visited by more and more apparitions,
which eventually became transfigured heavenly hosts—and along
with that responsibility now reluctantly fulfilled his duty as the
blacksmith of Moor.

For on rundown farmsteads with sour meadows and fields
tangled by weeds, what was needed were the services of a blacksmith who could weld cracked plows and sharpen reaper blades—

but not some mechanic like Bering, who was passionately interested in flying and gadgetry, knew how the valves of unusual motors worked, and created flapping bird wings out of rods, wire, rubber, and shredded blouses.

And so Bering now welded scrap from burned-out jeeps into tools for harvesting sugar beets more easily, constructed efficient windmills out of canvas and tin, and from scraps of iron and other metal that it took months to collect, he also made a generator, which, when the black market had enough fuel to pump into canisters and buckets, bathed the forge in radiant light for one whole evening.

Once the work was done at the forge, Bering had cabbage and potatoes to cultivate on a narrow plot, a coop of chickens to tend, a horse and two or three pigs to feed, and a sparse wagonload of hay to bring in come summer.

When the storm winds of March and April would sometimes drive red clouds of dust across the boggy fields—a fine sand that people in Moor said came on the south wind from the deserts of North Africa—Bering's father would start to feel the pain in the scar on his forehead again, notice sand everywhere, and curse both his fate and Bering's closed and taciturn nature. A woman! The house needed a woman, no doubt about it, even if she came from one of the army's whorehouses, even if all she did was at last rid the house of this gritty sand on all the windowsills and floors—and with it the pain of remembering.

But when he was not complaining, reeling off a list of reproaches, or shouting curses all through the house, Bering's father apparently wanted to spend his retirement years following his heir's every move with that relentless, meticulous talent retirees have for observation. And so when making his rounds to check on the neglected orchard, he would strike his cane against poorly pruned trees, hammer for hours on the rods of a clattering windmill, or sit in the dim parlor that was decaying with dry rot and, in the large hand of the visually impaired, keep records in a school notebook of his successor's mistakes and negligence.

Thursday, a dead swift in the well and the dog not chained.
Friday, a glove burned up in the forge and sand drifted in the
entryway again. At night, a weathervane in need of oil. Wind.
Cannot sleep. And so forth.

Assailed by figments of Mary and an unquenchable yearning
for Paradise, Bering's mother had long since ceased to care about
this world. By order of the Madonna, she had banned her husband and his blasphemous curses from their common bedroom
and entered all the other rooms of the house only after he had
vacated them. She spoke with Bering only in whispers, ate her
meatless meals alone in the kitchen, and considered every spark
that leapt from the stove's ashpan to be a sign from heaven.

Almost daily now, she beheld Celina the Pole floating above
the forge pond, bleeding from her gunshot wounds, and bearing
messages and advice from the Madonna. And Bering's mother
brought her wreaths of flowers, holy cards, and other sacrificial
gifts that she cast on the water, hoping to persuade her guardian
angel to find a wife for her lonely son.

Bering hated his inheritance. Perched above the roofs of
Moor, his farmstead seemed to be under siege by rotting jeeps,
gun carriages, and cannibalized armored vehicles that had been
left behind by departing troops and that he had dragged up Forge
Hill all on his own. The windows of his workshop were boarded
over or broken, their cracked stars of glass patched with wax
paper. Where even the paper covering these stars was ripped or
missing, branches from the neglected orchard now grasped into
the darkness of the forge. Even in the orchard, among tall pear
and walnut trees, vehicles crouched, overgrown with underbrush
and wild grape, abandoned, brown with rust, some already sunk
deep into the soft earth: here a moss-covered patrol car missing
its tires and steering wheel, there a tedder or the cannibalized
chassis of two limousines, and, like the heart of a dinosaur heaved
up onto heavy wooden trestles, an engine block without cylinders
or valves—black, greasy, and so huge that it could not possibly
have ever belonged to any of the vehicles under the trees.

Although the young blacksmith had long been unable to find any use for the rust-caked, rust-locked screws, drive shafts, and fenders of his iron graveyard, with the help of his horse he kept on dragging one more wreck, one more piece of corroded metal up the hill, as if trying to draw the circle of siege tighter and tighter around the farmstead he loathed. Forge Hill became as dreary and desolate as the rest of the world visible from up there.

But Bering, trapped in his duties to parents, forge, and farm, would perhaps never have abandoned and deserted his inheritance if, a few days after his twenty-third birthday, a gang of thugs had not forced him to taint his own house with blood and thus make it uninhabitable. It was a mild, windless April night when Bering, the blacksmith of Moor, shot a stranger.

Dead? Had that drunken thug who had leapt out of the darkness at him actually bled to death from the gunshot wounds that ever afterward in so many dreams, by night and by day, the blacksmith saw burst open over and over: two *eyes* boiling up in a black, leather-encased chest, wounds that transformed a metallic man into a soft, infinitely soft, boneless shape that did not collapse, but instead, in a fraction of a second, rose up! and then with a clumsy turn fell back into the arms of his buddies storming up behind.

Dead? Did I kill him? Did I? Was his pursuer, of whom there was no trace within minutes after the shots—or the next morning or all the days that came after—except the blackish trail of blood from his flight, drops and streaks that disappeared somewhere on the gravel path to the forge . . . was that drunkard, that filthy bastard truly and irrevocably dead?

However often Bering asked himself that question, with a steady stream of new curses for the nameless enemy of that night, memory always forced him to repeat: *I killed him, I shot him dead, I did.*

The stranger with a shaved head, a "city boy" armed with a chain and pipe, one of six or seven men, had already beaten him bloody beside the monument to Stellamour, Bringer of Peace, had chased him over the parade grounds overgrown with wild oats and up the gravel path to the forge and across the farm-yard—chased *him*, the shy blacksmith, who had nothing to use against his pursuers but a handful of horseshoe nails that he grabbed out of an open box as he ran past and flung back over his shoulder.

Gangs of thugs like those that April night were constantly leaving the ruins of deserted cities or hideaways in labyrinthine mountain caves to invade defenseless backwater towns like Moor and its neighboring villages. Ever since the army had retreated into the lowlands, leaving the desolate, forlorn lake country on its own, any determined horde, even when armed only with clubs, was invincible.

If a few sugar-beet farmers or granite-quarrymen did not join together to defend the road into town with axes and sling-shots, nothing stood in a gang's way. For years now, military patrols had defended only the roads connecting scattered head-quarters with the lowlands and were deaf to cries for help from the backcountry.

Occasional retaliatory expeditions ordered by some sympa-thetic general to the lake country or a mountain valley did not frighten these hordes—not operations that took two or three days to move through villages, with columns of soldiers, visible from a great distance, who pitched their tents in the lee of plun-dered farmsteads and sometimes had to bury the dead in the rubble. . . . They questioned the victims of a raid, wrote reports, now and then shelled a stand of trees or some long-deserted ravine as a sign of their resolve—and withdrew.

The army's few designated local agents were just influential enough to profit from their privileges, but as stipulated by the provisions of the Stellamour Plan, they were all unarmed and too weak to protect the no-man's-land under their charge from attack.

Gangs appeared and disappeared everywhere, smashing any-thing that stood in their way, demanded protection money, and did not shrink even from assaulting Societies of Penitence and Reconciliation, who in those days moved in long processions across former battlefields and gathered at the mass graves of demolished camps to erect memorials and shrines.

Although dozens of martial-law decrees protected these penitents, the thugs chased them across the fields, set fire to their flags and banners, and ripped up the placards they carried of Stellamour, Bringer of Peace, throwing those in the fire as well.

Escorted by two motorcyclists, the horde had likewise appeared in Moor that night out of nowhere, driving a truck that was stolen from some agricultural enterprise and whose bed they had filled with stones and bottles of gasoline. The truck rumbled along the shore promenade and through the narrow streets, slowing at times to a crawl—and then firebombs would hail against windows and entrance gates. Armored in leather, the thugs stood swaying at the truck's side panels, and while the driver laid on the horn, they yowled and tossed burning bottles at Moor. This obstinate one-horse town had better realize that there was only one remedy for this evil: fire insurance, protection money.

Finally they pulled onto the parade grounds, jumped down, stormed the house of Moor's secretary, dragged the wailing man outside, poured gasoline over him, threatened to ignite it, and hustled him in that state down to the old steamer dock. There they tied him to the anchor of a derelict excursion boat and dragged man and metal across the planks to water's edge; he was screaming, begging for his life, when they suddenly gave it up, like some game that had grown too boring, and left their sobbing victim behind on the pier.

From the broken windows of the secretary's stall, chickens now flapped out into the darkness, and a watchdog, mortally wounded by blows from chains, crept howling across the parade grounds.

Not until months later would Bering come to realize that from the moment that first blow struck his head as he bent down over the dog, he had thought of only one salvation—of the blue-black army pistol his father had hidden in an unused chimney at home. The same year he had given up the farm, the old man had demanded this weapon from a deserter—even though its possession by a civilian was punishable with death—in exchange for dried apples, clothes, and jerky, had then wrapped the precious object in oilcloth and hung it up the chimney.

That Bering had not only known his father's secret all these years, but had also regularly fetched it from its linen bag, disassembling it and putting it back together, and was as familiar with its marvelous mechanism as with the incomparably cruder tools of the forge—his father would not learn all that until this April night. The weapon was dangling in the chimney, polished and loaded.

Although his route of escape from the parade grounds up to the forge was pitch-dark, several hundred yards long, and strewn with potholes, Bering later recalled his flight as a single bound out of defenselessness into the omnipotence of an armed man.

The weeds of the parade grounds fly away beneath him. He takes those pothole traps with the assurance of a fleeing animal. But he is making a dash not for the forge, not for a hiding place, a burrow, but only for the weapon.

As Bering reaches the farm, the stairwell, the stairs to the loft, he can hear his pursuer tramping on the plank floor, hear him panting, hear the heavy shoes of his buddies. *Go on! Up the stairs!* And finally, fighting for air, screaming for air, arcs of light dancing before his eyes, he reaches the iron door to the furnace, throws back the bolt, grabs for the dangling linen sack. Oilcloth drops in the darkness.

Now he has the pistol in his hand. How strangely light, light as a feather, it is at this moment. Whenever he secretly played with its mechanism, it always lay heavy as a hammer in his hand.

Four steps, three steps in front of him, at very close range—his pursuer at last becomes visible in the light of his own hurricane lamp—the man laughs. He has caught up with his prey, knows he has the superior force of his buddies at his back, and takes a triumphant stride, his chain hissing—when his voice is suddenly swallowed up in a monstrous blast.

The first shot throws Bering's arm back as if that chain—rattling off into the night—had actually struck him. The crack of the blast rips at his eardrums, thrusts deep into his head and hurts more than any sound has ever hurt. The flash at the end of the barrel has gone out, went out an eternity ago, but he can still see the reflected face of his foe, that mouth gaping wide, a speechless amazement.

When the face turns pale and threatens to go out as well, he doesn't want to release it into the dark—and squeezes a second time. Only now does the weapon assume its old weight. His arm falls. He stands trembling in the night.

Strange, how he can think now of only one sentence, again and again just this one sentence in which he begins madly to wrap himself, that he whispers, barks, screams into the depths where something is thumping on its way, something is leaping, something is vanishing. . . . And so while life around him simply strides on ahead and makes a rustling noise here, a thumping noise there, and yet elsewhere scurries off almost soundlessly, he just stupidly screams away: *That's how it is, that's how it is, that's how it is. . . .* He simply cannot stop.

At some point he sees his mother climbing the stairs with a smoky stall lantern, hears his father, who grabs him and roars at him. He does not understand what he is asked. Something bursts inside him, unleashing a flood—he cannot hold his urine, it runs hot down between his legs, tears stream down over his face, and his shirt is soaked with sweat. All the liquid in him flows, drips from him, and turns to steam in cold air that reeks of pitch, feels icy now. But he stands there hot with fever, leaning against the chimney. He speaks. He wants water.

He lets himself be led down to the kitchen, begins to answer questions, but does not know what he is saying. He drinks water and gags. He drinks and drinks, but again and again the water spews back out of him before he can swallow.

As morning dawns, the old couple and their heir are still

sitting in the kitchen together, for the first time in years. The father's head has slumped to one shoulder, his jaw hangs open; a long thread of spittle drips from the corner of his mouth to his chest, but breaks at irregular intervals whenever he starts to snore. The mother has twisted the rosary around her hands and sleeps with eyelids only half closed. The stove is cold. Bering is huddled by the window, staring out into his iron garden, and with each pulse his blood stings as if it has crystallized in his heart and veins, has turned to sand, to fine, glassy sand.

CHAPTER 7

THE SHIP IN THE VILLAGES

S NOW HAD FALLEN IN THE NIGHT. SNOW ON
blossoming trees, snow on thistles grown tall already, on
the sagging roofs of limousines, and snow like an attempt
at camouflage on all the junk that surrounded the forge. Snow
in May. No one in Moor could recall its ever having snowed
this close to summer in all the twenty-three years since the end
of the war.

· The gusty winds of a North Atlantic cold front had even
driven little waves of snow across the lathe bench by the workshop window; a file stuck up out of one of the drifts, so did the
claws of a vise. And yet the year had begun milder than any in a
long time—laburnum in bloom ten days before the Feast of the
Forty Martyrs!

But on this day in May even an icy thunderstorm could hardly
have disrupted the festive excitement in the villages on the road
to Moor and its lake. Along poplar- and chestnut-lined roads and
muddy main streets, farmers and crofters in their Sunday best
had been waiting since early morning; in some places the
employees of stone mills or sugar-beet factories, organized as

reception committees or choruses, waited with bouquets and paper flags for the Transport.

Triumphal arches of pine boughs were displayed over dirt roads whose puddles and potholes had been hastily patched with gravel, tree bark, and wood chips. Only the ill and infirm stayed in their houses on this snowy morning. Whoever could walk had lined up expectantly, the most impatient even before sunrise, so as not to miss a moment of the grand procession that had been heralded for months now. In Moor, a turn in the road had been widened and shored up, a bridge at the millpool, plus one across a gorge, had been reinforced, and a roving construction crew had carried off, sawed off, or hammered off anything that lay or merely seemed to lie in the way along the planned route.

Wherever the view was not blocked by trees or war ruins overgrown with nettles, the flashing red lights of the procession could already be seen at a great distance. Led by a military unit with rotating spotlights, the transport approached like one of those freight convoys that had left the region in the first years of the Peace of Oranienburg—hundreds of trucks loaded with turbines, steel rollers, the machinery from whole factories. The land had turned sallow under the dust of their ranks.

Veiled in a cloud of diesel smoke, what crept along behind the military unit this time was just one tractor-trailer spotted with camouflage, a rig whose motor was obviously too weak, so that in the mountains and finally even on the easy grades of the hills near Moor the tractor constantly had to be augmented by plow horses hitched on up front, or by ten, twelve pairs of yoked oxen.

And so only with immense effort and often at the plodding gait of draft animals, the rig advanced its burden, both a great promise and simultaneously a vague memory of summer afternoons before the war, when the dock in Moor had threatened to sink to the bottom under the weight of happy excursion parties and when spa guests had crowded around the bandstand in the park of the Grand Hotel . . . advanced its burden, held fast to the flatbed trailer with chains and steel cables: a ship, a steamer with paddle wheels and a black-striped funnel. Perfumed with the pungent odor of fresh paint and caulking tar, still caked with wreaths of barnacles below the waterline, a fresh coat of white on the rims of its portals corroded by the salt of the Adriatic, a railing of mahogany polished smooth by the hands of countless passengers . . . ancient in its magnificence, it swayed toward the fresh water of Moor's lake.

The word in the waiting villages was that this steamer was a gift of the shipyard in Istria, a token of reconciliation and friendship in this third decade of occupation. Word was that a former conscripted laborer in the quarry, an engineer who had escaped from the barracks by the gravel works, had been promoted after the war to the top position at a shipyard in his Adriatic homeland and had sent this ship from the docks in Pula. A belated thank-you, it was said, to those farmers by the lake who had hidden the escaped prisoner back then from the quarry's search parties and bloodhounds. Word was . . .

The secretary of Moor, a retired quarryman, who could walk only with crutches since his mistreatment in the most recent attack, knew better of course. To be sure, this morning he had ordered not only his office but also the maple trees lining the parade grounds flagged with the colors of the victorious powers, but, like all the other middlemen and agents of the army, he kept it to himself that this ship was no gift, no token of reconciliation between former enemies, but simply junk to be scrapped, junk withdrawn from marine shipping along the Adriatic coast. . . . And the farmers by the lake, at least those who were old and retired, knew better, too—each knew in his heart that none of them had ever hidden a camp escapee and surely remembered that in his day fear of the military police and the quarry's mastiffs had been greater than any pity.

But who wanted to disrupt the biggest festival since the end of the war with such memories? Scruples had no place in the excitement over this steamer that had been dragged across the Alps from the Adriatic. The Danube shipyards that supplied inland waterways had long since either been dismantled and carted off or had never been rebuilt after their destruction. No shipyard in the lowlands would have been in a position to deliver a ship of this size to the lake by Moor.

The *Sleeping Greek Maid*, a paddle-wheel steamer that had adorned postcards of the prewar years as the emblem of the lake country, had gone up in flames on Moor's night of bombs amid a hail of shells and a roaring forest of spraying water; since then, cradled in algae and kelp, it had lain in the green depths beside the pier, easily visible when water and wind were calm.

With equal persistence and lack of success, the secretary of Moor had been requesting a new ship for a long time now. The carbon copies of forwarded petitions and denials received in reply filled two file notebooks in his office of lost causes. In the end, however, the basis for solving the ship issue had been found right under his nose, in the place that weighed upon Moor's history as no other: in the quarry by the lake.

An Adriatic insurance company, wishing to restore its home office in Trieste to its original splendor, had researched the source of the battered stone facing of its headquarters—and came up with Bering's hometown. Granite like that, dark-green primal stone, was won from only two quarries in the world. The first and larger lay on the Atlantic coast of Brazil, the other on the lake by Moor.

After much lengthy correspondence and complicated negotiation, the High Command of the region approved delivery of green granite to the Adriatic—and it was from there that this steamer, the centerpiece of the negotiated compensation, now swayed toward Moor in return.

The ship had to be dragged to the lake not just over Alpine passes, but also through the even more formidable barriers of trade restrictions and tangles of barbed wire laid out beneath the black eyes of gun barrels—all of which was a far greater sensation than the mere fact of a steamer in the mountains. There suddenly seemed to be justification again for the hope that the great

freedom of the Mediterranean coasts and the riches of the
booming south as well—even of America!—perhaps really were
closer than the devastation around Moor, than ruins, ripped-up
tracks, and empty, abandoned factories might suggest.

The waiting villages dreamt.

Amid the jingle of their brass bands, they dreamt of the ele-
gance of Italy, of palaces and promenades under palms, of the
inexhaustible warehouses of America, and of a remote world
without want, where after the war everything had only kept on
growing bigger, kept on growing more beautiful than before. In
the conversations of those who waited this snowy morning there
was probably no hope from recent years that was not evoked in
all its rich colors, casting the future in a glowing halo of freedom
and luxury.

This steamer that now crept so agonizingly slowly toward
Moor behind a cast-off army rig, behind nags and yoke oxen, had
been traded for nine loads of stone and yet was worth infinitely
more. . . . To be sure, it was not an especially large ship, only an
outmoded excursion steamer, which even in its best days had carried no more than three hundred passengers from the harbor at
Rijeka to the rocky islands of Kvarner Bay. It was not an especially beautiful ship, could not be compared with the fabled brass
luster of the *Sleeping Greek Maid*, to which even now, on every
anniversary of its sinking, divers glided down in a race to fix bouquets and pennants on its mired wreckage. Whichever diver was
the first to shoot back up with some scrap of rotted ornament
from the previous year could, after all, expect the prize of a trip to
Vienna, or to even more distant and exotic occupation zones—
Hamburg, Dresden, Nuremberg.

In the long years of want, with the burned-out hulk of the
Sleeping Greek Maid lying there in its depths, the lake had never
carried anything better than speedboats on army maneuvers or
the wooden skiffs of fishermen, who spent their days smoking
their catch in clay ovens and hanging their nets on the meadowed
banks. Wild oats and grasses grew from the windows of the

Grand Hotel by the lake, and the collapsed roof of the bandstand was covered with a chaos of broken chairs and sunshades, their canvas rotted long ago.

No, it was not an especially imposing ship, but it was the largest that the postwar generation of villagers had ever seen. After all, for the most part they knew the world's splendors only from foreign-language magazines, which were hotter items on the black market than citrus fruit or coffee.

It was—a magnificent ship. Huge and mysterious, an ocean giant!, whose precious freight consisted solely of the hope that now at last everything might once again become what it had been before the war.

CHAPTER 8

THE DOG KING

I N   T H E   S N O W - L A D E N   S I L E N C E ,   T H E   C R A S H
could be heard all the way up to the forge. Bering had just
dragged a crusher gear weighing several tons as far as his
workshop and was removing the heavy harness from his horse, a
long-maned draft animal, when the noise mounted from the
lakeshore, broke against the farmstead walls, and died away.
Only the sound of splintering glass lasted a breath longer, a faraway chinking rain of fragments.

The horse threw its head high in fright, giving its master such
an unexpected shove that he lost his balance and tumbled across
the gear and into the slushy mire of the farmyard. Soaking wet
now and smeared with muck, but with not a word of anger at
his mishap, the blacksmith hobbled to the gate, the horse's bit
and headpiece still in one hand, the other pressed to the pain in
his side.

Far below, the shore road lay deserted; plowed by the transported ship and trampled by rows of spectators, it was only a
dark border between the wintry land and the lake's leaden gray.
The road led first down a boulevard named after Stellamour and

lined with chestnuts, whose clustered blossoms were balled fists of snow, cut across a peninsula with thick stands of rustling reeds, took a sharp curve down toward the bay and the dilapidated Hotel Bellevue—where it was abruptly blocked by a shiny barricade. At the fork leading to the Bellevue's beach, and decorated now with boughs and garlands for the launching and christening to take place that afternoon, stood a wrecked limousine, its hood wrenched to form a bizarre sculpture, a bumper ripped from the chassis and bending upward like a chromed distress signal. A muddy track in the snow described the path of this transformation in a single, elegant arc. The car had been borne out of the Bellevue curve by overwhelming centrifugal force, had crashed against a newly erected stone shoring wall at water's edge, and bounced back onto the road. Two hubcaps had sailed off and now lay undamaged and sparkling in the snow.

Even from this distance, Bering had recognized the wreck at first glance. It was the commandant's car, a blue-and-white Studebaker, a luxury liner, the kind that otherwise you only saw illustrated in the mildewed magazines soldiers left behind in the barracks rubbish: eight cylinders, whitewall tires, two-tone paint job, brightly polished chrome trim, and headlights that could frisk a whole block of buildings in the night.

As a young teenager, Bering had joined a horde of other enthusiasts in chasing after this wonder whenever Elliot drove it through the villages at a snail's pace, sometimes tossing bitter chocolate and licorice from the window. These inspection tours had left deeper ruts in Bering's memory than in the muddy roads of Moor. As unstoppable as a tank, the luxury liner had dipped into every great pothole and sinkhole, only to come lurching back up out of it more beautiful than before.

Although, following a grand farewell ceremony in the quarry, the major had withdrawn years ago to the lowlands with the rest of his unit, the Studebaker kept reappearing on country lanes at irregular intervals, like some stray, ghostly symbol of authority. For on the day of his departure, Elliot had bequeathed the most impressive token of his power to the only inhabitant of Moor whom he had come to trust in all the years of occupation.

This man, who as a favorite of the army was equally envied and hated in these backwater villages, had the commandant to thank not only for this precious gift, but also for everything that fanned hatred against him: his almost aristocratic position as administrator of the granite quarry, a confiscated house—with a two-way radio inside!—plus limited, but nonetheless unprecedented, freedom of travel. And, ultimately, even his name. For in his final speech, the departing commandant had, with almost tender ridicule, called his favorite *my Dog King*. And by now there were only a few along the lake who still knew the Dog King by his real name, Ambras.

Ambras was a man above and beyond all doubt. As a liberated former slave laborer he bore a thumb-wide scar on his left forearm. It was the imprint of the red-hot file with which, after liberation, he had forever erased the prison number tattooed there. He spent his days out on the quarry's working terraces or in its dusty administrator's shed—and his nights in a country house called the Villa Flora, which was slowly falling to ruin and stood on a rise in the middle of a park now run to seed. He was the sole resident of this two-story, half-timbered house with wooden verandas, bay windows, galleries, and salons—yet was content to live in just one room facing the lake, the former music room. Here he slept on a sofa embroidered with scenes of paradisial gardens and used a card table covered in green felt as both dining table and desk; here he devoured his cold evening meals and tossed his clothes each night over the closed lid of a grand piano. He left all the other rooms—the cloth-draped furniture, the moldy wallpaper and ragged brocade curtains, the plaster fauns and the plundered library—to a dozen half-wild dogs.

The Villa Flora had known no human beings for years. Its owner, a hotelier named Goldfarb, had operated the Bellevue and its affiliated spa as an old-fashioned sanatorium and always on the edge of bankruptcy; but one November night during the war, he, together with his wife and deaf-mute daughter, had been shoved into an unmarked car by officials of the secret police and hauled off to some unknown destination. Word in Moor at the time was: to a camp in Poland—but also, camp? Poland? Ha! to the next best woods.

The cook, a carpenter's daughter from an upland valley near Leys, recalled in one of Major Elliot's interrogation sessions that her employers had knelt there in the salon in great confusion, packing and unpacking winter clothes, but finally all they had taken from the trunk was a stuffed plush giraffe and children's woolen things, cramming them into two bags, because the officials had permitted only hand-baggage. And she recalled in particular that one of those officials, the one without a coat, had smoked cigarettes in the master's study—in Herr Goldfarb's study!—where until that hour no one had ever smoked.

In any case, there had been no word of her employers, neither news from Poland nor mail from some other camp, and they had never returned, either, not during the war, not in the Peace of Oranienburg.

Like the Grand Hotel, the Bellevue became a place for wounded frontline officers to convalesce, or die, and the Villa Flora served as the summer home of some party functionary until Russian infantrymen overran Moor and found the functionary in front of his dressing-room mirror with a bullet through his head; he was holding the pistol in such a fierce death grip that it did not even fall from his hand when the infantrymen rolled the corpse up in the blood-caked carpet and threw him, plus a wreath of oak leaves and a chromed bust, out the window.

But the victors as well found only temporary quarters in the villa. Following a succession of military occupations and pullouts, the house was taken over on occasion by refugees from bombed-out cities, then by people driven out of Moravia and Bessarabia, and at last by vagrants, until Major Elliot finally closed up the ravaged house and ordered it be kept for the vanished hotelier—until, that is, the matter of his life or death was clarified.

At that point, Elliot had Moor's blacksmith hang the gates, which had been forced open, with chains and padlocks, ordered broken windows boarded shut and the park fenced with barbed wire. Then he set two dogs free on the grounds, large Irish wolfhounds that had been given him as mascots by the allied regiment of Highlanders. These huge dogs ate whatever was flung to them over the barbed-wire fence by military patrols, rushed to leap at every intruder, and even snapped up the carp in the park's lily pond. When at times the thunder from blasting at the quarry rolled over the lake to their domain, they would stand erect, bestial, with front paws extended against the veranda railing, and howl across to the Blind Shore opposite. The Villa Flora was inaccessible.

In the villages, people called those times the dog years: meat and soap and all the other necessities of everyday life were and remained scarce, for Stellamour's peace plan demanded that even the most wretched communities manage on their own. Whoever had fields and gardens that bore fruit also had food to eat, and perhaps enough to trade on the black market—a chicken for cigarettes, and potato schnapps for batteries. So that in those years—not just in the cities of ruins, but also on many a farm—a dog was one hungry mouth too many.

Mongrels were chased away, left by the road, or hungrily took off on their own, and out in the forests and upland valleys they banded together in fierce packs that even attacked red deer and dragged the bones of the hastily buried war dead back into the light of day. If hunger drove these dogs from the wilderness into the vicinity of the barracks, Elliot had his soldiers hunt them down and shoot them by the dozen, but did not permit the disarmed locals to avail themselves of gins, snares, and iron traps. For, like all hunting, dog-hunting was also reserved for the army. And the army winked when several of these mongrels who had run wild found their way through the barbed-wire fence to the refuge of the Villa Flora—and either groveled before the Irish beasts or perished under their fangs. And so an untamable pack on the villa's grounds gradually grew larger, breaking through the

barbed wire sometimes to attack the town and then retreat—
until one rainy summer a new master moved into the house
of dogs.

Early in August that summer, nine years after being liberated
from the barracks by the gravel works, the photographer
Ambras—Prisoner No. 4273, who had worked the quarry under
the whip—returned to the lake by Moor. A destitute specialist in
landscapes and portraits, but without camera, studio, or dark-
room, Ambras arrived that day in reply to the army's call for an
administrator of Moor's reopened granite quarry.

No one recognized the newcomer. Even one of his former
fellow prisoners would probably have had difficulty identifying
this stranger as the wretched, emaciated skeleton who on the day
of liberation had tottered along the frayed electric fence in the
direction of the laundry barracks. Too exhausted to wait in line
for the laundered jacket or shirt of some dead man or even to slip
out of his own zebra-striped uniform, Ambras had lain down in a
run-off ditch of steaming lye water for his first bath in months,
had lain there in the open air, staring up from the shallow water
to the snowy clouds. He saw the sky creeping above the quarry's
terraces and toward the mountains; he heard distant voices, commands, shouts, heard distant motors and the wind in the pines
and in the legs of a watchtower and wanted just to lie there, lie in
this warmth flowing around him at last and so milky and lazy—
when two gravediggers, citizens of Moor whom a tank crew had
conscripted for the job, grabbed him by the arms and legs and
tossed him on their wagon of corpses.

I'm still alive, Ambras had whispered into the snowy sky, and
could feel something round, hard in his back, feel hair against the
nape of his neck, cold bristles—*I'm still alive,* and did not take
his eyes off the mountains, off the clouds.

Even nine years later, in his first conversation with Major
Elliot, the rescued man could reproduce on a sheet of foolscap
the laundry, crematorium, bunkers, tunnels, and barracks of the
camp by the gravel works—to perfect scale. All during the job

interview, his victim's passport, blackened with stamps and entries, lay open on Elliot's desk beside a glass of schnapps. And although Ambras answered all the questions about his years in the camp with apparent composure, at times he would also stop unexpectedly, reach for the glass, and turn it in his hands for a minute or two before drinking.

That afternoon the commandant and the stranger were seen on the dock, talking, gesticulating, and Elliot was even heard to laugh. Or was it only his companion who laughed? The two of them waited for the ferry to the Blind Shore, were then conveyed across to the quarry on that dusty pontoon boat, and did not return before dusk—huddled in the wheelhouse, still talking.

In the following weeks, right below the new quarry administrator's name—on both flyers and the bulletin board at headquarters—stood the warning that any insubordination toward the administrator would be punished as severely as if it were an attack on Elliot himself. Thus even before he gave his first orders at the quarry, Ambras's name was already a threat.

Moor first learned to fear the newcomer, however, on the evening when he subdued the dog pack at the Villa Flora.

"The villa? . . . The house of dogs?"

That was Elliot's incredulous question, of course, when Ambras said he wanted to take up quarters there of all places and would not accept lodgings offered him at the Dock Inn or at any of Moor's farms vacated by émigrés. But in the end, it did not matter to the commandant who protected the missing hotelier's property from plunderers. And so he agreed.

That same day, at the hour the dogs were fed each evening, Ambras stood outside the chained gate to the villa. In one hand he held a bloody gunnysack full of bones and meat scraps from the barracks, in the other an iron rod as thick as a club. The pack was waiting for him.

Villa Flora. How often during his years in the camp had he seen this house as a minuscule pale beacon on the far shore. On many evenings, the beacon had suddenly begun to glow brightly

in the light of the sun low on the horizon; then invisible windows, banged shut by a draft or closed against oncoming night,
would reflect the sun's image across the lake in a frenzied succession of flashes.

Each time he had been dazzled by these lights from the
beyond, Ambras had stood there for the space of a breath—
among the barracks, maybe, or on the camp road, even under the
watchtower by the grinding mill—deaf and blind to the inferno
of the present. And for hours, days, after the signal went out, he
would imagine the faces—always new faces—of those faraway
people he did not know, who squandered the happiness of a life
lived in freedom.

In the eternity of his years in the camp, these traces of light
ultimately came to be the only evidence that Moor Quarry was
not all there was and that beyond the electric fence another world
still had to exist—even if it seemed to have long since forgotten
him and those like him.

Breathless from the steep path leading from the dilapidated
boathouse up to the villa, he sets down his sack of meat. The
dogs began barking while he was still hidden deep in the slope's
underbrush. They now leap savagely at the gate's rusty grillwork,
at its wrought-iron tendrils, leaves, and clusters. He throws them
bones and innards, one piece at a time, in high arcs over this
thicket of metal.

The pack lunges for the offal with a greed he knows from the
camp. Hungry, they forget the enemy at the gate and are now
only enemies among themselves. And so he can open the padlock. The chain falls into leaves that years of wind have drifted
against the bars.

Twelve, thirteen, fourteen . . . dogs—he counts them out loud
and when he is done, he starts over again, pronouncing each
number soothingly and insistently, never taking his eyes off any
of them as he counts, goes on speaking, numbers, nicknames,
whispers the commands of obedience training, and crazy stuff,
too, keeps it up, never stopping, while pressing his weight against

the grille until, with a deep groan, one side finally yields and opens just wide enough for him to enter.

The Irish wolfhounds have dragged their share of the meat to the edge of the lily pond, but they stop their ripping and gorging now and lift massive skulls toward the open gate. Stock-still, they stare at him, but do indeed begin to growl, to pull back lips and bare fangs, and yet they remain by the pond as if turned to stone, as if they cannot fathom how anyone can dare do what Ambras dares at this moment: speaking, whispering, he advances toward them.

It is neither of the Irish wolfhounds, but a grayish-brown spotted hunting dog, blanketed with scars, that suddenly, as if obeying some inaudible command, abandons a pig's foot and leaps without warning at the intruder.

For a long time now, Ambras has had no need of warnings when dealing with enemies. He strikes his attacker across the eyes and muzzle with such a blow of his iron rod that the dog, still in midbound, is sent reeling back to the gravel path. There it coughs, barks, blood until it can no longer close its crushed jaw and its head sinks to the stones.

While the fiercest of them dies, the dogs have eyes and ears now only for its subduer. Not a one is still eating. The slain dog lies open-mouthed in the gravel. Ambras walks on ahead to the house and has already begun to talk to the pack as before, soothingly and insistently—when over by the lily pond one of the Irish wolfhounds stirs from its torpor. It is the larger of the two.

How slowly, almost hesitantly, it sets into motion. But now, both speed and rage gradually increasing, it flies in monstrous leaps at the intruder.

Then the iron rod strikes it as well, thrusts like a lance into gaping jaws, files at the fangs, and rams shreds of the dog's own palate deep into its throat.

With a grinding movement of its head, the wolfhound still manages to pull the weapon away from Ambras, is able to vomit the lance back up and set its teeth into the arm of the Villa

Flora's new master—even though it is already starting to strangle on its own wounds. But whoever wants to stay alive now, has to kill. And it no longer has the strength to kill.

So it is Ambras who with a cry of anger or pain, more like a bay than a human voice, hurls himself at the dog. Clamping its muzzle tight with both hands, he feels the body beneath him become a single, untamed muscle. He squeezes the raging beast between his legs, clutches as tight as he can, dares not let go of this huge skull, this maw, ever again. And so dog and man roll off the gravel path into the brambles. Only there does Ambras end up straddling his enemy like a rider.

As if he now would like to set his own teeth in the animal's throat, he bends forward, bringing his eyes up next to the dog's eyes, his mouth next to the dog's mouth. Then he gives the dog's head, still clamped in his arms, a jerk, pulling the skull backward with all his might, farther and farther, until it is dipped in the raised hair on the nape and the beast has at last become the victim. The neck breaks with a sound audible for a good distance. And as he takes a deep breath, Ambras truly feels as if he has a horse beneath him, a warm, silky foal relaxing exhausted beneath its rider.

Later in Moor, there were always new "eyewitnesses" claiming to have watched this battle from some hiding place or other—a shed next to the barbed wire, a sheepfold, even a cave. In tales as dramatic as they were richly varied, they described, for instance, how the Dog King had squatted atop the cadaver for a while, before getting up and staggering toward his house, his new residence. Many witnesses also reported a third attack by the dogs; others had the conqueror stumble unmolested up the stairs to the veranda and swore that the mongrels hung their heads and slunk away to let the Dog King pass.

The fact was that all these witnesses were merely passing on and reworking the account of a fisherman who happened to be in the Bellevue's bay at the time, catching blind bream—eyeless, strangely sweet-tasting fish that prowled the bottom in this deepest part of the lake.

The fisherman had dozed off waiting for his float to jingle and was awakened by barking dogs. Through his binoculars he watched a man—whom he thought he recognized by his bomber jacket as the quarry administrator—push open the gate to the villa. And then saw the attack. The battle. And although his binoculars lost focus a few times and bobbed in sync with his pulse, the fisherman saw quite enough to give his account at the Dock Inn that same evening.

But there was something the fisherman did not know, nor would it ever be known in Moor: besides all those who simply retold the story, there was in fact a second witness to the battle. Bering, who at age nine felt magically drawn to the dilapidated villa and visited it over and over, had been looking that same day for wild orchids within view of the gate, when suddenly Ambras had burst from the underbrush. Hidden by vines of moorland long left fallow, Bering had not only seen how Ambras dealt with his enemies, but had also heard strange nicknames and commands that the conqueror called out to the confused pack as he strode forward. And, though frozen with fear, the witness had also observed how, after all that had happened, the subdued pack returned to its meat.

And then Ambras buried his enemies. He threw the dogs' carcasses into a ditch overgrown with elderberry and covered them with trash and rubbish that he dragged from the villa into the garden.

For a long time Bering did not dare leave his hiding place. Only fear of oncoming night drove him at last from cover. He ran as if for his life. But the house behind him kept silent. Only one window, restive with the flicker of a candle or torch, illumined the path behind him. The pack was invisible and made no sound.

In the years that followed, Bering never again came so close to the Dog King as in those hours of conquest. Ambras had long ago taken over the commandant's luxury liner, pitching and rolling through the villages, a shadow at the wheel. Ambras stood at the railing of the pontoon boat that conveyed him to the quarry every morning, sat surrounded by his dogs under the Villa Flora's giant pines, or watched the ceremonies of Societies of Penitence from a reviewing stand shaded by an awning. . . . For Bering, the quarry administrator remained a distant figure who for all those years seemed omnipresent only in his father's curses or in Moor's nasty gossip.

It was only when Bering recalled the subjugation of the dogs that the man's face assumed features, though they increasingly came to be those of a biblical hero, like the one pictured on the blacksmith's wife's pious calendars: an unconquerable king, who slew a lion with his bare hands and drove his enemies, golden-helmeted Philistines, into the desert, and to their deaths.

The face of this biblical warrior was still in Bering's mind at age twenty-three when he stepped out of his gate on the morning of the ship's christening and recognized the wreckage in the curve by the Bellevue. The Dog King in his chariot. The Dog King after battle. The king in his smashed-up car.

The many spectators who were marching to the Bellevue's bay this cold, snowy May morning to celebrate the launching of the *Sleeping Greek Maid* regarded the wrecked Studebaker on the road as an additional festival attraction. An automobile accident in a land of horse-drawn wagons, carts, and pedestrians—a carnival sideshow! Amid the wispy pennants of his curses, the quarry administrator stood beside the wreck, occasionally kicking the wheels sunk deep in the mire, but asking no one for help. And so the locals stood back at a little distance and inspected his misfortune—some rejoicing in it, others asking the administrator patronizing questions about how it had happened and calling out useless suggestions. But since you only did for a favorite of the army what you were expressly commanded to do, Ambras was left alone with the wreck.

He had pulled the torn metal of a front fender away from the wheel and tried to no avail to start the motor two or three times, when Bering, up on Forge Hill, yielded to the lure of this marvelous machine down by the lakeshore and laid the heavy harness on his horse again. Still muddy from his fall, he painfully mounted the unsaddled horse and rode it down the snowy slope to the lake.

The Dog King was just banging the last splinters from the frame of a window, when the shadow of a rider fell across him. Bering bent down from the height of the steaming animal as if to his squire. It was the first time that he had ever looked Ambras in the face.

"I can help you." His voice sounded cracked and thin in the cold air. He had to swallow.

"Help?" the Dog King asks, rising up and staring at him, and Bering suddenly thinks that the quarry administrator and chief justice of Moor is staring only at his hand, the one that held a pistol. Only at the hand that once killed a vanished victim.

"Help? With that old nag there?" Ambras asks. His jacket is torn, one sleeve damp with blood.

"With this old nag here, my horse . . . and my gear. I'll get the car back on the road, get the car running again."

"You?"

"Yes, me," Bering says and doesn't know how one speaks to a king, but does not dismount.

"Are you a junk dealer or a magician?"

"No, I . . ." Bering says, all at sea. And suddenly from far away a word flies to him that he has never heard, but has indeed read on his mother's calendars, and he corrects himself:

"No, *Excellency*, I am the blacksmith."

CHAPTER 9

MAJOR REPAIRS

THE DOG KING AND THE BLACKSMITH OF Moor were missing that day at the ship's christening and launching, and at the festival. They did not watch as the last supports were pounded out from under its stern, did not see the ship cast aside glistening banners of snow as it rushed into the water. The bow dipped so deep into the lake that a breaker leapt over the deck, tearing two lifesavers and several floral displays from the railing. Like a cradle that has been set rocking too hard, the steamer first canted dangerously toward the mountains and their Blind Shore, then toward the dock black with people, and only gradually came to rest, lying quietly at last in the waves beneath the ruins of the Hotel Bellevue.

Only now did Moor's secretary fling a bottle of wine against the bow. In the confusion, as the ship suddenly rushed into the water, he had almost forgotten it—the signal! They hadn't waited for his signal. And so he was as belated in shouting its new name at the colossus as the brass band on the ferry was in striking up its tinkling racket or the gala crowd along the shore in shouting its bravo. It was a familiar, faded name that now rose at last from the bottom of the lake—and immediately submerged again in the noise of excitement.

"I christen you . . ." the secretary shouted, cried in vain against the din and had to cough and begin anew, and finally sang the ritual in a feeble, stilted voice that could no longer be heard: "I christen you the *Sleeping Greek Maid!*"

The snow that had fallen from superstructure, decks, and benches drifted in the bay like fleeting memories of ice shoals and turned to mossy green water amid the echoes of jubilation. And while a choir broke into song on the pier, while speeches were made, flags raised, and, for lack of fireworks, signal flares were set off, a warm, gusty wind came up, ruffling the bay with blackish-blue shadows, devouring the snow from hillsides and marshy meadows, and disclosing a great morass.

While all this was going on, Bering and Ambras did indeed see fireballs from the flares, but they heard only the distorted, unidentifiable scraps of choir and band music that the gusts carried to them across the reeds. The Dog King and the blacksmith were not among the passengers who thronged the gangplank to board the ship, and a nervous master of ceremonies inquired in vain both along the pier and on deck about a missing guest of honor. With a great company aboard, the *Sleeping Greek Maid* pulled out for its first panoramic voyage without Ambras.

Bering's absence was not noticed; he hadn't been invited. But that the quarry administrator and Moor's chief justice had stayed away from the biggest celebration since the end of the war gave rise to rumors, both on shore and on board: there had been an accident, the Dog King lay maimed, slightly injured, severely injured in Moor's infirmary, lay dying, had just kicked the bucket—one dog less, no great loss . . .

What? Dead? That guy dead? Never. People like him would survive doomsday, and, at worst, within days of an accident just scratch the scabs off their faces and be as ironclad and unapproachable as ever.

"Him? He's sure to be up in the rocks somewhere with his

binoculars, reading lips and taking note of anybody who's talking about him. . . ."

At the wind-tousled banquet table on the *Sleeping Greek Maid*'s upper deck, Ambras's chair remained empty. None of the guests dared take his spot. In course after course, food served on plates intended for him turned cold and was removed untouched , from the table: carrot soup, pearl barley with beads of cheese, fatback, tripe, pickled blind bream, smoked pig snout in aspic, and even poached California peaches filled with chopped walnuts (from an abandoned army depot)—it all steamed and smelled so good and turned cold at the place reserved for the Dog King and was denied to the others at the table, whose eyes looked long and greedily as it vanished again into pots and kettles belowdecks.

The two hungry absentees spent these same hours doggedly struggling to drag the wrecked Studebaker up Forge Hill. Bering long since regretted his ride down to the shore. The Dog King had accepted his help without a word of thanks, and as he pulled now—with his Excellency angrily shouting commands—the frayed rope was rubbing the palms of his hands raw. And bent like a slave laborer, he strained toward his own house. And did not dare protest when Ambras pulled the coachman's crop from the shaft of Bering's own boot and began whipping the horse, *his* horse!

Flecks of foam snowed from the mare's nostrils. With each blow of the crop she pitched into her draft harness, making it hum like a bowstring. But neither her exertions nor Ambras's blows helped. Nothing helped. Gazing up at the steep rutted slope just below the gate to the farm, even Ambras had to recognize that two men and a horse could not drag the wreck up such an incline.

"Enough. Unharness her."

Bering freed the sweat-drenched mare from the gear, ripped a few bunches of spindly wild oats from the balk, and began to dry her flanks with them.

"Forget that."

The horse waited a few more moments in vain for her master's caresses and then, hanging her head, plodded up to the gate. The blacksmith was not allowed to follow.

"You come with me."

Mute, each locked in a different anger, the two now wandered down toward the Bellevue's bay after all. From there the Dog King could order up a jeep or at least a team of oxen that the blacksmith could drive.

"You can handle a team, can't you? . . . And a jeep? Can you drive, too?"

The blacksmith could do it all. For someone who had cannibalized vehicles junked by the army or had got the engines running again, armored cars and jeeps were as familiar as jukeboxes and burned-out toasters taken from the deserted barracks.

Halfway to the festival, just as the Bellevue's collapsed pagoda roof came into view above the crowns of a few giant pines, they saw coming toward them six of the draft animals that had helped transport the ship. A stableboy for a Society of Penitence, who led a monkish life in the high meadows of the Stony Sea, had lined up again and again for the bitter dark beer being given away down at the dock and had been ordered back home by an equally drunk foreman. Immersed in a whining conversation with himself, he now staggered along behind this team of oxen. Bering knew him. The half-wit. He had brought Bering a basket of knives to sharpen only a week before and, grunting blissfully, had stared into the fiery rain of a welding job until he could no longer see the world for all those dazzling visions. With a wet cloth draped over his eyes, he had then lain for an hour or more on the lathe bench beside the forge.

When Ambras started shouting at him from some distance, the terrified idiot began to sob. Thugs, he thought; only last February one of the gangs had beaten him badly, stripped him half-naked, and chased him through snowdrifts into a brook. He now picked up a stone, and was looking around for other weapons and some route of escape, when he recognized that man up ahead and was clear-headed enough not to resist his orders.

With six oxen in front of the luxury liner and a drunken stableboy as their driver, with Bering and Ambras now behind the wreck, now stumbling alongside, constantly trying to keep the skidding vehicle on track—like a caricature of the great ship procession that had crept through the villages that morning, the Dog King and his retinue advanced toward the forge, and, arriving at last at its gate, were greeted with wild curses from Bering's father. The old man took this parade for just another load of useless junk, threw clods of earth at the team, and waved threatening fists until one of the figures, which he saw only as phantoms, bellowed at him in the voice of the quarry adminis-trator and ordered him to shut his mouth and get out of his sight. He promptly fell silent and withdrew to the black interior of the forge.

With a deftness that seemed totally unhampered by his tipsy state, the stableboy led the team into the farmyard, turned them around, and, following Bering's instructions, placed the wreck out of the wind but still in the entrance, so that the car's broken headlights stared down over Moor and across the lake. For his help, the stableboy was given two coins and a few prunes that Ambras took from his jacket pocket. He tried to kiss the gentle-man's hand and bent so low in farewell that his cap tumbled from his head.

In the days after the festival, Moor saw the Studebaker, missing its hood and grille, and finally wheels as well, sitting on a dais of red logs in the entrance to the forge. Both doors of the gate stood open. From the farmyard came the racket of major repairs.

Even as a wreck, this car was still a threat. Until now, gangs of thugs had always kept clear of a house or farmstead whenever the Studebaker stood outside. For even when the vehicle stood apparently deserted on the fens or beside a dead campfire at the end of some ravine, at the merest hint of approaching footsteps a growling ash-gray mastiff would rise from the back seat and with teeth bared throw itself at the window until the glass was fogged over by its breath and only a maw and fangs could be seen behind the murky smears left by paws and muzzle. Not a trace of the beast was to be seen, however, at the entrance to the farm. The blacksmith went to work on the car with impunity.

Moor's world seemed changed since the launching. To avoid any disruption of the *Sleeping Greek Maid*'s maneuvers when arriving or departing, Societies of Penitence were no longer permitted to use the dock as a platform for their elaborate rituals, during which paper boats scribbled with names and dates were set aflame and pushed out onto the water. A month before the launching, in fact, the wind had driven one such ship of the dead back to shore, setting the encircling rushes on fire.

But it was with particular satisfaction that Moor noted that the Dog King—though he had not vanished, was neither wounded nor dead—was without his buggy at least. Every morning, accompanied sometimes by three mongrels from his pack, he took an upland path leading from the Villa Flora to Forge Hill to inspect the wreck, Bering's mechanical plans for the repairs, and their progress; then he descended to the dock and boarded the ferry for the quarry. He was now its sole passenger. For since the great launching, it was not just this dusty pontoon boat that steamed across the lake twice a day, but as Moor's new hallmark, the *Sleeping Greek Maid* likewise sailed as far as the Blind Shore—white and seductive beneath its banner of smoke, from whose elongated, plumed, or tattered shape the villagers learned to read coming changes in the weather. When the shriek of the ship's siren brushed along the shoreline and then returned from the heights of the Stony Sea, swarms of coots and gulls fluttered up from Moor's promenade, traced uneasy arcs out over the lake, and then, laughing shrilly with relief, glided back to the reeds.

Granite-breakers, miners, and stonemasons—anyone who had work to do on the Blind Shore or was merely a participant in one of the Stellamour Parties—now made the trip on the excursion steamer, and returned on it as well. The *Greek Maid* was a faster, more dependable connection between the villages and the far shore than the winding and often mired Shore Road had ever been, and in following its route, the ship stitched up the abysses of the lake. The bullet-riddled steamer of the same name, still lying amid pennants of algae just beyond the piles of the old pier, seemed to grow more invisible with each crossing, as if its successor's paddle wheels, screw, and rudder blade could muddy the view by stirring up not only the sand and muck of the bottom but also oblivion itself.

The world *had* changed. The iron garden that encircled Bering's farmstead, and was already starting to run wild, bore fruit at last. For now that the Studebaker stood in the entrance to the farm, that arsenal of junk overgrown with elderberry and nettles no longer merely supplied spare parts for dilapidated farm machinery, whose crude mechanisms had always seemed utterly ridiculous to a lover of birds—but now, finally, the iron garden became a laboratory for the creation of a work of art.

Like a man possessed, the blacksmith searched the junk for anything that might be a useful building block for his vision; he pulled back into the light what had long ago sunk beneath underbrush and cushions of moss, liberated all the raw material from lichens and rust, and laid the old iron in an oil bath.

When his hands disappeared into the tarry brew and could only grope for parts he could no longer see, he would stare sometimes for minutes on end at the stumps of his forearms—and then it seemed to him as if those missing hands had never held a pistol. His invisible forefinger slid along the thread of a screw until it touched the slot—and then he started up out of his daydream and suddenly felt the gun kick again and heard the echo of the shots fired that night as a painful tolling deep in his head. Only working on the car for the Dog King drowned out that tolling and at times even let him forget that somewhere out there among the rocks, in the reeds, or in one of the old, labyrinthine bunker systems in the Stony Sea lay a dead man, his victim.

Ambras asked no questions. He was the only inhabitant of Moor who, since the departure of Major Elliot, was authorized to arrest, convict under martial law, or hand over to the army anyone owning a gun and shooting to kill—and he had no interest in Bering's deeds, or in his dreams. Every morning, Ambras trudged up to the blacksmith's, where he stood and drank two cups of chicory coffee that Bering brewed in a pot over the forge. Then he strode around the wrecked car in the entrance and listened to the blacksmith's explanations, or stood in the farmyard, legs spread wide, and examined the construction plans that Bering sketched in the mud and dust with a poker.

As bewildering as these sketches sometimes appeared to Ambras, one thing he did see at first glance: the Studebaker, Major Elliot's legacy, could not be restored to its old glory. But this blacksmith knew how to wrest a new form out of every dent and every tear in the metal. This blacksmith was more inventive, and above all more persistent, than the army mechanics who in years past had repaired or serviced the car with no particular zeal. (And had not an order signed by Major Elliot forced them to perform the task, the Studebaker would surely long ago have found a place in one of the junkyards behind the barracks.)

With the title and Elliot's grease-spotted orders always within reach in the glove compartment, Ambras had until now undertaken the trip to the lowlands twice or three times a year: mile after mile on gravel roads, across rickety bridges spanning rivers and gorges; long hours of waiting at checkpoints and zone crossings, then days of loitering in some barracks courtyard outside a garage; nights spent in enlisted men's quarters or in a sleeping bag thrown down between scrapped tanks and armored cars— and all of it just to demand that some bored sergeant perform the scheduled service Elliot had guaranteed. . . . And after all that, it suddenly turned out that the blacksmith in Moor had a mysterious talent for motors! Already by his second visit at the forge, Ambras was so satisfied with progress in repairs that he left behind two cans of corned beef and a jar of peanut butter, delicacies that even softened Bering's father's mood and interrupted his curses for a day.

Of course nothing the blacksmith found in the garden fit the wreck, nothing worked just as it was. Of course he had to hammer, bend, and weld parts of the car's twisted, torn, and dented body back into shape, just as he crafted the scrap iron from his garden, had to place the pieces on his anvil and make them match under his blowtorch, join them into something new. But why had he gathered junk for years, why had he stood in a shower of sparks and endured the piercing clang of his own hammer blows if not in preparation for this task, the greatest mechanical challenge of his life until now? "Fine. Agreed. Do as you like," Ambras had replied to each of his suggestions thus far, not even waiting to hear any further technical explanations. "It's fine. The thing has to run, that's all, do you understand? Run."

To think someone could talk about a *car* like that. That someone did not understand that it was up to the mechanic whether a vehicle remained a mere machine or became a catapult that could hurl even an invalid out into a world, racing away at speeds impossible for mere humans . . . into a world where fields dotted with poppies became rivers striped with red, hills turned into shifting dunes, Moor's narrow streets into scurrying walls, and the horizon a pulsing boundary that flew toward the driver—and right under him.

Bering had trudged Moor's dirt lanes too long and had hauled too many loads with oxcarts and horse-drawn wagons not to see an automobile as the supreme convenience—and speed as an intimation of the life of birds. But what had he been permitted to try his hand at thus far? Creeping tractors, the motors of buzz saws, hay balers, and on rare occasion a stranded jeep or trans-porter whose driver rewarded him for his help by letting him take a quick thrilling spin or two. The hulks and engines of those two limousines rotting away under the pear trees in his garden had been there merely for him to study their mechanical secrets, the way an archaeologist studies the winches of some forgotten epoch; wrecks like those existed only to be cannibalized, and no art in the world could ever set them in motion again.

But here now was this Studebaker. A luxury liner! Within its

engine, after only one day of repairs, there again began to pound
not just the staccato of all mechanical mobility but also the
rhythm of travel itself—rappings from a world that had seemed
attainable again, even for Moor, ever since the launching of the
Sleeping Greek Maid.

"Fine. Agreed. Do as you like . . ."

Bering made purposeful use of the freedom Ambras granted
him—as if he had tested every stratagem while waiting so long
for this chance. He cut and welded tail fins, extending them till
they looked like tail feathers! He took carburetors that had lain at
the ready on his junk arsenal's shelves for years and attached one
to each pair of the Studebaker's cylinders inside a monstrously
enlarged engine compartment. He rebored cylinders and ground
their heads; he modified and shortened the induction manifolds
and polished their rough interiors in order to increase the flow of
the gas mixture—increased the speed and power of *everything*
about the luxury liner and finally even set to work on the doors
with hammer and blowtorch, until they took on the shape of a
bird's wings tucked tight to dive, and the long tapering hood
now resembled a crow's beak. His pattern for the grille that he
forged was two talons opened to snatch their prey.

As bizarre as this transformation was, as often as it was discussed anew each day at the Dock Inn or on board the *Sleeping
Greek Maid* during crossings to the quarry, the Dog King was
apparently not disturbed by either beak or talons.

A crow? A vehicle like something from a spook-house ride?
When one of the miners risked speaking to him one morning
about the blacksmith's strange bodywork and happened to mention the disrespectful comparisons made in the tavern, Ambras
only laughed in amusement. Crow, jackdaw, or chicken—any
bird was all right by him. For in the shower of sparks that came
with every blow by which this young blacksmith turned a wreck
into a new vehicle, Major Elliot's legacy was taking on a new
form as well—a limousine that was close to being junked and
depended on army workshops would become *his* car at last; a

second-hand, rolling token of Elliot's power would become the unmistakable harbinger of *his* will; its new paint job, a brightly polished blackish gray, would mirror *his* strength.

Early one morning during the seventh week of major repairs, a brigade of mowers was busy cutting the first hay on the slopes below the forge, when one of them suddenly stopped and pointed up the hill with a cry of amazement—soundlessly, as the sun's image reflected off the windshield, chrome, and enamel in a chaos of dazzling light, *The Crow* rolled out of the entrance gate up there.

Even before the last mower had lifted his eyes from the drooping stalks up to that shining phenomenon, the motor started with a noise that was more like a bellow than any engine sound the brigade had ever heard before. The car rolled down the hill the length of a tall tree and then stopped in a quickly scattering cloud of exhaust and dust. The bellow sank to a steady thunder that now brought face after face to the windows of Moor. They all stared up at the forge.

As if coming to themselves after their first fright, four yelping dogs leapt out of the black void of the entrance. Their master followed at a leisurely pace, swinging his pack's steel collars in his right hand like a lash. The dogs circled the car, snapping at its freshly blackened tires, until Ambras caught up with them, opened one of the rear doors, and had them jump into the back.

Only now did the driver, did Bering let go of the wheel, intending to get out and yield his place to the gentleman. With the hand in which he still held the collars, Ambras blocked the door from opening more than a crack, grabbed Bering's shoulder with the other hand, and pushed him back down onto the upholstered seat: "Sit!"

With his dogs' eyes following him and as if led on some invisible leash, Ambras circled the sparkling vehicle once, twice, flung open the door, fell into the passenger seat, pulled the door to with the usual force—so that, given how easily it moved now, it banged shut loudly—and clapped the blacksmith on the arm: "Let's go."

"I'm . . . driving? Now? Where to?" Bering would have liked to get out again, at least to take off his leather apron and tell his father what was going on, and there was still a pot of chicory coffee simmering above the embers in the workshop, too.

But as always, whenever he surprised the blacksmith with one of his sudden orders, the Dog King would brook no delay. "Let's go. Anywhere . . . home. To the Villa. Drive to the Villa Flora."

CHAPTER 10

LILY

L ILY'S MOST SECRET POSSESSION CONSISTED
of five rifles, twelve bazookas, sixty-three hand grenades,
and more than nine thousand rounds of ammunition—all
packed in excelsior, cardboard, and oilcloth and kept in crates
that were painted black and so heavy that she could not carry but
only drag even the smallest of them.

Lily's most precious possession, in contrast, weighed no more
than an apple; it was a doeskin pouch that she had pulled from
the rubble of a bombed-out movie house on one of her expeditions in the lowlands and filled with those clouded emeralds
she sought and found in the ravines and high corries of the
Stony Sea.

Lily knew, however, not only about forgotten weapons caches
dispersed among the rocks during the war and about eddies in
glacial streams where emeralds rolled among the pebbles, but she
was also familiar with all the paths into the mountains, including
forbidden ones through mine fields above the timberline, and
even in the dark she could bound down the steepest scree
without stumbling.

78

Her agility in the wilderness offered better protection from the attacks and brutality of the gangs than any of her rifles, though on rare occasion she did carry one, disassembled and hidden under her worsted coat. On the same day the *Sleeping Greek Maid* was christened, while fleeing from two scouts of a marauding horde, she had climbed so high into the mountains that after eluding them she had to take a shortcut back to the lakeshore in order not to miss the launching. Without ropes or pitons, she scrambled that day down an icy, north-facing overhang. No one could follow her on routes like that.

Lily was the sole remaining resident of the weather tower that stood in the meadow near the shore and rose high above burned-out ruins that were once the galleries, sunbathing terraces, and spring-water pavilions of Moor's lakeside resort. Within the tower's circular walls and beneath its cupola and cast-iron weathervanes, she felt more at home than in any other building along the lake. At one time a thermometer, hygrometer, and barometer—all oversized and set in wall niches—had informed the spa's guests about the temperature, humidity, and pressure of the salubrious lake air, while a chromed water gauge had scribbled the lake's gentle rise and fall as a needle-fine diagram on an endless roll of paper. But those once-glass-paned niches had long since become empty, sooty holes, just like the windows in the old shoremaster's house under the linden trees near the beach.

With a pack of tail-wagging dogs pressing around her, Lily was about to tie the reins of her mule to the arm of a stone faun next to the stairs leading up to the Villa Flora, when the Crow cracked a loud backfire and turned off the lakeshore road and into the villa's drive. Lily gave her mule's neck a soothing pat, pulled a last strip of jerky from her saddlebag, cut it up, and tossed it to the dogs, who were now so torn between the meat and the vehicle rolling slowly toward them that they began to whimper.

The car glided along between the giant pines of the drive, disappeared behind their towering trunks, reappeared with a glint—

and as it came to a stop at the staircase was surrounded by the barking pack. Lily clapped her hands and laughed—so this was the junk bird, the monster that over the past few days people had been describing for her at farms, at checkpoints, at every stop along her trip back up from the lowlands.

Wild with joy, the dogs sprang at the metal wings and tail fins as Ambras, before getting out himself, opened the door and released the mastiff, two Labradors, and a black Newfoundland from the back seat to join the others: "Last stop, blacksmith. Turn it off."

Bering turned the engine off, but his hands clenched the steering wheel and his eyes were not on the flaking splendor of the Villa Flora. He stared across the dance of the dogs at the laughing woman. All his life he had never looked into a stranger's eyes for more than a heartbeat. And he lowered his gaze now, too, the moment Lily looked at him.

As Ambras walked around the car toward Lily, his hands flitted over the frantic pack, stroking muzzles and heads and pushing muddy paws away. "A visitor from the beach! What a surprise. Have you been waiting long?"

"Long enough to feed your beasts a week's provisions."

"They'll dream about you in gratitude. . . . I was at your tower on Wednesday and Friday. Were you on a trip?"

"I was outside."

"*Outside?* And?"

"There's a new barricade at the hanging bridge by the waterfall—four leathermen with slingshots, steel rods, and a walkie-talkie."

"And they let you through?"

"Me? Is my name Ambras? I went over the pass."

"With your mule?"

"Who else would have hauled my stuff?"

"Did you trade a lot?"

"A lot of crap."

"How long were you outside?"

"Eight days."

"And how's Elliot doing?"

"He's gone."

"Gone? What do you mean, gone?"

"Our major has got himself transferred. He's gone back to America. . . . Left six weeks ago. He left something for you at the barracks. I brought it along." The mule threw its head back in defiance as Lily pulled it toward her with a tug at its halter and took a small package out of a leather bag dangling from the pommel; it was wrapped in blue paper and tied with a dog collar. "Elliot's sergeant said you probably forgot the collar on your last visit." Lily threw the package at Ambras so abruptly that it fell among the dogs.

Ambras seemed strangely confused. He bent awkwardly to pick up the package, an irresistible attraction for dogs' noses. "Forgot? I've never left anything behind in the barracks." As he lifted the bundle from the pack, a pyramid of muzzles rose up under his hands. The dogs grew less curious only after he unfastened the collar, letting it fall to the ground with a rattle, and began to tear open the paper.

With the first rip in the blue paper a deeper blue shone through. Against this blue background gleamed white stars. Then the paper sailed away over the dogs' heads, and Ambras was holding the folded flag of the United States of America in his hands.

"That can't be everything," Lily said, "the thing was too heavy for that."

Ambras weighed the cloth in his hands, testing, and shook it like a pillow until it fell apart, unrolled, began to flap in the wind—and for a second time something dropped among the dogs, striking the stones with a metallic clang. Startled by the harsh sound, the pack pulled back for a moment, leaving a small circle clear, in the middle of which something inedible glistened. Ambras stared down between his outstretched arms at Major Elliot's farewell gift. At his feet lay a pistol.

"Stellamour Doctrine, paragraph three," Lily said, imitating the voice that, amplified by a battery of loudspeakers on the parade grounds, occasionally echoed through Moor from the radio at the secretary's office. "Private possession of firearms will be prosecuted under martial law and is punishable by death."

Ambras gathered the flag up, tossed it over his shoulder, a toga, and supplemented Lily's recitative with a stanza that had never been written down. "Villa Flora Doctrine, paragraph one: Martial law is Ambras. Paragraph two: Exceptions embellish the law." Then he bent down for the pistol, grabbing its barrel like the handle of a hammer and pointing it at Bering, who had rolled down the car window and was still sitting at the wheel, mouth agape. "Get out, will you. Come here!"

The abashed blacksmith obeyed, took ten steps, and was standing now, head lowered, in front of the Dog King and the woman; he fumbled awkwardly at the strings of his leather apron—the knot at the back would not undo. The pack sniffed at him, and he flinched in alarm when he felt a dog's wet tongue on his fingers, which were still tangled in the apron strings. "Off!" Ambras said, and the tongue desisted.

"You untie a knot with hands, not clumsy mitts," he heard the voice of the woman suddenly say, and in the next moment felt wonderfully soft, cool hands take his fingers from the knotted string, felt Lily's hands brush fleetingly across his back, sending a flush to his face. From the center of this touch a shudder rose up his spine and was lost in the roots of his hair. And then the oil-smeared apron finally fell from him—an ancient skin.

"Here, a tool for improving the world," Ambras said and held the pistol out to Bering as if wanting to press it into his hand. "Do you know what this thing is?"

The question came at the blacksmith so unexpectedly that he was still sailing along in his delight, light as a feather, before he understood—and felt his palms suddenly grow moist. As if his pores were about to release the dampness and moisture of that *one* night in April, a bead of sweat formed at a temple and crept down his cheek, then another. He saw light reflected off the nick-eled barrel of the weapon in Ambras's hand, and in the flash of two fired shots saw a stranger tumble into the darkness. And heard the rattle of a lost chain. . . . The Dog King knew about those shots that night. Knew about the dead man. Knew everything.

"Don't worry," Ambras said, popping the magazine out of the pistol handle and then shoving it back in again with his free hand. He held the weapon up as if for a skyward salute, pulled the breechblock back, then let it spring into place with a sharp click. "Don't worry, it's not loaded."

The weapon. It was the same model. Bering knew this weapon better than any other mechanism he had ever disassembled and put back together. On the morning after the shots, his father had picked it up like hot, glowing iron with a pair of hooked tongs and taken it to the workshop. There he had laid the thing on the anvil and demolished it under raging hammer blows and between blows had screamed: *Idiot, that idiot! The fool will get us all hanged yet! Shooting in his own house!*

Cock, grip safety, safety lever, magazine release, slide, trigger, and all the other parts that had glided so often through Bering's hands in the years before, that he had oiled and puzzled together into a never-changing toy—under those hammer blows, they whizzed through the workshop like unpredictable bullets. Only after a fragment crashed through a window, splintering a pane of rare glass, which was hard to replace, did the old man come to himself again and order Bering to gather up the pieces and bury them. Which he did, while his mother wiped the bloodstains from floorboards and stairs with water from Lourdes and a conse-crated sponge from the Red Sea.

"Well, what is it? Are you deaf?" Ambras was holding the pistol up so close to Bering's eyes that he could read what was engraved on the metal.

And in the low, resigned voice of someone charged with a crime who has at last ceased to resist and confesses, Bering read the engraving on the metal, the same words that during hours of mechanical play had grown so familiar to him that even in the dark he could have decoded them like Braille with his fingertips:

"*Colt M-1911 Automatic. Government Model. Caliber 45.*"

Ambras lowered the weapon. "Very good. So? Do you know how to handle tools like this, too? Can you shoot?"

"Shoot?" So it had *not* been an interrogation? He was *not* being charged? Had in fact the Dog King merely asked one of the many, countless questions a man could answer one way or another, and afterward time would still fly off into the void, its course and meaning not changed in the slightest? Everything remained as it was. Ambras knew nothing about that night.

"A lieutenant," Bering said slowly, "a lieutenant showed me a weapon like that last year. We . . . we took shots at the sundial on the washhouse wall."

He did not even need to lie now. The lieutenant, part of a retaliatory expedition that had decided to camp in the Bellevue's park, had paid him for repairing a broken diesel generator with target practice and a pair of boots that had hardly been worn. The numbered dial on the hotel's dilapidated washhouse had made an apparently easy target. The fan of hours pictured the riders of the Apocalypse—a faded horde on flaking plaster. But that day Bering had fired a whole magazine at one gaunt rider's coat-of-arms and had not hit it once.

"So he can shoot, too," Ambras said. "Well, take the thing then. It belongs to you. Martial law says, 'The blacksmith needs a hammer.' "

Lily had knelt down beside one of the Labradors and was scratching it behind the ears, when under the old magic of the weapon Bering was suddenly seized with a desire to feel her fleeting touch again. Hardly daring to breathe, he looked into her eyes. Then he reached out his hand and took the weapon from Ambras.

CHAPTER II

THE BRAZILIAN

S he came over the pass. *Down the avalanche cut, through knee-deep snow, she came over the pass. We ran into her at the Eishof Inn. Yesterday evening. Her mule had a heavy load!* She had been down at the army base again.

She brought a whole crate of cigarette lighters with her this time—and nylons! The mule had a portable radio around its neck; some kind of radio or tape recorder at any rate, and it was playing that American music. As if she couldn't come up with anything better to do with her batteries. American music.

She's probably on her way to Leys now. She was at the dock this morning, selling sunglasses to the quarrymen belowdecks on the Sleeping Greek Maid. *She offered the boatswain a bottle of cologne if he would let her bring her animal on board and put in at Leys Bay on the way back from the quarry. Leys Bay, just for her alone! No one else wanted to get off there.*

And?

You ask? Of course she got what she wanted. And the boatswain almost grounded the Sleeping Greek Maid *docking at Leys . . .*

Whenever Lily returned from the lowlands with her mule,

Moor eagerly followed her every move. For the girl from the weather tower was the only person in the lake country who still crossed the border with scarce black-market items whenever some army maneuver or other had once again blocked the road to the lowlands until further notice and no more safe-conduct papers were to be had from Moor's secretarial office, not even for a bribe.

Lily did not care about restricted areas or safe-conduct papers, but simply went her own way, supplying whatever anyone wanted. For the people of Moor that meant tropical fruits, tools, or green coffee beans from army depots; and for the logistics officers and soldiers who ran those depots, it meant the hellish souvenirs she found in caverns, caves, or simply under moldering leaves on her expeditions across the Stony Sea: antiquated weapons—for shooting or stabbing—from the final battles and skirmishes of the war, bullet-riddled helmets, bayonets, iron crosses, and all the junk that the army of Moor's men had lost or cast aside on the road to ruin. The war and its triumphs had long since become at least as faraway and inexplicable a memory for the victors as their own ruin was for the defeated, and so such trash was now collectible, its value steadily growing and constantly determined anew by Lily's trading. The victors offered scarce goods in return for the abandoned insignia of their foes. At army bases, then, Lily traded helmets for honeydews, daggers adorned with skulls for licorice and bananas, medals for nylons and cocoa.

The Dog King lacked none, *none* of these bartered items, since under the shadow of the army he enjoyed every privilege and knew no want; yet even for him Lily found something for which in the end he was prepared to pay almost any price: gemstones. For a single emerald washed from the sediment of a glacial stream, Ambras gave her more food and luxury goods than she ordinarily realized from a whole muleload of war junk traded at the bases.

The Dog King was addicted to stones. Even dozing, he some-

times whispered his calculations of the cubic mass of those huge
blocks of granite he had his miners blast from the slopes of the
Blind Shore, and he dreamt of the ponderous hewn stones he had
carried on a wooden barrow in his years under the whip of the
camp. . . . But since that February day when Lily offered him an
emerald in exchange for one of his puppies, and then over time
had sold him more than a dozen of her finds, he had been losing
himself more and more often in the shimmering depths of crys-
talline structures. Even the dull sheen of freshly quarried granite
now reminded him of the inner patterns of precious stones, and
during the day he often sat for hours in his administrator's shed
examining an emerald's floating inclusions under a magnifying
glass. In those tiny crystal gardens, whose petals and hazes
gleamed silvery green against the light, he saw a mysterious image
of the world, without sound or time, which for a moment let him
forget the horrors of his own history, and even his hate.

And so Ambras had become not only Lily's most magnani-
mous trading partner, but he was also the one person along the
lake who called Lily by her name. For although she had spent
most of the years of her life thus far living in the same poverty
and under the same sky bounded by mountains and chains of
hills as any other resident along the lakeshore, for Moor Lily was
and remained simply "the Brazilian." An outsider. Someone from
somewhere else.

In the year Bering was born, Lily had ended up beside Moor's
lake as part of a stream of refugees from the rubble wastelands
of the city of Vienna—a five-year-old girl, burning up with
scarlet fever and lying under a horsehair blanket in her father's
wheelbarrow.

For how many days and weeks had this column of wagons,
gaunt saddle horses, and heavily burdened people on foot been
moving through the scorched countryside? Much later, Lily
remembered the nights most of all: beds made under frosted
trees, cones of light where milky-white figures appeared and vanished again, drafty barns with empty birds' nests stuck to the

rafters, and a burning train station, its windows bright red as if lit for a festival. Snow-covered people lay in a house with no roof, and one evening the column came to a halt, blocked by cadavers of cows, with crows hacking at the nostrils and eyes. . . . Above all, however, Lily remembered the promising sound of the one word that the refugees spoke as a charm to ban all the pain and terror of their trek, that was whispered in sleepless hours and sometimes even *sung* by the driver of a large covered wagon: *Brazil. We're headed for Brazil!* . . .

But just as a rivulet always seeks the path of least resistance, burying itself in sandy soil here, washing around a boulder there, branching out over pebbles, and simply lifting lighter pieces of rubbish and wood to carry them away, so in those days the column had steadily avoided dangers—burning villages, rivers with no bridges or ferries, tollgates, barricades, and at times mere rumors of the cruelty of some band of highwaymen—and had chanced increasingly large detours in great mad arcs and spirals, always in the hope of a coast, of a sea that bore ships to Brazil. And so the great harbors of the Adriatic, of the Ligurian Sea, and finally even of the North Atlantic had served as the column's wavering polestar, until at last, on a day in late winter, it arrived somewhere, nowhere, in Moor.

As at so many stops along their flight, what awaited them here was a promise of quick transport, of potatoes, bread, a roof over their heads. After a few days, a week at most, of waiting in the empty hotels of this former spa, so it was said, they could proceed by train across the snow-blocked passes—across the Alps!—to Trieste, and from there by ship to a paradise.

It was evening when the column reached the lake and the railroad embankment, which in those days still had tracks and a train of empty cattle cars—a deserted beach. But the pillaged, ice-cold hotels—the Bellevue, the Stella Polaris, the Europa, and the Grand Hotel, where long pennants of snow wafted from pagoda roofs—were already filled with other weary souls, expelled, homeless, bombed out, who huddled around open fires in the lobbies and defended every spot to sleep with canes and fists.

Suddenly the word was: Everyone turn around, go back, everybody down to the beach. The commandant, some commandant or other, had assigned them the old lakeside resort as quarters.

That evening, the little girl Lily thought she had arrived at her goal. Stucco roses, garlands of plaster shells, the grand pump-room's shimmering mosaics, white statues along the galleries, the dusty splendor that slipped past her eyes as her father pushed and tugged the wheelbarrow into the spa's interior—she thought she recognized it all as a token of the land that had been described to her in so many tales and promises as she fell asleep in a barn or out in the cold fields. And so despite her exhaustion and burning brow, she tossed the horsehair blanket aside, leapt up from her father's wheelbarrow, skipped with arms outspread around the spouts of the defunct fountain, and called out over and over, "Brazil! Brazil! We're here, we're in Brazil!"

But what awaited the girl that evening at Moor's lakeside resort was more than just disappointment that no one else wanted to call this snowy shore *Brazil* or that beside the promenade lay only a frozen lake and not the promised ocean. . . . For camped alongside the refugees from Vienna, among long rows of cots and straw beds in what had once been a gymnasium, were about thirty liberated slave laborers, who existed on meager rations provided by ever-changing occupation forces and were waiting to be returned at last to places from where, an eternity ago, they had been dragged away to this lake. Too emaciated or badly injured to join up with any column passing through and leave Moor on foot, these last-remaining souls had been hoping for months now that someone marching home would forget the rules of self-preservation and burden himself with a cripple or an invalid, had hoped for hands to carry them, for a shoulder to lean on or a wagon that would bear them out of this chaos and back home.

Among these figures cloaked in blankets and rags, there was a linen-goods dealer from Bessarabia, who had watched his wife die in a cattle car. Even now, after the three years of unending camp life since her death in the suffocating crush of the deportation train, he still saw her face before him—always when he lay in the dark, always when he closed his eyes, and always. An empty bowl still warm before him—so hastily had he eaten—he was crouched against a set of wall bars, scratching scabs and great patches of dead skin from his arms and the backs of his hands, when Lily's father entered the room.

Her father did not notice this gaunt figure that suddenly stopped scratching and stared at him open-mouthed. He had picked his daughter up out of her feverish dance around the fountain and wrapped her in a sheepskin jacket, and was now carrying her to one of the straw beds assigned the newcomers for the night, when the linen-goods dealer arose painfully and, scrambling, stumbling over blankets and bundles and sleepers and cardboard suitcases, came toward him, saying: "That man there, the one there with the girl"—did not shout, but simply said over and over again in a not especially loud voice: "That man there. The one with the girl." But as he lurched forward, he kept one arm outstretched, pointing unwaveringly at Lily's father.

In the flickering uneasiness of the room, it did not bother anyone at first that when the gaunt man finally reached him and began to pound his back with fists, the father, still bent over and pressing his daughter to him, simply stood there without straightening up or turning around or raising a hand to defend himself. Strangely undaunted by these weak blows, he laid his daughter on her bed and spread the jacket over her.

Only now does he stand up erect. He does not defend himself. Eyes open wide, mute and rigid with terror, Lily lies there on the straw.

The gaunt man is no longer pummeling her father, but has latched on to a sleeve, as if he does not rightly know just how he should grab hold and continue attacking someone who just stands there and does not defend himself—but does not flee, either. At a loss, he turns to his companions and now begins to shout across the hall after all, as if crying to them for help: "That's him. That's one of them." How gaunt even his voice is!

And, of course, here and there loud curses are heard in the gymnasium: "Shut up! Are they crazy?" And one fellow even tries to calm the gaunt man: "Cut it out, stop it, we want to sleep. . . ." But why should an exhausted man, who has had to see a lot worse than a fight, get involved when some stranger starts hitting another stranger somewhere in the dark? If only these idiots don't step on your feet. Or in your bowl of potatoes. No one tries to separate the two. They're not really hitting each other, anyway. The one has got his claws set in the other.

And then the gaunt man is suddenly no longer alone, but surrounded by his companions. They have understood better than all the others that there at the end of the room one of their own is seeking revenge on *one of them*. But they have all dreamt of revenge at some point in the past years—one man alone is too weak for such dreams. And so they lend the gaunt man a hand. And crowd around the father and ask him something and kick him, although he hasn't even answered. They kick and shove him out of the room ahead of them, and aren't even sure themselves where to—just outside. They want to go out into the night, where they will be alone with him. The newcomers from a devastated city don't understand any of this. They want to sleep. It suits them fine that the room has quieted down again.

No one could say later whether a former linen-goods dealer from Bessarabia was the only liberated slave laborer that night who recognized a refugee from Vienna as one of his tormentors from the war years, as *one of those* who had appeared in their black uniforms on train platforms, in camps and quarries, under gallows—wherever not just the happiness and life of their victims came to an end, but a whole world, too. Perhaps each of the liberated prisoners saw a different memory before him in

Lily's father. There was enough to remember. Wasn't he the one from the ice party, who in winter poured water over naked prisoners at roll call, until they lay encased in ice as if under glass? Or was he the Stoker, who after shooting a group of hostages had tossed his mortally wounded victims alive into the pit of hot coals? . . .

The linen-goods dealer at any rate had no doubts. He would have recognized this one face among the faces of all humanity—the man who was stumbling out into the night ahead of him and who fell now was the man in the black uniform who had looked into the cattle car through an air hole with barbed wire nailed over it. That day. At a train platform in Bessarabia. This man had strolled back and forth in the midday sun and smoked a cigarette while the people crammed inside the car had screamed for water and help. He had walked back and forth as if promenading, but when an arm had stretched out to him through the barbed-wire mesh of the air hole, a hand holding an empty tin bowl, he had pulled his pistol and shot at that hand.

The linen-goods dealer feels the scar burn as hot as the wound did that day.

And while the man simply walked on and the bowl rolled across the platform and came to rest between tracks, a woman was dying of thirst inside, in the darkness, in the midst of the screams. All her life she had loved to wear starched blouses and a silver brooch, and now she was lying on straw in her own excrement and no longer knew her husband, who crouched beside her and whom she called "sir" when she begged him for water. He did not want her to see his empty, bleeding hand, and in that single hour whispered a hundred times and more: *Don't leave me.*

But where to take him?

What to do with this swine?

To the shore, where else? To the water. The lake is the only place for him. They drag the father through the meadow's wet snow, down to the water. So let him go under now the way his army went under, and his city. They leave a wide track behind them, and streaks of black. Is that blood? They reach the yacht landing, a long wooden bridge that ends invisibly in the night. They trample across the planks. They toss him off the pier down into the darkness.

But the ice covering the narrow bay does not break as he lands hard and lies there. He falls six feet. Onto black ice. The water level is at its winter low.

He doesn't want to go under! Well then, down they go. After him. But a few of them remain behind now, including the linen-goods dealer. He did not even grab hold as they tossed him over. Even on the way across the meadow to the shore, his hate was growing much smaller than the pain another face has brought back, *her* face. And there is no room left beside that face for the battered features of that man there. He has vanished. He is lying in the ice.

But several of his companions are now deep into their anger. They don't give up. They want the ending they are entitled to. The swine won't go under!

As if it had sprouted there on the shore that very moment, they see the old diving tower high above them, a wooden scaffold with lots of arms, from which in summers almost forgotten now headlong dives, somersaults, and elegant pikes had been executed into the green water. A black silhouette against a clear starry sky, the tower looms in the night—a gallows.

Lily's mother was never able to say at exactly what moment she recognized her husband among the torches that came dancing across the ice on the bay toward the diving tower. She was standing in line with her blue enamel pot outside a field kitchen set up in the arcade and watched as a horde of ruffians or drunks dragged their victim along—but maybe it was only some sort of rough game. And suddenly felt her pulse race when she recognized first the coat, then the figure. And probably at the same moment she heard her name. Only now, after a long delay—as if the horde had stormed right on past time faster than any scream, as if the groans, the slaps of blows, and all the noise of revenge had to echo toward her in the stillness first—only now were the father's cries to be heard. He was crying for help. He screamed his wife's name.

But they have already reached the diving tower. They are standing on the firm ice. Who brought that rope? Where did that rope come from? It is long enough and it is strong enough and it falls out of night down to them there on the ice and loops around the feet of their victim. *And now pull! Pull him up!*

Who is this fury who suddenly starts shrieking behind them and tries to push her way between them? Does she belong to him? She is simply shoved aside. They are standing in closed ranks now. That raving woman won't help him. "Higher!" Others like him hung from worse gallows than this during the first days of liberation. Just once, if for the first and only time in their lives, they are going to turn red, *red!* in their black uniforms. And if not for shame, than at least with the blood that rushes to their heads in their final hour.

Hands tied behind his back, the father swings above the ice. Under the force of jostles and blows, he swings through the emptiness. Finally hangs motionless in the night. A dripping plumb bob.

What happened then happened so suddenly that witnesses to this act of revenge—participants and onlookers alike—later had to merge several often contradictory fragments to form a single memory. A searchlight seized the diving tower, bathing the horde and its victim in white light. Orders barked over the ice. Soldiers tramped across the yacht landing and up the tower's winding staircase. The liberated prisoners' tight circle around their victim broke apart under kicks and the blows of rifle butts. There was also the crack of one or two warning shots. Then a jagged bayonet gnawed through the rope, and the father fell to the ice a second time. A soldier who tried to catch him could not hold on.

That plunge, however, was not a rescue, but only the beginning of a riddle that in coming years Lily's mother would simply

call "Father's fate." For the father was in fact still alive and
babbled and pleaded with the soldiers who grabbed him under
the arms, propped him up, and though he was dripping with
blood, drove off with him in an army truck, along with the linen-
goods dealer and several of his companions. . . . But wherever it
was they took him that night or in the days or weeks or months
that followed—he never returned.

With no more success than she had before with the horde, the
mother now tried to battle her way to her husband through
the cordon of his ostensible rescuers. The soldiers kept shouting
the same incomprehensible sentence and pushed her back. She
ran after the truck as it lumbered across the meadow, but got
only as far as the lake promenade, where she had to stop to catch
her breath—and then waited all night beside Lily's bed for
someone to fetch her.

The next morning snow was falling in watery flakes, when,
under the escort of a military patrol, the linen-goods dealer and
his companions returned to the lakeside resort to tie up their
bundles. "Home, we're going home"—that was their sole reply
to the refugees' questions. The linen-goods dealer said not a
word. Never budging from the side of the soldiers in the patrol,
Lily's mother received answers just as curt and cool, which an
officer finally translated for her, saying that the war criminal
was at headquarters, was being interrogated. But when Lily's
mother, her feverish daughter in tow, arrived at headquarters
with her questions not an hour later, the transfer had already
occurred—Moor's commandant had turned the father over to
the Red Army.

Where would they take him? To what city? To Russia?
Where? . . . To these and all other questions there were no more
answers. The father did not return. Not the next day, not the
next week. The column of refugees moved on. Were the emigrants supposed to miss their train, the only train to Trieste, for a
stranger, who had joined them with his wife and daughter on one
day and had got lost again on another? There were other ways to

get to Brazil, and those who missed the lost man should wait for him. But there were only two of them.

So Lily and her mother remained behind, and Lily's fever receded, even as she realized that this trampled beach with its black trees . . . that these mountains and statues, that this fountain . . . that none of this was Brazil. But her mother wanted to stay. Her husband had disappeared in Moor, and it was to Moor that he would—he surely *must*—return someday. Lily's mother, who until the devastation of her city had painted scenery in a workshop of some Burgtheater, began to paint again—first, a Last Judgment on a freshly stuccoed wall of the rebuilt cemetery chapel; later, the solemn faces of farmers, miners, and fishermen. She painted pictures of the boats of a Society of Penitence moving through the reeds, of the mountains in shades of blue, of the lake at sunset with sailboats, of the lake at sunset without sailboats—and for them she was given flour and eggs and what they needed to live.

On Sunday afternoons, however, she would often sit before a life-size, half-length portrait of her husband, which she never completed. She painted the picture from a photograph that she carried with her until her death and that showed Lily's father smiling in front of the Vienna Opera. He was wearing his black uniform with all his medals and a cap whose brim left his eyes in deep shadow. The mother sat and painted and, brushstroke by brushstroke, substituted a loden suit with elkhorn buttons for the black uniform and a felt hat with a jaunty spray of heather for the brimmed cap.

When the last column of the steady stream of refugees had left the halls of the lakeside resort in search of better days, the commandant, seconded by Moor's secretary, authorized the painter and her daughter to move into the vacant shoremaster's house. The commandant would accept no gift in exchange; the secretary gratefully let her paint his portrait. There in the house's old scullery, designated now as a studio, Lily found her mother beside an upended easel in a puddle of linseed oil, turpentine, and runny paints—it was the nineteenth year of the Peace of

Oranienburg. Lily carried and dragged the unconscious woman to the pier and laid her in a skiff and rowed madly across the lake—and only as the clinic at Haag came into view did she notice that her mother was already dead.

Not until a year later, however, did Lily leave the house they had shared and lay claim to the weather tower. For by then, of all the buildings of the lakeside resort, only the top floor of the tower had been left untouched by the conflagration with which Moor had paid for refusing to buy fire insurance from one of the gangs from the Stony Sea.

The arsonists had gathered up rotted lounge chairs, sunshades, and folding screens from the grand pumproom and the galleries, tossed the kindling of broken doors and shutters onto the pyre, lit it, and used slingshots to drive off anyone from Moor who attempted to put it out. A hail of glass and fist-size stones kept raining down in the darkness on anyone who tried to approach the flames with a bucket of water or merely out of curiosity, until finally nothing was left to be saved and the lakeside resort collapsed in an incandescent cloud.

Lily had been in the mountains that night and from her camping spot had seen only a puzzling soft reflection in the fog banks far below, a pulsing light that might just as easily have come from a wedding fire or the burnt offerings of a procession of penitents. Two days later, suspecting nothing, she returned to the lakeshore, to a scene of burned desolation, and within an hour after her arrival began clearing her things out of the shoremaster's house.

The arsonists—and after them, apparently pillagers—had left little of any use behind; even the gas lamps had been ripped from the charred beams; all her provisions locked in tins were missing, every glass jar had burst or been broken, the black shards strewn like seed across the floor. The only things left untouched—because they could be reached only by a trapdoor hidden under the ashes—were the remnants of her parents' lives: a trunk full of clothes, photographs, tubes of paint, brushes, and old paper. . . .

In that trunk Lily found a cracked and brittle map, which on her first day in the weather tower was the only decoration she tacked to the freshly whitewashed wall. Although the ocean's blue was mildewed and the coastline broken in many spots by a torn fold, above the network of longitudes and latitudes and in a strangely intricate hand was written the word that brought back her childhood and a forgotten longing: *Brazil.*

CHAPTER 12

THE HUNTRESS

LILY COULD KILL. A WOMAN ALONE IN THE mountains, alone somewhere in the hotel ruins high above the lake, she had to flee again and again from the lust of the gangs, had to bound down slopes, escaping into the wilderness, often into the night, running from murderers and arsonists, had to hide in the ravines of the Stony Sea, in some thicket along the lakeshore, or in caves. There she crouched, her heart racing, a jackknife clutched in her hand, readying herself for that one moment when the steps of her pursuers would come to a halt outside her refuge. . . .

But twice, sometimes three times a year, unpredictably and by no regular schedule, Lily changed herself from a fleet-footed victim who was hard to hunt into an equally swift huntress, who always remained invisible high in the rocks and, from as far as a quarter of a mile off, held her prey under the spell of cross hairs and killed. Twice, sometimes three times a year, Lily hunted her enemies.

At the dawn of such days, and often still deep in darkness, she would start up out of a dream, rise from her bed under the beams of the weather tower, pack camping gear, bread, and dried fruit in a knapsack, dress for the region of ice, and walk down to the boat landing. There she tossed a few buoys and some carelessly gathered nets into her skiff and rowed toward a bay to the east of Moor. Anyone seeing her at that hour—the helmsman of the *Sleeping Greek Maid*, perhaps, who liked to stand in the wheelhouse in the early morning and gaze out over the water with his binoculars—saw only a fisherwoman rowing to her fishing grounds. Without ever arousing suspicion, Lily glided toward invisibility, toward the deep shadows of the cliffs. There she pulled her boat out of the black water, hid it behind a curtain of blackthorn bushes and willows at the bank, and set out for the Stony Sea.

On those days, Lily climbed without rest for more than four hours through a pathless world that fell away ever steeper below, until she reached a spur of rocks overgrown with dwarf mountain pine. No more than a stone's throw from that spur, and just beneath the tongue of a glacier covered with debris, yawned the entrance to the cave in which years before, while searching for amber and emeralds, she had discovered the cache of weapons, *her* weapons.

Lily did not know who had dragged these black crates full of grenades, rifles, and bazookas up into the mountains to arm himself for coming battles once the war was over, perhaps even well into the Peace of Oranienburg. The weapons came from the arsenals of various armies: American grenades, English Enfield rifles with scopes, even a Russian Tokarev, and a German carbine lay bedded in the excelsior among boxes of ammunition that had a phosphorus charge that sent up a smoky flash as it hit its target, signaling to the marksman where his shot had landed. . . .

Lily had never attempted to ferret out the true master of this stockpile or move the cache to some better hiding place. For from the cover of the dwarf pine, she could see the cave's entrance, camouflaged with brush and stones, and could check to see if since her last hunt anyone had found his way up here or

perhaps had returned after all, decades later, to fetch his booty—
and the undisturbed camouflage, the lack of any tracks in the sur-
rounding firn, were also a sign to her that it was, had to be, her
fate to do what she did.

Let the penitents in their processions of reconciliation by the
lake and all those other grovelers, pious snivelers, and hypocrites
go ahead and illumine their shrines with candles for the dead,
entreat their souls, and believe in some supernatural justice or
at least in the decisions of military courts—Lily believed only in
the black maw of this cave. Whatever power or chance it had
been that had brought her here and shown her the means of an
earthly justice—this maw cried out for her and demanded that
she make use of her find and strike her foes and scatter them in
the wilderness.

And had there been a single sign, a strange footprint in the firn
or a branch torn from the camouflage, to suggest that she was not
the only person who armed and transformed herself here, she
would perhaps have left the cover of dwarf pine and returned to
the lake, actually relieved, never to come again. But except for a
single Enfield rifle, except for *her* rifle, the weapons had lain
untouched for years.

And so she did what the maw commanded and broke through
the brush of camouflage into the mountain, and deep inside it
opened one of the wooden crates (always the same one) and
armed herself. And when she returned out of the darkness into
the light of day, she was not carrying some antiquated, useless
collector's item—like those she found buried in the leaves and
soil of old battlefields and combat zones and exchanged at army
depots for scarce goods and provisions—but a shiny sharpshooter's rifle without a trace of patina.

Among the soldiers of the occupation forces, who had non-
chalantly shown her how to handle such weapons—when, for
instance, at the end of a trading session they would boast of the
accuracy of their own rifles and fire them at tiny balloons at the
base's shooting gallery—among them, there was not one who was

a better shot than she by now. But Lily always let her un-
prompted instructors believe she watched these demonstrations
with frightened awe and could be persuaded only with difficulty
and lots of applause to try a shot now and then herself. And
under the soldiers' eyes, she always placed her shots convincingly
just outside the balloons, bull's-eyes, or cardboard enemies.

Armed for hunting season, Lily walked, climbed, crept, and
scrambled over the Stony Sea for hours, sometimes days, glean-
ing a pretty fossil here and there along the way or even splinters
of emeralds as she forded streams, but searching for nothing
except her game. For none of the gangs made permanent camp in
the remains of bombed-out mountain garrisons and blown-up
bunker systems; only those who wanted to be safe from swift
reprisal after a raid, or from a rival gang or perhaps a retaliatory
expedition, retreated to these stony labyrinths, staying here a
few days or weeks, then returning to swoop down on a farm,
an entire village, or a Society of Penitence. Lily knew many of
the gangs' dens, but usually found them empty on her hunting trips.

It was always the same fever that seized her, an overwhelming
feeling of fear, triumph, and rage, when at last she came across
her enemies: the huntress silent and invisible among the rocks—
and far below her, looking like faceless insects through her scope,
a horde of leathermen or a column of veterans wanted for arrest
marching along the path of the slope opposite, or across a
meadow, a field of scree. Even at that distance, the laughter and
shouts were audible at times—and unmistakable. It was their
deceptive belief in their own strength that led those little figures
down there to this loud self-betrayal. If they had a battle behind
them, they roared drunken recollections to each other of especially crushing blows; if they had looted, they often stumbled
along in grotesque costumes, in the bloodied clothes of their victims, aping the wails of their battered prey, laughing, bawling
cries for help in this stony wasteland, which reverberated with the
call of just a single jackdaw if the wind was calm.

Pressing the butt of her rifle to her cheek, Lily brought her enemies, man by man, into the bluish, quivering focus of the cross hairs. At such moments she did not care if those moving targets down below were relics of the war—veterans who had been fleeing the victors' military courts for decades now and led the lives of outcasts in these limestone wastes—or if that was the late-born brood of ruined cities lurching along down there, dull-witted thugs who had eluded all the welfare and educational programs of Stellamour, Bringer of Peace, to join together in packs that glorified a life without pity. . . . At such moments, Lily knew only that by tomorrow night each of these figures might appear below her tower or outside any house or farmstead in Moor, with a torch or a chain in his fist, demanding *everything* and killing with his bare hands.

Once the huntress had decided on a target, she followed the last moves of her prey with her rifle barrel so slowly and unfalteringly that it was as if her hands, her arms, shoulders, and eyes had merged with the weapon's scope and mechanism to form a single, half-organic, half-metallic machine. For the space of three or four breaths and to the rhythm of her pulse, she let the head and chest of her prey sway out of the cross hairs and back into the cross hairs, until she finally squeezed the trigger and at almost the same moment saw the swaying object drop—and the horde scatter.

For even before the echo of the shot had returned from the vastness of the Stony Sea and died away, all those for whom the bullet had *not* been intended took cover, vanished—roaring, strong, and invincible one moment, and in the next hidden in thickets of dwarf pines, among scree, and behind boulders. They reminded Lily of riders on a whirligig, whose circling chairs are suddenly torn from their moorings and flung with wild centrifugal force in all directions. . . . To watch a dreaded horde fly apart like that was such a ludicrous sight that sometimes she instinctively began to snicker and dropped her rifle with a giggle.

Below, amid the busted carousel, the smoke of the phosphorus charge rose up, the pungent signal of a hit. And it probably stank a little like hell there, too. Lily's nostrils spread as she spotted this drifting pennant of smoke with her naked eye. Under the pennant lay something tiny, inert, dark. Her prey.

But woe to that dark something in the distance if it dared to move, to wag its head, if it wailed or cried for its comrades. Then Lily's giggle died away at once. Then she pulled her prey into the cross hairs again, drew it very close, fired a second time, and cursed amid the echo. And stared through the scope at what was at last a dead man.

He lay in that total solitude into which only a man who has been shot—who has entered the line of fire, endlessly far from any cover—is hurled. On the borders of that solitude, invisible behind rocks and dwarf pines, his comrades crouched under the spell of deathly fear and did not dare to do anything—not to flee, not to move, not to cry. . . . Only now did Lily release her prey from the cross hairs into an eternal distance in which everything once again appeared small and meaningless.

CHAPTER 13

IN THE DARKNESS

THE POPPY GREW HIGH IN THE FIELDS that year and with it came weeds. Even potato and cabbage patches, the steepest clearing, every parcel from which—no matter how hard the ground—the people of Moor tried to extract some harvest was sprinkled with red, hemmed in red, marbled with the red of poppy blossoms.

But only the blacksmith's wife knew that poppy meant blood and was a sign from the Virgin. *She* had strewn this silky red over the land as a daily reminder to her last-remaining son that among the many whose deaths had never been atoned, who lay somewhere in the soil of Moor, along the shore, or under a thin layer of gravel, there was surely also a victim who had not been slain by thugs or in the war or in the quarry, but by *his* hand. . . . *Holy Mary have mercy on him and pray for him*—so began and ended each devotion the blacksmith's wife prayed before an altar she had erected in her bedroom, a wax Madonna encircled by empty cookie tins and animal bones wrapped in silver paper—*and lead my son back to Thy kingdom.*

Ever since Bering's mother had seen the gentlest of her children vanish along with the Dog King in that smoky cloud of dust billowing up behind the Crow, she had left the gate to the farmstead standing wide. For on the very first night that passed without the heir, Celina the Pole had appeared above the reeds of the forge pond bearing a message from the Madonna. The blacksmith's wife was to keep the gate open day and night for the return of her lost sons. Weakened by many days of fasting and the exhausting night vigils at her altar, the blacksmith's wife would not have been able to close the gate in any case without the help of the Madonna—it was too heavy and dragged in the gravel, and ever since the days of major repairs, her half-blind husband no longer cared about the gate or the farm. This was no longer his house. And whoever left this house without a word— in a leather apron smeared with oil and at the side of a dog man who was protected by the occupation army—was no longer his son.

The heir had been gone a day and a night, and did not return until the next evening. Dressed in strange clothes, without his apron, he arrived in twilight, coming up the hill on foot like a sinner, and the blacksmith's wife hoped he had finally understood the Madonna's sign and was returning to make atonement and to cleanse his house of what had been. And she ran toward him with open arms.

But he simply held out a net bag full of white bread and canned peaches and walked on past, pushing aside her hands and her questions. She followed him into the house and up the stairs to his room. He did not say much; kneeling on the planks in front of his wardrobe, he stuffed clothes into a cardboard suitcase that had no latches, and tossed back into the cupboard what he did not need; he removed from the wall the photo showing him on the dock with his brothers, a tattered piece of crape still dangling from its frame. He laid the picture with the clothes, looped some wire around the bag, and said, "I'm taking the horse."

"For heaven's sake, my little boy," the blacksmith's wife whispered, "are you leaving us? But for where? Where are you going?"

To the house of dogs. The heir wanted to live at the house of dogs—and now he carried his suitcase out to the stall. Not until he was putting the packsaddle on the restive horse, and ripped his jacket on a strap buckle, did the blacksmith's wife notice the weapon in his belt. The gentlest of her sons was carrying a weapon! Hadn't that cursed thing been shattered on the anvil under the blows of his father's hammer? Had she not with her own eyes seen steel springs and fragments of metal whiz through the workshop, on the same day she washed blood from the cobblestones at the gate? Was time running backwards now at last and putting together again *everything* that had been shattered—and not just what was unjustly destroyed, but also the whizzing debris of the weapon her son now bore in his belt? Was this the way the Madonna had answered her prayers and entreaties for restitution? . . .

"May Satan remove his claws from you," she whispered, but did not dare touch him. "For heaven's sake, what has become of you?"

"Be quiet," he said. "I have a job at the villa, and bed and board. Be quiet. You'll get what you need. I have to go. I can't spend my whole life here as a blacksmith. I'll send you two what you need. Be quiet! I'll be back."

So he left for the house of dogs, leading the horse out of the farmyard. She stood there at the entrance and stared after him, as if with her eyes alone she could force him to turn back. She felt her husband's gaze at her back; as on every other day, he was sitting at the kitchen window. She felt his eyes, which could now distinguish only bright and dark, only phantoms, and even at this terrible moment did not want to turn around to him and tell him who it was that she had seen vanish in the darkness outside.

She was still standing at the entrance gazing into the night, long after the heir had become invisible by the lakeshore and no sound of a hoof was to be heard. When the pain in her legs became unbearable from standing so long, she walked, groaning, to the forge pond and sat down in one of the cannibalized wrecks stranded among the rushes. There in a jeep with no tires or steering wheel, she waited for a miracle, for the appearance of Celina, who would soon hover above the water and tell her what to do now. She waited all night. This time the soul of the Polish woman kept silent and hidden in the reeds. And the Madonna Herself gave no further sign, either. The pond remained mute and black and by the light of dawn revealed only her own reflection.

When she heard her husband shouting through the open kitchen window for matches to light the stove, she finally stood up—and suddenly knew what must happen, even without Celina's counsel. She had to sacrifice herself. She had to follow the example of the saints and martyrs who had also sacrificed themselves and in so doing had saved souls.

She returned to the house unnoticed, softly opened the trap-door to the cellar and pulled it softly shut behind her, descended the stone steps, and sat down on the hard clay between two empty barrels. In that same darkness in which she had brought her lost son into the world on Moor's night of bombs, she would give him life a second time. In the cellar of his house polluted by blood she would take his guilt upon her and there on the bare floor, with no bed, with no warming blanket, and with no light, she would pray the rosary, so rich in suffering. From the depths she would unremittingly and insistently beg heaven to be gracious to the heir, until Celina or the Madonna Herself took pity on her and told her at last that it was enough and that her child had been received again into the host of the redeemed.

But this time the Madonna was implacable. The blacksmith's wife whispered rosary after rosary into the darkness and withstood all temptation, all the entreaties and threats of her husband, who had fumbled and searched through the house and had not found her between the barrels until the second day after her disappearance. She did not climb back to the light of day. She did not want to return to the world again.

In the first weeks of her penance, the old man often groped his way down to her in the darkness, where they were now equally blind at last. He never carried a lamp, had not needed one for a long time now. He brought bread, chicory coffee, and cold potatoes. She accepted bread and water. Coffee, blankets, but all the rest she refused. He saw to it that she did not starve. He brought her clothes and, when the stench became intolerable, a chamber pot. He capitulated.

She remained steadfast for weeks and months, and confuted even the evil spirits who on frosty nights kept conjuring up the image of the kitchen stove. And when the Brazilian, snow clinging to her shoes, found her way down to her and offered her tea, gingerbread, and news from the house of dogs, she stopped saying her rosary only to tell her that she should go, vanish. As long as the heir did not relieve her of this penance himself and as long as the Madonna kept silent, she would have to hold out. She no longer felt the cold.

In December, the blacksmith was feverish for three days and did not make his way to the cellar; he lay in the kitchen with his head burning up and watched the shadows of chickens between the legs of the table and chairs. He did not have the strength to chase the chickens from the kitchen. They strayed through the cold house searching for food and pecked the mildew from the furniture. But even during those long days he never heard a complaint from the cellar, or any other sound from its depths.

When Moor's charcoal burner was attacked on New Year's Eve and so badly wounded that he died before the Feast of the Three Kings, the old man finally, painfully, and with great difficulty closed the gate to the farmyard—it was as if it had taken root in the earth. His wife could hear the hinges scraping and creaking even down there in her darkness. She no longer cared. Up there the gate was being closed on her lost sons. And the Madonna was silent about that, too. Up there it was obvious that heaven had forgotten the house of the blacksmith.

CHAPTER 14

MUSIC

B ERING'S FIRST TEST AT THE VILLA FLORA came in overcoming his fear of the pack. The dogs did not take their eyes off him, followed him everywhere at first, growling as he moved about the house and park, and probably did not attack him only because Ambras had forced each of them to accept this new resident's scent as the smell of an untouchable. He took Bering's hand, brushed it over their muzzles and flews, forced the hand into each mouth, and said in a voice equally low and insistent: *He is one of us, he is one of us, of us* . . . and concluded by whispering into their twitching ears that he would kill any dog that dared set its fangs in that hand. Then he gave Bering a bloody sack and ordered him to feed the beasts.

(Lily! Lily had no need of such threats in her dealings with the dogs. Although she took the precaution of leaving her own watchdog, a white Labrador, at the weather tower when she visited the Villa Flora, she was nevertheless at laughing ease with even the largest of Ambras's dogs, allowed them to leap up on her and roughhoused with them, letting the pack grow wilder and wilder, until at last she shouted "Enough!" and gave a signal that the animals obeyed instantly, the way they normally obeyed only their king's command.)

In these early days, Bering kept his pistol loaded for the first time, out of fear of the dogs, and when Ambras mockingly called him his *bodyguard*, he did indeed think of defense—but only of his own. He was determined to use the weapon to protect himself from the fangs of the pack.

Except that as days passed, the mere weight of the pistol proved so reassuring that he gradually learned to deal with the dogs with less fear. True, they did not obey him, but they no longer dared bare their fangs at him, either. And if he did not love the beasts, he came to feel something like gratitude for the way they understood his determination, no longer even barking when he returned at night from the lake with a basket of fish and walked through the darkened house, which was his house now as well.

It took several weeks before Bering found *his* spot in the house of dogs. He first spread a mattress in the library, and lay awake all night under the eyes of the pack; on other occasions he tried sleeping on the bench next to the cold kitchen stove or, after numbing himself with two glasses of malt whisky, the first of his life, he tossed until dawn on a cot on the veranda.

He finally spent a dreamless, peaceful night on a couch in the former billiard room, which lay bathed in moonlight on the second floor, and the next morning he carried his cardboard suitcase up to the room and tacked up the photograph showing him with his lost brothers. From a large, semicircular bay window in his new quarters, Moor's landscape looked like some still undiscovered land never trodden by man: the reeds along the shore, the lake, the ice fields and precipices of the high mountains—all were without paths, without a trace of humans. Neither the quarry's distant staircase nor the villa's dilapidated boathouse could be seen from this window.

Although the house of dogs lay in the shade of giant pines, barely an hour's walk from Moor, it sometimes seemed to Bering as if it were not the wind that swept across those needled crowns, but the surf of some invisible sea that now separated him from his inheritance and his old life.

The path back to the forge had been lost. Barely a week after his departure, when he had rolled up the hill in the Crow with a box full of scarce items, his father had thrown stones at him. Stones at the high-polished luster of a luxury liner! He pulled the car back to a safe distance, got out, and still crediting all this to some misunderstanding, to his father's blindness, he approached the old man a second time, holding his CARE package up high, and, by way of greeting, listed for him all the things this box contained. . . . But the old man did not stop throwing stones and clumps of dirt at him, feeble shots that missed him by a wide margin, and responded to the list of lavender soap, menthol cigarettes, and after-shave by shouting just four words at him: "Out of my sight!"

Without having been so much as grazed by a stone, Bering left the box behind on the gravel path that day. (And from then on he left gifts and groceries only clandestinely at the entrance— until Lily offered to bear his packages from the Villa Flora up to Forge Hill once a month. The old man always took whatever the Brazilian brought him, and never once asked about the donor.)

Many things at the house of dogs could not be found at any other house on the lake: canned seafood, peanut butter, Brazilian cocoa, Belgian pralines, and cellophane bags of cloves, bay leaves, and dried chili peppers. . . .

Delicacies from army depots and black-market deliveries filled the kitchen shelves, while in the unoccupied suites and salons— through which only dogs roamed, since the master of the house sometimes did not enter them for months on end—the possessions of vanished residents rotted away: tapestries depicting Flemish winter landscapes and hunters in the snow, leather easy chairs and sofas, the arms ravaged by dog bites, the upholstery hanging in tatters. The marble tub in a second-floor bathroom was half filled with rubbish and fallen plaster, and the star-parqueted floor of the plundered library rustled with leaves blown in through a broken window by every storm.

More than all the delicacies and the frayed splendor of a past era, however, what irresistibly attracted Bering here, too, were machines and technological mysteries—for instance, a singing turbine that was housed in a wooden shed and, with current won from a stream rushing through the park to the lake, could illuminate the whole house on some evenings until it lay like a festive ship in the darkness; plus a two-way radio, from which, on certain set days and at set hours, there burst the voices of the army, of the miners in the quarry, and a cracking and hissing silence in between news, orders, and questions. And a television—it was one of a grand total of three in the whole lake country. . . .

The other two television sets were located in assembly halls, kept under lock and key by the secretaries of Moor and Haag and turned on only once a week to show an eager public black-and-white melodramas, pictures from America and the rest of the world, and sometimes even an ancient Stellamour gesticulating at a lectern decorated with flowers and bunting. But the apparatus in the empty library of the Villa Flora often flickered away for hours unwatched, except by the pack of dogs to whom it presented the weather maps of a military broadcast or uniformed speakers who changed into sparkling phantoms amid the snow squall of electronic interference.

Of all the technological wonders of the Villa Flora, however, it was not this wood-encased picture tube that intrigued Bering the most—he had gawked at a similar Cyclops eye in the assembly hall before; it was nothing new. What fascinated him and would not let him go was a gadget that came from the estate Major Elliot had bequeathed to his Dog King and that since the commandant's departure had gathered dust between two cloth-fronted loudspeakers out on a glassed-in veranda—a record player.

Ambras had no objection to Bering's putting this junk back into working order, to his patching cables and cloth fronts frayed by dog bites, soldering connections, and then sitting for hours before the loudspeakers, enraptured by the same pieces played over and over—for most of Elliot's records, lying about in piles for years, unjacketed and unattended, had been rendered useless by the winter damp and summer heat of the veranda.

There were inspection tours of the quarry, repairs and menial chores at the villa, fishing trips to Leys Bay, and bumpy rides in the Crow through forests and along the shore—but amid all that, whenever Ambras left him the time, Bering gave himself over to the music the Dog King had inherited from Elliot.

Ambras first learned the names in his inheritance, however, from Bering, and only through his bodyguard did he slowly begin to take pleasure in these new sounds in his house, which were so totally different from the tinny music of his quarrymen or the crude marches of a sugar-beet workers' band. And so he raised no protest when for Lily's first visit after Bering's arrival, an electric guitar solo was turned up so loud that some of the dogs began to howl along.

"What's going on with you two?" Lily shouted and laughed. And before Bering could answer, Ambras shouted back, "That's rock 'n' roll!"

CHAPTER 15

KEEP MOVIN'

C OMING BY WAY OF LEYS, THE ARMORED
car had rolled through Moor at dawn, leaving colorful
tracks of posters behind on walls, gates, and trees.
Down by the dock, a navy-blue and gold one adorned a weathered advertising pillar encircled by poppies at its base; another
covered the faded flyers and now illegible orders on the bulletin
board at what was once army headquarters; and anyone walking
the shore promenade noticed that every third or fourth chestnut
tree lining the road was decorated with a poster:

CONCERT

it said, in gold letters against a blue background. Friday. In the
Old Hangar. After Sunset.

Even the door of a dilapidated shrine of the Leys Society of
Penitence had been pasted over with posters. Navy-blue and
gold. They were so wonderfully colorful that no sooner had the
armored car disappeared than kids in the streets (and not just
kids) promptly pulled them off and ran away to hide their shreds

of precious booty. . . . But if such a craving for color and rare paper had left only one observer time to read the message and pass it on, that would have sufficed to spread the news at the same speed usually achieved by flyers.

A concert! On Friday, after a long silence, things would get loud again at last in the hangar of Moor's old airport. Loud with the songs of a band that Supreme Headquarters had sent out on a tour and that would make stops not just at large bases but also in the remotest corners of the occupation zones—there, as per the wishes of Stellamour, Bringer of Peace, to thrill the offspring of the defeated foe and so bring them under the victors' magic spell.

The first of these concerts had taken place years before under Major Elliot's supervision and had not been much more than a variation on a Stellamour Party at the quarry. The hangar of the old airport, which lay protected from the wind in an upland valley above the lake—and after being used briefly during the war now served as a landing strip only for hooded crows and flocks of migratory birds—had been at the time (and still was) the only hall left standing that could contain an audience drawn from the entire lake country.

On Elliot's orders, the stage's steel frame and the beams of the roof, still peppered with grenade holes, were draped with banners inscribed with *Never Forget* and other Stellamour slogans. At the doors to this concert hall (which was still wearing its camouflage colors) a giant army tent was erected in which documentary films were run simultaneously on several screens, silent, endless loops of film, showing over and over the perfectly straight rows of the barracks by the gravel works, a pile of corpses in a white-tiled room, over and over, a crematorium oven with its firing door open, a column of prisoners beside the lakeshore—and in the background of all these reminders, over and over, the snowy and sun-baked and rain-drenched and ice-coated walls of Moor Quarry. . . . Anyone trying to get to the stage in the hangar had no choice but to enter by way of this flickering tent.

But since Elliot's departure and the army's retreat from the

lake country to the lowlands, no more banners were draped on
concert days and no movie tents were erected, and even Stellamour Parties had degenerated into poorly attended ceremonies
put on by Societies of Penitence, which were growing smaller and
smaller and had not disbanded only because even from a distance
the army continued to support the organized activities of all
penitents. Neither Moor's secretary nor the Dog King nor any
other agent of the occupation forces would still have had power
enough to force the locals to enter a tent full of hideous scenes or
attend a party in the quarry in their former numbers.

And so from the erstwhile pomp of those rituals of penitence
and remembrance, all that was left was this concert, which took
place twice or once a year, or even more infrequently, depending
on the mood and zeal of the officer in charge, but no longer
awakened any memories of the war years. The stage in the hangar
had long ago ceased to host big bands, orchestras in army uniforms, whose slide trombones and clarinets played tunes to
which, after a dash through the tent of horrors, you were allowed
to dance the fox trot. These days it was the musicians themselves
who danced!

Like ecstatic technicians, they leapt and ran around among
loops of cable and stacked loudspeakers and wrenched from their
instruments tone sequences that could be heard clear above the
snow line—the staccato of the drums, the shrill riffs of a tenor
sax, the scales of electric guitars ascending into howls. . . . A
diesel generator on an army truck was attached to amplifiers that
transformed every roll on the drumhead into thunder, and it also
supplied power to a battery of spots that bathed the band in a
light seen nowhere else around the lake—a chalk-white light. In
deafening cascades, the songs roared over the heads of Moor's
children and rang in their ears for hours afterward and evoked
nothing except wild excitement.

Bering, the crier of Moor with his delicate hearing, was
addicted to this music from his first concert on. For days after—
and days before—the performance of an army band, he dreamt

of its voices and drummed his fingers to its rhythms on tin pails and tables, even in his sleep. And when he stood beneath the stage in the middle of an ecstatic crowd and surrendered himself to the overpowering sound, he sometimes slid back deep into years past, back to the darkness of the forge, and was floating and rocking again in his cradle suspended above cages of chickens, a screaming child whose ears pained him and who fled from the world's racket and clamor into his own voice.

Deep inside a band's great music, he no longer had to drown out the painful noise of the world with his own lungs and his own throat, for here was a strange sound curiously related to his own primal cry and the voices of his birds, a sound that embraced and defended him like a coat of armor made of rhythms and harmony. And even when a concert sometimes grew so loud that it threatened to burst his eardrums and left him deaf for a few seconds, even in that sudden, ringing silence he still *felt* the mysterious closeness of a world in which everything was different from what he knew beside the lake and in the mountains of Moor.

The few English words, the vocabulary, that had stayed with him from his lessons in army tents and a stark schoolroom and that he recognized again in the songs of a band led him by way of *highways* and *stations* to shoreless dreams; he and those like him were serenaded with *freedom* and *broken hearts*, with *loneliness* and the *power of love* and *love in vain*. . . . And the heroes of these songs lived in a Somewhere where everything was not only better but always *in motion*, too, and where time did not stand still and run backwards as it did in Moor. There, *somewhere*, there were cities and not just ruins, wide and perfect roads, train tracks stretching to the horizon, great harbors and *airports*—and not just a shot-up hangar and not just an embankment overgrown with thistles and elderberry and missing its tracks for decades now. There everyone could walk or ride wherever and whenever he wanted, and didn't have to depend on safe-conduct papers or army trucks or horse-drawn wagons and didn't first need to cross mined passes and checkpoint barricades on the way to freedom.

"Keep movin'!" was what the singer at a summer concert had screamed into the microphone, thrusting his arms up, a figure of redemption in the garish spotlight, high above the enthusiastic throng in the darkness before the stage, high above the heads of his audience, who were trapped between the walls of the Stony Sea. "Movin' along!"

When Bering sat behind the wheel of the Crow, at the steering wheel of *his* creation, succumbing for the first time to the fever of speed, of movin' along, the band's sung invocation, its howled invocation of that yearning, seemed feasible as never before. "Keep movin' "—up and away! If only down a gravel road strewn with potholes and along a drive lined with giant pines and up a rise from which he could see no farther than the Blind Shore.

Ever since the record player had been rediscovered, Lily came more frequently than usual to the house of dogs. She always arrived in the late afternoon, sometimes bringing new records along with her other bartered items from the lowlands, but always departed with the onset of dusk and never stayed overnight.

Bering closely observed his master and the Brazilian as they traded items, but he never detected in either gestures or speech even a hint of anything more between them than the bonds of a peculiar familiarity and stoic empathy. It made no difference if they were discussing business or weighing the dangers of an attack by thugs, they always spoke to each other in the same cheerful, sometimes ironic tone that stripped things of any excess of meaning, even relieved danger of its menace.

A few days before the announced concert, Lily offered the Dog King a cherry-sized, clouded emerald—and two boxes of ammunition for the pistol that the bodyguard, as Ambras now called the blacksmith without a mocking smile, always carried stuck in his belt, hidden under jacket or shirt.

In exchange for the emerald, whose floating inclusions merged to form a crystal garden under Ambras's magnifying glass, Lily demanded maps that were to be had only from army archives— and for the ammunition, a place on the stage at Friday's concert, plus two quarrymen as guards to escort her there. After all, drunken hordes could be expected (as always) this time, too.

"I'll get you the maps. You can have a place on the stage. You don't need the quarrymen," Ambras said, nudging his body-guard, who was cutting meat for the dogs; "*we* will be your escorts."

Bering forgot his disgust at the sticky meat, and for a moment he again heard the ecstatic audience's roar, a hurricane of voices sweeping him along with it at the last concert—a guitar player was dancing at the edge of frenzy to a driving beat, a goblin whirling in the distance, leaping and rampaging like a prisoner inside the cone of light that followed him and would not let him go and transformed every movement into a flying shadow. As if trying to free himself from the light, the dancer ripped his guitar from its shoulder strap and to the thunder of a drum roll, grabbed it by the neck with both hands, swung it high above his head like a club, smashed it against the floor, jumped over frag-ments, splinters, coiling steel strings, and bounded finally out of the light and into the black depths of the stage, only to reappear the next moment, a frantic runner who flew toward his audi-ence—and threw himself into the raging throng with a scream that was drowned in the hurricane of voices!

But he did not fall into the darkness and vanish among hun-dreds of faces; he rode a wave of lifted hands and arms, as if these were not the reveling children of Moor who held him high and protected him from striking the cracked concrete floor of the hangar. He floated. Glistening in his costume, he floated like prey in the waving arms of sea anemones on some ocean floor.

A place on the stage! On Friday he would be closer than ever to breakneck dances and plunging leaps, to those floating idols. And above all, in that wilderness of cables, gliding lights, ampli-fiers, and towered loudspeakers, while great music raged around him, he would be next to this woman, be next to Lily somewhere in the night.

But when Bering finally lifted his eyes from the kitchen knife in his hands and the scraps of meat for the dogs, to search for Lily's eyes, she was already on her way outside. He heard her mule plodding in the gravel and resisted the urge to run after her. The dogs pressed around him and were so frantic for their food that he did not dare ignore their greed.

CHAPTER 16

AN OUTDOOR CONCERT

L ILY ARRIVED ON THE EVENING OF THE
day of the concert, riding her mule up the tree-lined
drive—and she was as beautiful as a pagan princess in the
blacksmith's wife's illustrated Bible. She was late; Ambras and
Bering had been waiting impatiently on the ground-floor veranda of the house of dogs. The Crow stood ready to go in the
evening sun. The beak of the hood, the hammered pinions of
the doors, even the taloned grille open to snatch prey were as
shiny as on the first day after major repairs. The bodyguard
had spent the afternoon tuning the bird's valves, brushing spark
plugs, filing points, and polishing enamel and chrome with
doeskin. The car doors stood open. On the back seat a scruffy
terrier was dozing; it suddenly raised its head and pricked up its
ears, although the rider was still hidden deep in the shade of the
giant pines.

Lily had tinted strands of her hair silver blue; around her neck
she wore strings of freshwater pearls and from her ears dangled
chains of finespun silver that fell to her shoulders. Two bobbing
bouquets of reddish-blue feathers and horsehair were attached

with silver buckles to the sleeves of her leather jacket. The steady swaying of these ornaments seemed to be connected by some invisible mechanism to the nodding head of the mule, which wore a similar bouquet on its brow band. It plodded up the hill at a leisurely pace. From the saddle pommel hung a leather net with a transistor radio inside that tootled and crackled Lily's music, which she often played to accompany her when riding secure paths; these were the pop tunes of exotic short-wave and AM stations that usually produced only whistles in the lake country's other still-functioning radios.

Through his master's binoculars, Bering watched the rider approach, but his heartbeat made the image flutter and lose focus.

"Have you seen the *Greek Maid*?" Lily called as she emerged from the shade of the trees and took a shortcut to the veranda through a stand of brambles; the mule calmly obeyed the pressure of her heels and broke through the thick underbrush. "That ship's as overcrowded as a lifeboat after a battle at sea."

Barely an hour before sunset and the start of the concert, and still following its course through rough waters between Moor and the villages along the shore, the *Sleeping Greek Maid* came steaming into view from the house of dogs. Although the evening sky was cloudless, winds off the mountains came in short, violent gusts, raising whitecaps on the lake. The hiss of waves breaking in the reeds was audible even from the villa.

With the binoculars, Bering could bring the clumsily maneuvering ship into close enough range to see that its decks were black with passengers. Beneath a ragged pennant of smoke, the steamer was just approaching Moor's pier again, for the fifth or sixth time that day. The stream of concertgoers moving toward the old airport had begun early that afternoon and kept on lurching forward in pulses regulated by the rhythm of the docking schedule.

Four jeeps, a troop carrier, an armored car, and two army rigs heavily loaded with the band's equipment and a generator had arrived at the hangar the evening before. The armed escort had had trouble keeping curiosity seekers away from the musicians' cooking fires and tents. In their enthusiasm, Moor's children had threatened to storm the camp. They thronged around the vehicles, drumming hoods and side panels with their fists and singing snatches of the songs that they wanted to hear, *had* to hear, at the concert the next day.

"I had to make a detour," Lily said, jumping down from her saddle. "A military patrol has blocked the shore promenade. They're searching bags, checking IDs, and flashing cameras in people's faces. We'd better not drive your bird to the hangar. The drunks are already brawling by the tollgate at the airport entrance and are managing to stay on their feet only because the crowd's so dense."

Ambras knew about the jostling crowds along the steep gravel road to the airport, just as he knew about every other obstacle on the way to the hangar. At the last concert, two years before, a band of skinheads with chains, brass knuckles, and axes had taken up a position at the old tollgate and tried to charge a music tax from everyone passing through. In the end, the skins had clashed with the military police, and when it was over, three wounded men and one corpse lay in the gravel. . . . Ambras knew everything about these concerts—about attendance records, disruptions, accidents, brawls, attempted arson. Ever since the concerts at the hangar had begun, he had observed them as a bystander, because the army demanded that Moor's secretary write a report and that the quarry administrator sign it as a witness.

Now he took the binoculars out of Bering's hand and gave the shore promenade a quick survey. "*We*'re not walking. We're driving." He whistled for his ash-gray mastiff. "Let's go."

As Bering started the Crow, the mule, which had begun grazing by the lily pond, bounded to one side in fright. Bering could feel how damp his palms were against the cool, dry steering wheel. Lily sat beside him on the front seat. Lily had not been so close to him since that moment when she had untied the knot of his leather apron. Ambras sat in the back beside the mastiff, which laid its head in his lap as soon as the car began to move.

Even the old truck trail that followed the rocky slopes high above the lake to Pilot Valley was jammed with people now; from every corner of the lake country the audience streamed toward the hangar. After only a mile or so on this road, the Crow was trapped deep inside a procession moving toward a glow that grew brighter and brighter.

Although people may have gawked greedily at the winged Studebaker and furtively stroked the silky smoothness of its finish, its owner had as few friends here in this procession as at the quarry or anywhere else in Moor. And at that moment it was probably less the fear of the Dog King or his allies in the army that protected him and his Crow from fists and stones than it was fear of the mastiff. Ambras had rolled down both back windows, and, tugging at its chain, the beast thrust its massive head out the openings, now left, now back to the right, and its deep, angry barks cleared the space that Bering's short honks demanded.

Even the soldiers of a military patrol that stopped the car at a wooden bridge to stare in amazement at this bird vehicle from all sides did not dare touch the chrome beak and forged talons until the Dog King had closed the windows and got out. In his conversation with the patrol, Ambras motioned at one point toward Bering (or was it Lily?) and laughed and said something that could not be understood inside the Crow above the dog's barks. Without showing any ID, without even getting the back of his hand stamped, something demanded of every concertgoer—at the very latest at the entrance to the airport—the Dog King climbed into the back seat again, and they inched forward.

They spoke little on this trip. The procession parted reluctantly ahead of them and filled in again so closely behind that the faces in the crowd glowed in the reflection of the taillights.

Many of the potholes in the truck trail were so deep that the band's advance team had stuck poles and branches in them to warn those following of the pitfalls. When Bering avoided these gaping holes, the road sometimes grew so narrow that the pedestrians he pushed aside began to shout in protest and bang the windshield with the flat of their hands. Here, too, no one dared raise anything except an open hand against the Dog King's car.

When Ambras bent forward unexpectedly and clapped Bering on the shoulder, Bering, completely engrossed by now in creeping ahead inch by inch, jerked so violently in alarm that he nudged the Crow's beak against a costumed man in white makeup, bumping him into the underbrush.

"Let him be. Keep driving," Ambras said. And then: "Did you bring the thing?"

The *thing*. The Dog King seldom called any object by its name. The car, *the thing*. The two-way radio, *the thing*. The television, a glass cutter, the acetylene lamp, a jackhammer: this *thing*, that *thing*. But for his dogs he was constantly inventing new, often crazy nicknames, terms of endearment or insult, which, however, changed so quickly that the animals recognized themselves better in the special, unvarying pitch of the call and whistle he had for each. Nonetheless, just to be sure, all heads lifted when he meant only one of them.

"Bring what thing?" He might be Ambras's employee, but Bering was unwilling to give up names. How could anyone live without names! For every tiniest part of a mechanism, a function went with its designation. . . . Although over the past few weeks he had learned to understand both his master's *thing* language and his curt gestures, he occasionally tried to wrest a name from him by questions of apparent incomprehension. At best, however, every such attempt ended in his having to say what the Dog King meant.

"What thing do you suppose? What thing do you suppose would most impress those people shouting out there? A feather duster? So, did you bring the thing with you?"

"Here," Bering said, laying his hand for a second on the pistol hidden at his belt. In the past weeks Ambras had not asked him once about the weapon.

The drive dragged on. With no traffic, it would have taken barely a half hour. But on this Friday the sun had long since set before they reached the airport's plateau. They could already hear in the distance the practice runs of the instruments, the booming of a bass guitar. The door to the hangar lay in glittering light. The crowd was jammed up against it—a black flood of silhouettes and dancing shadows. There must have been thousands.

Bering knew no wider and better preserved piece of highway in all the lake country than the airport's old tarmac. Three times in the past weeks he had driven through this uninhabited valley to open the Crow up for a few seconds to speeds unachievable on any of Moor's gravel roads. But the pavement that had then been like a river rushing toward him through suddenly opened locks was now a single, sluggish stream of people, and lost somewhere in its midst was the Crow—flotsam, rocking in a walking cadence toward the hangar.

"I can't remember—" Lily said, and did not complete her sentence, because everyone in the car was thinking the same thing: none of them could remember ever having seen such a great throng for a concert. And this storm flood was intended for just one name, which could be found on all the posters and now stood flickering in flaming electric letters above the entrance to the hangar:

PATTON'S ORCHESTRA

That this blazing name throbbing in flashes had proved to be such an immense attraction apparently baffled even Moor's secretary. From out of the mob ahead, he suddenly emerged, gesticulating wildly, motioning them to a parking spot in the barricade of military vehicles. And on the way through the area around the stage, kept clear by soldiers, he repeated over and over in fussy confusion that this mass of people would never fit in the hangar—impossible. He had already discussed it with the military police earlier in the evening. The concert had been moved outside. Only the stage was still under a roof.

The stage, a steel framework draped with camouflage nets and ribbons of lights, had been moved to the open sliding doors and was still occupied by uniformed technicians. The empty hangar in the background, now just a sound box through which giant shadows flitted, seemed to quake under the test runs.

Led by the bodyguards of Moor's secretary, the Dog King and his retinue climbed up into the blinding light of the stage, where they were shown to their places. Stage seats—those were narrow spaces in the darkened background between instrument cases, amplifiers, and towered loudspeakers. And there each of the group now stood, ill at ease in his or her own way, stood suddenly amid a shrill barrage of whistles. The audience wanted to see its idols.

Patton's Orchestra! In the occupation zones, no name (except perhaps that of the Bringer of Peace) had been more famous—or infamous. This band's songs, heard every Wednesday evening in local assembly halls in shows broadcast by army stations, had been transformed into hymns and street ballads sung in the remotest backwater villages and could thrill an audience even when booming from receivers distorted by interference.

The band leader, a skinny guitar player, who wore his waist-length hair in a braid, had baptized his orchestra after Patton, the highly decorated general and commander of tanks. And the motto the leader ordered written both across the head of the band's bass drum and on the tarps of the column of trucks with which he toured the Peace of Oranienburg—under the protection and in the pay of the army—had long ago become more familiar to his fans than any slogan of Stellamour's: *Hell on Wheels*.

Wherever Patton's Hell on Wheels stormed the stage, grabbing their instruments and tuning up by playing several bars at brutal volume, a wild jubilation welled up that no other music could unleash. "Hell on Wheels!" had become a battle cry that sometimes terrified even their heavily armed escort, for that cry would often be followed by storms of enthusiasm that could scarcely be distinguished from a general insurrection. Then stones and bottles flew through the air, iron rods and burning flags. . . .

Whatever it was that General Patton and his band triggered in the heads and hearts of their enraptured audience, it could not be controlled and was often quelled only with force. But despite brawls and melees in front of the stage, there was not a commandant who would ever have forbidden a Patton performance—these concerts actually appeared to transform the unrest in the occupied areas into wild, but ultimately harmless celebration. Besides, Patton's concerts also had a magic attraction for the hordes from the Stony Sea and ruined cities. As bawling fans, their faces whitened with chalk, even skinheads for whom there were arrest warrants out sometimes came right up to the stage and, occasionally, walked into the military's trap.

The human tide moving across the tarmac had still not come to a halt; Ambras was giving the secretary a vigorous talking-to—something about a truck loaded with stones that had broken down. And Lily and Bering were standing beside each other, not saying a word, dazed by the bright daylight of the immense stage yawning before them—when the concert began without any announcement.

What looked like a soundman dressed in a spotted camouflage outfit, who had only just been concentrating on tuning a guitar, repeated several bars, increasing the tempo each time; a drummer, who had been striking a triangle in boredom, suddenly thrust his arms up and let loose a rattling flurry on his drumheads. . . . That was the signal. Three costumed figures leapt into the light. Hung with chain upon chain of amulets, their faces whitened with chalk, and holding their guitars ahead of them like swords, they waited for the hand signal from the bass player and then strummed a throbbing chord—and it drowned out every other voice.

Lily touched Bering's arm and shouted something to him. He had to put his ear right up to her mouth, had to get closer to her than ever before, until he finally understood her. "That—isn't—Patton." Her hand, which had rested on his shoulder for a moment, slipped away again, and he did not have the courage to hold it fast.

It was not Patton. It was only the opening act, a band whose name no one had ever heard before, either on the Wednesday evening shows or on short-wave hit parades. But although their riffs pulsated away, bursting at times into dissonances, the audience gradually started stomping and writing rhythmic fiery signs in the darkness with their torches and burning sticks. When the opening act ended in an orgiastic snarl of voices and the nameless band had vanished as suddenly as it had come, the light from the spots dimmed to a violet glow. This twilight, in which only a microphone or a piece of chrome flashed here and there, screamed for Patton to appear.

A spotlight flared up, its conic beam fell from high in the night onto the stage and slid across Bering, and from out of the darkness fingered a man whose face was blue with tattoos. He ran. He ran as the light grasped him, ran farther into the cone of light, through the dusk of the stage, dragging a mike cable behind him, and as he ran he screamed the name that was amplified into a monster rolling over the crowd and across the tarmac: "General Patton and his Orchestra!"

Bering sees the runner grab imaginary levers. He rotates or pulls them all down and leaps back into the depths of the stage, where in a fury of magnesium flashes Patton's musicians come storming in from all sides. There are seven men and four women. The audience knows each of them by name.

They grab their instruments and mikes just as the audience has seen them do on television on Wednesday evenings, and at no discernible signal they start playing one of Patton's most famous songs at such a frantic tempo that no one in the crowd at their feet can sing along and or even stomp out the rhythm.

Then the music breaks off again as abruptly as it began. Only a chorus of fans singing in hopeless catch-up goes on roaring for a few seconds in the sudden lull before they fall back again into an amorphous jubilation, during which, as the last of his orchestra, General Patton takes the stage.

Patton does not run. He strides. He is coming toward Bering, who turns pale, feels short of breath, and instinctively tries to flee deeper into the shadows of the towered loudspeakers. But Lily is already there. Ambras is nowhere to be seen.

Patton is so little.

Little?

Patton moves past, moves past so close to Bering that he could touch him by stretching out an arm. Patton brushes him with his gaze, stares through him, and moves on, out into the exultation. Bering watches him, a shadow against the sun of a spotlight, stride toward the crowd, which stretches all its arms out to him—and someone like Bering, standing among the cables and all this black apparatus, might well believe all those arms are stretched out to him. Or to Lily.

They mean it for us! he wants to shout to her, *They mean it for us!*

But Lily has eyes only for Patton's shadow. He has found his place far ahead in the jubilation. There, at the very edge of the stage, he lifts his hand as if to calm the frenzy, but he is really only shading his eyes to gaze out into the sea of enthusiasts below him, and now roars with a voice that is eerily larger than his own figure: "Good"—and after a long pause in which the crowd returns that cry as a thundering echo—"evening!"

Good evening! For someone like Bering, that cry alone is enough for him to recognize the unmistakable voice he has heard so often from the television set in Moor's assembly hall, from crackling radios, and finally from one unchanging record among the collection Major Elliot left behind. But he has never *really* heard it.

Those of his excited fans who thought Patton would now pick

up again at the same frantic tempo as his band and unleash the same unbroken storm of sound, suddenly, amazingly, hear him all alone now. Patton needs only to lift his voice and with that very first note high above the frenzy of the crowd, above all the noise of the world, he is alone. He sings.

Far from his musicians and so close to the lifted arms of the crowd that some of them grasp for his feet, Patton clutches the mike in his hand and accompanied only by a single guitar—which makes the glittering arsenal of his silenced orchestra seem strangely useless—he cries, sings, speaks, whispers, husks long, melodic phrases that Bering takes to be the lines of a love song. *He* at least hears words whose mere sound touches him and makes him think only of Lily's presence, of her hands, whose fleeting touch he already knows, of her mouth, which he does not know.

No one from along the lake has heard this song before. The exaltation has died away to a silence in which Patton's voice sounds even larger. Standing radiant in the darkness, as if he has grown with his own voice, he looks large, larger than any expectation of his fans.

Bering shivers, although the evening is warm and calm. As always when he loses himself in a beautiful sound, a shudder from his heart raises goose flesh, scuffing his skin till it is like a bird's. He feels so good that he is afraid the beautiful sound will let go again now—and drop him. (How often he has had to come to himself again in a jangling world—feeling a bit ridiculous, those tiny hairs still raised here and there. He always came to like that at the end of some great emotion.)

But this time the shivering doesn't stop and the sound doesn't let go of him and nothing forces him back into the world. This time the beautiful sound only increases in power and brings others voices with it—above all, the sound of a bass guitar, on which a dark-skinned woman slowly, then almost imperceptibly faster, begins to echo Patton's voice. As if an archer were testing a long, sinewy bowstring, the bass tones purl behind Patton's voice, follow it up and down a spiral staircase of notes, grow denser, come closer.

And Bering climbs and runs and leaps, flies behind the hands of the dark woman, behind the voice she is following, and finally loses all weight—just as in those moments when, through his master's binoculars, he tries to follow the swift, arrowlike patterns of a bird in flight and grows lighter and lighter just by looking, until he abandons the earth beneath his feet and hurls himself into a spinning sky. Patton sings.

Bering flies. Eyes closed, he makes loops in the sky and is sailing along between cloud mountains, when two arms gently pull him back to earth—not down into a jangling world, but into a nest. They are two arms in black leather, as cool and smooth as wings, reaching from behind around his shoulders, around his bird's neck. And a warm body, as light as a feather, nestles against his back and begins to rock with him to the rhythm of Patton's voice.

He does not first have to recognize the silver bracelets at the wrists or to feel the dangling chains of finespun silver against his neck to know that these are Lily's arms. Her breath turns his goose flesh bumpier still. And finally he leans back and lets himself be held and rocked. That was how it was at the beginning of his time. That is how he had floated through the darkness of the forge and been sheltered in the voices of captive chickens. What should he do to keep from crushing things underfoot in this paradise? He has never held a woman in his arms. He does not know what he should do. If only the voice that holds them both in this marvelous suspension does not stop singing.

Hell on Wheels!—As if Patton has sung his orchestra awake, as if those awakened can feel this floating, disruptive peace behind their backs and are reminded of their motto, all the instrumental voices suddenly throw themselves at Patton's melody and assault his voice with such fury that it drowns in the surging flood of notes—only to re-emerge in the surf barely one breath later. Bering sees a waterfowl swimming among the breakers, and each time, just as a wave caps and is about to bury it, the bird takes off, fanning the spray with its wings. Inspired by the power with which this voice pierces even the thunder of the percussion, Bering feels himself lifted now and strong enough to reach for Lily's arms—and to extricate himself from them.

He turns around to her, to her face, and his eyes are suddenly so close to hers that he has to lower them, just as at their first meeting. He cannot endure such closeness without embarrassment. He feels as if she is gazing right through him, to the very bottom, and has to close his eyes and—only in self-defense, really, and to evade that beautiful, bewildering gaze—dares something that until now he has dared only in his sleep and only in the presence of a fantasy.

Blindly he pulls Lily to him and kisses her on the mouth. And is deep within his dream, when in the next moment he feels her tongue between his lips and against his closed teeth.

Now it is Lily who extricates herself from *his* arms. Although she takes scarcely a step back and continues to hold his hands in her own, she is already so distant again that he yearns for her and wants to tug her back into that unsettling closeness.

But she doesn't want that. He has done something wrong. He must have done something wrong. He takes fright. Now he *has* to look at her. But her eyes reflect no mistake. How quiet it has become inside him. Only now does he hear the excited roar—there below, to the very edge of night, a field of raised arms waves. And all arms are flying toward *them*. In the black depth of the stage, they hold unseen hands, hold each other tight. Patton's song is over. Moor's children cheer him.

Now Lily releases Bering from her gaze and pulls her hands away and turns toward Patton and begins to clap her raised arms in rhythm with the crowd: "More! More! More! . . . "

Bering has never seen a woman like this. He still feels the moistness of her tongue on his lips and he cries out her name. And she hears him. She hears him and smiles at him—*More! More!* She grabs his wrists and pulls his arms up. He's supposed to clap, too! and as he does, be so close to her that he can feel his heart against her breast. She does not let go of his wrists. She claps with his hands. He has actually kissed her.

Now something inside him tears away and rises from those same depths to which Lily's gaze sank just now. It is one of his lost voices. He wants—yes, he wants to join in the great cry, and he stretches his neck as he did on that snowy February morning, stretches his neck like a bird, a chicken. But it is not cackling, not clucking that rises in his throat and rips his mouth wide, but a human sound. He cries in triumph. Cries as he has never cried, and adds his voice to hers to form a single, exuberant voice.

CHAPTER 17

THE HOLE

O F COURSE MOOR'S CHILDREN, AND THOSE
from Haag and Leys, too, would have stayed on till
exhaustion set in this Friday night and would have
screamed themselves hoarse and dumb until dawn, calling out
Patton and his band for encore after encore. . . . But at some
point, it was long past midnight, the musicians disappeared into
the black depths of the hangar (and from there, unnoticed, to
their tents) and did not return to the stage despite continuing
applause. Then the spotlights went out. The dismantling of all
the gear was illumined by only a few low-wattage lamps.

Out on the tarmac, brushwood fires and torches blazed. After
more than half an hour of chants protesting the band's disappearance, the crowd, first grumbling, then simply murmuring, began to
withdraw from the valley. Anyone who stumbled through the night
toward the lakeshore and carried a flashlight hid that precious item
until he branched off from the tide of pushers and shovers and was
alone at last—for fear that he might provoke the craving for artificial light, electric guitars, and other tokens of progress unleashed in
the ecstasy along with so many other emotions.

Most incidents listed by the secretaries in their reports to the army occurred on these and similar paths home. For in the sudden silence after the hurricane, after so much wild enthusiasm and abandonment, the old laws and rules of the Peace of Oranienburg did not seem to be in force again yet: prohibitions were meaningless, threatened punishments did not intimidate. A great deal that was done in the hours after a concert happened in the moment and with no concern for the consequences.

But this time the crowd was unusually peaceable for such a night. As if this Hell on Wheels had vicariously vented the fury of Patton's fans, there were only a few isolated scuffles between hostile bands of leathermen, but no battles. There were a couple of fistfights and bloody noses, but no punches with brass knuckles, no flying chains, no crowbars. The band's escort and the military police had apprehended barely a dozen suspects in the audience, and had not once made use of their guns.

The crowd might have appeared chaotic in the darkness, but it was almost genial as it sluggishly crept out of Pilot Valley. Apart from a few of their drunken buddies, no one tried to come to the aid of the detainees, who were left behind, handcuffed to the side panel of a transporter. Whoever that might be pulling at his shackles or bellowing curses or protestations of innocence—plunderer, black marketeer, or wanted killer—as they thronged past, Patton's fans simply lamented that yet another concert had come to an end.

While Lily sat sleepily on the Crow's front seat and, protected by the mastiff, waited for him to return, Bering searched for his master in the barricade of escort vehicles, in the area around the stage—and ended up wandering aimlessly in the throng. Under the spell of Patton's voice and Lily's tenderness, he had not noticed that Ambras had vanished until shortly before the spotlights were extinguished. All through the concert, he had been certain that Ambras was standing in the deep shadows of the wings, not thirty feet away. Had that *not* been Ambras? At one point he had been sure he felt Ambras's gaze on them and had tried to pull Lily closer in the darkness and whisper in her ear, "He's staring at us."

"Who's staring at us?"

"*He* is."

"Ambras? Why should he be bothered by us? He only kisses his dogs."

And then Lily had been so close to him, and Patton's music sped right on past their embrace, and Bering forgot something he had never forgotten for a moment since moving into the house of dogs—the presence of his master.

Battling now against the current of people, he grew increasingly uneasy at the thought that here in the darkness and confusion, a horde of drunken leathermen might recognize Ambras as the quarry administrator, as a friend and agent of the army. . . . How many hours had Ambras been gone? Maybe he had been mistaken up on the stage and the figure in the shadows was only a stranger, maybe even an enemy.

But *if* it was the Dog King who had seen his bodyguard blinded by tenderness and shame there among the loudspeakers and amplifiers, then he certainly had seen not just the secrets of an embracing couple, but above all—perhaps nothing else but— their arms! Their raised, intertwined, happy arms. For Bering and Lily had raised their arms high above their heads with a dancer's grace to form a single waving field with thousands of other excited fans tonight—and Ambras would never be able to raise his arms like that again. Ambras was a cripple. And Bering knew his secret.

As he roamed through the throng, he heard again the thunder in the quarry—it had been only yesterday morning. An explosive charge had gone off too soon. A hail of stony fragments had rained down on him and Ambras.

They ran for the administrator's shed through a cloud of sand and stone dust. Ambras kicked the door open with a curse and shook the sand from his shoulders. Then he took a brush from the cupboard, bent his head toward Bering, and ordered him to brush the dust and sand from his hair.

"I can no longer do it today," Ambras had said. "When there's a change in the weather, no matter if I'm standing in the rain or in the snow, I can't lift either arm anymore."

A change in the weather? It was a sunny day—except the wind was picking up. Bering was repulsed by this dusty head that snowed dandruff at the first touch of the brush. He did not want to be this close to a man. He had never once brushed even his father's hair—not even his father, who could no longer see himself in the mirror and had his wife comb his hair on Sundays with a staghorn comb. Hair! . . . He was a mechanic, a chauffeur, a blacksmith—or was he just an armed hairdresser?

Although Ambras's order enraged him, he did as he was told to do and pulled the brush through the wiry, partially graying hair as carefully as if brushing the coat of a vicious dog.

Ambras's shoulders turned white with stone dust and snowy dandruff, and as he performed this tedious, humiliating service, Bering began to comprehend what this secret, confided to him so offhandedly, really meant. Bodyguard was no mere nickname.

The Dog King was not joking when he called Bering his bodyguard. Ambras could no longer raise his arms above his head or against an enemy, and he had every reason to hide such an infirmity from Moor. If one of the army's protégés could no longer help himself, the power of an occupation force steadily retreating ever farther into the distance would soon no longer help him either.

After this chore, they sat crouched in the administrator's shed in front of a broken and disassembled jackhammer and could hear gusts of wind driving sand across the corrugated tin roof. An hour passed, and only then did he dare ask his master, "What's wrong with you, what sort of condition is it?"

"It's the Moor disease," Ambras had said. "A lot of people got it on the Blind Shore."

"In the quarry? Doing what sort of work?"

"It wasn't work. It was the swing."

The Swing—Bering knew the name for this torment from a poster-sized, grainy photograph that had been exhibited in the army's show tents and at some Stellamour Parties, along with other mementos of torture. The poster showed a giant beech tree, from whose lowest spreading branches five prisoners in striped fatigues hung in the most hideously wrenched position. Their hands had been tied behind their backs and a rope then pulled through the knots. They dangled from this rope, they swung from this rope. Their agonies had been described in English and German along the bottom of the picture, but Bering had retained only this one word, *Schaukel*, and its translation, *swing*.

"If you looked a guard in the eye," Ambras had said in the administrator's shed, stroking his thumb on a lock washer from the disassembled jackhammer, "just looked him in the eye, you understand . . . you weren't allowed to look him in the eye, you had to keep your eyes lowered, you understand, just looked at him, that could suffice—and it might also suffice if out of fear you stared at the tips of his boots *too* long or didn't doff your cap fast enough, and it might suffice if you bent over a little because you couldn't stand up straight anymore after he had kicked you and roared *Look at me!* roared *Look at me when I'm talking to you*, you understand—all that and a great deal less could suffice for him to say, 'Swing! Report after roll call.' And then you began to count the minutes until they would finally drag you out under the tree.

"Once there, they twist your arms behind your back and tie them with a rope, and, like most of those before you and most of those after you, you are in such anguish you start screaming for mercy. And then they pull you up by the rope and slap at you to start you swinging—and you, you scream and try with all your strength and for God's sake to hold yourself in some sort of slanted position, so that for God's sake it won't happen. But it happens—your own body weight steadily pulls your bound arms higher and higher, until you have no more strength and your own terrible weight yanks your arms up behind your head and rips the ball joints of your shoulders out of their sockets.

"The sound it makes is one that you know, if at all, only from the meat market, when the butcher rips the bones from a carcass or breaks a joint by bending it the wrong way—it doesn't sound all that different with you. Except you alone hear the cracking and splintering, because all the others—those swine still holding the rope they pulled you up by and your fellow prisoners staring up at you from below, still unhurt, although they'll be dangling up here themselves tomorrow or within the next minute—all the others can hear only your howls.

"You dangle there in pain you would never have believed anyone could feel without dying, and you howl in a voice that until that moment you knew nothing about, and never, never in your life will your arms ever again be so high above your head as at that moment.

"And if someone wants to make a total cripple of you, then he clasps your legs now and tucks his body up and hangs his entire weight on you and starts to swing with you. I was spared that," Ambras said, "but only that." He had scratched his thumb on the jackhammer's lock washer and licked the blood from a tiny nick.

This was the first time Bering had heard a former prisoner from the barracks by the gravel works talk about his torments. In the army's show tents and at school during the first years after the war, it had always been Stellamour's preachers (which is what Moor secretly called them in those days) who had talked about the tortures and misery of the Blind Shore, but never one of those who had been tortured himself. And at the parties at the quarry or in penitential rites at the dock, the liberated prisoners remained so silent and faceless that, like many of Moor's children, Bering sometimes believed the prisoners from the camp barracks had never had a voice of their own or any other face than the rigid features you saw on dead people in the army's posters, their naked corpses piled atop one other outside barracks or lying naked and staked in great ditches. No show tent and no history lesson had ever failed to have such pictures, and they were often carried by sandwich men in the processions of the Societies of Penitence.

It had taken a long time for Bering and those like him to realize that not all the unfortunates from the barracks had vanished into the earth or the great brick ovens by the gravel works, but that some of them had escaped to live in the same present, in the same world, as they themselves. Beside the same lake. On the same shore. But once the Dog King and other former zebras, who had exchanged their uniforms for army coats and bomber jackets, assumed positions of responsibility by order of the occupying army and under its protection—and not just at the quarry but also at sugar-beet factories, saltworks, and secretariats—then even those born after the war in the most remote village by the lake were forced to recognize that the past was not past by a long shot.

But Moor's children were bored by memories of a time before their time. What did *they* care about black flags at the docks and at the ruins of the gravel works? Or about the message of the Grand Inscription at the quarry? Veterans and men crippled in the war might be outraged by a Stellamour Party and protest the truth of the victors—for Bering and those like him, the rituals of remembrance, whether ordered by the army or nurtured by Societies of Penitence, were only gloomy shows.

What Moor's children saw on billboards and heard about in "history courses" promulgated by the Bringer of Peace was just Moor after all—dilapidated barracks, the barnacle-encrusted piles at the dock, the quarry, ruins. They knew it all. What they wanted to see looked very different: the superhighways of America, down which rolled long lines of the kind of cars that only the commandant, and later his Dog King, drove here beside the lake. The skyscrapers on the island of Manhattan, where Lyndon Porter Stellamour resided, or the ocean!—that's what they wanted to see, not yellowed black-and-white pictures of the Blind Shore. They wanted to see the Statue of Liberty at the entrance to New York harbor and the hollow torch in her raised arm—not the colossal letters of the Grand Inscription: *Here eleven thousand nine hundred seventy-three people lie dead.* Sure. Dead people lay in the ground most anywhere. But who, in this third decade of the Peace of Oranienburg, still wanted to count corpses? Moss was creeping across the Grand Inscription.

Once the concert was over, Bering had run into neither drunken rowdies nor leathermen, but he kept shoving his way through the throng ever more ruthlessly. If something happened to the Dog King, the Villa Flora would revert to the army, and he would have to go back to the forge. It angered him that the crowd was so sluggish. Using both hands, he pushed aside Patton's fans, with whom he had only just felt a kinship, and bawled out the name of his master. But that name merely evoked nasty looks here, and as hard as he fought against it, the crowd slowly carried him along.

The barricade of escort vehicles was only a remote black fortress in the darkness when he finally discovered the Dog King. He was standing leaning against a junked tank overgrown with grass, besieged by people with torches, so that his face flickered in the glow of burning branches and flares. He looked as if he were totally engrossed in watching a brutal spectacle performed in a semicircle around him. Seven or eight Iroquois—skinheads, who sported a narrow stripe of hair, dyed garish red like a cockscomb—lunged at him and then leaped back, thrusting their torches at him, but not touching or singeing him, and bellowed questions or curses at him: what they were bellowing could not be made out. He did not answer them and made no attempt to defend himself. He simply stood there and watched them. How tired he looked.

That was supposed to be the Dog King? The army's friend, who issued verdicts and could declare martial law for the entire lakeshore? The invincible man—whom Moor still feared as someone who could batter the skull of one beast with an iron rod and break the neck of another with his bare hands? This tired man?

"The dogs . . . how could you kill those dogs that day?" Bering had asked yesterday morning in the administrator's shed, and Ambras had given him no time to say that he wasn't just asking about some rumor in Moor but that he had been crouching that day, freezing with fear, among wild grapevines beside the fence of the Villa Flora and with his own eyes had seen the pack subdued—and saw it sometimes even now when he closed his eyes.

"With these arms, you mean? Dogs don't strike at you with chains," Ambras said. "Dogs don't dive at you like birds. Dogs don't force your arms up, they spring at you from below." Even now, Ambras had said, any dog that sprang at him would be springing to its death.

Bering could move closer to his master only slowly, much too slowly. The crowd took no notice of his agitation, nor of shouts from a couple of fire dancers, nor of the beleaguered man whose face kept disappearing behind circling torches. Wedged in by a group of sooty figures who were dragging a wounded man with them, Bering started flinging his arms about—when Ambras looked at him, when Ambras looked at his bodyguard over the tops of twenty, thirty heads.

Was he really looking at him?

Bering at least thought he not only recognized that look, but also the question, the command it contained, and automatically reached for the pistol in his belt.

Was *that* what was demanded of him now?

The look said *yes*.

So he tugged the weapon from his clothes so hastily that the trigger got caught in his shirt and ripped it. When he finally held the shiny pistol in his hand, it was warm with his body heat and yet it was strange and totally new to him and did not remind him either of shots fired on an April night or of the fading face of an enemy.

He released the safety, pulled the slide along the barrel, heard a bullet pop from the magazine into the chamber and held *his* weapon up, ready to fire—showed it to a dark world, in the midst of which his master stood, awaiting his help.

And suddenly a space opened up before him, a space of fear, which began to expand farther and farther around him in a rising jumble of voices: "He has a gun." "Careful, there's a guy with a gun." "Say, it's the blacksmith, and he has a gun. . . ." The crowd parted before him like the Red Sea in that woodcut he had examined so often in the illustrated Bible of the blacksmith's wife.

The people, the sea . . . the whole world pulled back from him into the dark. "Get out of here, take cover!" "That madman there has got a gun." What were torches and burning branches, what were stones, clubs, and bare fists against the shiny nickel of the gun in his hand?

He felt dazed as he strode through this empty space toward the motionless Ambras, whose face seemed to grow ever more shadowy, ever darker. The torches and, with them, all light pulled back from him. Whoever carried fire tossed it away, doused it, or stomped it out, so as not to provide the armed man with an illuminated target. Blind in the sudden night, the fire dancers and assailants shoved and stumbled into the darkness.

Bering picked up a torch that had been tossed aside and held it high. Who would hurl a stone now or dare so much as raise a fist against him? The fire in one hand, the gun in the other, he came to his master's aid.

When he finally reached him, the Dog King was standing all alone. "Did they do anything to you? Are you . . . are you hurt?" As strong as he was at that moment, his voice quivered now nonetheless.

"I'm alive," Ambras said. "Those idiots wouldn't have touched me."

"Not touched you?" Bering thought he could hear the shards of his triumph smashing to the ground. Confused, he put his pistol back in his belt, tucked his torn shirt in. "And me? What should I have done?"

"Nothing. Don't worry," Ambras said, "you did everything right." Then he asked about Lily.

"She's waiting in the car."

"And the dog?"

"The dog is with her."

On their way back to the barricade of vehicles, the tarmac emptied so rapidly it was as if Ambras's bodyguard had opened a gate somewhere into the night, a floodgate, through which the stream of concertgoers now vanished toward the lakeshore. The Dog King did not say much as they walked.

Why had he left the stage, why had he ended up so far out in the crowd?

He hadn't wanted to go deaf up there.

They met no one else on the road except a machinist from a sugar-beet factory, who wanted to beg the quarry administrator to issue him safe-conduct papers for the lowlands and tagged after them, talking and gesticulating, all the way to the hangar. And even this petitioner, who would not back off until Bering finally physically pushed him away, was terrified the next day when he was told that the Dog King had made Moor's young blacksmith not just his driver, not just his servant, but had also armed him and given orders to shoot any assailant.

At the hangar Bering had to stand off to one side and wait for more than an hour while Ambras discussed something with a captain inside one of the armored escort vehicles. He was freezing, and shifted from one foot to the other, but did not dare go on ahead to the Crow. From a brightly illuminated troop tent he heard shouts and laughter and thought he recognized Patton's voice, too. The driver of the armored car offered him a cigarette, but then, when Bering did not understand his jokes or a remark about the concert, he put his earphones back on and stared off into space.

Ambras smelled of schnapps when he finally climbed out of the vehicle and by its headlights found his way to the Crow. The mastiff was sitting up on the front seat as if made of porcelain, while Lily sat leaning against him and slept—but woke when Bering opened the door. The dog did not make a sound. Bering made it crawl over the seat into the back, took the dog's spot behind the wheel, and started the motor.

Was what he felt on the way home called happiness? Lily sat beside him and as he took the gentle curve to exit the barricade of vehicles, she leaned against him just as she had against the mastiff and let him secretly stroke her hand with his. And Ambras, sitting in the back seat and scratching his lead dog, could confirm that Bering, the former blacksmith of Moor, knew how to rescue not just himself but also the most powerful man on the lake from danger. And all the while, Patton's music was still ringing in his ears!

The tarmac was deserted. Only along its edges did figures sometimes emerge into the Crow's headlights—people squatting beside a fire or lying in the grass wrapped in blankets. In his happiness, Bering could not resist the temptation of this broad runway, cracked here and there by only a few thorn bushes—and stepped on the gas. The sound of the motor made the dog's grunting snorts inaudible. The acceleration pushed Lily against his shoulder. The runway streamed toward him out of a black infinity and then under him and on back to where he had first kissed a woman and rescued his master. The bushes on each side swept past and out of view like chalk-white stripes.

"Are you crazy?" he heard Ambras's voice say at his back. Lily appeared to be asleep. The rumbling Crow flew through the night.

Bering let a few seconds elapse before he slowly took his foot off the pedal—and a few more seconds until he put his foot on the brake, and in that wisp of a delay he felt a strength that no longer had anything to do with the gun in his belt. Then he stepped on the brake and decreased speed so aggressively that the dog's head slid off Ambras's lap and struck the back of the seat. Ambras said not a word, but Lily sat up startled, laughed softly, gave Bering a nudge, and whispered, "Down, boy!"

Shortly before the end of the runway—there where in the last year of the war, fighter-bombers had reached their maximum take-off speed and no longer touched ground and had to climb in a tight turn to keep from crashing against the walls of the Stony Sea—the Crow slowly rumbled off the tarmac and onto the old truck trail. The ponderous, serpentine ride over potholes, ditches, and washed-out ruts began anew. This road was empty now as well. Patton's fans had draped the warning poles with scraps of paper and clothes, turning some of them into scarecrows. The rags snapped and fluttered in the cold wind rising from the lake, they waved at Bering. The night was turning stormy.

Maybe that sharp pain in his shoulders hadn't misled the Dog King after all, maybe the weather was turning around. Were the slopes hidden in the clouds already? Visibility was getting worse. Weary from the strain of staring at the rutted, potholed road, Bering rubbed his eyes. He did not recall from the drive up to the valley the holes being so close together. More and more of these pits were showing up in the headlights now as sudden black shadows, and not all of them were marked with poles. At times he steered the car to the very edge of the drop-off because there was no other way through.

"What are you doing? Be careful," Lily whispered when he made one such evasive maneuver, and she instinctively grabbed his arm. But she was too sleepy to stay awake, and let her head sink back on his shoulder. Ambras was talking to his mastiff in the dark and paid no attention to the road.

Was it the trail of smoky dust thrown up behind the Crow that was blurring his view so strangely? Could the gusty wind be forcing the dust through cracks and vents into the car's interior? No sooner had Bering wiped his eyes with the back of his hand than they began watering again, and he had to summon all his powers of concentration to make sure whether that was a hole in the road or only just a shadow.

But maybe his trouble seeing, maybe these illusions, simply

came from the Crow's poor headlights. During the week of repairs, he had tried in vain to find parts. Was he even on the right road? No, no, there was nothing wrong with the road. But where was he to get new headlights in Moor? The Dog King should have asked the captain about it. Or could Lily locate some in the lowlands?

By asking questions like that, Bering slowly, imperceptibly drove out of his happiness. He turned toward Lily, but the light was so poor that he recognized her face only on second glance. She was fighting off sleep. She was no less tired than he.

But Bering was awake now, wide awake, because a shadow, a hole without any warning pole stuck in it, opened up so unexpectedly that he missed plowing the car into it by only a hair. He hit the brake so violently that Lily barely managed to keep herself from being thrown against the windshield. Bering could not see what had happened to Ambras and the mastiff, but he heard the curses: ". . . what's wrong? What's wrong with you?"

"A pothole."

"Where?" Lily asked.

Bering experienced the shortness of breath and drainage of blood that comes with shock as he took his eyes from the road and looked at Lily—and the shadow, the hole *moved* with his eyes!, sliding from the beam of the headlights, flying up to become a black spot darkening Lily's face. The shadow moved *with* his gaze. The hole that opened up was not out on the truck trail, but in his vision! When he turned back to the road, the hole traced the movement of his eyes—when he stared into the beam of the headlights, the shadow lay quiet again on the road, an oval smudge, not as sharply outlined and not as black as real holes and traps, and yet barely distinguishable from them. His vision, his world had a hole in it.

"Where?" Lily asked a second time, "where is there a pothole?"

"Are you seeing ghosts?" Ambras asked. "What's wrong?"

"Nothing," Bering said. "Nothing." And drove on and drove right toward the hole in his world, which receded before him and danced away with every movement of his eyes like a will-o'-the-wisp, down the road and up the dark cliffs and out over the drop-off—and yet was always just ahead of him, as if pointing the way back to the lake. And he followed this sign that no one saw but him, followed it mutely and helplessly into the night.

CHAPTER 18

IN THE KENNEL

THE NIGHT WAS SHORT. IN THE EAST THE
ridges and peaks of the Stony Sea were already towering
into the dawn when the Crow finally turned onto the
shore promenade and swayed toward the fire-blackened walls of
the lakeside resort.

The gusts had condensed to a warm wind that chased ragged
banks of clouds across the lake. A clear early summer morning
filled with birdcalls broke above the cliffs of the Blind Shore. But
the hole through which darkness forced its way into Bering's
world did not close with the light of day either.

The mastiff's head on his knees, Ambras sat silent in the back
seat, and Bering could not tell in the rearview mirror whether the
Dog King was awake or asleep. Bering shivered, though he could
feel Lily's warmth as she leaned against his shoulder and slept. He
was clenching the wheel as tightly as if it were his last and sole
support in a landscape that rumbled past and fell back to nothing
along the sides of the road.

Lily woke up when the Crow came to a stop beside the
weather tower. A yelping white Labrador bounded across the

shore meadow—*her* dog. Ambras had to hold his mastiff back by its chain; above the barking, he shouted, "Good morning!" to Lily. Then he laid his hand across the lead dog's eyes and said, almost inaudibly, "Enough." The mastiff fell instantly silent. Only the Labrador outside would not stop jumping at the car in wild joy.

Coffee? Didn't Lily want to come with them to the Villa Flora? Lily was not hungry, just tired. She wasn't going anywhere else. The Labrador snapped at the tires.

What with the two belligerent dogs, there was not much time for good-byes. Lily brushed a finger across Bering's cheek, tracing an invisible wavy line over the skin—a signal he didn't understand—and got out, hastily slamming the door behind her to avoid provoking the mastiff to attack her watchdog. Ambras let go of the chain and laughed. Outside, the Labrador leapt up on its mistress and, with a surprise thrust that she could not parry, it licked her face.

"What are you waiting for?" Ambras asked, tapping Bering's shoulder.

Without turning around to them again, Lily undid the chain and padlock on a metal-plated door and entered the tower; already invisible in its dark interior, she called for her dog.

Bering put the Crow into reverse, rolling back over a stand of nettles, and with one hand tried to keep the mastiff in the back seat, which otherwise would have lunged right through the windshield for the Labrador. Lily's watchdog was standing out there, with no collar or chain, bent down over a puddle from which it drank a few laps of muddy water before bounding into the tower after its mistress. "Down!" Ambras said, and Bering could feel the mastiff's slobber turning cold on his hand.

As the Crow glided between rows of pines toward the Villa Flora, the sun rose above the mountains. Over the past few days, Bering had filled the potholes in the drive with hundreds of shovelfuls of gravel and sand. The drive was smooth, the boulevard flooded with light—and that calmed the driver. If he held his left eye closed for a few seconds now, a great deal vanished from view—but the spot vanished as well. His other eye, then, was intact. Was *intact*.

The pack pressed around the returnees but did not bark and, tails wagging and tongues lolling, followed them down the halls of the villa to the kitchen. There Bering was ordered to prepare food for the dogs, even before Ambras would let him make a fire and put water on for coffee—and was so tired that he cut his hand. His blood dripped onto the pig stomachs and offal, dripped onto the oats he intended to mix with the meat, and splattered the stone tiles of the kitchen floor. The hungriest dogs in the pack sniffed at the blood, but then tucked their tongues back in their mouths—they would not touch it.

Ambras re-entered the kitchen just as his bodyguard was trying to stop the bleeding with a rag and cold water. He told him to get rid of that dirty rag and dressed the wound with iodine, gauze dressings, and tape from an army first-aid kit. Then he divvied the dogs' food into bowls, emptied the ash-box in the stove, helped Bering build a fire, and made the coffee himself.

Ambras, who during the warm part of the year spent a good many nights in a wicker chair surrounded by his dogs out on the veranda, did not seem to be tired despite a night of no sleep. He gave Bering the day off and, accompanied only by his ash-gray mastiff, walked down to the boathouse, where he set off a flare; he occasionally used these fiery signals to call the pilot of the pontoon ferry to the boathouse by the villa and then jumped aboard from a rotting swimming dock. The ferryman, who as on every morning had been waiting for the quarry administrator at the dock in Moor, responded to the fiery signal with a long tone of his foghorn, which resounded across the bay and through the hallways of the Villa Flora, piercing even Bering's exhaustion. Then he cast off his lines and set the pontoon boat's course for the boathouse in the field of reeds.

Bering lay in his clothes on the couch in the billiard room, and with open eyes and to the music of the record player, he dreamt of Patton's concert and Lily's arms. The dark spot in his eye was now only just an annoyance that would surely disappear after a few hours' sleep. He had already forgotten the deep cut in his hand. And he was no longer alarmed even when he closed his eyes and the dark spot went on dancing across the murky, pulsing, bloody red to which his eyelids had muted the morning light. His exhaustion was greater than any fear.

Amid a drum roll from the dusty loudspeakers at the foot of his couch, he fell asleep and began to dream of an opening, of a drain, a hole, a vortex, that sucked the blue right out of the sky. Nothing was left behind but total blackness. He did not awaken when the music came to an end and the tone-arm needle jumped its spiral of grooves and, accompanied only by a rhythmic, crackling sound, now began to describe unguided circles around the spindle. Meanwhile the wind fell. In the stillness, the crackle of the circling needle beat with the regularity of a ticking-clock pendulum and triggered in Bering's dream little bouncing balls that suddenly glowed and then went out again.

The Villa Flora was a very quiet house this morning. The dogs dozed in the shade of the veranda, stretched lazily across the stairs leading to the park, or roamed the hallways—and did not bark once. Sometimes it seemed as if they pricked up their ears just to listen to Bering breathe. They remained silent as well when a man collecting firewood appeared on a hill just beyond the barbed-wire fence, which, though overgrown with ivy, still protected the villa. The man was too far away to notice that seven or eight of the dogs followed his every move, nor could he hear that they were still growling long after he had disappeared with his dosser between the trees, never once suspecting danger. The sun climbed high above the park. Birdcalls grew rarer and died away in the midday heat. Summer came on. Afternoon arrived. Bering slept.

Of course the first thing he saw when he awakened in the early evening was the black spot. The hole. It had not disappeared. He blinked as hard as he could, rubbed his eyelids, even filled a sink

to the brim to immerse his head in it, and repeatedly opened and
closed his eyes underwater, until his vision grew even darker from
his holding his breath—and still the hole did not go away that
evening

or the next day

or in the following weeks.

But it did not get any bigger, either.

During those weeks, when Ambras asked him about the cut
on his hand, which was healing poorly, when he spoke to him or
merely looked at him, Bering always lowered his eyes for fear that
the Dog King might notice the spot in his eye. He began to
counter questions with questions and tried to draw his master's
attention from himself by casually mentioning that some dog in
the pack had a sore paw, by referring to some needed part for the
Crow, or simply by pointing to an empty skiff near the shore, to
an approaching rider or a column of smoke on the Blind Shore.
What's going on there? Are you expecting visitors? Isn't that the
secretary's boat? He was so adept at diversion that even the mis-
trustful Dog King would never guess that his bodyguard was
avoiding his glances and asking questions simply to keep a secret
from him.

The lively, nervous vigilance with which Bering guarded his
secret during those weeks ultimately led Ambras to believe that
his bodyguard was being especially cautious, taking special
interest in things at the Villa Flora. Ambras attributed Bering's
vitality to his having grown completely accustomed to life at the
house of dogs. Whereas in reality, Bering was growing accustomed only to the hole in his world, to an infirmity that he found
worse on some days, better on others, and for which he knew no
better cure than silence—a chauffeur with holes in his vision. A
servant, a mechanic—a bodyguard with holes in his vision! There
was definitely no place for a blind man in the house of dogs.

And Lily . . . Lily, to whom he might perhaps have entrusted
his secret, to whom he most certainly would have entrusted his
secret—during those same days and weeks, Lily came to the villa

only for her usual brief afternoon visits. She did her customary trading with Ambras, but never tried to be alone with Bering, and acted as if they had never held each other in their arms and never kissed. When he came too close to her, she smiled, made some casual remark, or patted him like a dog—and moved away from him.

Bering nevertheless touched her tenderly once as they sat with Ambras on the veranda and he had to bring a carafe of wine out from the kitchen, and he bent down over the table so that he could stroke a hand across her back; she did not exactly pull away from him, but she simply went on speaking with Ambras and gazed so vacantly into his eyes as she said good-bye in the dusk that he began to doubt his own memory. He had held this woman in his arms? *She* had come up to him, after all, and had laid her arms on his shoulders, and carried him off to where he could not sleep now for yearning for her.

Compared to the hole that Lily's puzzling withdrawal tore in his life, the hole in his eye lost its importance, and on many days he even managed, without ever being conscious of it, to augment the missing fragment of his world darkened by this blind spot— and *saw* a dog's head, *saw* a stone, a strand of Lily's hair, or the channels of growth in an emerald under Ambras's magnifying glass, where in reality there was only darkness.

"She comes when she likes, and she goes wherever she likes. Let her come and go, leave her alone—or you'll be in her way . . ." Ambras said one stormy afternoon as he sat with Bering on the veranda, going over a sketch of the quarry. Because of the threatening thunderstorm, they had boarded the *Sleeping Greek Maid* to return from the quarry to Moor's shore earlier than usual. The waves had already been too high for the pontoon boat, which rode low in the water. Ambras was circling the blasting areas for the next few days in red pencil, when they saw Lily leading her heavily laden mule along the lake at the edge of the park. She waved from over the barbed-wire fence. *She comes when she likes. She goes wherever she likes. Leave her alone.*

Even under the roof of the veranda, the wind from the on-

coming thunderstorm was so strong that the sketch of the working terraces spread out over the table rose and sank in the draft
like a bubble, like a wave. Bering was told to weight the paper
down with glasses or empty bottles. But he did not hear Ambras's
directions. He saw only Lily and heard nothing except the
rustling of the pines.

The sky above the Stony Sea turned black. In the heat lightning, scudding clouds looked like the ships, lighthouses, palaces,
and fabled beasts of some gigantic shadow play. Lily was in a
hurry. She waved *no* when with an arm gesture Ambras offered
her a chair on the veranda. The arm gesture could have meant a
glass of wine, an invitation to trade or simply to chat. But Lily
wanted none of it. As she passed by, Bering stared at her so lost in
thought that Ambras rapped the table and sketch with a compass
to remind him of layers of stone and boreholes. *Leave her alone.*

Lily's last visit had been four or five days ago. She appeared
now to be coming from the pass, from the lowlands. From the
army base. The first drops splashed against the glass of the
veranda. Maybe there would be hail. That sickly yellow breaking
through rents in the black sky looked like hail. Storm-warning
beacons were blazing on two platforms out in the fields of reeds,
although all the boats, skiffs, and rafts that the fire was supposed
to call back to shore had been tied up long ago. The deserted lake
roared like the sea.

How confidently Lily led the mule down the steep path. The
animal started to balk as a bolt of lightning struck far out in the
water, but then it appeared to nod when Lily turned around and
called some soothing words. Bering thought he could hear her
voice above the bluster of pines and lake.

Several dogs in the pack grew so excited at seeing Lily appear
under the stormy sky that they fought their way through the
brambles and took the barbed-wire fence in mad leaps just to
greet her and be petted. But neither the foul weather that was
certain to reach Moor within moments nor the tempestuous joy
of the dogs could deter Lily from her path.

Deep in his quarry again now, Ambras shaded in the circled

blasting areas with his pencil, whereas Bering's attention was still out there with the dogs, with Lily. He watched her bend down over the mastiff to scratch its neck and ears—and could feel her hands on *his* neck, teasing the nape until it gave him goose bumps.

Lily showed greater tenderness to a dog than to him. She was in too great a rush to go a few steps out of her way or at least to take shelter at the villa—but she spoke with the pack, laughed and whispered into the mastiff's ear. Then she stood up straight, tugged the bridle taut, and hurried on. The storm had reached Moor's shore. It ripped at the pines along the drive, boomed like an organ in the Villa Flora's stairwell, and drove dust from the shore promenade in long banners across the whitecapped lake. But the expected hail, which had also been forecast on the radio by the army's weather service, held off. Even the rain drifted away in a leaden-gray veil high above the villa. The pattern of those first drops on the white limestone stairs faded and evaporated. And the hail fell elsewhere, too.

Lily had vanished and was perhaps already at her tower when the mastiff returned to the house and, in trying to crawl under the table on the veranda, dragged the sketch to the floor. As if awakened only now by the angry command with which Ambras chased the dog back into the house, Bering bent down for the sketch, fussily smoothed it out, and spread it over the table.

"Upside down," Ambras said. "Turn it around. I'm sitting here. The quarry has to be at the bottom, and the sky at the top. Where are your eyes! Are you blind?"

Leave her alone. Damn it, why did Lily stop for that mutt, with hail clouds overhead, and pet its stinking hide—and yet walk right past the gate-sized hole in the barbed-wire fence and not even offer him her hand? Just waved at him in passing, after being gone a week, and then went her way. Lily! After all, he had kissed her. Had she forgotten that? Was that over and forgotten?

But however monotonously Bering repeated these questions and accusations in conversations with himself or simply in his thoughts, he could barely utter a sentence when face-to-face with Lily in the Villa Flora or out on the dock or among the booths of fishermen, poultry dealers, and trappers on market day in Moor. Then he would grin in embarrassment and say something for which he would curse himself angrily the second the opportunity had passed and he was alone again with his helplessness. Sometimes he would begin to stutter simply when asking Lily if he should take the packsaddle from her mule as it grazed beside the villa's pond.

Only if it was *she* who began a conversation—by asking for a pinch of salt for her mule, by asking him about how things were at the forge, about a hawk circling above the pines or the mechanics of a combustion engine—did he sometimes find his way to weightless conversation. Then for a few seconds he believed she was moving back toward him. Then he told her about his fumbling father, about the bone structure of a bird of prey's wing, about how a transmission worked, and about the impossibility of returning to Forge Hill.

During one such conversation, he also accepted her offer to take CARE packages to the old people on Forge Hill—groceries, soap, and greetings scribbled on yellowed index cards from the filing cabinets in the administrator's shed. But if Bering dared so much as the gentlest physical advance, even a look directly in her eyes, Lily turned away or backed off from him. Never again was she the way she had been to him on the night of the concert.

What had he done to her, what had he done wrong to make her a stranger again? Day after day he waited for the right moment when he would finally demand an answer—even at the risk that she would distance herself from him even more. But as the weeks of summer passed, of all those many unasked questions, only one question remained. Imperceptibly, yet persistently, it began to pound its way into all the other accusations, finally into all his thoughts about Lily, tormenting him even in his sleep. This one question was no longer directed at Lily, but at himself, at the vigilance with which he now followed her every move during her visits to the villa—until he almost forgot the hole in his world, the blind spot in his eye.

Was the only woman he had ever held in his arms, ever kissed, avoiding him

because the Dog King

was her true

and secret lover?

Leave her alone. That was what Ambras said. That was *his* wish, not his bodyguard's. Leave her alone. He wasn't bothering her! He did not risk the gentlest reproach out of the fear and shame of being rejected. He had always left her alone and would never have dared touch her if *she* had not laid her arms around him—that night. He could still hear the delicate jingle of her bracelets. He remembered in painful detail. He remembered her embrace as he sat with Ambras, the sketch of the quarry before them, and stared at the outline of the rows of now dilapidated barracks by the gravel works. He remembered when he stood next to Ambras among the tipcarts on the dusty pontoon boat, when he cut up the meat for the dogs, and when he lay awake at night, and he remembered when he awoke exhausted the next morning. He was leaving her alone. He did remain silent. But that left *him* alone, and gave him no peace.

Whenever the Brazilian and the Dog King haggled now in his presence over the value of an emerald, its worth in trade, examining its purity under their magnifying glasses, and gushing over clouds, liquid inclusions, and healed fractures, over black kernels, pennants, orthorhombic prisms, over the great wealth of shapes in the floating gardens deep within a stone, Bering suspected that in their comments, in every word he did not understand, were coded messages of love, and he searched their most casual gestures and movements for some hidden proof of the truth of his suspicion.

Sometimes he heard them both laugh, thought he heard them laugh on his way down to the villa's cellar to fetch wine or blue cheese. . . . Were they laughing at him? Was he the dupe in some

game? One cool, windy day in July he could bear these constant
questions no more.

Two nights before that summer morning, an attack on a farmstead near Leys Bay had left one person dead and an unknown
number wounded, and Ambras had ordered him to check all the
Villa Flora's door locks, to fix any that seemed in need of repair,
and then to reinforce every shutter, every opening to the outside
world with metal stripping. He left him alone to do the job,
whistled for his mastiff, and with it and four other dogs set out
for the quarry.

The first hours of these repairs and fortifications, which would
keep him busy for days, maybe weeks, Bering spent just mea-
suring windows and doors, calculating the materials needed, and
pondering how he might acquire them. In the process he passed
the door of the former music room—Ambras's door—four
times, without stopping once, since the shutters in this ground-
floor room already *were* made of iron, and its door led only into
the hallway and not out into the wilderness.

But when he finally pushed down the brass handle of the door,
as carefully as if he feared to find someone asleep or on guard
inside, his private justification for the intrusion was a noise
coming from the room—it sounded like someone hammering.
The door was unlocked.

Had the Dog King himself not taught the pack that Bering
was never to be attacked, the dogs, who were lying about on the
stone floor of the hallway, would probably not have allowed him
to lay a fingertip on that handle. But as it was, they simply stood
up and stared at him as he gave the door a push and took a step
into the darkness.

Bering had entered the music room only once. That time,
about three weeks previously, he had to help Ambras haul an
embroidered, moth-eaten sofa from the dusk of this room to the
library upstairs. As they pulled the heavy piece of furniture away
from the wall, a section of the fabric had torn off—a lion done
in embroidery floss and lying among water lilies, with birds

swarming around him, birds even in his mane and on his paws, as if they were combing his pelt with their beaks. Weighed down by the sofa, Bering had hardly had time to look around the room that day, but thought he sensed he was the first stranger to enter this darkened asylum in years.

The music room lay in twilight on this summer day as well. As before, the wide wooden blinds had been let down and clattered as he entered; brocade curtains, shredded now by time and dogs, billowed like sails—and all at once it was so bright, bright as day, that Bering reached for his gun in alarm. The next moment it was dark again. The banging sound was merely one of the iron shutters. One gust of wind flung it open, the next slammed it shut with a bang.

Bright.

Dark.

Bright.

Bering reached out through the slats of the blinds, pulled the shutter to, and pushed the bolt into place.

Dark.

The open door at his back now became a garishly white lamp illuminating the interior of room in which the Dog King resided. This swath of daylight led from the door to a corner nook. There stood a narrow cabinet as tall as a man, with dozens of drawers, its front decorated with inlay. Above the handle of each drawer sat, or sang, a bird carved in various veneer woods. Although the wood had been cracked or warped by fluctuating temperature and humidity, Bering still recognized *his* birds at first glance—the wren, the blackbird, chimney swallow, buzzard, sparrow-hawk . . . the birds of the lake country.

Beneath a withered palm at the window stood the grand piano, closed now for decades. It was draped with tarps and covered with stacks of papers, articles of clothing, and piles of books. One of the brass wheels on its elegantly turned legs had broken off, probably during some attempt to roll the instrument as booty out of the room. The tracks of its final move were engraved in the parquet. Since then, the piano had stood in its spot, a little askew but unmovable.

The piano and the cabinet were the only furnishings. There was no chair. No table. No bed. The walls were bare. In the bay where the sofa had stood until several weeks before lay mattresses, army blankets, and a few pillows, alongside some carelessly folded maps, military magazines, and sheets of paper scribbled full.

Like a bloodhound, Bering sniffed at these cluttered sleeping arrangements, at the pillows, the coarse blankets; he plucked hairs from a sheet and examined them in the swath of light, but nothing here smelled of Lily, of the perfume on her neck, of the woven leather of her arm bands, of the reddish-blue feather bouquets at the shoulders of her jacket—nothing smelled of smoke, reeds, and lavender, the unmistakable fragrance of her hair. He would have recognized any slightest whiff.

The hairs on the sheet came from the dogs. Everything here stank of dogs, nothing else. Did in fact only dogs curl up on this bed to warm their king by night? This was not a room. It was a den. A kennel.

Strange, but looking at Ambras, you saw no sign of slovenliness. He permitted no spots, no tears in his clothes. Once a week, Bering had to take a sackful of laundry up to Leys, where the wife of a lime burner mended, washed, and ironed Ambras's clothes for two bars of soap or a packet of instant coffee. (Bering always looked forward to these laundry trips, because then the Dog King let him have the Crow all to himself for hours and never asked where else he drove—up to deserted Pilot Valley, for instance, and then down the runway in ecstasy.)

If Lily had ever been in this kennel, she had left no trace behind. Loose pieces of the star-parqueted floor lifted under Bering's steps and fell back into their pattern with a bright clatter. The dogs sat outside the door, sat in the light, and their ears alertly followed the intruder's every move. Bering groped through the dingy emptiness and avoided the eyes of the pack.

He was ashamed. He was deceiving the man who had liberated him from the forge. He was deceiving his master. But he had to confirm or obliterate the suspicion that was devouring his life.

The sheets of scribbled paper he found on the piano and in the bedding contained nothing but calculations—long, vertical rows of numbers and not a single word. He did not even understand the titles of most of the books—English novels and works about the war in English. And no matter how violently he shook and frisked the clothing on the piano—a bomber jacket, a macintosh, faded jeans—not the slightest hint of a secret love fell from the pockets. Fine stone dust was all that he could beat out of Ambras's clothes.

And then the cabinet. The cabinet! Behind each wooden bird, in each drawer, Bering found a nest of gauze and cotton balls. And in each nest, nothing but stones: rough emeralds, amethysts, pyrite sunbursts, pink quartz, opals, and splinters of unpolished rubies that lay like dull, congealed drops of blood in their white nooks. Only Lily brought such finds from the mountains back to Moor—but she peddled her stones to anyone who offered enough money or goods in trade. Little labels, no wider than a thumb, were tucked into the nests, but all that was written on each was the stone's name, finding place, the date acquired in trade. On some Ambras had also noted the goods bartered: 6 maps scale 1:25,000, 1 bottle iodine, 2 carbide lamps, 1 ammunition belt. What did Lily need miners' lamps for? Or an ammunition belt?

Not until Bering gave up on the cabinet and, in hope of finding some hidden or lost token, crept on all fours in the bedding, opening and closing the books strewn over the pillows, shaking blankets, even lifting the pieces of cardboard slipped under the mattresses to prevent dampness—not until then did he discover the photograph. It lay face down next to the wall—something was written on the back. As he picked it up, raising it to the light, sand and a few flakes of whitewash trickled onto the sheet. The nail with which it had been tacked to the wall above the head of the bed was still stuck in the photograph's serrated border. The outline of the photograph was still visible there, a bright shadow. The plaster, splotched with damp and nitrate stains, was so brittle that the nail had probably pulled from the wall in the draft as he entered, or had simply fallen under the weight of the paper itself.

Bering waited a long, a very long time before turning the photograph over, because the writing on the back, that large, florid script—that was Lily's handwriting. That had to be Lily's handwriting. He had his proof now and did not dare look at it.

> *North Pole, Friday.*
> *I waited an hour for you in the ice.*
> *Where were you, my dear?*
> *Don't forget me.*
>
> L.

Don't forget me. L.

Lily.

But when Bering finally and slowly turned the picture over in his hand, like some deciding trump card, what he saw was the face of a totally strange woman. She was laughing. She was standing in the snow and waving to some invisible photographer.

In his surprise, in his relief, Bering did not hear the dogs get up from in front of the door and run outside without barking. They bounded silently like that only for their king.

Bering had no ears for the footsteps in the hall and no eyes for the shadow that fell across the open door. He stood there in the kennel, his back to the world, and stared at the mildewed picture:

It was a young,

it was a laughing,

it was a totally strange woman.

CHAPTER 19

A LAUGHING WOMAN

I N WHAT YEAR HAD THIS SNOW FALLEN? FOR whom was the woman's laughter intended? And to whom was she waving so happily? To Ambras?

Ambras.

Bering almost started laughing, too, as he laid the photograph back on the rumpled bedding and tried to leave everything just as he had found it by strewing a pinch of plaster and sand over the picture. Then he stepped over to the black window and checked the bolt once more, as if the shutter banging in the wind had really been the only reason he had entered the kennel, as if that would undo what he had done.

The cold iron bolt suddenly felt as hot in Bering's hand as if it lay glowing on his anvil, and he jerked his arm back when he heard the voice:

"Good day, sir."

Ambras spoke slowly, as if with great exhaustion, was speaking there behind Bering's back.

He turned around.

Ambras was standing in the doorway, the shadow of a man in

white light, and behind him the dogs panted and jostled and did not dare enter the kennel because their king was still standing at the threshold.

"You have . . . you . . . you're back?"

"Do you know what happened in the camp to anyone caught looking under someone else's straw bed," Bering heard the shadow say, "just *looking*, you understand—for bread, for cigarettes, for a potato, for anything that could be eaten or at least traded for something to eat? They threw a blanket over the man's head," Bering heard the shadow say, "they threw a blanket over his head, sir. And then each prisoner was allowed to strike the bundle until his anger or his strength gave out or until the room corporal ordered him to stop. In my barracks, that could mean the anger of more than a hundred men, my good man.

"But whether it was a hundred or only forty or thirty, they beat him—and no one called the guards in such cases, you understand? The guards came only if a thief was beaten so badly that he could no longer get to his feet for roll call. Only that would bring the guards. I've seen how the guards came then, my good man. I've seen the guards take someone beaten like that and drag him by his feet to roll call. We stood there in the snow. We stood there at attention in one long line in the snow, and the thief had to crawl the length of our line all the way to the crematorium.

"They made him crawl, crawl at our feet through the snow, as if he were trying to save himself in the crematorium. He could no longer walk. And the guards always right beside him, right above him, right behind him with booted kicks and blows from rifle butts; one even had a whip. But the crack we heard at the crematorium wasn't from a whip. We lost sight of the thief behind a snowdrift. The last thing I saw of him were the white soles of his feet. He crawled past us barefoot. . . . And you? What are you looking for here, my good man?"

Bering reached for the bolt on the shutter. The iron was once again as cold as it had been in the silence before his master's return. The iron told him he had regained his composure. He turned away from the shadow and pulled the bolt down. The shutter sprang open. The kennel turned bright. The shadow in the doorway was transformed into the Dog King, who held up a hand to shield his eyes. Then the heavy shutter banged against the wall outside.

"I wasn't looking for anything. I haven't stolen anything. It was this shutter. It was open. The wind was banging it open and shut. You forgot to close it when you left. I heard it banging clear down at the boathouse. I had gone to the boathouse to get a file and heard the banging, and first thought it was an intruder—and then I thought of the dogs. The dogs would have nabbed him, after all. It was only this shutter. I closed it."

How easy he found it now to speak, to lie. He lied, even though he did not know how long the Dog King had been standing in the door watching him. Could Ambras have seen him open the drawers to the bird cabinet and find the nests of stones inside? And did he know that he had picked up the photograph of the strange woman and put it back, had strewn sand and plaster over it?

Bering did not give it another thought. He simply went on speaking. He lied. Told how the dogs had almost leapt at him when he went to open the door to the music room, and praised their vigilance, and also said: "Should I wait next time till the wind has shattered the glass?" He felt sure of himself. With each word that Ambras had said about thieves who stole bread, about beatings as punishment and a prisoner in the snow, Bering's sense of security had grown. Ambras would believe him. He was so caught up in his memories that he forgot the present, that he saw only someone stealing bread, whereas his bodyguard had been rummaging through what was once a music room for proof of a secret love.

"Why did you throw the bolt open after you had just locked it?" Ambras asked. "Close those damn shutters, why don't you."

Which he did, too.

"And now go get your tools. We're on our way to—"

"I want to ask you something," Bering said. "Might I ask you something?"

Ambras said nothing.

"Why did you come back?"

"To get you," Ambras said. "The pontoon boat is anchored at Leys Bay, something's wrong with the engine."

"The pontoon boat? I . . . I don't mean now, not today. I mean . . . why did you come back *here*? Here, to the lake, to Moor. To the quarry."

Bering was wondering if his sense of security had betrayed him, was afraid he had gone too far, and was expecting a brusque reprimand in place of an answer, when after a long silence Ambras suddenly bent down to one of the dogs, held its head in both hands, pushed back the flews as if to check its fangs, and then said, more down the dog's throat than to his bodyguard:

"Come *back* to the quarry? I didn't come back. I *was* in the quarry even when I was walking through the rubble of Vienna or Dresden or any of the other harrowed cities of the early Stellamour years. I just needed to hear the din of hammers and chisels somewhere or watch someone climb a staircase with some burden on his back, even just a sack of potatoes—and I was in the quarry. I did not come back. I never left."

Ambras let the dog slip from his grasp and stood up; his stare was so vacant that Bering countered it effortlessly. "Come on. Get your tools. The pontoon boat has drifted halfway down the lake. The engine sputters and smokes and can make no headway against even the gentlest current. The ferryman can't locate what's wrong."

"What about you? How did you get to shore?"

"With one of the brace fishermen. They caught more fish last night in Leys Bay than they have for the past two weeks."

Today Bering had no trouble carrying his toolbox, although on other occasions he found it hard to lug it out to the Villa Flora's diesel unit, to the quarry's conveyor belt, or down into the machine room of the *Sleeping Greek Maid*. The relief he felt at seeing that picture of a strange woman made every burden light. For a brief while he even forgot the hole in his vision. All the same, he allowed himself time—on the way down to the boathouse and then for more than two hundred strokes of the oars—before he made use of his new, peculiar freedom and attempted to resume a conversation beyond routine questions dealing with matters of everyday life. It was as if by intruding into the kennel he had simultaneously advanced into Ambras's secret interior and could move about there with the same impunity as in the dusk of the music room.

During the boat trip to Leys Bay, the master and his servant sat as they always did on boat trips together—back-to-back and each to himself. Ambras was perched on a pillow in the bow, where the fishing gear was stowed, his eyes directed ahead toward Leys Bay, to where the pontoon boat drifted in the reeds but still out of sight. Bering was bent over, rowing. His hands on the oars, he stared back to where they had come from, to the shore of Moor, to the boathouse, the swimming dock. With each of his strokes, the dogs left behind grew smaller. Their disappointed barking seemed gradually to turn into the distant sound of a sputtering engine, audible only in the short silences between strokes of the oars.

The master and his servant did not look at each other, and for more than two hundred strokes of the oars did not hear each other either. But when Bering at last spoke the words of the question that, as on so many other occasions, had been only a thought until that moment, it was as if the dogs suddenly froze and stopped shrinking, even though the boat kept gliding farther and farther out into the lake. "Why," Bering asked into the void, back toward Moor's shore, "why did they put you in the camp back then?"

He spoke loudly, spoke above the splash of oars and waves cast by a dropping wind against the sides of the boat. Although he did not turn around to the Dog King, he could picture him clearly:

Ambras had dipped one hand in the water flowing past below him. Bering could feel its slight tug to starboard—even the little paddle of a human palm could disrupt the boat's smooth ride. Ambras took his hand from the water now. Bering heard water dripping, the tug eased, ceased.

"Why did they put you in the camp back then?" *In the camp. Why had anyone ever been taken from his home, his room, his garden, or some refuge in the wilderness and been put in a camp? Why had half-starving construction gangs built long, straight rows of barracks beside these gravel works—and at other quarries, too— with crematoriums just behind them?*

During the quiz games and question periods—almost forgotten nowadays—that had been held on Moor's parade grounds on days preceding and following a Stellamour Party, an information officer kept bawling questions like that through his megaphone or wrote them on a giant blackboard. With a correct answer, likewise bawled through a megaphone or written on the board in chalk, each participant in these proceedings could win sticks of margarine, some powdered pudding, or a carton of unfiltered cigarettes. Even nowadays a shrinking congregation gathered every Friday evening in Moor's assembly hall to hear a radio program in which, between musical interludes and lectures on the history of the war, the old questions were still asked. By scribbling the old answers on a military postcard and sending it to army broadcasting, a person could enter a drawing that promised small prizes and even trips to distant zones of occupation. The courier who took Moor's mail to the lowlands once a week had to deliver those cards post-free.

Bering, too, had sometimes secretly filled out postcards for the blacksmith's wife (he dared not let his father know anything about it) and mailed them at the secretary's office; he once won a catalog of American luxury cars, and another time a pass to see a baseball game at the largest army base in the lowlands. But his father would not permit his son—or anyone *he* could order around—to take trips on a troop transporter belonging to his

former enemies. The pass was now a bookmark, still stuck between brightly colored illustrations and schematic drawings of a
motor in the catalog he had won—the only book Bering had
taken with him from the forge to the house of dogs.

"Why did they put you in the camp back then?" Here in a
boat far out on the lake, in view of the Blind Shore, the question
sounded strangely different from those radio-quiz questions that
every resident of Moor could answer in his sleep.

Bering had often seen the Dog King angry, but had never
heard him raise his voice, and certainly never shout. And Ambras
did not shout now, either, although the first sentences of his
answer were so vehement that a brace fisherman crossing their
path a little distance off raised his head in curiosity.

"Why? Because I ate at the same table and slept in the same
bed with a woman. Because I spent each night with that woman
and wanted to go on living with her. And because I combed her
hair with just my bare fingers. She had long, curly hair, and my
arm was still very limber then, you understand. Nothing has ever
again flowed through my hands like her hair. I did not see hair
like hers again until the camp, in a warehouse where it lay in a
great pile—pigtails, locks, handfuls of chopped-off hair stuffed in
gunnysacks—to be used as the raw material for mats, wigs, mattresses, or whatever. . . .

"That morning I combed her hair for her while she slept, and
it did not wake her. It was starting to grow light, but sunrise was
still an hour or more away. We were lying in our bed, I had just
thought I should close the window, because the pigeons in the
courtyard were so loud, when the bellowing and drumming and
pounding on the door started, it was like an avalanche. 'Open up!
Open up at once!' "

Ambras's narrative had grown so soft that Bering stopped
rowing and turned around. The Dog King was sitting atop the
tackle box in the bow, hunched over and talking to the water—
and there on the tattered green of his bomber jacket, large and
conspicuous, just below the shoulder blades, Bering saw his blind

spot dancing, saw the hole. The barking of the dogs on the shore had died away, and from the reed fields of Leys there now came the unmistakable sound of a motor—a clattering that instantly died away.

"She awoke only then, amid that hellish noise, amid the bellowing and banging on the door," Ambras said. "She was so frightened, sat up so suddenly in bed, that a few strands of hair got caught in my fingers. She cried out in pain, and I embraced her and held her tight and held myself tight against her and thought, They're not banging on our door, they don't mean us, they can't mean us. They always came at dawn—that much I knew. They always come when you're most defenseless, entangled in some dream, they come when you're far away and yet easier to catch than at any other time.

"They didn't have to kick in the door. Back then, I often forgot to lock it of an evening. It was open. They just had to push down on the handle, that was all, and then they were standing in the middle of our life. There were four of them. All in uniform. We had only the sheet. It took all their strength to tear us apart. They beat us with clubs on the head and arms and screamed, 'Herr Ambras beside his Jew whore!' and 'You're fucking a Jew sow, asshole!'

"She had grown very quiet. She was totally silent, mute. She was, I don't know, breathless, as if turned to stone. The last thing I heard from her mouth was that cry of pain when she sat up in fear and a strand of her hair got caught in my hand. They had beaten us, needed all eight hands and fists to tear us apart. But she remained silent. She looked at me. I was almost blind, blood was dripping into my eyes. They kicked her into the kitchen and threw some wadded-up clothes after her—she was to get dressed, get ready. There were clothes draped over all the chairs and on the sofa. We had been taking photographs for a textile firm till late the night before. The lamps, the camera—it was all still there.

"She had been my model for each new dress and was probably

dragged away in one of them—I can't say how that was. Because when she came back from the kitchen and bent down for a shoe, one of them pulled her up by the hair and yelled, 'Jew whores go barefoot!' The others hadn't been watching me closely enough at that moment. I was down on all fours from the kicks and blows, but had just enough breath left to grab the camera tripod and slam the thing against his knee. His skull was far too high, beyond reach. I managed to see her hair slip from his fist. Then something exploded against my forehead. I woke up in a cell under a mask of congealed blood and was still naked."

How small, almost puny, Ambras seemed to his bodyguard in that moment. It was as if the Dog King, sitting hunched over there atop the tackle box, had been transformed from the most feared and powerful man in Moor back into the portrait and landscape photographer that he had been before the war—before his years in the camp—but that he had not been allowed to remain.

"I think the dress she had on when she came out of the kitchen was red," Ambras said, turning around now toward Bering for the first time in his story. "I think it was one of those summer dresses she didn't like to be photographed in because they were too showy for her taste. Red. But it may be, too, that the color was just from the blood in my eyes. Everything was red. Everything dripping. Everything fading. And so that was the *blood* they kept harping on in those days: *pure blood, the disgrace of mixed blood, blood sacrifice.* Well, in my case, blood was merely dripping into my eyes."

"And the woman? Where is the woman now?" Bering asked, thinking of Lily. He had been thinking of Lily the whole time—saw her in a red dress coming out of a dark kitchen, saw a uniformed thug pulling her hair.

"It was three years before I could search for her," Ambras said. "After three years and four different camps, I was able at last to return to where we had lost one another. Lying in an American field hospital, I had heard about the carpet-bombings, the firestorm in Vienna, but I didn't know where else to start looking for her. No more was left of the house where we lived, of the whole street, than was left of the rest of the city. The street was a pile of rubble.

"I did a lot of digging in the first months of peace—for broken dishes, clothes, enamel pots, and the remains of our life, later for copper cables and brass. The only trace I found of her was her sister's address in some Red Cross records. This sister had been married to one of those pure-blooded, racially pure bastards and had survived the war in a Swiss sanatorium. She had been looking for her with as little success as I. She had a photograph of her and a letter written from a camp in Poland. But that last news from her contained familiar words: *I am healthy. I am doing fine. . . .* Words like that were required. We had written sentences like that in our barracks by the gravel works, too. People who the very next day would go up in the smoke of the crematorium wrote sentences like that home. We were all healthy. We were all doing fine.

"And in the photograph she was standing in the snow, laughing. I fought with her sister over that picture. It belonged to me. I took it the winter before she disappeared. She was standing in the snow, laughing. That picture belonged to *us.* For weeks, it had been wedged into the wooden frame of a little mirror in our kitchen. At some point she had used it as a card and written a message for me on the back. She never wrote even the simplest messages on just a slip of paper, but always on one of the post-cards or snapshots forever lying around our place. Once I even found an apple on which she had written that she would be late. She must have tucked that photograph away on the same morning they threw those clothes to her in the kitchen. She included the picture with her letter from the camp. *I am healthy. I am doing fine.*

"Her sister didn't want to give me the picture. There wasn't a single lab left in the whole neighborhood that could have made us a print. Finally, an army photographer helped me out—one of those guys who at the time were filming and photographing the empty barracks, the ovens, and quarries for the Stellamour Archives. We got our copy from him, we got two copies. Her sister had demanded that the writing on the reverse be copied as well—her handwriting, her message to me. But those few words were so blurred and dark on the copy that she asked if I could imitate the handwriting. She would then give me the original. I tried. I reproduced the writing on the reverse as best I could with a pencil. It was the only letter I've ever written to myself.

" 'I waited an hour for you in the ice,' I wrote. 'Where were you, my dear?' I wrote. 'Don't forget me.' "

In the silence that followed his story, Ambras suddenly knelt down on the wet floor of the boat, bent over the side, scooped water with both hands, and washed his face as vigorously as if he had just returned covered with dust from a blast at the quarry. Once Ambras, still dripping, had sat back down, Bering reached for the oars and with a few strokes turned the boat to its old course for Leys Bay. They had drifted.

The photograph. The strange woman. Bering could no longer recall the features of the woman's face. It had sufficed to see a stranger. What made him uneasy now was his carelessness—he had put, tossed, the picture back on the bedding in the music room without paying attention to whether traces of his morning's work with the iron locks and bolts of the Villa Flora had been left on the snow where the lost woman stood laughing. Perhaps a black fingerprint in that snow or one or two filings clinging to a bit of grease would betray him. Even now he could feel the grease and the filings on his hands.

He dipped the heavy oars deep in the water and watched as the spinning waves and eddies of his strokes were quickly left behind and tried to calm himself with the notion that any clues left in that kennel could be read not only as traces of an intruder but of a dog as well. After he had worked on the door to the garden, the threshold lay in a snow of fine iron filings. Every dog would have to have filings on the pads of his paws by now.

Bering rowed sturdily, swiftly, as if with each stroke in the water he wanted not only to draw nearer to the reed fields at Leys but also to pull away from Ambras's memories. Although the day was cool and a dense, gradually lowering cloud cover was now almost at the timberline, sweat dripped down his chest. Each time he tried to wipe a rivulet of sweat from his face by pressing cheek to shoulder so as not to break his stroke, he turned to steal a glance at Ambras. He had not moved. He was wrapped in silence, was not looking at Bering, and gave no signal, did not even wave when the pontoon boat, loaded with tipcarts full of gravel, came into view at the edge of the reed fields at Leys—and aboard it, a black figure flapping its arms, the ferryman. The man waved, shouted a greeting or a question, but they were still too far away to understand him—and then bent back down over a wooden shed scarcely bigger than a doghouse.

There, inside that engine room, stuttered and banged a motor that, years before, Bering and his father had taken from a truck that had struck an ancient tank mine. In the process of remounting it on the gravel barge, he had learned how a truck motor can be retooled into a ship engine, and later, in countless hours of service and repair of this burly eight-cylinder motor, he had transformed it into one of *his* machines.

The ferryman was apparently unwilling to give up on the attempt to start it. At irregular intervals, the exhaust pipe, which towered like a flagpole above the engine shed, would pump out a fist of black smoke that scattered in the wind as a bouquet of plumes.

Whatever was wrong with the engine—throttle valve, intake manifold, a filter—Bering could tell even from this distance that the ferryman's angry attempts were doing more harm than good, and he shouted: "Turn it off! Turn the motor off, idiot!"

Ambras paid no attention to either the ferryman or the bodyguard's shouts. He had got up, was standing erect now in the bow like a picture from the blacksmith's wife's calendars, and said not a word. The boat glided through a sheer, iridescent film of oil that ripped open beneath the strokes of the oars and closed again in their wake. Two cormorants took off, gulls and coots as well—the slap of the oars had come too close for them.

When the boat bumped against the planks of the pontoon ferry with a thud, the ferryman finally turned the motor off, flung a black rag into the shed, stomped his way between tipcarts toward the newcomers, and began to curse and describe the motor's puzzling problem even before Bering had tied a line to an iron ring in the planks. Piece of crap! The engine was a piece of crap! In the middle of the lake it suddenly started smoking, shit! Wasn't putting out, suddenly had no power, nothing. . . . And this fucking raft full of fucking stones had got caught in the Leys current and drifted, at full throttle, drifted off course! And the truck was waiting at the dock in Moor, shit! The only one this week, and it would head back down to the lowlands early that afternoon, with or without a load, *had* to head back to pass the checkpoints by sundown.

Ambras shoved aside the grease-smeared hand the cursing man held out to him, boarded the pontoon boat in one quick step, cut the ferryman off, saying, "Don't bother me with this!" and pointed an outstretched arm at Bering. "Tell it to him."

"I *am* telling him. I am telling him!"

But Bering wasn't listening. He was already alone with his engine. He was standing at the open shed now and had started the motor and had ears only for what he heard coming from the insides of this oil-blackened, vibrating hunk of metal. He bent down over the rows of cylinders, surrendered himself to them, as if in the hammering of a diesel motor, of all places, he might find refuge from the memory of fists banging on an apartment door, from the memory of clubs raining down on an embracing couple, from the memory of how a woman in a red dress had vanished. The motor's driving pistons hammered away until it all was inaudible, even the ferryman's rantings. What he was saying was now meaningless noise at Bering's back.

Even in his early years at the forge, when standing in front of a wreck in the workshop or lying on his back under some tractor that had conked out in a sugar-beet field, Bering had always preferred to listen first to what the engine itself was saying rather than to the babblings of its angry or helpless operator. For whatever he might learn during the hours of repair from the machine's operator—whether vague guesses about the cause of the problem or whole life stories—the information could never be as reliable as the jingling of a valve, the whine of a V-belt, or the rattle of a loose gasket. To someone with delicate hearing, that interplay of the most disparate sounds of a running motor—which in a world of horse-drawn wagons and wheelbarrows was perceived as mere (and rare) engine noise—revealed itself as the harmonic orchestration of all the sounds and voices of a mechanical system. Within this system, each voice, each noise, however trivial, bore an unmistakable significance that led to conclusions about the functional capability of those hammering, stomping, hissing parts.

Bering listened with eyes closed. He was all attention now. He unraveled the knot of intermingling and layered voices, followed each thread of sound to its origin, and heard the engine's construction. Like a blind man, he groped along the fuel lines, fingered pieces of iron that he had forged himself years ago for lack of spare parts, opened and closed ventilating screws, listened to the machine's breathing in the bubbling oil bath of the air filter, gave the throttle cable a tug and let go, loosened the feeders to the cylinders and blew shrill tones on them—nothing, no wedge of dirt was clogging the lines, diesel fuel was pulsing unimpeded through the engine.

It was the air. This motor here was short of air. It could not breathe. It smoked, struggled to get oxygen, until the piston stroke stopped, and it burned its fuel so badly that only soot, but no power, was released. The strange thing was that it had no problem idling—no stutters and gasps, no plumes of soot. Not until Bering pulled the throttle cable out as far as the catch, demanding full power from the motor, did a fist of smoke shoot out the exhaust with a bang. Not until then did the bark of a metallic cough spread out over the lake, and instead of tracing a churning, powerful curve in the water, the raft merely rotated lazily around its anchor chain, as if to show the reeds and all the cormorants, gulls, great white herons, and coots hidden there the dead freight it was carrying: tipcarts full of primal stone, green granite, blasted, pounded, and ground to gravel, gravel for railroad embankments and roads to be built somewhere, roads to lead from somewhere to somewhere—but never up to this lake, never to these upland valleys and over the passes of the Stony Sea. Every pebble of this load rotating in the reeds by Leys beneath a grimy sky was a reminder of Moor's inaccessibility and remoteness, of its empty railroad embankment, of truck trails and muddy roads that led no farther.

Bering discovered what ailed the engine when he loosened the clamp rings on the air hose that fed the outside world's bad air into the air filter and its seething oil bath, from which the cleansed air rose in black bubbles to fan the fire of the cylinders. The hose slipped from the intake manifold's nozzle and fell like a severed organ among the metal innards. When he pulled the air hose out again, he found a defect so simple that the ferryman, who was busy rolling himself a cigarette, did not even notice the actual repair.

The ferryman was standing with his back to the wind, holding one hand to shield a match flame, trying to light his cigarette, when the engine suddenly began to roar with its old power. A gust of wind dived into his cupped hand and put out the match flame. With a cry of surprise that soon became a coughing laugh, he turned to Bering. "What did you? . . . How did you? . . ."

The Dog King was sitting in the wheelhouse and barely raised his head as the raft began to tug at its anchor chain. The shadow of a swarm of frightened gulls flitted over reeds and tipcarts. Water roiled at the stern.

Bering let go of the throttle cable, and for a brief moment as the roar ebbed he gave himself over to the wonderful, fleeting sense of relief that came over him whenever he solved a mechanical problem, but that he could never hold on to or prolong. At such moments it made no difference whether he had sought a solution for hours or days or only a few minutes—whenever a defective mechanical system began to run flawlessly again under his hands, he felt an intimation of that triumphal ease that otherwise he thought he observed only in the ascent of birds. Then all he had to do was push himself off from the world—and it sailed away beneath him.

On the ferry one simple maneuver had sufficed—the trouble had been hidden in the air hose. The insulation lining the inside of the engine's air hose was starting to fray, dangling in tatters at some points. Although these tatters fluttered and swayed in the soft breeze of an idling motor and did not retard the burning of fuel, in the strong suction of an open throttle they became a kind of flap valve, a hand laid over the mouth of the air filter, suffocating the fire inside the cylinders.

Bering didn't even have to open his toolbox, which still lay rocking in the boat. The broad blade of his jackknife sufficed. He scraped the brittle tatters of insulation out of the air hose, then screwed the clamp rings tight again.

The raft rocked clear to move out through the reeds. The ferryman kept shouting, "Better than before!" down into the vibrating wooden shed. The engine was running better now than before. But, evidently uninterested, Ambras was sitting in the wheelhouse on a stack of empty sacks and paging through a grease-stained cargo register. The ferryman did not want to lose another second and urged haste. Coughing and sputtering as if, with repairs completed, the engine's troubles had been passed on to him, he labored at the capstan and rolled an iron spider up out of the lake. Bering hardly recognized the rust-eaten, barnacled thing. During his first apprentice year, he had welded this anchor from the track links of a cannibalized tank, then appended the four iron tentacles and barbs.

As the iron spider and its chain clattered against the side planks, Bering beheld his work veiled in the black cocoon of his perforated vision, wrapped in a hovering scrap of darkness, but, despite the eclipsed light, he saw thin, shiny, silvery rivulets run down the welds and drip back into the lake. He had once hammered the lance blades of the tentacles on the anvil into the form of barbs, without any help or instructions. The welds were poor. He could have done better now. But his patching days were over. Had to be over for good. He carried a gun. He lived in the house of dogs. The fire in the forge had gone out.

Without getting up from the pile of sacks, Ambras now shouted commands to his bodyguard: "Hey! Come here. Listen." He would not be going back with Bering. He had things to do at the steamer dock and at the secretary's office in Moor. Bering was to row home and start working on the bolts and door locks again and—*do you hear!*—there was to be no more snooping around in rooms he had not been invited into.

There was nothing in Ambras's voice of the exhausted tone of his story in the boat. His voice now sounded brusque and cold, the way it usually did when it came through a megaphone at the quarry or on days when penitents assembled on the drill field where prisoners had once stood for roll call.

"I was just bolting the shutter," Bering shouted above the engine and jumped into the rowboat. "I didn't touch a thing. *Not a thing!*"

But the Dog King spoke to his bodyguard as if he repented his weakness in having confided to him not only about his crippled arms but about a lost love as well. He spoke so coldly, as if the trip to the reeds at Leys had merely proved to him that his bodyguard was more likely to be touched by a defective machine than by a defective life. After so many speeches, flyers, and messages of the great Lyndon Porter Stellamour, after countless penitential

and memorial rites in the backwater villages along the lake and
on its Blind Shore, the first man, the only man among the men
of Moor in whom Ambras had ever confided, still would rather
listen to the pounding and hammering of engines than to the
words of memory.

CHAPTER 20

TOYS, BREAKDOWN,
AND HAVOC

E ARLY IN AUTUMN OF THAT SAME YEAR,
during the sugar-beet harvest in October, what few machines there were in the lake country began to break
down; some suddenly just stopped altogether. Gear teeth locked,
flywheels, camshafts, and piston rings broke, even the hands on
the big clock at the steamer dock fell clattering from the face one
morning and sank into the lake; wear and tear devoured the simplest cotter pins, pipe clips, regulator screws, and hoop irons.
Again and again, at a sawmill, a sugar-beet factory, or a gravel pit,
some presumably irreplaceable truck had to be replaced for days,
weeks, or forever by a team of oxen, a conveyor belt ready for the
junkyard replaced by shovels, wheelbarrows, and bare hands.

Machines! With each passing year, you could depend less and
less on machines, people said at the Dock Inn, in the offices of
Moor's secretary, in any room where this breakdown and the passage of time were discussed. Those who tried to plow with tractors and harvest with steam-driven threshers would soon have
nothing but stones to eat. Better a nag in a horse collar and mud

up to your ankles than the most powerful tractor and no fuel or parts. . . .

The great expectations bolstered by the christening of the *Sleeping Greek Maid* in the spring had not been fulfilled. The Crow kept by the Dog King was the only, the last limousine to bounce along Moor's gravel roads. In the garages of once-grand summer villas, mules and goats stood beside derelict convertibles, and the people along the shore and all those forced to live their lives in the shadow of the Stony Sea still obtained most of their engines and spare parts from the army's junkyards or from iron gardens like the one sinking deeper and deeper into the weed-grown earth of Forge Hill.

Along the lake, what was and remained new was always old—every piece of scrap iron, no matter how bent and rust-eaten, had to be laid in an oil bath, brushed, polished, filed, and hammered into shape, and used over and over until wear and tear finally ended its usefulness, leaving nothing but junk for the smelter. Gardens of scrap iron may have kept piling higher and higher around houses and farmsteads, but the number of useful spare parts in them kept dwindling; and the smelter at Haag, the only one in the lake country, supplied only substandard metal that lost quality and durability with each new smelting.

But service and repair—and, ultimately, transformation of junk into a fiery liquid to be poured into new forms—required skills and tools still at the command of only a few craftsmen. Each of them was supposed to be blacksmith, mechanic, locksmith, and iron-founder all in one and in some hamlets was already revered as a shaman, who by simply repairing a diesel generator could lift a farmstead into a present illuminated by electric light—or, then again, let it sink back into the darkness of the past.

The best-known and most frequently visited of these mechanics was still the young blacksmith of Moor—or had been at least until that autumn. For although he had abandoned his inheritance to hole up in the house of dogs, during the first weeks and months of his new job, even behind the tangled barbed wire of the Villa Flora he had remained available for Moor's needs and could always be fetched to repair some inoperable machine. But now, at the very time when there were so many problems and a general breakdown, he no longer so much as raised his head if someone shouted "Blacksmith!" to him through the barbed wire. "Help me, blacksmith!" Now that he seemed to be attached to the Dog King like a Siamese twin and—in plain view of a miner at the quarry—tied that army spy's shoes and brushed the dust from his hair, that damned blacksmith no longer answered to his name.

Even the people in Leys and Haag who operated machines had long been trying with gifts and pleas to lure him out of the Villa Flora and back to his workbench, to the forge, to his iron garden high above the lake. How often had they stood as petitioners at the Villa Flora's barbed-wire fence, waiting with poppy-seed cakes, smoked brace, sides of bacon, and baskets of pears and mushrooms for the blacksmith to step out on the veranda, to drive by in the Crow, or to come strolling up from the boathouse at the side of the Dog King. A few had even brought the defective parts of their machines along in sacks and been bitten by one of the dogs when they tried to lay the stuff in the driveway so that as the blacksmith came and went, he might at least cast it a glance and perhaps even call out some advice in passing.

But the blacksmith, whom the ferryman and miners at the quarry now called the bodyguard in their conversations as well, could not be softened by either pleas or promises. Only when the Dog King specifically ordered him or if a petitioner could induce the Brazilian to put in a good word did Bering occasionally still take on a mechanical problem. He brusquely refused all other machine operators, chased some of them off by threatening to let the dogs loose, and in the case of one particularly stubborn salt-worker—who for three days running was waiting for him every morning at the dock with the dismantled generator from a truck—he pushed the fellow away so violently that the helpless man stumbled and fell backwards into the water.

Bering wanted nothing more to do with the junk of his black-smith years. For although his passion for all things mechanical was still unbroken, the neglected machines of Moor—these monstrous iron mutations, rebuilt again and again over the decades by so many bungling hands and paws—confronted him above all with his own infirmity. More than any other kind of work, steady examination of these corroded motor blocks, cracked cylinder heads, sooty spark plugs, hopelessly worn gears, and rusty ball-and-socket joints made him unsettlingly, painfully aware of his blind spot, of the hole in his world.

Perhaps it was because the days were growing shorter, because there was a general lack of light and a seemingly impenetrable cloud cover during these weeks—but there were times when, instead of screws, springs, and boreholes, instead of the cause of a mechanical defect, he saw only the hovering blind spot in his eye. And when, as on occasion, there was also some impatient machine operator gawking over his shoulder and tormenting him with questions about how long repairs would take and how serious the problem was, the blindness in his eye sometimes expanded like a cloud of soot. With each botched repair, with each mistake he made while a machine operator watched him stare into the void, groping for filigreed parts, the danger grew that the hole in his world would not remain his secret much longer.

When dealing with his own familiar mechanical creatures, however, he did not need daylight, had not needed a falcon's eye for some time now. For the inner workings of the Crow, for the Villa Flora's generator in the turbine shed, or for the mechanism of his gun, even blind he could have recognized any problem by touch, or just by sound—and could have repaired the problem blind as well. In hour after hour of fine mechanical work, he had expanded his pistol's magazine, increasing its firepower by more than twenty shots, and his blind spot had never once proved a serious hindrance.

He worked alone and unobserved in the shed beside the house

of dogs, and however tiny a component in some mechanical complex might be or whenever darkness hid a borehole, he *saw* what he wanted to see with his hands—or *heard* a worn-out spring, the play in a hinge, and did not need his eyes. With each new autumn day, it seemed to him as if his fingertips were growing more sensitive and his hearing so acute, sometimes painfully so, that he began wearing gloves much of the time and on stormy October nights, when the whole countryside moaned, cracked, and howled like a single organic machine, he stopped his ears with cotton balls and wax.

On those days when he would rumble down the runway of the old airport in the Crow and during the moments of greatest speed surrender to the illusion of flight, he sometimes voluntarily renounced every view of the world for a few breathtaking seconds and *closed* his eyes and flew ahead in an exultation beyond compare. When he opened his eyelids again after four, five heartbeats—always at the same weatherbeaten stripes across the runway—he hardly noticed his blind spot. Then the runway, an avalanche of cracked asphalt, thundered and roared on through him as if he himself were as bodiless as the air that bore him.

Moor no longer recognized this blacksmith, this bodyguard. He was letting his inheritance go to ruin and did not care if a stranded tractor was rusting in the field during the weeks of harvest—but he had plenty of time to drive the Crow up to Pilot Valley and waste gas racing up and down the runway. A shepherd claimed he had seen the blacksmith shoot at a horde gathering scrap metal up there. They surprised him one day outside the hangar and tried to block his retreat with iron rods and wooden clubs. Traveling at full speed, he shot from the open window at those plunderers draped with strands of cable and copper wire. He missed. He didn't wound anyone. But he shot, without hesitation. With no one to stop him, he flew away in his Crow.

The change in the blacksmith was a rich source of conversation for the stonemasons and miners who commuted to the Blind Shore aboard the *Sleeping Greek Maid* each day and often got drunk on potato schnapps on the return trip of an evening. Of course the guy liked driving along the shore promenade in the Crow with the Brazilian at his side, liked playing chauffeur, carting her back and forth between the lakeside resort and the house of dogs, liked all that better than striking sparks at the forge. The Brazilian had the boy eating out of her hand. At harvest home, he had mounted a windmill on the roof of her weather tower, one that made an attached glockenspiel play the first bars of three different melodies depending on how strong the wind was—and it lit a hurricane lamp, too. And on the eve of All Souls' he had flown an electrical kite in the skies above the Villa Flora; constructed of sticks, light-bulb wire, and parachute silk, it had panicked a procession of penitents moving through the reeds with their lamps for the dead and had driven the dogs wild. Their howls had kept half Moor awake till dawn. And then, two or three days later, mechanical chickens or pheasants made of paper and wire—toy birds!—were seen fluttering among the giant pines in the park near the house of dogs.

That madman was playing at the Villa Flora, while Moor lost one piece of machinery after another to the general breakdown and even the works of the handless clock at the steamer dock had been turned into a pigeon nest covered with bird shit. And the Dog King gave him free rein everywhere, let him have the Crow, let him confirm all safe-conduct papers, and sometimes even had the blacksmith supervise work at the quarry while he himself sat on a folding chair outside the administrator's shed and stared at the mountains through his binoculars.

But wherever the people of Moor talked about the blacksmith and the change in him, there were differences of opinion about who was actually driving him to do such crazy things: the Brazilian, some said, of course the Brazilian; she admitted him up into her weather tower, something no one from Moor had ever managed until now. And hadn't she also tricked him out of the horse he brought with him to the house of dogs from the forge? The Brazilian had only to whistle, and he jumped. Now she had his nag to ride on her smuggling trips and could have her mule trot along behind with just that much more of a load. What do you suppose she gave him for that nag? The miners, stone-masons, and sugar-beet farmers would have enjoyed being paid *that* price themselves.

The Brazilian? Oh go on, others said, it had been the Dog King after all who had lured the blacksmith off his hill, no one else. That escaped convict was crazy himself. First he had made the blacksmith as unpredictable, frisky, and ferocious as one of his mongrels and then put him between himself and the world. And now—whoever wanted just to *speak* with the quarry admin-istrator never got past the bodyguard. He apparently had not only to protect his master from drunken thugs and plunderers, but also to keep at arm's length *anyone* who confronted the two of them at the quarry or the secretary's office with a petition or complaint.

There was no avoiding such surmises and rumors as they spread among the backwater villages by the lake, but Ambras took no interest. Let Moor talk and, as far as he was concerned, it could hammer hoes for its fields from the scrap of defunct machines—the Dog King appeared as untouched by rumor as by stranded tractors or by anything that was the present. Ambras did not suffer from the present.

The unusually cold and wet autumn made his shoulder joints ache much worse than had any change in the weather since the year of his torture. Some days the pain crippled him so badly that his bodyguard not only had to comb his hair but also had to help him dress and undress. And even when his searing hot joints left him time to think about Bering's strange behavior, unlike the rest of Moor, he regarded the lad's recent display of reluctance to repair farm equipment ready to be junked simply as a sign of growing reason, as a slackening of a perverse mechanical passion that began at junkyards only to end in junkyards. As long as Bering kept the Crow's motor and the villa's generator in the tur-bine shed running and supplied him with a pair of arms if need be, he could, for all Ambras cared, either assist or chase off local machine operators and go right on tinkering with his windmills and fluttering model birds until the dogs had snatched the last of his paper chickens out of the air. Such whimsies did not disrupt order in the house of dogs. What really gnawed at that order, even threatened to undo it at times during the first days of November, was the pain—this pain in his joints.

Sometimes Lily helped. If Lily happened to arrive at the Villa Flora during an attack of pain, Ambras allowed her to sprinkle his shoulders with an alcohol essence of moss blossoms, arnica, and anemone, and to rub that in until the fire went out.

On those days, Bering saw not just the signs of torture on his master's bare back, violet scarred stripes left by blows of clubs and strokes of whips received decades before . . . but above all, he also saw an aging man in pain, shivering there in the cold kitchen. And he saw Lily's hands circle over the scarred skin—those were not the hands of a lover. For as tenderly as she touched him, Lily assisted the freezing man no differently from the way someone brushed stone dust from his hair. That was no caress, but merely the old familiarity between the Dog King and his friend from the beach. Or was it simply pity?

When Bering first saw him like that one chilly afternoon, Ambras was sitting half-naked and hunched on a kitchen chair, submitting to the procedure in silence. When Bering entered, Lily was bent over him, a glass bottle in one hand and a rag in the other, dripping the concentrate on his shoulders. The lotion ran down over Ambras's scarred skin in a tangle of rusty-red arteries. Without hesitating, without thinking, as automatically as if he were following orders, Bering walked over to Lily, took the rag from her hand, and began to dab at the rivulets on this bludgeoned back. Lily's astonishment lasted only a moment. Then she nodded and accepted the bodyguard's help.

In the wake of that afternoon of sudden, wordless closeness, Bering began to abandon himself to Lily, dogging her every step. He showed her his longings by constantly inventing new pretexts to escort her from the Villa back to the lake or to drive her in the Crow along the shore or into Moor or anywhere else. In the hope of once again approaching the magic of the concert night, he offered her everything he owned, everything at his disposal, and whenever she attempted to ease Ambras's pain, he was standing at the ready with rag in hand. He forged protective grilles for the weather tower's ground-floor windows, shod her mule after it threw two shoes on the road over Frost Pass, and when Lily failed to come to the house of dogs for six or seven days, he led his horse down to the lakeside resort, tied it to the rail of her stairway, and shouted up to her that he had no time anymore to care for the animal, he had the Crow, after all, he was giving her the horse. And when she expressed delight in a flexible model of a bird of prey's wing that he once showed her out on the veranda, on one of her next visits he surprised her with an artificial pheasant he sent fluttering toward her between the rows of giant pines lining the villa's drive.

Then, during an inspection tour of the Hotel Bellevue made by Ambras and Moor's secretary, Bering found a glockenspiel in the rubbish. The secretary recalled that before the war this music box buried there under tiles had been rung to call the spa's guests to meals. Although the laws for plundering also applied to any trash found in the ruins, Ambras permitted his bodyguard to take the thing along; it was as large and heavy as a cast-iron sewing machine. After only one evening at his workbench in the shed beside the Villa Flora, Bering had the music box running again. When he played the glockenspiel for Lily and she merely laughed at its schmaltzy melodies, he hammered away at its pinned cylinder for many more evenings, until it played the first bars of three of the songs of Patton's Orchestra. Now Lily applauded and, even before he could give her the thing, she suggested a trade: binoculars for the music box!

He agreed to the deal and, by installing the glockenspiel between beams in her tower's roof, upgraded it to an ingenious machine that could announce oncoming storms. He attached the

music box to a windmill, which now not only made a light flash
in time to the strength of the gusts but also turned the cylinder,
so that three different songs, each appropriate for a given wind
speed, were broadcast out over the lake from the ruins of the
lakeside resort. The storm light could be seen on the Blind Shore,
and an east wind would carry the music as far as the reeds at Leys.

Moor began to hate this sound after the first storms of
October—not only because bad weather always followed but also
because it was audible proof to everyone that Bering's skills
would have sufficed to get every inoperable machine running
again before the first snowfall. But whatever the bodyguard did
during those cold weeks, it was done solely for the Brazilian.
After a few sleepless stormy nights, Lily asked him to uncouple
the glockenspiel from the windmill and to set it atop a trunk that
stood in her tower room, like an altar beneath a map of Brazil.
Bering did what she requested of him.

In the middle of November, several machine operators from
the villages tried to make do by plundering spare parts from the
abandoned iron garden and shelves on Forge Hill. They offered
the old blacksmith smoked fish, schnapps, and moldy tobacco,
plus pictures of Mary and bone relics for his Virgin-crazed wife,
and in exchange took oiled ball bearings or an assortment of
stainless-steel screws and bolts. Bumbling through the house
behind his visitors, the blacksmith regarded these trades, which
he made with no nose for business, chiefly as punishment for his
heir—let Bering's collection of precious spare parts be lavished
on the next best stableboy or stone-breaker.

Word soon got around among these scrap-iron collectors that
the old man took whatever he was offered for his junk. He got
drunk on the rowanberry schnapps and wood alcohol he took in
trade, then perched himself for hours atop the anvil and sang
army songs; he brought the smoked fish, pictures of Mary, and
the silver-plated collarbone of some martyr to his wife in the
cellar. The blacksmith's wife sat crouched on the dirt floor in
the shackles of her rosary, did not speak with the drunken man,

and did not touch either the relic or the fish. Rats or martens had dragged the gifts away by morning.

When Lily arrived at Forge Hill once a month with CARE packages from the Villa Flora, she found little need of them. The blacksmith, who was often deep in loud conversation with himself, did not see her and was unwilling to listen to her speak at any length. Sometimes she would find CARE packages from the previous month unopened in the pantry. He would let her ask a question ten times or more before he finally answered, "It's all right," said, "We're not in want, we have everything, miss. Thanks for coming. . . ." (He simply wanted the Brazilian to see that someone who had survived the Sahara and the war needed nothing from killers and deserters—let her go ahead and announce to the house of dogs that Moor's last blacksmith, unlike his silly wife in the cellar, hoped for nothing, for nothing more at all from his heir.)

The shelves of spare parts quickly emptied, and the iron garden was bare before the first snow. In the end, even the anvil disappeared in the wheelbarrow of a scrap-metal collector. It was all the same to the blacksmith. The farm could be cannibalized like a wreck for all he cared—the heir was never coming back anyway. The house turned icy. Sometimes hens laid eggs in the unused kindling of the woodbin. A fire might not burn in the stove for days.

After a last, fruitless attempt to persuade his wife to return from the darkness, the blacksmith gave up and did not even build a fire in the tin stove he had dragged down to the cellar the week before Christmas. Down there, in the depths, the air temperature remained as untouched by the seasons as water at the bottom of the lake, growing neither hot in summer nor cold on frosty days; nevertheless, it did sometimes seem to the blacksmith—despite a fierce winter, when even wild brooks froze over and the waterfall at Haag turned into a rigid monument—as if there in the darkness of the cellar, each day grew milder, each day grew warmer. When he went downstairs to refill his wife's water pitcher and box of provisions, it might happen that he would crouch for half an hour or longer between barrels, listening to the whispered stanzas of her rosary. He would feel cozier and warmer then than he had for such a long time now upstairs in that snowy light, of which he saw only an icy gray shimmer.

At New Year's, when he lay feverish for three days and chickens stalked across his featherbed in search of food, a compassionate visitor built a fire in the good tiled stove.

The visitor could make nothing of the old man's mutterings and did not understand why he should take bread and a jug of water to the cellar, but in return for building a fire he appropriated three bottles of schnapps, a box of horseshoe nails, an ax, and a sheepskin jacket, and before leaving he told the feverish man that Moor's charcoal burner had been killed in an attack by a horde of skinheads. "If those skins knew you're lying up here all alone by your stove—" the visitor said. "Well, just be glad the skins don't know. The Dog King has ordered the swine hunted down," the visitor said. "He radioed the lowlands and sent his bodyguard to a meeting at the secretary's office to announce that a retaliatory expedition was on its way . . ."

The blacksmith barely understood what he was being told and so nodded to everything.

Ten days after the charcoal burner's cremation—which took place in front of the stone letters of the Grand Inscription and ended with the strewing of ashes on the lake, as prescribed by the rites of a Society of Penitence—a military column dressed in camouflage white came marching along the shore promenade. Bering counted more than eighty men at the trooping of the colors outside the secretary's office. The soldiers once again set up their main camp in the ruins of the Hotel Bellevue and over the next few days sent out forays of various sizes. Granted, they discovered no trace of the charcoal burner's murderers, but they found seven vagabonds in an abandoned salt mine near Leys and took them prisoner, and on a lumber trail up to Pilot Valley they chanced upon an ammunition stockpile from the war years: ton upon ton of forgotten artillery grenades, bazookas, and mines from the arsenals of a foe defeated decades before. The entrance to the cave, which was barely visible under the snow and a frozen layer of earth, had been exposed by a mine-searching unit only because a suspicious sergeant had mistaken a frozen fox trap near the trail for an explosive device and had sounded the alarm.

With Ambras's approval and against the protest of Moor's secretary, who feared unforeseeable damages and casualties, the captain in command of the retaliatory expedition ordered the stockpile blown up, and for three days a jeep outfitted with chains rattled through Moor's snow-drifted streets. For hours on end, a loudspeaker mounted on the jeep's roll bar blared brass-band music and the warning that on January 22, at eleven on the dot, a great explosion and shock wave was to be expected. The people of Moor should unhinge their windows or at least keep them open, nail planks over the window frames, and take shelter in underground cellars or other appropriate safe places. The fallow land between the edge of the forest and the Moor town line, marked off now with red pennants, was declared off-limits and was to be avoided by all means, because the shock wave would be unbroken there. Anyone caught in the open in the vicinity of this zone at that hour would do best to huddle in the snow and keep the mouth open to prevent the eardrums from bursting.

By the morning of January 22, the feast of St. Vincent of Saragossa, snow-blown Moor was like a town deserted by man and beast. The *Sleeping Greek Maid* lay at the dock under a cover of snow, and even work at the quarry had been halted.

Shortly before eleven the sky cleared. Tiny ice crystals sparkled in the air, but nothing was to be seen or heard of soldiers preparing for the blast. When the sun broke through the clouds, the countryside began to glisten so brightly that the Dog King had to raise a hand to his blinded eyes. He was standing with Bering and two army agents behind a boarded-up window in the office of Moor's secretary, and through a narrow slit in the planks he stared at the open slope a mile and a half away, above which, within the next few minutes, a dome of fire was to lift. Four of his dogs dozed in warm proximity to the cast-iron stove, its black column looming in the semidarkness.

The nervous secretary checked the fire once a minute, offered his guests bitter coffee and dried apples, and spoke of a letter of protest sent to the High Command in the lowlands. He had invited the army agents to his grimy office so that they could witness the blast and any subsequent damage, and he listened to Ambras's soothing words—at *that* distance, there was no danger to buildings in Moor. The barricades were a superfluous precaution. That little bit of wind would not harm the people of Moor.

Bering could feel the warmth on his brow from the blinding winter light that pierced the slit as if probing the interior of a bunker, and at first he assumed the line of tiny figures who suddenly appeared in the distance at the edge of the off-limits zone were soldiers. Perhaps they were busy with final preparations for the blast and would vanish instantly again among the snowdrifts. But a look through binoculars revealed a procession, revealed the unmistakable sight of a Society of Penitence—twenty, twenty-five, thirty figures in striped fatigues, their faces blackened with soot. They were shielded by nothing except the blind spot in his eye and were moving out across the snow fields beneath flags and banners as if the red warning pennants fluttering there were merely road markers.

"Who are those idiots entering the zone now?" Ambras asked, grabbing the binoculars from his bodyguard's hand.

"There are thirty or more of them," Bering said. "There are at least thirty. Maybe they're from Eisenau."

"From Eisenau!" the dumbfounded secretary cried.

They had to be from Eisenau. The salt mines of Eisenau lay so high in the Stony Sea that it was quite possible no one from the mining village had heard any warning of the blast. The snow was so deep that it was hardly likely any of them had come down to the shore, and certainly no one from Moor had made his way up to them with news from the lake. . . . They could only be from Eisenau. They had fought their way through the snow. On January 22, the feast of St. Vincent, they always left their valley of salt to come to the Blind Shore to lay wreaths at the base of the Grand Inscription and light bouquets of torches along each of its stony lines. All in memory of the fact that the commandant of the barracks by the gravel works had been a man from Eisenau, who, one January 22, had punished ninety prisoners for an attempted mass escape by sending them down a mined tunnel and then ordering the mines detonated.

The rest of the camp inmates had to line up in rows at the mouth of the tunnel that day and stand there in the cold until the ninety would-be escapees had been driven into the mountain. And then their drovers returned. Then it was quiet for several minutes. And then the black stony mouth of the tunnel suddenly began to roar and spewed fire and chunks of boulders at those standing there at attention, and a massive shock wave breached their ranks. When the smoke cleared and an icy dust descended over the witnesses, the mouth was closed forever.

"Idiots," the army agent from Haag repeated and squinted at the Dog King as if expecting applause. The penitents were now deep into the red zone.

"There are more than thirty," the agent said, and kept on counting to forty under his breath. The people in Eisenau had perhaps heard nothing about the warning, but they had probably heard about the army's arrival, and that had brought them in such numbers. Even now, the army always liked to see these Stellamour processions and occasionally rewarded participants with fuel, powdered milk, and batteries.

"Run," the Dog King now said to his bodyguard. "Run if you can and tell them not to take another step. Tell them to bury themselves in the snow. And if they're praying and singing, just have them leave their mouths open. Tell them to open their mouths wide."

As he stormed out of the semidarkness of the secretary's office

into the blinding winter landscape, Bering was not thinking of
the penitents from Eisenau or of the shock wave or of the
impending rain of fragments. He was thinking of Lily's face, of
her eyes, of the look she would throw him when Ambras told her
of his dash through the snow. "You should have seen him,"
Ambras might well say to her. "You should have seen him running through the snowdrifts toward those idiots."

The snow was dry and bottomless. Bering sank to his waist in
some drifts and was out of breath when he reached the line of red
pennants. He assumed he was now within shouting range of the
procession and began to cry out. But as he fought for breath in
the cold, his voice was too weak for the white land. Although the
sky was now deep blue, wind gusts tore swatches of snow from
the drifts' ridges, wrapped his warning cries in them, and bore
them back to where he had been. "Stop! Don't move! Don't
move, damn it!" The penitents did not hear him. Undaunted,
they advanced toward an invisible volcano.

He had to move out deeper into the off-limits zone. Those
idiots! They were leading him into the impending storm, into a
hail of fragments. And now he really was afraid of the tempest,
like the one that had exploded without warning above him and
Ambras in that blasting accident at the quarry. He had been
lucky that day and had only had to comb dust from his master's
hair. But that hail of stones then was probably nothing in comparison with the hell that threatened now. But should he turn
back? In view of witnesses assembled at the secretary's office, with
the binoculars of the Dog King trained on him? It was too late to
turn back. The sooty faces in the distance were already nearer
than the witnesses behind the office's boarded-up windows. *Run
if you can.* Did the Dog King want him to demonstrate his
strength on this field of white? He had to go on.

As he plods on, runs on, he plucks one of the red pennants
from the snow and draws loops and circles with it in the air. At
last he reaches the procession's tracks and yet even by following
in footprints quickly erased by drifting snow, he closes in on

them only slowly. His panting precludes any more cries. *Eleven o'clock.* Even at this distance, the clank of the hours from Moor's clock tower sound more like a hammer and anvil than the ring of a bell. In the silence that follows the last stroke, Bering can hear the penitents' singsong between gusts of wind, but has to stop to catch his breath and still has no voice. *Run if you can.*

Only now does he recall that someone like him does not need a voice. Enraged at being unable to reach the procession, he tugs the pistol from under his jacket, holds it high above his head, and fires into the winter sky. And if the noise not only alerts those fools up ahead but also reveals to the army a man bearing a firearm—that's fine with him. He just wants those people up ahead to halt, wants to stop fighting for breath and to accomplish what the Dog King expects of him.

Now, finally, a few of the penitents turn around toward the lake, toward Moor, toward him.

Bering lowers his pistol and swings his pennant. Wants to cry out but manages only a squawk. The procession comes to a faltering stop and stares at the armed man staggering toward it. Is he drunk? The penitents are already holding the poles of their flags like lances. What does he want? Is this an attack? Does he belong to some horde that in the next moment will come storming out of a white ambush and assault their act of remembrance? Are flags and banners to be burned once again out on this open field, though they bear only the slogans of the great Stellamour: *Never forget. Thou shalt not kill?*

An attack?

But he's all alone.

No one's following him.

But he has a gun.

By the time Bering reaches the sooty faces, he has stuck his pistol back under his jacket. The shaft of his pennant is now just a crutch that keeps him on his feet. Bent low, fighting for breath, he gasps, "Into the snow. Everybody into the snow. . . ." He cannot say anything more now. It takes minutes, an eternity that almost has him enraged again, before all the penitents have gathered round and finally understand what he is trying to warn them about.

An explosion?

They don't know anything about an explosion. No one in this pilgrimage to the Blind Shore has heard of any other explosion than just that one, the one now long past, the one in their litanies and prayers.

I'm too late, Bering thinks in amazement, *am I too late?* It is well past eleven. He sees the penitents sink into the snow, slowly, stiff with cold—and with open mouths, just as the Dog King commanded. Only their flags and banners still flutter above the icy swells like the sails of a sinking ship. Between snowdrifts, in the troughs of their waves, there is almost no wind. Veils of snow waft over them as they crouch and lie there—spindrift flags. It is well past eleven. But nothing happens.

How much time elapses in the anticipation of disaster? Minutes? An hour? Bering will no longer remember later. Racked by exhaustion, he lies among sooty faces in the ice and feels safe there, feels as safe in a trough of snowdrifts on an open field as if it were a nest. Above him the glass blue winter sky, before him the glistening ridge of a dune of wind-pressed crystals—that's how silent and lustrous it must be inside those floating gardens where light gathers and bursts to form chrysanthemums and petaled stars, inside the crystals that the Dog King keeps in the drawers of his bird cabinet. Bering lies in a nest of light and thinks of Lily, lies as stiff as an insect millions of years old, its form preserved for eons in a flood of amber—and might very well have fallen asleep if the cantor of the procession had not stood up beside him and brushed the snow from his fatigues and said, "We're freezing here. Are we supposed to freeze to death?"

Freezing? Bering doesn't feel any chill. As if he himself were part of the cold, he watches, never stirring, as one penitent after another rises from cover, from the ice, and tugs his ragged costume to rights. The procession is reaching for its flags again, making ready to resume the chant of litanies and endless lists of names from the death registers of the camp barracks—when the sky, the glass blue winter sky above the waves and drifts and dunes begins to burn.

In a single moment a dome rises high above the white land—a house of fire, a fortress of flames. It towers into cloudlessness. And then, simultaneously with thunder that seems to come not from above but to have been thrust from the fiery core of the earth, a hurricane darkens the land. The red fortress is extinguished by a surge of snow, earth, and stones, founders as the breaking wave howls and whistles and races toward the penitents, quenching all light to a sallow gray. Like a flock of frightened birds, whirring brushwood and splintered rock precede the flood. Clumps of ice and frozen earth, stones, everything that only just now had seemed fused together, cold and inert, is light as a feather, leaps and spins out into space as if freed from gravity.

No one, nothing can hold in such a storm. The hurricane seizes the cantor and the flag bearers, seizes everybody who emerged from the lee of the trough—lifting one almost hesitantly, flinging the next violently into the air—and pitches them all back on the ice, into the snow, hurling their tattered flags and broken poles after them.

Strange, how in the midst of this tumult, Bering clearly hears the unmistakable sound of cloth tearing, the hiss of a rending banner. The shock wave—or was it a tumbling man?—has turned him onto his back and flung his arms from his face. Now he lies in the hurricane with eyes open and sees that the hole in his world has been only a ridiculous scrap of a larger darkness, just one of countless blind spots whirling about him, shooting right over him, and forming a single abyss, a single darkness—only to be broken again, in the very next moment, by the winter sun.

CHAPTER 21

EYES OPEN

THE ARRIVAL OF THE MADONNA AND MOST
Blessed Virgin sounded like the impact of a bomb
dropped from the air, and the roar of Her attendant
heavenly hosts descending to this vile earth could scarcely be distinguished from the thunder of artillery. . . . Ears ringing in the
tumult of a long-awaited miracle, the blacksmith's wife crouched
in her cellar darkness and instinctively recalled the noise of battle.
The Virgin's return sounded like Moor's night of bombs.

There were no hymns of praise this time. No harps and trumpets either. Only this thunder, as if heaven itself had burst.
Nonetheless, the blacksmith's wife had no doubt—the Mater
Dolorosa had heard her prayers at last. The Star of the Sea, the
Queen of Heaven, had returned. But this time She did not
appear enfolded in the music of the spheres, but wrapped in the
surging clamor of the world, so that Moor and Haag and the
whole lakeshore might hear what She now proclaimed to Her
most faithful servant: *It is enough!* Enough prayers. Enough
penance. The lost son, the little boy, the heir, had been received
again into the host of the redeemed.

This message was bathed in great light, but of all those comets and aureoles, the blacksmith's wife saw only the pale reflection that reached her through the cracks of a hatch down which potatoes, beets, or heads of cabbage usually tumbled into the cellar.

And the Madonna? Why did She not graciously descend to the depths Herself? Why did the heavenly host squander its radiance in the desolation above rather than cast golden light over the solitude of a penitent? The blacksmith's wife understood and smiled. The Madonna wanted Her servant to climb back to the light of day, too, to ascend to the heights, to *Her*. It was indeed enough.

The stabbing pain she felt in her heart, her struggle for air as she ascended the stone steps—those were but the final adversities on the road to the light, the last scourges at the end of a great penance. Just this one steep bit of the path still caused pain and took her breath away, but beyond it lay endless release. The Madonna was surely waiting for her now above the forge pond, was floating above the reeds.

The pond was frozen. The reeds were withered and bent from the wind. The crowns of the trees, the roofs of Moor, the thicket—everything that only just before had borne the weight of snowy cushions, was now bare, empty, freed of all burdens. The shock wave of the greatest explosion since Moor's night of bombs had swept the snow from the branches and treetops and roofs and exposed the shabbiness of the shore. But as she stepped through a stall door into the open, the blacksmith's wife saw it differently. After the long darkness, purple and blue-green shadows danced in her eyes, and she took them for blossoms. Blossoms in the black treetops. In the midst of winter, the Madonna had made the trees bloom. Wherever *She* was, it was spring.

The tumult of the visitation yielded now to a silence at whose farthest edges, in a far-off somewhere, dogs were barking. There, too, in a snow-white distance, flames shot into heaven, a silent fire blazed, flames without the slightest sound. But the pond! The pond was empty, its water polished ice.

How tired the blacksmith's wife was in the light, endlessly tired. The miracle of the blossoms had swept the snow from trees and roofs, but not from the wooden bench, which still stood white and wintry against the wall of the house. The old woman sat down on this bench, sank onto a pillow of snow, leaned against the icy wall. Gradually the blossoms faded.

That fire there in the distance—was that supposed to be the great radiance that had found its way to her in the cellar and lighted her return from the depths to the world above? The blacksmith's wife stared a long time at those flames as they grew smaller and smaller, and tried in vain to discover the form of the Queen of Heaven in the glow. The radiance slowly sank back into the barren land, and her gaze sank with it, sank until her eyes reflected only a burnt-out wasteland plumed with black trees and branches.

The day after the explosion, Bering's father groped his way down from his hill to Moor for the first time in months, leaving a drunken man's tracks behind in the snowy streets. At times he lurched so badly that he had to prop himself for a few minutes against a wall or the parade-ground flagpole before he could continue on his way. He paid no attention to the military column falling in for retreat outside the secretary's office, or to a firewood dealer, either, who called a surprised greeting from the box of his horse-drawn wagon and tried to tell the blacksmith how yesterday a procession of penitents from Eisenau had walked into the blasting zone, trumpets blaring, drums rolling, and had escaped, as if by a miracle, with only a few wounded. "And your son, of course," the man shouted down from the box as the blacksmith staggered by, "that madman was mixed up in it again, too, of course!"

It took the old man hours to leave Moor, the terraced vineyards, the shore promenade, behind him and, taking a strenuous shortcut up a stairwayed path, finally arrive at the portal to the Villa Flora. He cursed the dogs that came storming out of the park and leapt, slavering and baying, at the wrought-iron tendrils of the gate. He banged his cane on the iron, tried to push one

side of the gate open, and without hesitation would have
bumbled into the fangs of the pack if Bering had not come running out to his father. Bering calmed the dogs, chained three of
the fiercest barkers, and stepped to the gate, without opening it.
"What do you want?"

Separated by iron leaves, by iron branches and bars, they stood
facing each other, the one the strange image of the other—the
one a disabled war veteran, the other wounded only the day
before. Flying shrapnel (perhaps it was only the nailed shoe of
one of the shock wave's victims) had made a gash across Bering's
forehead from the right temple to the hairline, leaving him
looking even more like the old man, whose brow bore its fiery-
red scar in token of battle.

The arduous path to the house of dogs had sobered the old
man up. All the same, he took an unsteady step backwards and
almost stumbled when Bering opened one side of the gate after
all. "Well, what do you want?"

The old man saw his son's face no differently from the way he
saw all other faces—saw only a shadowy oval with dark smudges
for eyes, and said to this face that was like all other faces, "She's
sitting outside the house. She wasn't in the cellar this morning. I
go down to bring her bread and milk. But she's not there. I look
for her in the kitchen, in her room, in the stall. Then I find her
outside the house. On the sunning-bench. She's dead. You have
to bury her. You killed her."

He says nothing more. Not at the gate and not on the drive
back to the forge, the first ride he has taken in a car since the
war—and he got in only because exhaustion forced him to. The
heir asks twice about his mother's final days. Did she say anything in between beads and penitential prayers? The old man
does not know himself, but he keeps even that from his son.
He does not want to speak to him, will never speak to him again.
Now they both are silent and sit beside each other in the Crow as
if the rattling of its snow chains has taken the place of anything
they might say.

The road up to the forge is drifted deep with snow. Chains are no longer any help. They leave the Crow behind next to a drift as tall as a man and plod up to the farmstead, following the old man's fresh tracks. Bering slows down with each step and finally, as if in exhaustion, stops halfway up when he sees his mother at the top, on the bench beside the stable door. No snow fell in the night, yet she is covered with snow, white with frost or the crystallized evaporation of her body heat. She is snow-white.

When, after pausing there, he comes closer, very slowly comes closer, he sees that her eyes are still open. Her mouth is open as well—as if she, like himself and the penitents from Eisenau, has simply followed the orders of the Dog King and is waiting mute and open-mouthed for the great explosion, for the firestorm.

Bering was unable to close either his mother's eyes or her mouth when, late that morning, he laid her in a coffin, in a box knocked together out of pine planks with which he had planned to rebuild the chicken coop last year, in that almost forgotten life.

While he sawed and hammered, his father sat, as always, on a stool at the kitchen window, staring down over the roofs of Moor, and did not even answer when Bering asked about a shovel. The forge had been visited by so many scrap-metal collectors that there was not a tool left for digging a grave.

When Bering returned to the Villa Flora around noon to fetch a pickax and shovel from the garden shed, the Dog King was sitting close to a glowing-red stove in the main salon and examining a piece of amber under his magnifying glass. He hardly looked up and merely nodded when Bering entered the room with his grave-digging tools and asked for the afternoon off and use of the Crow for the second time that day. Ambras was so immersed in studying the latest item in his collection that he apparently did not catch even the description of a frosted-over corpse. The amber contained an organic inclusion of great rarity, a lacewing surprised in take-off by the drop of resin in which it had been frozen. Bering shouldered his grave-digging tools and turned to go. The Dog King held the amber up to the light. Wait! He did want the bodyguard to tell him one thing before he left— How old? How old did Bering guess this insect inside the stone was?

Bering obediently put down the pickax and shovel again, obediently accepted the magnifying glass, and felt tears come to his eyes and had no answer and could only say, "So I'll be going now."

"Forty million," the Dog King said. "Forty million years."

On the drive back to his father's cold house, Bering had trouble pulling out of the way of the departing military column, and almost did not get the Crow out of the deep snow and back on the shore promenade. A few soldiers applauded the skidding bird vehicle. In yesterday's excitement over the wounded pilgrims from Eisenau, whose injuries had been tended to in one of the column's tents, neither the captain of the retaliatory expedition nor any of his sergeants had asked about the shot fired shortly before the explosion in the red zone.

The column plowed a wide trail through the wintry countryside, and Bering withstood the urge to follow it as far as the lakeside resort. Instead of rattling down to the weather tower, he drove to the secretary's office and reported a death. The office windows were still boarded up. The secretary pressed his seal on a death certificate and said it was probably too late for a burial today. . . . Wasn't it?

No, it wasn't, Bering said.

Should he have the lay missionary fetched from Haag then, or at least the preacher from Moor's Society of Penitence? The secretary couldn't understand the hurry. And the brass band?

No sermon, no music. The bodyguard wanted none of the usual stuff. He required only one or two men to help with the grave and two more to carry the coffin.

It was already dusk when Bering and three laborers from a sugar-beet factory lowered the coffin on hemp ropes into what seemed like a bottomless hole. The ropes were too short for the grave.

"What now?" one of the laborers asked.

"Let go," another one said.

All three of them were drunk. For a wicker bottle of schnapps and sixty army cigarettes, they had run alongside the Crow all the way from Forge Hill to Moor's cemetery, making sure that the coffin, bound makeshift-fashion to the roof, did not fall off. They had switched off digging the grave. When it was the last man's turn—Bering's turn—they retreated to the leeward side of the stone shrine built next to the chapel and illumined by candles, and there they passed the bottle and smoked blond cigarettes, with which you could buy most anything in Moor. Then the bottle was empty, and they reeled back to the grave and found the madman from the house of dogs in a hole that deep. By the light of two funeral torches, clods of earth leapt up out of the depths and fell onto a mound higher than any other in the cemetery.

Bering did not hear the laborers' laughter. Alone in the pit, panting, sobbing, he had dug at the earth with pickax and spade until the winter sky above him was only a fading rectangle framed in black clay—when suddenly a snowball burst against his shoulder and one of the laborers, whom he had long since forgotten about, called down laughing from the edge of the sky, "Hey! What are you going to bury? A horse?"

The laborers had to help the madman out of a pit whose bottom was no longer visible. And when they finally bent down over the hole, they watched the coffin disappear into the gloom until it dangled in the darkness on ropes that were too short. Now the first of them let go of that damned rope, then the second and third, and only the bodyguard was left holding a limp end in his hand. Then there was just the sound of a box tumbling into the depths and landing with a thud. A fraction of a second later, ropes slapped against wood. Then it was quiet.

The five women standing at the foot of the clay crater interrupted the drone of their appeals to martyrs and saints, and crossed themselves. They had come that afternoon to decorate the shrine with candles and brushwood in the hope that, like every commandant before him, the captain of the retaliatory expedition would make an inspection tour of Moor's memorials and perhaps reward their efforts with packets of instant coffee. But instead of the captain, just this heathen vehicle bearing the coffin of the blacksmith's wife had rolled into the cemetery—a bit of variety, in any case.

Mourning along with these women were two vagabonds who had spent the night in the chapel and were trying to warm themselves on the shrine's candles. Their hope of a swig of schnapps and a few cigarettes from the gravediggers' cache proved in vain. The mourners also included four or five curiosity seekers, who had presumed the Dog King was in the coffin atop the Crow and had followed the funeral procession through the streets of Moor and out to the cemetery.

By the time the hole was filled and the clay stamped down to a great mound, the mourners had drifted off. The laborers likewise thought they had done enough for their schnapps and cigarettes and shoveled only as much dirt back into the hole as was fitting for a woman's grave. Let the madman worry about the rest of this insanely deep crater. He said not a word as they left.

Bering assumed he had long been alone, when he noticed his father standing among the warped crosses and illegible gravestones, there at the edge of the flickering circle of light cast by the torches—and beside him, Lily.

Lily laid a comforting hand on the old man's shoulder, stepped away from him, and came toward Bering as if she had some message for him, and said, "I'll take him home." Then she took Bering's grimy, ice-cold hands in her own and breathed her warmth on them. When he pulled his hands away from her because he had to cover his face, she took him in her arms. But he could not endure such closeness and, not knowing what else to do, he took a step toward his father. Now she gently held him back and said, "Let him be. He's talking crazy. I'll see he gets home."

As the old man took the Brazilian's arm and vanished among the crosses, Bering pulled the funeral torches from the snow and planted them on the grave mound, which now looked like the earthen pyramids that Societies of Penitence had erected on battlefields and above the foundations of demolished camp barracks, and that even nowadays were crowned with torches on the anniversary of peace. Then he squatted wearily in the snow and scraped clay from the grave-digging tools so as not to soil the Crow's soft upholstery on the ride home.

When at last he left the cemetery and drove between the rows of chestnut trees on the shore promenade, crawling slowly toward his future, light was still burning in only a few of Moor's windows. In the night, which lay clear and moonless above the mountains and turned the lake into an abyss, each of them was alone: the bumbling blacksmith on his cold hill; Lily—who left him there after warming some soup—in her tower; and the bodyguard in the house of dogs. That night he lay on the floor of the main salon with the warm bodies of the pack and cuddled in his sleep against his master's gray mastiff.

CHAPTER 22

A BEGINNING OF THE END

H E HEARS THE WHISTLE OF THE KING-
fisher and the husky whir of the startled wren. When
he grows drowsy listening to the chatter of chimney
swallows or the monotone territorial song of titmice, he is awakened sometimes by the metallic alarm call of a yellowhammer.
He is not deceived by the starlings, those grand frauds that can
imitate the cry of a kestrel and the lament of an owl as easily as
the song of a thrush or a blackbird—and this spring, unlike those
of years past, he often hears a nightingale, too, which always
begins its mad stanzas with a melancholy fluting.

He hears the birds at dawn when he lies awake in his bed in
the billiard room or among the sleeping dogs on the parquet of
the main salon. He often sleeps with the dogs now and has to
smile every time their ears dance in their sleep to the sound of
birdcalls. Then the old, familiar names of birds come to him, as if
fluttering up from those lost lists he wrote in the blacksmith's
empty order-book during his school days: little egret, ivory gull,
pied wagtail, hen harrier, and whistling swan. . . . But it is not
only their names that have returned to him this spring, but also

the ability and above all a *desire* to mimic birdcalls—to whistle, hum, or click his tongue inside the resonant hollow of his mouth, with such beguiling results that sometimes the confused dogs trot the length of the Villa Flora's tangle of barbed wire when he sings for them the song of a pheasant or a partridge in the underbrush.

His hearing is as sensitive again now as in his first year, when he floated through the darkness in a basket, listening spellbound to the voices of chickens. Sometimes he sits on the veranda, his eyes closed, scratching a dog's neck, and he can feel the strength or weakness of each animal in the pack simply from the elasticity or brittleness of the skin—and then it is as if his hearing, his sense of smell, his skin and his fingertips were trying to decipher the world anew as a pattern of rough, cracked, and smooth surfaces, of painful or soothing sounds and melodies, of fragrance and stench, of cold, warm, fevered temperatures, of the breathing and torpid forms of existence.

He has difficulty recognizing sheer, delicate inclusions in the crystals Ambras sometimes tries to show him when he waves Bering over and holds a tourmaline or an unpolished emerald under his eyes. But when the Dog King lets him examine a piece on his own and the stone turns warm in his hand, he thinks he can *feel* not just the most filigreed inclusion, but also the very refraction of the light. And although his poor vision dims the floating gardens inside the stones, he still understands what Ambras is talking about so excitedly. He then nods, perhaps more often than necessary, to divert any suspicion about his eyes. Yes, sure, of course he sees it, sees everything Ambras wants to show him. But he is—and he still guards this secret as if not just his staying on at the house of dogs but also his life is at stake—he is on the road to darkness.

A man gets like this, he thinks, his ears and fingertips become this sensitive only if he is going blind. For ever since he buried the blacksmith's wife in a hole as black and bottomless as the depths of the earth, there is not just *one* gaping hole in his vision, the one with which he has learned to live, but, like a double image of that clayey pit, there is a second as well! And sometimes he thinks he can see night coming on at the shadowy rim of his field of vision—an impenetrable, all-enshrouding darkness.

The day after the burial, as a cold sun rose above the mountains, setting Moor's shore sparkling again, the snow revealed that there could be no doubt of this second hole in his eyes, either. He could test what until now had been his good eye as often as he liked against the unmerciful white of the snowy fields—the morning snow showed him, over and over, that he had *two* blind spots.

In the weeks that followed, as if all the white had now fulfilled its purpose, winter faded in a thaw and was later lost in days of gurgling rain, which came earlier and harder than any in years. The flanks of the mountains were veined with white streams of melting snow, and veils of waterfalls blew down across some of the quarry's working terraces. The lake flooded the steamer dock and even the loading ramps by the gravel works. Work was halted at the Blind Shore for over two weeks.

But later, when the high water had receded and the slopes and cones of granite waiting to be transported re-emerged like islands and gradually fused to form a chain of sludge-covered hills, the Dog King assembled all the miners and stone-breakers at the foot of the Grand Inscription and announced to the more than fifty men that

as of tomorrow

only a third of the crew would be needed on the working terraces. The rest should claim their wages at the administrator's shed and look for new jobs in the sugar-beet fields, at the logging mill, or in the salt mines of Eisenau. The High Command had issued an order to cut back production. . . .

Ambras added neither words of comfort nor of encouragement to the notification and, having delivered his shortest speech ever to the stone-breakers, abruptly turned his back on the assembly, whistled for his mastiff, signaled the ferryman on the pontoon boat, and ordered him to return him to Moor—leaving both the laid-off men and those unaffected to their stupefied silence.

The outrage first become vocal when Bering, who was told to remain at the quarry, nailed a poster with the names of all the laid-off men to the door of the administrator's shed. Suddenly the bodyguard could barely fend off the indignant crowd— "Who wrote this list?" "Who chose these names?" "What swine put my name on the list?"

Bering pushed away the angriest men, who wanted to rip the notice off the door, and at the same time he felt angry at Ambras himself, who was now well out of reach, a figure on a gravel barge far out on the lake. Why had the Dog King left him alone to face this furor?

Although the bodyguard stood menacingly at the door to the shed, his gun clearly visible at his belt, the men barely stepped back. The assembly finally calmed down for a few minutes when the blasting foreman moved in beside him, raised a megaphone over the men's heads, and began reading off the sequence in which those who had been laid off were to claim their pay envelopes.

"You all saw it coming!" the blasting foreman shouted into the megaphone. "Ever since last fall, we've been sitting here on a pile of gravel nobody wants."

Bering saw that some of the men had picked up stones and were holding them at the ready in their fists. The fools. Had they really not noticed that for months now, only the stockpiles had grown with each day of work? Along the narrow-gauge tracks down which tipcarts rolled from the working terraces to the loading ramps, at the mouth of every tunnel, and all around the pond—cones, ramparts, and piles of gravel, of primal stone, towered everywhere. It already looked as if a new mountain range was forming at the foot of the Stony Sea, a bulwark behind which the gravel works' conveyor belts and grinding hoppers, even the last line of the Grand Inscription—WELCOME TO MOOR—were all slowly disappearing.

But those mountains of gravel were merely the sign that Moor Quarry had been exhausted. With each cubic yard their digging ate into the cliffs, the dark-green granite grew more brittle and banded with fragile streaks as crazy and unpredictable as the lines of tectonic energy that had dislocated this primal stone in prehistoric catastrophes and then, over the course of ages, thrust it up through the softer limestone reefs of the Stony Sea.

Where in better days great blocks and plates of solid, flawless granite had once been blasted, cut, and hewn, now miner's wedges, chain saws, and borings produced only rocks that rattled as they fell on the working terraces—rubble barely good enough to grind into gravel for filling potholes on truck trails and mountain roads or for raising levees along banks of marshy meadows.

But in the lowlands they needed blocks and ashlars from which to hew monuments and ever more statues of the Bringer of Peace and his generals. In the lowlands they needed stone pillars for the colonnades of shrines and slabs for memorial plaques as big as portals. But gravel? There was gravel and rubble enough down below. Gravel didn't have to be carted down out of the mountains. Since the first snowfall last winter, the army had not sent any more semis up into the lake country. Gravel and stones could stay where they were.

At one point people said the hauling had been delayed because of a danger of avalanches in the narrow valleys; later the word had been it was the threat of mudslides from melting snow, and rumors of mined viaducts and imminent attacks by gangs likewise provided a steady stream of new reasons why a long-overdue convoy of trucks from the lowlands never seemed to arrive. The truth was simpler and was not to be drowned out even now in the uproar at the administrator's shed. The quarry was scheduled to be closed. "Close it! You just watch, they want to close our quarry!"

Had the blasting foreman not shown such composure, Bering's only defense against the crowd's rage would have been his gun. It was the blasting foreman who got those who had been laid off to calm down enough that they dropped the stones from their fists and then, man by man, stepped up to the pay counter in the administrator's shed and received the rest of their wages—food-ration coupons and a few bills in plain brown envelopes. But to all questions about the closing, the blasting foreman could likewise only repeat what the Dog King had already said: There was no longer enough work for everyone at the quarry.

Were no new roads being built anywhere? No levees, even in the lowlands? The blasting foreman shrugged.

So this was what had become of Moor's granite. For decades the deep green of this stone had been the pride of the whole lakeshore; it even appeared on the region's coat-of-arms as a lustrous background to a miner's hammer and a fish, stylized as a hunting knife. . . . Only last year, the secretary had tacked an army geologist's report on his bulletin board: In addition to the upheaval zone of the Stony Sea, a comparable deep primal-green granite was to be found only in a small section of the coast of Brazil. Except for Moor, only in Brazil! And now it was supposed to be all over?

"Not over," the blasting foreman said, "just different."

Not over, the bodyguard confirmed, happy for any words that took the place of a hail of stones. Maybe at some point their continued work would uncover a new compact layer of granite; he himself had heard Ambras speak of a temporary measure—

"I don't believe a word you say," one of the laid-off men broke in, and spat on the pay counter.

No one believed such soothing words. And no one—not those who would be unemployed tomorrow and not those who had been spared—returned to the gravel works. As if on strike, the men stood around among the pyramids of gravel and rock, or stretched out in the grass under a pale-blue sky, comparing the contents of their pay envelopes, trading food coupons for schnapps and tobacco, and waiting together for the last time for the *Sleeping Greek Maid*, which, as on every other workday, came steaming across the lake only toward evening to transport them back to Moor's shore.

This time the bodyguard had no choice but to board along

with the stone-breakers; he had waited in vain all afternoon for Ambras and the gravel barge. During the trip home, he stood alone at the railing—the thumping of the paddle wheels sounded like the rhythm of a huge drum. Once he had carried out the orders of the Dog King, the blasting foreman left no doubt as to which side he was on, and was sitting again now on the quarter-deck among the stone-breakers.

The house of dogs lay in deep twilight when Bering returned from the Blind Shore that evening. There among the stubbled flowerbeds beside the pond stood Lily's horse; it stopped pulling at the black stalks and raised its head with a whinny when it recognized its old rider.

Lily was still here? She almost never stayed till nightfall. Bering entered the dark house, absentmindedly petted a few dogs who greeted him, tails wagging, and in the entryway could hear Lily's laughter coming from the main salon, followed by Ambras's voice calling his mastiff.

A bottle of red wine and the scraps of their supper still before them, Lily and Ambras were sitting at the salon's large table, on which were also scattered gemstones, rough crystals, plus two boxes of bullets, packages of soap and tea—and a dud grenade shell as large as a vase, the kind you found only seldom these days around destroyed bunkers and crumbling gun emplacements up in the mountains. Did these two need the cover of night for this trading session? By now, not even retaliatory expeditions cared about the detritus of war, about rusty weapons and a few bullets.

Ambras was just saying . . . "why don't you put him in an asylum?" when a draft banged the salon's heavy door shut behind Bering. With the futile, apologetic gesture of an eavesdropper caught in the act, he gently opened the door again and then shut it softly, acted as if he had not been standing silently on the threshold, invisible beyond the circle of yellow light—and yet could not hid his embarrassment. "They say the quarry's going to be closed."

"Good evening," Ambras said as he turned to his bodyguard, lifted the wine bottle as if to his health, and drank.

"They say the quarry's going to be closed," Bering repeated, without returning the greeting.

"So? What would be so dreadful about that?" Ambras tossed the gray mastiff a piece of bread dunked in oil, which it snapped in midair and devoured.

"The men who were laid off . . . they say it's just the beginning. They went wild. They would have loved to stone me."

"Wild? That's how they always are. Did you calm them down?"

"The blasting foreman did. . . . Was that really just the beginning? Yesterday you said it was only a temporary measure."

"There is no mine that doesn't give out someday. Everything, every hole, even a notch you make in a mountain, has to close someday."

"They're afraid that soon there'll be no more supplies delivered to Moor, no groceries, no medicine."

"So what?" Ambras was getting louder with every word. "They've got their sugar beets. Their vineyards still grow, the lake is full of fish, and the strongest medicines come from wild herbs anyway. In the camp, we ate nothing but turnips for years—"

"And this evening we've nearly emptied a second bottle by ourselves," Lily said, interrupting the rising anger with that cheerful tone that once again made Bering feel how little he shared in the familiarity between these two.

"A quarry administrator without a quarry." Bering looked into Lily's eyes. "What becomes of a quarry administrator with no quarry—?"

"And of his bodyguard, you mean?" Ambras broke in. "Don't worry, good sir, there are gravel works in the lowlands, too."

"Does that mean we're going to the lowlands?" Although he had not noticed before just how drunk Ambras was, Bering suddenly felt as if he were standing at the edge of his world, beside a sea he knew only from pictures. It was the same feeling he felt when he sat in front of the record player with his eyes closed and listened to Patton's music. *To the lowlands.* He had left the lake country only once before, back when he was twelve or thirteen, when even teenagers and children had joined the great pilgrimage to Birkenau to take part in the dedication of the largest shrine of the Peace of Oranienburg, an edifice built from the wood of hundreds of camp barracks, a wooden cathedral into whose columns and stained walls had been burned the names or simply the numbers of millions of the dead . . . names and numbers from its foundations up into the very top of its dome.

The pilgrims never reached that towering edifice. They did make it across Frost Pass, and after another day of marching and praying they saw cornfields, roads, and a gray city in the haze below, but the commandant of their section had ordered them to turn around and go back over the pass, because the army was hunting plunderers and isolated sharpshooters in the area. Bering, however, had never forgotten the sight of a long row of power pylons in the distance, or the straight line that cut through fields, meadows, and woodlands, reflecting shiny, silvery light here and there, which a pilgrim that day had reverently said were the tracks of the railroad—those tracks led to the sea.

"What I mean, good sir, is that we'll go to the lowlands if the army offers us a gravel pit there," Ambras said. "We'll go to the lowlands if the army wants to have us."

"Ah! The gentlemen are emigrating," Lily now cried. "The lake air is no longer healthy, is that it?"

"The air is getting thinner, at least," Ambras said. "You should find yourself a new tower when the time comes, too." He toasted Lily and finished the bottle.

"A new tower? In the lowlands? I get to the lowlands often enough. If it's to be up and away, then let it be farther away. A lot farther."

"Off to Brazil again?" Ambras grinned.

"To Brazil, for example," Lily said seriously and very slowly.

"Well then, bon voyage!" Ambras was laughing now.

"You're probably on your way there right now." Bering made a vain attempt to join in the conversation. He was too slow. As so often when the Dog King and Lily were talking, he would make a remark or crack a joke after she was no longer in the mood. "Is your horse already saddled for overseas?"

"I'm here on your account." Lily ignored his attempt this time, too. "I've been waiting a good hour for you. I found your father up on Frost Pass. He was playing war."

CHAPTER 23

THE WARRIOR

L ILY HAD BEEN ON HER WAY TO THE LOW-lands with her mule and horse, their packsaddles loaded with items to trade—war scrap, beautiful fossils and crystals—when she found the half-blind blacksmith in the mountains, a day's journey from Moor. He had only the clothes on his back—no coat or blanket to protect him against the cold mountain night, no provisions, not even matches to build a fire.

It was shortly before twilight fell and, as on her many previous trips over Frost Pass, Lily planned to spend the night in the shelter of the ruins of the fort at the top of the pass. Her animals were just plodding past the mossy vault of a bunker, which not even two direct artillery hits had destroyed before the fort was overrun, when a warrior with a soot-blackened face emerged from the rubble and shouted, "Halt! Don't move! Password!" It was Bering's father.

He was waving an iron rod and evidently could not decide if he should hold the weapon like a gun or a sword or simply like a club. He wore the dented helmet of a Moor fireman on his head and an iron cross around his neck; the lapels of his loden jacket, which was smeared with mud as if for camouflage, sparkled with medals and decorations, even badges and pins that were souvenirs from pilgrimages, livestock exhibitions, and veterans' conventions. "Password! Password!"

When Lily did not stop her animals, but let them plod ahead toward the warrior, he took cover behind a ruptured wall held together only by twisted bands of steel. Lily laughed. Although startled at first and then perplexed to run into the old man so far from the lake and so high in the mountains, she laughed at what she presumed was a joke.

The old man did not recognize the laughing rider who now approached him with arms raised. But when she got off her horse in front of where he had taken cover and handed him a flask through a wide crack in the rampart, he nonetheless lowered his gun, his sword, his club.

"Rowanberry schnapps," she said.

Although the voice was unfamiliar to him as well, the warrior was in a conciliatory mood. "Take cover, miss." He grabbed the flask, took a hefty pull, and seemed to have already forgotten his demand for a password. "Attack is imminent. Those dogs are trying to break through to Halfayah. They won't. Never!"

"Don't shoot!" he then shouted into the black gaping ruins of the fort. "Don't shoot, she's one of us!" He shouldered his iron rod and, without returning the flask, started to grope his way through the reinforced-concrete rubble, like a frontline officer on a tour of inspection. As he went, he called and wheezed questions or orders into the shafts and embrasures of bunkers and caverns—from which came only the cold odor of rot and damp earth. Although lurching and bumbling, he was so businesslike as he made his way through the dark field of rubble that Lily tied her animals to an antitank obstacle and left them there to follow him.

She needed all her powers of persuasion, even had to pretend she was a disguised courier bringing orders from his battalion headquarters for a well-ordered retreat, before he was willing to accompany her to her campsite in subterranean quarters.

On her trips to the lowlands, Lily had spent many nights in this empty cellar room buried under the debris of bombs and also kept here a cache of fuel, baled hay, and canned food. The old man lent a friendly hand as she tended to her animals and prepared a meal of tea, cornmeal mush, and dried fish on a camp stove. For a few moments he seemed even to rid himself of his delusions and to recall Lily's earlier assistance and visits to Forge Hill, but then responded only with "Yes, sir," and "Very good, sir," when the courier told him she would accompany him to Moor the next morning. "Very good, miss!"

Lily gave her sleeping bag to the madman for the night and wrapped herself in two saddle blankets, but the warrior would not let her sleep, suddenly acted as if he heard the alarm signal and had to return to his machine gun in the rubble up above, but then began singing army songs again, as if he weren't at the front but on a barrack drill field—and drank her flask empty.

By sunrise, which arrived in the cellar's darkness as only a narrow band of light falling from an air shaft, he was fast asleep, and Lily had trouble waking him. He had again forgotten that she had been a courier the evening before, and he now believed she was a partisan who had surprised him in his sleep and taken him prisoner. She first had to refer to some new order of the day to get him to help her hide her load of goods in one of the caverns. The order read: "Prepare a cache at the fort and return to Moor at once."

To Moor? To a lake? The warrior had never heard of a town or a lake by that name. But how many of this world's names had not already appeared in orders, names that grew bright only under artillery fire and darkened again when it ended—El Agheila, Tobruk, Salum, Halfayah, Sidi Omar. . . . Names, nothing but names. And in the end only the desert remained.

And so the warrior was obedient this time as well, carried packages and bundles tied with twine to niches in the wall, which he had to plug again with stones and camouflage with moss— and suddenly his hands were grasping a rifle whose butt stuck up out of a saddle basket. His vision was too clouded for him to *see* the weapon's stamp or its unmistakable magazine, but he recognized it with just his hands. It was an English rifle. He had captured guns like that in the desert, on Halfayah Pass.

"Don't touch that gun!" the courier, the partisan, the strange woman cried.

"We're taking the gun with us," she said now, much more gently, and helped him up on the horse. Silent and still dazed from the schnapps, he sat on the animal's broad back, sat again at last as high as he had during the war, while this woman, who definitely did not belong to his army, tied the reins to her mule's packsaddle. She rode ahead on the mule.

The mule track to Moor was rocky and steep, and at times they heard rising from below the roar of streams filled with melted snow. Twice at the very last moment, Lily was barely able to keep the old man from tumbling off the horse into the depths; still, she avoided the more level roads in the valley in order to bypass the barricades and checkpoints set up by the military—which were just as likely to be manned by skinheads and leathermen. And although the fact that the old man had made it to Frost Pass on foot by himself indicated that the barricades were unmanned for now, Lily trusted such peace as little as she trusted peace in general and preferred her usual route to any easier one.

But when the old man slipped from the saddle the second time and was saved from tumbling into the depths only because his crude shoe got caught in the stirrup, she mounted the horse with him, ordered him to hold on to her, and soon felt his head against her shoulder and heard him snoring.

By early evening they arrived at the Cross of Moor, at the bullet-riddled watchtower by the switch that had sunk back into wasteland, at the abandoned embankment where the trains of the past had rolled down to Moor's shore or to the quarry. Here the warrior suddenly sat up in the saddle, as if the clatter of a switch, the clang of iron had awakened him. "Pretty," he said and, like a child, he pointed at the lake lying dark and smooth below them. "A pretty lake." Far out, a bright ship split the surface with a wake that grew ever broader—the *Sleeping Greek Maid* was steaming toward the Blind Shore.

Lily did not take the madman back to Forge Hill that evening, but rode with him to the Moor infirmary, a barrack with a corrugated tin roof, where members of a Society of Penitence provided some scant care to men injured at the quarry or to victims of a gang attack, until they could be transferred to the clinic in Haag. Although patients occupied only two of the barrack's five iron-frame beds, an attendant, who was sitting at a table beside the entrance playing cards with the gravel barge's ferryman, said this was no place for the senile and insane. If Lily was determined to leave the old man there, fine—but, first, that would cost her and, second, she would have to fetch him within three days at the latest and take him to Haag or wherever. While Lily was dealing with the attendant, the warrior began to give off a pungent odor. "He's shit his pants," the attendant said. "He'll have to be diapered. That costs extra."

The warrior believed he was in one of the enemy's field hospitals, and when the attendant led him to a scullery, a shed with a wooden tub and several tin buckets, he was unwilling to part with either his fireman's helmet or his medals. Only after Lily told him he was an official prisoner of war, and would be treated honorably as long as he obeyed the medic, did he give in and let them remove his helmet and medals and undress him. Then, after giving the attendant some chewing tobacco, schnapps, and a coupon for a can of gasoline, Lily made her way to the house of dogs.

"I told her your father didn't belong in our infirmary barrack or in a clinic, but in a veterans' home," Ambras said for the second time that evening, after Lily had finished retelling for his bodyguard the story of the warrior and her turnabout on Frost Pass. Responding to a signal by the Dog King, Bering had uncorked another bottle of red wine and joined the two of them at the salon table. "In a home? The one in Haag?" he asked. An organization of former frontline soldiers in Haag operated a veterans' home in a hotel whose façade still bore a weatherbeaten name—Hotel Esplanade.

"Not in the Esplanade," Ambras said, "not in Haag. In Brand."

In Brand? But that was on the other side of Frost Pass. On the other side of the zone's border. The lowlands began in Brand. Whoever wanted to go to Brand needed safe-conduct papers— issued only for valid cause—or, like Lily, had to know the back ways. "Why Brand?" Bering asked.

"Because the army would take care of him in Brand and because the old man can't stay in Haag for very long," the Dog King said. "He can't—nobody can."

Lily, who had just bent down to the mastiff lying under the table to whisper her childish nickname for him, sat up straight so suddenly that the dog leapt up in alarm. "What do you mean by nobody? He can't, nobody can. What's that supposed to mean?"

Nobody. As if he had mistakenly blurted out a magical word conjuring up a wilderness, a wasteland devoid of humanity, and now had to consider whether to go on, to retract that word, or simply to fall silent, Ambras replied after a long pause, in which only his mastiff's panting could be heard. "Along the lake . . . nobody will be able to stay along the lake. Next year the army wants to declare the lake country a restricted military zone for troop maneuvers. . . . The entire shore, the villages as far up as Eisenau, the sugar-beet fields, the vineyards—it's all to be a theater of operations for bombers and tank squadrons. Pilots, artillery, sappers, shock troops, the whole circus is already on its way. . . ."

"That's . . . that can't be . . . I don't believe it!" Lily was apparently as speechless as Bering.

But as drunk as he was, Ambras had evidently decided to reveal prematurely a secret guarded by himself and Moor's secretary, and went on speaking: "Tanks will plow the fields. The navy will torpedo the *Sleeping Greek Maid*. Divers will splash in the reeds. All by way of preparation. All as an exercise. Ready for combat at any time . . ."

"Are they crazy? Are they completely crazy?" In her immediate rage, Lily grabbed her wineglass and hurled it through the open window into the night, where it fell on grass or moss, for no crash, no breakage was heard. As if roused by an invisible attacker, the mastiff bounded in pursuit of the trail of drops left by the tossed glass, and stood at the window barking into the darkness until Ambras roared an even louder curse. Bering had never seen Lily so angry.

"Crazy? Yes. Probably. They're probably all crazy." With a single motion of his hand Ambras chased his lead dog back under the table.

"And what's to become of the people here!" Lily shouted. "Have they withstood attacks and bullying by the skins all these years only to be driven off in the end by the army, by their protectors?"

"The people?" Ambras said. "Next year the people will finally be allowed to go where most of them have wanted to go for a very long time now anyway—to the lowlands, you understand, close to army bases, close to supermarkets, railroads, gas stations. Next year these people will finally be able to leave their backwater towns. Up and away. The lake country will be disbanded."

"And us? What about us?" Bering asked as hastily, as if he was afraid that Ambras's announcement might prove to be some misunderstanding, that departure for the lowlands might be just drunken talk. "What about us?"

The Dog King was close to slurred babbling. He raised the wine bottle and waved it like a trophy. The bottle was empty. "We're going, too. . . . If everybody's going, we're going, too."

It was shortly before midnight when Lily left the Villa Flora at the end of a conversation that grew only louder and crazier. For the first time since Bering had become a bodyguard in the house of dogs, Lily had let Ambras coax her into staying until well into the night, and Bering was excited as he watched her disappear into the dark on horseback. When, in two days, she would once again depart for Frost Pass, for Brand, he would be accompanying her!

We're going to the lowlands! I'm going with Lily to Brand. The dogs and their drunken king had long been asleep that night, but Bering was still perched by the loudspeakers in his room, and to the guitar riffs of Patton's Orchestra he thought about the road that lay before them. *I'm going with Lily to Brand.* What did it matter really that his war-obsessed father would be going with them, too.

Of course Lily had said "no" at first, "out of the question," when Ambras had suggested that she take the old man, the warrior, right back with her over the pass again—there were enough veterans and disabled soldiers in Moor already.

"It's not some mountain excursion for sanatorium patients," Lily had said. "I can't be constantly worrying about him on a trip like that. He falls off his horse. He has to be bathed. He has to be diapered. He's already ruined my sleeping bag. I brought him back to Moor. That's all I can do."

"And what if *he* escorts you?" The Dog King appeared to be so taken by this notion that he began to laugh. "Let the bodyguard escort you! We'll send him on maneuvers. Let him practice! Let him practice the retreat to the lowlands. Let him see to it that a warrior arrives safely at the army base. Let him be his father's keeper for a few days. Let him . . . let him honor his father and mother. . . ." Ambras was laughing so hard as he exclaimed these last sentences that Bering barely understood a word. *Honor*—that he understood. "Honor?" he had asked. "What honor?"

"You are to escort her!" Ambras grumbled. "You are to deliver a madman to Brand, and you are to escort her—but you are not to honor anyone or anything, you understand, not anyone, not anything. That was just a joke, you idiot. The stuff about honor has always been just a joke."

CHAPTER 24

ON THE WAY
TO BRAND

THE PAST SPRING'S ROCKSLIDES AND
cascades of melting snow had left the road to the lowlands barely distinguishable from the bed of a brook.
Trucks, military vehicles, or high-wheeled oxcarts could make
headway on such roads—but a *limousine?*

By following the former railroad bed, which led through ivy-
hung tunnels and across viaducts, you could have reached Brand
in a day or two on foot or with pack animals, but now that the
army cleared the roads and truck trails of rubble, snow, or mudslides only for their own columns and transports and no longer
manned posts at the exits from valleys, the tunnels on this route
were often transformed by the gangs into traps from which there
was no escape.

Which left the mule tracks. But the mule tracks led through
mine fields and up into the region of crevassed glaciers. In fog or
bad weather you could easily go astray on these trails, and astray
meant the abyss or the flash of an exploding mine.

During the two days before their departure for Brand, Bering climbed and drove and rode through the mountains over and over in his mind, thought only of the shared path that lay before them. He spent one sleepless night at the window of his room, surveying the dark crests of the Stony Sea with his binoculars, until he thought he could see connections between the bright patches of cliffs and scree and the black, impenetrable swathes of mountain forest—the radiant lines of *his* path.

"In the car? What car? Oh, in the Crow!" On the eve of departure, Lily did not give a moment's thought to a suggestion that Bering, after much hesitation, had brought to the weather tower. Drive to Brand in the Crow? That was all they needed. Did he have any idea of the condition of the road to the lowlands? The Crow, Lily said, would have to be able to fly, would have to be able to sail across ditches and mudslides, to take the road to the lowlands without breaking an axle. No, she still preferred horse and mule to any vehicle. Bering would be better off to leave his bird behind at the house of dogs and mount his horse again for the trip to Brand, because the safest way to the lowlands was still the one via the old fort, the one over the pass.

Although Bering had pictured a different, more dramatic departure for Brand—driving off in the car in a billowing pennant of dust that dispersed very slowly—he was almost feverish when he saw Lily approaching the house of dogs between the giant pines the next morning. The dogs made a dash for her. She was sitting on her mule and listening to news from an army station on her transistor. The riderless horse plodded behind her, *his* horse. She came to fetch him. It had rained in the night. The hooves left deep imprints in the soft earth, little wells that filled with water, mirrors where patches of sky quivered.

Ambras was sitting in his wicker chair on the veranda and responded with only an absentminded nod when Bering offered a fussy farewell this morning, as if before him lay a long journey and not just a path through the Stony Sea. The bodyguard listed the supplies in the cellar, described how to deal with the generator in the turbine shed if the power went out, and was trying to explain the latest difficulties in starting the Crow, when Ambras simply nodded, waved him off. He didn't need to hear all that. He barely returned Lily's greeting, either, and was already engrossed again in a quarry inventory as the two of them departed.

They left the Villa Flora behind. The dogs leapt up on the portal's iron tendrils to no avail and barked after them in disappointment for a long time.

"Did you include your father in your provisions?" Lily asked her escort. "I can feed only one of you."

"Jerky, zwieback, dried apples, chocolate, and tea," Bering replied. "Enough for three of us for at least six days."

"That's too much," the woman on the mule said. "We'll be leaving your father in Brand, after all."

They had to dismount at the infirmary again and wait. The attendant was asleep and did not open up until Bering banged on the door and windows, shouting his father's name. Only last year, skinheads had raided the barrack at this same early hour, searching for drugs and bandages and smashing whatever they could not use.

The attendant had shaved Bering's father's head and beard and bathed him; the old man now smelled of soap and disinfectants and in his son's eyes looked as gaunt and strange as he had on the train platform the day he returned to Moor. And, as then, the scar on his forehead burned a dark red.

The old man was again deep in war, but he had no memory of either a courier or the partisan who had taken him prisoner in the mountains a few days before, and he no longer recognized the woman's escort either. That was some woman. That was some man. He saluted both civilians, who had probably come to this field hospital to bring him back to the front. It was indeed strange here. This desert was not his country. Everything seemed quiet at the front. No sound of battle showed the way—but the civilians would know. They surely had orders to lead him there. The warrior was ready. He received his helmet from the hands of the medic and then his medals, which were in a jingling paper sack that he would not let go of when the civilian fellow helped him into the saddle.

If he simply *had* to take that junk with him, the civilian said, then he damn well had to put the helmet on again, too, and buckle it—either that or tie it fast to his belt—and had to put that sack of medals in the saddlebag, because he would need his hands, both hands, to hold on tight. There was only this one horse, and they would both be riding it. . . .

But a civilian had no right giving him orders.

With the sack in one hand, he would hold on with just the other. That, however, didn't satisfy the civilian. He mounted the horse with him, sat there grand and lordly in front of the old man, turned around to him, looped a rope around his body, and bound the two of them tightly together.

Bering had not been so close to his father since childhood. He felt the old man's breath on his neck, and the smell of soap filled his nose—and, after a few hours on the road, the sour, acrid odor of sweat. But he felt no disgust and none of his old rage at the stubbornness of this codger lost in memories of the desert and the war. Holding the reins slack in his hand, gazing out over the horse's head to search the path for traps and obstacles, Bering spoke to his father as he would to a child, kept asking him whether he wanted to eat, wanted to drink or rest, and finally untied him and showed him a dwarf pine behind which he could squat and relieve himself.

The warrior was gradually coming to realize that this rider, who gave him food and drink and saw to it that he did not fall off the horse, had to be a soldier, after all, a good comrade accompanying him into battle. He began to mutter behind the rider's back, warning him of Halfayah's banners of white dust, of sand as fine as flour that entered the pores and eyes of a marching column, of a caravan, penetrating even sweat-drenched cloths over mouths and faces, blinding everyone and leading them astray. When the rider ordered him to rest, he let himself be helped down from the horse and sat on a stone. When the rider ordered him to drink, he drank, and when the rider said, "Don't talk so much, be quiet for once," he instantly fell silent. He did everything the rider ordered.

Lily astride her mule was always four or five horse-lengths ahead. At times she turned around to shout a warning of some especially precipitous or rough bit of road. The path grew steeper and so narrow that Bering had to devote all his attention to holding the reins and keeping himself and his father on the horse.

For hours, for days, he had wanted to be alone on this ride with Lily and had pictured himself swaying beside her through the Stony Sea, moving toward the lowlands; he wanted to sit beside her by the fire as night fell, to sleep beside her on stones or in moss, to listen to her tell about Brazil. . . . But now, finally on the journey he had yearned for, she was far ahead of him and at most called out from the distance a few curt warnings that had nothing to do with the darkness, nothing to do with the one danger that truly threatened him. And in between warnings he had no real need of, he heard his father's mutterings.

And even if Bering no longer felt rage at this madman who had made life on Forge Hill unbearable and now filled his ear with babbled memories of war, the disappointment of this journey was sometimes so great that he could no longer endure the muttering and said, "Quiet, can't you be quiet for once?"

The warrior wanted to be obedient and followed every command instantly. But each word was valid only for as long as he could retain the memory. And in seconds he forgot words, commands, forgot *everything* he was told and ordered to do over and over. His memory reached deep into the deserts of North Africa, and he could even describe the sky above the battlefields and still knew which clouds promised a sandstorm and which rain—but he forgot what happened in the moment, it vanished as if it had never been. His present was his past.

Be quiet! No sooner had he heard what the rider said than the memory of the war was already stronger than his obedience, and although after each command for quiet he would break off in the middle of a sentence, of a word, and fall silent for a moment, with his next breath he was already talking, kept on talking about the desert and the battle and Halfayah Pass, which he thought he saw up ahead, somewhere between those towering rocks and the clouds. Up there! They had to get up there. They had to take the pass.

"Quiet! Shut up. Be quiet for once."

Toward evening, on the final climb, with the fort already in view at the top of the pass, they came to a broad field of scree. To reach their campsite, they had to dismount and lead the animals by their bridles through a labyrinth of stones—so painfully, so slowly that dusk was beginning to fall. But Lily wanted to spend this night as well in the subterranean quarters of *her* bunker.

Bering was amazed at the size and features of this hide-out. The entrance between two piles of concrete rubble was so well camouflaged by a thicket that Lily suddenly seemed to have been swallowed by the earth, and he had to follow her shouts to find his way down inside.

The warrior, it seemed, also no longer recalled this refuge, where he had slept beside the fire a few nights before and had dreamt of an alarm signaling the start of battle. But now, after he tried to arrange wood for a new fire and then helped hide the animals in the thicket and started to drag a packsaddle that was much too heavy for him down into the darkness, it suddenly seemed to him as if that particular night was not yet over, as if it had never been gone at all, but was still *here*—and suddenly his hand was once again on the rifle butt that stuck up out of the partisan's baggage, and he remembered, remembered that on Halfayah Pass, and during the entire war, a lowly private was never allowed to touch a sharpshooter's rifle, and he felt compelled to warn his comrade: "Don't touch that rifle. There'll be trouble if you touch a rifle like that."

A rifle? All the way here, Bering had never noticed the weapon, which was rolled up in a raincoat tied to the mule's saddle. "A rifle! You have a rifle?"

"You have a pistol," she said. She threw a horsehair blanket over the sandy floor by the campfire, pulled the rifle out of the coat, gently laid the gun beside the blanket, and then plumped the coat into a pillow. *She* would be spending the night here—and the men on the other side of the fire. She wanted only her weapon beside her.

When Lily tossed the planks of a smashed ammunition crate onto the fire to prepare tea and soup, its flame was reflected like a flickering star in the lens of the scope. Bering had never seen a sharpshooter's rifle before in his life. Maybe Lily had found the thing at some abandoned army base and wanted to swap it in Brand or just hand it over to the army, as required by law. When, in confusion and under its magical attraction, he simply stepped across the fire and bent down for the gun, Lily said, in a tone he had never heard from her before, "Keep your hands off it. It's loaded."

"There'll be trouble. I told you so," the warrior muttered. "I told you so." And Bering understood only that he dare not ask any more questions and would do better to do what Lily requested of him—snow, he was to fetch some snow. He nodded and went out into the darkness to fill the kettle with snow, the coarse-grained, watery snow that lasted the summer in the shade of crevices and sinkholes.

The wind outside raced across the high plateaus and corries and drove banks of fog against the glaciers of the highest ranges until their cracked, ancient ice vanished in the undulating gray. Kettle in hand, Bering stood in the wind on a tongue of snow and watched as barren mountains sank into the clouds and into a night rising up to the pass from the abysses below. Then Lily called for him, for the water, and he climbed back down inside.

Only hours later—after she had cooked and they had eaten and the warrior, having taken a few deep pulls on Lily's schnapps flask, had fallen asleep wrapped in a blanket and they were now sitting by the fire in her bunker, in her smoky cave—only then was everything the way, or something like the way, Bering had imagined a night in the Stony Sea. Sheltered by a fort stormed in battle decades before, here he was in a cave with Lily, beside a fire, separated from her only by flames that grew smaller and smaller—here he was alone with her at last.

They sipped tea from tin bowls. They stared into the fire and spoke into the embers, spoke about the dangers that menaced a wanderer in these high mountain wastelands, about foul weather and fog that rose in a sudden wall of smoke. About rockslides and avalanches. And about drifting snow, which could cap ravines and crevasses and transform a fissured landscape into a softly textured surface that at every step could break open into bottomless black.

Many of the ravines and sinkholes hidden under the new snow that comes with a sudden change in the weather were so deep, Lily said, that you could count to twenty or thirty or more to the rumble and bump of a stone dropped down them. Tomorrow, Lily said, they would be crossing a plateau of such sinkholes, a sinkhole cemetery, down whose shafts the bodies of refugees had been thrown, members of a column that during the last weeks of the war had taken the same route they were on now in an attempt to detour around the mined valley roads. The refugees had probably been surprised by a snowstorm and strayed from the path, and had eventually frozen to death. A sapper unit from the allied armies had not discovered the bodies until the second year of peace and had entombed them in the sinkholes.

It was easy to talk about snowstorms, about rockslides and mudslides, and certainly about Saint Elmo's fire, the blue garland of flame that in the charged air before a thunderstorm licked the top of iron road signs or the steel cables of a suspension bridge, announcing an impending bolt of lightning. But they both said nothing about the rifle shimmering dully in Lily's shadow, nor did they mention the scattered gangs of skinheads, who in retreat before the army could come clear up to the region of glaciers and from whom, even at these heights, no one could be safe. Bering, blissful to be near Lily, had forgotten the danger of the gangs for now, and Lily said nothing to keep from getting too close to the secret of her hunting trips.

And they said nothing about themselves either. When they

spoke, it was as if their sole concern, their sole passion, was the Stony Sea. And when they fell silent, it was so quiet in their refuge that they could hear only the crackle of the embers, the breathing of the sleeping warrior, and, in between, their own blood tolling inside their heads.

In the flickering firelight, deep shadows scurried over Lily's face, and sometimes tears came to their eyes from the smoke, which could escape only through the low entrance and a small light shaft. Sometimes Lily's eyes became invisible in the flicker, and then Bering no longer knew whether it was those bouncing shadows or the holes in his vision that darkened her face. He wanted light—a hundred torches, spotlights, a forest fire, the glare of snow—so that he could look into her eyes. But he had only this dark-red flicker, and the log he threw in the embers was wet and smoked as it burned.

Lily was sitting on the other side of the fire, on the other side of the world, and yet was as close to him now as she had been for a long time.

Was that really *his* voice? Was that really *him*, who in the midst of a long silence spoke Lily's name so loudly that it startled her? To him it felt as if her name and all the words that followed spoke themselves and were simply using his breath, his vocal cords, his throat, the way bird voices sometimes flew through him and emerged audible only by way of his body and out of his mouth, without requiring any special act of will, any special effort. Sometimes his mimicked whistle, his mock song of a thrush or a blackbird, sounded like a stranger's voice, and that was how he spoke now.

"Lily!"

She was engrossed in watching the embers. A warning call could not have torn her more abruptly from her preoccupation.

"What is it?"

"I . . . have a secret."

"So do I," she said slowly. "Everybody does. There's isn't anybody who doesn't have a secret."

"But I didn't choose mine."

"Then let it go. Throw it away. Go outside, write it on the rocks, write it in the snow."

"I can't."

"Anybody can."

"I can't do it."

"Why not?"

"Because it . . . because I . . . I'm going blind."

Now that the awful thing had been said, he lost his voice, and suddenly a weariness came over him in which everything about him felt sluggish and heavy. Sitting there on the cold, sandy floor, he had to use his arms to prop himself against the urge to topple over and sleep. His eyes almost fell shut. He wanted to go on talking, wanted to say something else, but his voice had deserted him. He grinned without meaning to. He didn't even know he was grinning.

"Nobody could tell you're blind," Lily said, and smiled as if simply replying to a joke—and only then noticed the state he was in, his exhaustion. Bering could say no more than what he had just said. And Lily saw that it was not merely the acrid smoke that was making his eyes water.

Separated by the fire, they sat there in the night, and for a moment it seemed as if she was about to get up and come to him again and take him in her arms again, just as on the evening in Moor's cemetery when he had buried the blacksmith's wife. But she stayed on her side of the embers, after all, and watched Bering attentively for a long time.

"What's it like to go blind?" she asked him then, and poked at the fire with a branch so vigorously that she had to shield her eyes from the swarming jet of sparks. She asked him twice—and waited mutely until at last the clamp loosened that was constricting Bering's throat and would at most have permitted him a thin scream, a squawk, the cry of a bird.

And Bering began to talk about a concert at the airport, about a night when Lily had taken him in her arms—and not just out of pity. But he did not speak of her tenderness, but of their trip home together from Pilot Valley, about the drive in the Crow, and described—haltingly at first, but then more urgently, as if afraid to lose his voice again—the shadows and potholes that had flown up from the beam of the headlights that night and lodged in his vision as blind spots. He revealed his secret. He sought out Lily's eyes and found only a shadow: "What should I do? Ambras mustn't know anything about it."

"Mustn't know about it?"

"He mustn't know a thing. Not a word!"

Lily asked no more questions. She pulled the blanket up over the shoulders of the sleeping warrior, who had rolled out of the firelight into the dark.

"Black spots are a long way from being blind," she said. "If this weather holds, we'll be in Brand tomorrow." At the Big Hospital in Brand there was a medic who had occasionally supplied her with medicine for Moor's secretary. "Maybe he can help you. . . . You won't end up blind. If you go blind, then I'll go deaf." She smiled again now.

For Bering, the cheerful confidence with which Lily tried to comfort him was no comfort. Didn't she believe him? Couldn't she even understand his fear that someday he might be bumbling around like his father?

"I don't want to become an invalid," he said, and turned his head to the sleeping warrior. "I don't want to be like that guy."

"A few days ago that guy managed to find his way clear up here all by himself."

"And Ambras?" Without taking his eyes off the sleeping man, Bering began tracing lines, flat arcs, on the floor with his forefinger, setting one arc atop another in the sand. Ambras surely knew this medic himself, right? So sooner or later, in a radio message or from some casual comment by the secretary, he, too, would find out about how things stood with his bodyguard's eyes.

"He doesn't know him," Lily said. "In Brand everyone has his own friends. . . . And besides, the Big Hospital doesn't broadcast news about vision problems. They have worse cases to deal with there."

As absentmindedly as he had drawn them, Bering now erased his arcs, wiping the palm of his hand across the floor. To think Lily could talk about his fear like that. But he nodded. He would do what she advised. Only soldiers or favorites of the army were admitted to the hospital in Brand, which, even in the third decade of peace, was still simply called the Big Hospital in backwater villages by the lake. Anyone who suffered from an illness but had no advocate in the lowlands had no recourse but the Red Cross barracks in Moor or Haag—that is, if he didn't seek help from a saltworker's wife in Eisenau. She laid her hands on the brow of every patient who entered her dingy parlor, murmured unintelligible charms, and drew healing symbols on his body with a bird bone dipped in some black brew.

"We'll be in Brand tomorrow," Lily said. "You can depend on the man at the hospital. Or would you rather go on a pilgrimage to Eisenau, to see the saltworker's wife?"

Bering blew on his cold fingers and spoke more into his cupped hands than to Lily as he said, "I've been . . . to Eisenau before."

Although the flames were sinking into the embers tongue by tongue, Lily did not touch the supply of wood at her feet. The fire died out. And only darkness found its way down the light shaft into the cave. The blackness that finally enveloped them was as impenetrable as if they were inside a mountain.

The two of them sat erect in the silence for a long time, but let their conversation and their secrets be—and did not wish each other good night, either. Each sat on her or his side of the ashes, each listened as the other lay down to sleep, shifting into position on the chinked bunker floor. They would be in Brand tomorrow. In Brand. Unless the wind, which was now turning the fort's shafts and subterranean corridors into organ pipes, did not die down again and kept on jamming more and more clouds against the walls of the Stony Sea—snow clouds. It was summer in the lowlands. But up here it might very well snow during the night.

Tomorrow in the lowlands. Bering saw the towering high-voltage pylons pointing into the clear sky, saw the silvery strands of a railroad and a stream of cars and machines moving across the flat land as far as the horizon. The sky seemed embroidered with the darting patterns of flocks of birds, but had not a single blind spot, and the light was so dazzling that Bering had to shade his eyes—and suddenly he felt Lily's hands on his shoulders, her breath against his neck, a warm husk of breath . . . but no, he was already dreaming all that.

CHAPTER 25

KILLING

T HE PATH THROUGH THE MOUNTAINS WAS
strewn with seashells. The next morning the travelers
moved on toward Brand, across a fissured high plateau
east of Frost Pass, but even after five hours of riding, mother-of-
pearl from thousands upon thousands of petrified clam shells still
shimmered beneath the hooves of their pack animals.

In the language of smugglers and the people who sometimes
commuted between zones across this treeless, shrubless plateau,
these shells fused with the moon-white limestone were called
hoofprints, because in both size and shape they resembled horses'
tracks. The remains of a prehistoric sea, they lay scattered over
massive boulders and fields of scree like cast silver traces of an
immense, long-vanished cavalry. In years past, Lily had sometimes tapped especially beautiful prints from the limestone and
traded them for scarce goods in the lowlands. Oblivious now to
the mother-of-pearl, she guided her mule across it, and her
escorts had difficulty following.

The day had turned mild, contrary to the stormy omens of the
night before. An amber-hued sun lent even the scree a costly

243

luster. The wind, instead of bringing snow, had dried the clouds
from the mountains and then died down before dawn. High
above the travelers, between the towering rocks and black walls of
the Stony Sea, the glaciers and fields of firn now looked like
monstrous manta rays drifting over the deep, and the sky above
the icy banners on the highest peaks was such a dark blue that at
times Bering thought he saw constellations.

When Lily dismounted to lead her mule carefully alongside
ravines and sinkhole shafts that had suddenly gaped before her,
Bering followed her example, which left the warrior riding like a
commander high above his foot soldiers. The old man was lashed
to the load of goods that Lily had left behind at the fort a few
days before and that together they had pulled from camouflaged
hiding places at dawn and put back into packsaddles, and as he
rode now across the most dangerous stretch of their route, sometimes mute, sometimes lost in conversation with himself, he gave
in to the sway of his last journey across the Stony Sea.

How often he had walked this road to Brand before the war
and even during its first year, had climbed the path to do iron
work on the stronghold at the fort at the top of the pass—until a
fateful chain of commands had dragged him farther and farther
from his house and his town and finally landed him in the deserts
of North Africa.

And although the warrior had forgotten everything that was
not part of the war—his name, his house, even his son—he
would surely have found this path through the mountains on
pure instinct by himself, and without any help would have been
capable of groping his way, as resolute as he was blind, across
Frost Pass to Brand. . . .

But he sat lashed to the horse, tied down with ropes, nothing
but a load of goods himself, and to the animal's broken gait he
swayed and rocked and bobbed toward the stony ground, held
captive in his rope restraints, and could not have fallen even if a
rocky stairstep had set the horse on its haunches. He felt the
power tugging and pulling at him from all sides, trying to cast
him into the abyss, into those black shafts that opened up before

the horse's hooves, and yet were soon left behind to the right and left of the path.

"I want to get off," he said. "I want down. I want to march. I'm going to fall off."

"You're not going to fall off," Bering said, and lifted his head toward his father, but had to close his eyes at once in the dazzling amber-hued light. "You're not going to fall off. You can't fall."

Like straggling survivors of a perished caravan laden with their few remaining possessions, the travelers moved toward Brand across the bottom of an evaporated sea, through meadows of sea-weed, banks of mussels, coral reefs, and abysses—all of it thrust upward in an era beyond human time by the force of a tectonic catastrophe, heaved cloudward, and transformed over the course of eons into the peaks and ice fields of a mountain range.

When the path permitted it, Bering joined his father on the horse, and the old man spoke to him again behind his back—confused memories of the desert; incessant, monotonous conjurings of the war. But now he no longer forbade him to speak, gave no more orders, but let him talk and talk and sometimes even listened and smiled when the old man spoke of camels. Lily rode silently up ahead.

The Stony Sea certainly appeared brilliant and peaceful today—but whenever Lily stopped to search sunlit wastelands with her binoculars for danger, Bering saw her apprehensive watchful demeanor as simply a sign that the three of them, and each individually, had dragged something alien into this peacefulness, something inexplicable, the seed of an evil that always threatened to erupt wherever people were alone with themselves and their kind.

In the fifth hour after their departure from Frost Pass, they were trotting smartly in tight single file over extensive terraces of moss that lay like green stripes across the chalky-white rocks, when Lily reined in her mule so violently and unexpectedly that the animal reared up with a snort. Pressing close behind, Bering's horse tossed its head and barely managed to dodge the mule.

The mossy terraces led deep into the field of sinkholes that

Lily had talked about beside the fire the night before. Attached to
a boulder and almost illegible with rust, an iron plaque recalled
that in the bottomless shafts of this field, the army had interred
the bodies of refugees who had been surprised by a snowstorm
and had frozen to death here in the last weeks of the war. . . .

But it was not these yawning, eternally open graves that had
brought Lily to a sudden stop; it was what she saw in a wind-
protected hollow at the edge of the field of sinkholes. There, not
thirty yards away, were two crouching figures—skinheads.

They were evidently busy building a fire.

"They've never been here before," Lily said, but so softly that
Bering did not understand a word. He had spotted the crouching
figures as his horse made its abrupt evasive maneuver, and he
now elbowed his babbling father to warn him. But the old man
did not understand the poke and did not see the men and began
to curse the rider—and fell silent only when Lily whispered to
him the magic word whose meaning a warrior understands even
in the greatest confusion: "Enemies!"

Suddenly the old man was sitting atop the horse's sweat-
drenched back as erect and rigid as the rider to whom he still held
tight. It was too late, however, for an unobserved retreat. The
skinheads had turned toward them in the same moment that
Lily's whisper gave them a name.

Enemies. They have never seen each other before, but they recognize each other. They stare. They reach for their weapons like
falling men grasping to catch themselves—Lily for her rifle, the
skinheads for an ax, for a stone to fit into a slingshot, for a club
with a flashing scythe blade at one end.

Only the warrior lashed to the load of goods is still sitting
empty-handed astride the horse. Now, at last and for the first
time in his life, he is an officer, a colonel, a general! He needs no
weapon, but simply takes his hands from the rider. This guy, the
rider, *is* his weapon; he already has his pistol in his hand.

Pulling a pistol from your belt, taking a rifle from the camouflage case of a rolled-up raincoat—both make very little noise;

and picking up an ax or sickle blade from rocky ground makes no more noise than a barely audible clink.

But how still it grows between these enemies, deathly still, when the clink and rustle of arming is past and only the bare battlefield lies between them, a rocky, mossy basin riddled with sinkholes.

It is still. And suddenly Bering again hears the hiss of a steel chain, the tramping on the forge's plank floor, hears as well the laughter of a pursuer and sees a laughing face illumined by the flash at the end of the barrel, then fading in the dark of the stairs.

He once again has an enemy before him, and he slowly, but without hesitation, aims the barrel of his pistol at him. This time the enemy isn't laughing and is not so close as on that April night—he will never let an enemy get that close again. . . . And nothing else now is as it was back then on Forge Hill either.

For as his eyes adjust to looking into the dazzling sunlight, what Bering gradually sees no longer frightens him. It enrages him. And his rage no longer prompts him to flee and act in self-defense—but to attack.

The swine! One of the two skinheads looks like a bird, looks as if he is clad in whitish-brown feathers. Bound chickens dangle from his shoulders—live chickens bound together like a twitching stole! Claws bound, wings bound, they dangle from this man in leather, and their beaks must surely be bound as well, for the birds are silent. That's how chicken thieves carry their booty and keep the meat fresh for slaughter during day-long marches through these wastelands. Chicken thieves!

Maybe in some remote farmstead high above the lake there is a crofter who was slain for these chickens, who has been lying for days now beside an empty, lopsided coop. For a moment, Bering thinks of the blacksmith's wife, of her soft voice when she would step to the farmyard gate and call the chickens from the iron garden. . . . But then he sees only these bound birds. That is the sight that enrages him.

He can feel those bonds on his own body, can feel how his

own dangling weight causes the thin twine to cut into his flesh, but there is no easing that weight with a flap of the wings. The wings are bound or broken, the beaks tied shut! And he can also feel the cry that cannot leave a throat blocked by force and so bounces back into the lungs, reaches all the way to the heart, and shatters there painfully, inaudibly. Birds bound and gagged!

In the bluish tattooed faces of his enemies he now sees just one face whose light went out on an April night—and in the chickens he sees companions, old friends from his first, floating year in the dark. *These* chickens soothed him long ago. And now they are mute. Their questioning, clucking voices consoled him back then and joined him even in his sleep, and during all these years have been as close to him as his own voice.

The swine! Now the second skinhead pulls a bundled package of feathers and claws from the ground, a smaller bundle, only four chickens, and throws the booty over his shoulder—and turns away. Is he turning to flee? Then, more clumsily and slowly under a heavier feathered burden, his buddy starts to run, too.

Those bald-headed swine are running away!

But now Bering hears something else—laughter, a giggle. It is Lily. She has laid her rifle in front of her like a scale-beam across her saddle and giggles and waves, giggling, at the fleeing men. She quickly realized that the skins were picking up their weapons not to fight, but to flee, and are alone in this wasteland, without the superior numbers of a gang. Presumably they are not even scouts—scouts don't burden themselves with booty—but are only deserters, exiles who have violated the code of some gang of killers. When the riders suddenly appeared, probably what those two noticed above all was the dull sheen of guns, and from past battles with the army they must know that all they can gain now is their own lives. And they are running for their lives. Are they ever running! The chickens dance at their shoulders and backs, banging against black brittle leather. Lost down spins in the amber of the air.

There is no triumph in Lily's giggle, only relief. Without even having to fire a warning shot, she can watch the same fear, the same centrifugal force take effect that she has seen only on her hunting trips—but through a riflescope and after a fatal shot.

In this marvelous moment of playful, feather-light victory, her rifle slips away, and before she can grab it by the barrel, she has lost her gun. She is so elated by the ridiculous sight of the fleeing men, floundering under their burdens like two laying hens, that she hardly notices Bering—deep in a rage of which she takes no notice, either—jump down from his horse.

Bering won't, *can't*, let the chicken thieves escape. A skinhead got away from him once in the dark, a gaping, ugly face that afterward kept appearing to him by night. He wants to extinguish that vision forever. He also wants to see those chickens flutter and hear their voices, and he watches now as the distance between him and his enemies grows, step by step, and knows that a pistol will no longer suffice to bear his hatred to its goal.

If he is going to extinguish that ugly face, he needs a rifle— Lily's rifle.

In two bounds he is beside her mule. Without a word he grabs the gun, clutches the rifle, and is following the fleeing men through the scope before Lily can even drop her hand grasping at empty air.

She drops her hand. Sits motionless in the saddle. Should she believe what she sees? Bering runs to a boulder, a jagged rock, a mossy rest for the rifle, falls to one knee, buries the barrel in a pillow of moss, and pulls the skinheads into the cross hairs. That readiness, that determination and resolve to kill—that is how *she* lies in ambush on her hunting trips. That sharpshooter there, that's *her*. And that is *her* rifle aimed at fleeing chicken thieves.

Lily knows the quivering image the sharpshooter sees in the lens of the scope. It is as if by looking through the lens, Bering were seeing only images inside her own head, gazing at *her* secret, at memories of an unsuspecting, ludicrous victim stumbling along, unaware of the stigma of the cross hairs that he bears on his brow, his chest, his back. There in the exact line of fire, a skinhead hung with chickens is running off and thinks he has almost escaped, is almost safe—but he is only pumping the pedals of a wheel spinning toward no other goal than death.

Lily can no longer endure the sight. *Are you crazy*, she wants to shout at the sharpshooter. *They're harmless, they're running, they're running away, let them go!* But her energy and her voice are trapped inside this duplicate hunter, inside a duplicate of herself. And that likeness is silent and deaf to everything that is not a part of killing.

A hunter? That's no hunter. That's a killer, a murderer, no better than the tattooed enemy at which he

now

shoots.

The crack of the rifle tears Lily out of her numbed state. Like the echo of shots that she herself fired months, years ago, that horrible crack rebounds from the mountains.

Lily holds her ears, but can still hear not just a rapid sequence of shots, but in between them the metallic sound of the bolt as well and even the bright, almost merry tone of ejected cartridges clattering over the limestone. The sound of killing pierces the flattened hands pressed to her ears. She jumps from the saddle now, too.

Bering has never held a weapon like this one in his hands and yet handles its mechanism as naturally as if he were dealing with some old familiar tool from the forge or the gearshift of a wreck from the iron garden. He shoots, thrusts the bolt up, pulls it back, ejects the empty cartridge from the chamber, pushes the bolt forward and down—and at the completion of this flowing movement has his finger on the trigger again. He fires. Reloads. Fires.

The staccato of the shots explodes in his ears, causing a deafness beyond piercing pain, where there are no voices and no pain and no sounds left, nothing except a single, continuous singing tone deep inside his head.

He shoots five times—and shoots not only at his enemies but

also with even greater hatred at that dark, bobbing spot, at the
hole in his world into which the figures—growing smaller and
smaller in the cross hairs—have almost vanished.

The first shot hits stone. Panicked now, the chicken thieves
scamper on. The next two shots as well merely spray fragments of
limestone and mother-of-pearl across their path of flight.

It is only after the fourth shot, or is it the fifth?—they are so
close together it is hard to say which one hit—that one of the
fleeing men, the one with the heavier feathered burden, flings his
arms up as if to fly away.

But he doesn't fly. He falls. Wrapped in a dusty cloud of
feathers and down, he falls and hits the rocky ground with fluttering arms extended.

Bering, his eye still trained on the scope, is very close now to
his victim—and he sees *Ambras*. While his other enemy silently
and in fear for his life runs on and on and escapes into the wilderness, Bering is thinking of Ambras. He wonders if it had been
Ambras who was hit, whether he would have flung his arms that
high above his head. Would the shot have freed him from his
infirmity? Freed him forever?

Now, having hit his target at last, the bodyguard thinks of his
master. He is no longer thinking of his enemies. For Lily is beside
him now. She grabs him from behind by the hair, pulls him by
the hair out of his deafness, knocks the rifle out of his hand, and
screams, "Stop, stop it, you asshole, stop it now!"

This scream of outrage, which can really stop nothing now,
can save nothing now, is the only thing the man who has been
shot hears of his world—a sign of rage, which he probably
believes is meant for *him*, for him alone. And while the snowy
down tossed upward by that last shot descends on him, while his
eyes grow fixed so that they can stay open forever, he turns his
face, his gaze, slowly, endlessly slowly, to this distant, screaming
woman.

But neither the woman nor the sharpshooter—who is hidden
behind a boulder and kneeling beside her and invisible to the

man who has been shot—notices anything of his unutterable struggle. They have eyes only for each other. They stare at each other. They hate each other. In this moment they part forever, just as he—this skinhead, this chicken thief, this dying bird man—must now part from them and from everything.

CHAPTER 26

THE LIGHT OF NAGOYA

L IGHTS, COUNTLESS LIGHTS: THE BEAMS OF
headlights slipping past or crossing one another; fingers of
light grasping at the night, then dipping into it to re-
emerge at some other point of darkness. Signal flares in red.
Flashing lights. Rows, blocks, and floating patterns of illuminated windows. Swarms of sparks! Towers and palaces riddled
with light—or were those high-rises? Army bases? Sample books
of light, tracks of luminescence stretching to infinity along noc-
turnal streets and boulevards; runways embroidered with sparks,
spiral nebulae. Flowing lights, leaping, flickering, softly glowing,
and blue-beaming lights, tangled garlands of light and pulsing
lights, barely discernible and as silent as the constellations glistening through the thermal currents and eddies of this summer
night.

The first thing the travelers to the lowlands saw of Brand was a
chaos of light. Bering sensed how his rage at Lily and the tense
vigilance that had kept him scouting all day for the escaped skinhead or a vengeful horde were transformed now into relief, into
excitement. The field of sinkholes that had remained so close by

his side the whole time, as if his horse were merely trotting in place, was suddenly as faraway now as Moor itself, as the house of dogs; was as faraway as everything he was coming from. There below lay Brand.

In Brand at last.

On the entire stretch from the field of sinkholes, Lily had halted only once, beside a cascading torrent to water her mule. If the escaped skinhead was in fact a scout, then they *had* to make the lowlands today. And so they had ridden on into the night, across the Stony Sea's barren foothills, over gently descending ridges, and finally down a steep serpentine road toward the lights of Brand. The road was good.

Arriving at an unmanned checkpoint, they had just passed a raised tollgate and a dark guardhouse fortified with sandbags, when from the sparkling depths the first bundles of fire, yowling molten balls, began to rise—at first only here and there, then in rapidly increasing numbers. Lily had her mule firmly in hand, but there was almost no controlling Bering's horse, which kept pressing ahead as if refuge could be found only where the mule set its hooves.

"Is that a battle?" Bering said as if to himself, and gave his horse a soothing pat on the neck. "That's a battle."

"A battle?" Without taking her eyes off the lights, Lily fiddled at the knobs of her transistor. The crackling interference did not decrease. "That's not a battle. It's a celebration." How different, how strange her voice sounded after so many hours of silence.

Three silent riders—for even the warrior had been turned mute, as if forever, by the shots in the field of sinkholes—they had passed through the afternoon, through the evening, through the night, and had reached the edge of the mountains in silence and had even kept their silence at the first, marvelous view of the lowlands lying suddenly below them as they emerged from a high valley. And remained silent even though waves of light were hurled up at them in the darkness, as if they were standing on cliffs above a soundless surf.

"A celebration?" Bering asked. "What are they celebrating?"

The booming sprays of fire did not sound much different from the shots in the field of sinkholes. *That* was supposed to be the noise of a festival? Then had what happened among the sinkholes perhaps been a festival, too? A celebration of victory over a bald-headed chicken thief?

While Lily had cursed him as a murderer, a trigger-happy idiot who would do better with a hammer for a weapon, he had silently pulled the knife from the skinhead's belt and—rope by rope, knot by knot—had cut the blood-splattered chickens free from their torturer.

I killed this swine, I did.

In his memory he once again drags and yanks and rolls the corpse to the edge of one of the gaping holes in the rocks and pushes it over, and all the while the only thing he feels is disgust at the large gunshot wound sticky with feathers on the dead man's neck. How heavy a lifeless body is—like a piece of water-logged wood, it slaps, then bangs against the projecting rocks, against the walls of the shaft, on its plunge into the darkness and, even when invisible, flings the ugly sound of its fall back to the world above. *I defeated this swine.*

And then, while the liberated birds—wings broken, claws bruised—stagger off across the limestone as if mimicking the flight of their torturers, he, the victor, leads his horse back to the battlefield; to the staccato of the shots, it bounded off in panic, his father still lashed to it, and is now ripping lichen and moss from the rocks off in the stony distance. How skewed his rope-bound father sits atop the horse, and how silent—as if the shots had finally returned him to reality and to a frontline from which not just the alarms of war but also his own and all other voices have faded forever.

And as the victor, leading his horse by the bridle, approaches the battlefield, he sees Lily standing at the edge of the dark-ness, beside his enemy's bottomless grave. She has picked up the rifle. She is holding her rifle in her hand. She extends her hand slowly, to full length, and lets the weapon drop into the abyss, no, flings the weapon into it! The banging, splintering, clattering

that pierces the darkness lasts longer than did the sound of the
falling corpse. Then she mounts her mule without looking
around for him. But he cannot follow her at once, he must, he
must step one last time to the edge of the ravine, the grave, the
hole in the rocks, because he cannot bear to leave beneath an
open sky the body of the chicken whose wings and breast were
first pierced by the bullet that entered his enemy's neck.

He fights back nausea as he picks up the torn cadaver and
tosses it down to his dead enemy. It is the nausea that always
overcame him when the blacksmith's wife sat at a bucket of
scalding water and plucked feathers from the body of a slaugh-
tered chicken. The bird disappears soundlessly into the depths.
And as the victor finally mounts the horse to join his mute father,
all that is left on the battlefield are feathers and down and a
muddled trail of human and bird blood mingling and oozing
into the rock and ending at the edge of the ravine—a road
marker into the abyss.

"What are they celebrating down there? What sort of festival
is it?" Bering asked again—into a void, for Lily had given
her mule's flanks a light tap of the heels and was already well
ahead of him.

She had ridden far ahead, far out of reach, the whole way from
the field of sinkholes to the lights of Brand, and sometimes the
tootling and jagged crackling of her radio was the only marker for
him to follow through a labyrinth of dwarf pines, rocks, stunted
firs, and, toward the end, darkness. Whenever he lost Lily from
view, he stopped and listened to the wilderness. Drifting tatters
of pop tunes and commercials and a steady barrage of voices
reporting the news would then point the way. The reports came
at such frequent intervals and the tone of the voices was so
excited that he thought it had to be news of some sensation or
catastrophe that was being bawled by short- and medium-wave
stations clear out into the stillness of the Stony Sea. Twice he
tried to get closer to Lily, closer to those excited voices. But Lily
kept her distance.

Japan . . . victory in the Pacific . . . theater of war on Honshu island . . . impenetrable cloud of dust hides Nagoya after single bomb strikes . . . nuclear warhead . . . flash is seen hundred and seventy miles away from Nagoya . . . Japanese emperor aboard the battleship USS Missouri *. . . unconditional surrender . . . smoke seethes forty thousand feet . . .*

Nagoya. Honshu. The war in Japan. . . . What from a distance Bering more guessed than understood about the nature of the news was merely that they were probably talking about the war in Asia again, whose horrors, along with those of other wars and other battles fought somewhere, he had seen flickering across the screens in the assembly halls in Moor or Haag since grade school. And the television in the plundered library at the Villa Flora, which often glowed only for sleeping dogs, illumined endless hours of the night with pictures of the war. A jungle war. A mountain war. War in bamboo forests and war in pack ice. Desert wars. Forgotten wars. A war in Japan: one of many. All these reports from the front always ended with a reminder of the blessings of the Peace of Oranienburg bestowed upon the defeated by the goodness and wisdom of the great Lyndon Porter Stellamour. No, those kinds of reports and announcements no longer moved anyone in Moor. Why had Lily been paying attention to this army babble for hours now?

. . . harnessing of the basic power of the universe . . . atomic bomb . . . the voice bawled *. . . the force from which the sun draws its energy has been loosed against those who brought war to the Far East . . . surrender . . . unconditional surrender . . .*

But even in this third decade of peace, Bering understood not much more of the victors' language than a few commands and some scraps of songs by army bands, and so beneath flaming bouquets of fireworks, he felt thrilled to ride toward an illumined, radiant Brand, and had no idea that during the two days of his trip across the Stony Sea, the world had come to an end on an island named Honshu.

Nagoya. All alone with the terror for which, in the wake of the news, this name now stood, Lily stayed well ahead of her escorts. Every hurricane had a name, the voice bawled from her radio, and from now on *Nagoya* would be the name of the greatest firestorm in the history of warfare. The emperor of Japan had left his palace. Accompanied by his defeated generals, he had boarded the battleship USS *Missouri*. There he had made a long and silent bow and then signed the unconditional surrender. After more than twenty years of war, unconditional surrender!

As the mule crossed a steel bridge illuminated by crook-neck lamps and then plodded on toward the first houses of Brand, the radio reception became so clear that Lily turned the volume down. Between reports of the Japanese surrender and excerpts from barked oratory, the army stations broadcast not only marches and hymns but also, over and over for hours on end, an old hit tune: "Lay that pistol down, babe, lay that pistol down. . . ."

At the end of the bridge loomed warehouses, with colorful neon inscriptions flowing around them and long lines of trucks standing before them. Lily brought her mule to a stop next to a row of trailers loaded with rolls of cable and turned around to her escorts for the first time in a good while. They were far behind, still on the other side of the river, a blackness rushing through the sheen of the bridge. Bering noticed that Lily had stopped. He waved. Lily gave him no signal, but she waited. Now, finally, she was waiting for him.

Cars! Trucks! Bering had never seen rigs in such numbers. As if these shimmering rows of semis, dump trucks, and tractor-trailers were lined up beside the warehouses in honor of his arrival in the lowlands, he rode across the bridge and toward the parking lot, and withstood the temptation to dismount and check them out, truck by truck.

His father was as indifferent to the sight of these vehicles as to the fireworks and festivities, the noise of which could be heard as far as the river. From the glow beyond the warehouses, march music was clearly audible now; a tracer rocket ascended howling above the corrugated tin roofs, but the old man did not inquire, said not a word, and no longer held fast to his son, either, but sat on the horse with arms dangling—a weary, endlessly weary rider. He raised his head only once, when suddenly the ring of iron could be heard above all the festive noise, the clang of train cars being shunted and banging together, the clank of switches, the screech of brake shoes. And then, like a phantom from some forgotten era, a locomotive steamed past the warehouses and disappeared into the darkness so quickly that for a moment even Bering thought it was only a mirage. But then there was no doubt. Between the warehouses ran shining tracks, behind these buildings lay Brand's central station. Trains rolled from Brand out into the world.

Lily gave just a preoccupied nod when Bering asked, "The railroad?"—the way someone does who is learning to pronounce a new word. She pointed into the darkness where the locomotive had vanished. "Move out!" Down this ramp, then across the embankment. . . . She knew a shortcut that led between sidings, rusty freight cars, and signal boxes to the middle of the city, to the army base, to the Big Hospital. Although none of the hate and contempt she had shown Bering in the field of sinkholes was evident now, she still spoke only directions, orders: "Move out." "Halt." "Straight ahead." . . .

Before the riders left the deserted railroad yards to venture into triumphant Brand, Lily permitted Bering's horse to pull up close to her mule again: "Halt." Up ahead there, by that loading dock—Bering was to leave his weapon. There, under an iron trapdoor covered with coal dust, was a hiding place she had often used for similar purposes. If a military patrol found a weapon on a civilian, safe-conduct papers issued by Moor's secretary and even a letter of authorization by the Dog King would not be much help. Brand was not Moor. In Brand there were no kings. In Brand the army ruled. The walls had eyes here.

Throw away another weapon? Bury Major Elliot's precious pistol, Ambras's pistol, *his* pistol, in a filthy hole in a railroad yard? The bodyguard didn't want to do it. Even if Lily hated him forever and the Dog King no longer needed him and there was nothing left to protect and nothing more to save than his own hide, he would never again expose himself to this world unarmed—never. He kept his weapon well hidden. It was the secret behind his new, superior strength. He could attack—not simply flee, not simply defend himself. He could wound. He could lame. He could kill. No, *he* would ride armed, all the way to the Big Hospital and even to Army Headquarters. And on a night like this what military patrol would care about a rider sitting astride a plow horse loaded down with baggage and a slumped-over old man? Brand was celebrating. And there were lots of wretched riders like him.

Lots? Lily pointed with a hasty gesture back at the railroad tracks and the parked trucks. There were lots of riders only where there were no tracks, no roads, no vehicles. Brand was not Moor. . . . Bering still didn't want to be without his weapon for even a single day? Fine. "Move on." She had warned him.

The journey to the Big Hospital was a ride through a triumphant army camp. In the city's large squares, open fires were blazing, above which poultry turned on spits. Spicy soups and punch steamed in the kettles of the field kitchens amid pressing throngs of civilians and soldiers. At the main gate of the Stellamour Barracks—or so people in the crowd by the kettles said—they were even giving away cans of small beer.

In the squares and on the streets, every man was a victor. Some of them offered the riders from Moor a glass of schnapps or punch and shouted jokes after them, and when Lily declined their invitations, drank to the health of the poor mule that had to carry such a prude. "Straight ahead." Bering knew that these shouting men were insulting Lily, but he did not respond as he would have in Moor at such a moment. He did nothing to help her. He did not threaten the shouters. He rode past them as if he were following some woman or other, some stranger who knew the town and was showing him the way.

In the throng of this great festival, an armed man would

probably have remained unnoticed even if he had not carried his weapon as well hidden as Ambras's bodyguard did. Lily had been wrong—there were other riders here. Not just mounted military police—before whom the crowd parted, though they kept right on drinking, talking, and laughing—but also an entire cavalcade, a caravan, whose horses, donkeys, and mules carried heavy loads much like those borne by the animals of the newcomers from Moor. Were they refugees?

Bering quickly lost sight of these riders amid the brilliance of the city. Brand—it was a rushing sequence of images. And although the fireworks had died out and only stray tracer rockets still ascended above the roofs, all the streets, houses, and squares were lit as bright as day. Neon lights flowed past, stoplights swayed above intersections—a flashing play of color above the crowd, through which flag-decorated jeeps and limousines drifted like honking barges on a languid river of heads, shoulders, faces. And the crookneck lamps of a boulevard illumined even the treetops, lavishing, wasting light where only sleeping pigeons were perched. Electric light everywhere!

Brand squandered light so prodigally that even the spots and holes in Bering's vision grew brighter and seemed transformed into mere blurs of deep darkness spilling over into a gray now rimmed by transparence. In Brand even a gas station gleamed like a shrine, and all the riches and overabundance of the low-lands lay displayed in store windows or under spotlights—here an illuminated fountain, a waterworks spraying light, there a façade of diagonal neon lines and antenna trees draped with flashing lights. . . . And displayed in a department-store window the size of a stage were heaped pyramids of fruits he had never seen before, mannequins in shimmering pajamas, shoes in all colors, candy boxes, and silver-plated gadgets—and rising up out of the chaos of all those wares was a wall of light, a flickering rampart built of nothing but television screens! A wall of glowing images.

Move on!

No, Bering simply *had* to stop here. He nudged his father.

"Look." But the old man was too exhausted. He didn't even raise his head. He didn't hear him.

Look. On all the television screens in the wall—there must have been thirty or more—were pictures of a festive city, its houses draped in flags, its avenues and streets hung with lanterns. Pagodas. Gardens. Wooden temples. Then people beside conveyor belts. People in huge factory halls. Industry. A harbor—cranes, silos. A lighthouse. Battleships. Breakwaters—surf crashing beyond.

From a battery of loudspeakers around the edge of the window, the same voice that Bering had heard on Lily's radio was bawling Nagoya and Japan and other names over the heads of a noisy audience that was slowly gathering now at the window, attracted by the bawling voice and the pictures.

Move on.

And suddenly the festive city and its harbor vanished behind a sun that rose and set again immediately in a pillar of cloud, set in an immense mushroom that rolled skyward out of the depths of the earth, ripped the sky open, seemed to tower up into the blackness of space. . . . The wall went dark and as flickering light returned, it showed the sea aflame, a charred coastline, smoldering tree trunks with no ruins behind them, only basements, foundations as far as the horizon. Black arms of cranes, the lost blade of a windmill or turbine, a statue—a metal god or general—half-melted, half-fused with the blackened rubble. No people anywhere.

And then, to the applause of the spectators at the window, who acted as if they were quite familiar with these pictures, a small, stooped man in a black formal coat climbed the gangway of a ship, took a seat at a card table surrounded by military men hung with medals, and wrote something in a book. The audience hooted. Then the stooped man in the formal coat faded and, to the American national anthem, the light of Nagoya erupted once again—a flash became a star and a star became a chromium white nova that froze in frame at the zenith of its blinding power.

Move on. Bering could barely tear himself away from this light, which pierced and brightened even the holes in his vision. It was like staring into the arc light of the welder at the forge, into a garish, painful brightness that even through closed eyelids revealed the outline of his tools or of his own hand. The image of an exploding sun was transformed into a mere backdrop, scenery for a uniformed reporter, who read the news in the language of the victors—and only then did Bering finally turn away and search for Lily and spot her far ahead, almost at the end of the street, saw her outside a well-lit entrance above which shone a red neon cross. The Big Hospital. They had reached their goal.

The crowd at the window began to disperse. The reporter was reading names and numbers that were evidently no longer news in Brand: the explosive power of the bomb in megatons, the total presumed dead, the number of vaporized buildings, the temperature of the charred earth. . . . None of it news by now.

But the unsuspecting rider—with the neon cross ahead of him and the flickering wall of the display window at his back—was gradually, slowly catching on. Directly in his path was a man selling lottery tickets, and, bending down from his saddle, Bering asked about the chromium white light and the city and names he could barely pronounce.

"Na . . . go . . . ya?" The man selling lottery tickets did not have much time for this gypsy or stableboy or groom or whatever he was, and appeared not to understand his question. Nagoya? Everybody knew that. What hole had he spent the last few days in? Or didn't he have ears? Eyes? The bomb. Two days ago. The emperor. Unconditional surrender!

The man selling lottery tickets tossed catchwords, scraps of old news, to the ignorant fellow on the horse and laughed when it appeared the rider still had not caught on: "Are you from the moon? It's peace, moonman. They've beat them all. It's the Peace of Japan. They've won!"

CHAPTER 27

MORBUS KITAHARA

WOLF HOURS. IN MOOR THE HOURS AFTER
midnight were called wolf hours. . . . That made
him think of Moor now.

Lily was gone. She was sleeping in one of these buildings here.
She was lying behind one of these windows in the dark. Alone.
Or in the arms of a stranger. That he didn't know.

His father was gone. Lay practically buried under army blankets at the head of a long row of iron-frame beds in one of the
barracks of the Big Hospital. That he knew. He had seen him
lying there himself. Had left him in that empty hospital ward.
Under those blankets.

And the mule? The horse? Lily had taken the horse with her,
too. Was the horse that had carried him across the Stony Sea to
the lowlands and warmed him with its great body—was it
standing in a stall? A barn? Given all the many machines, were
there any stalls left in Brand?

Deep in this night of triumph now, as he was pushed and
pulled along by throngs that would not settle down till morning,
Bering realized he was alone. He drifted along in the crowd,

drank schnapps and cold punch from half-empty cups that had been left here and there, ate cold scraps of meat from paper plates before stray dogs could lick them clean, joined some drunks on a folding bench before the podium in a festival tent, and fell asleep sitting there, awakened with a start, let himself be carried farther along, and tried to stay close to the jeeps, trucks, and limousines that stood unguarded in the streets. Cars in front of every house. He was in the lowlands. He had reached the lowlands. He was in Brand, late at night, surrounded by people, voices, light, music. But he was alone.

Now, finally at his goal, was what he felt called longing? He longed for the black shores of the lake. For the silence of the Villa Flora at night and for the warm bodies of the dogs when, as so often, they pressed close against him in the wolf hours. Was Ambras sitting in his wicker chair on the veranda now? The night here was summery and mild. But up there?

Sometimes the festival spat him out. Then he crouched like a beggar beside the gatekeeper's shed at a factory, tried to make out the schedule in the glass shelter of a bus stop, strayed from dead-end streets into backyards, grew curious and rummaged through garbage cans until somewhere a window was thrown open and a suspicious voice shooed him off. He stepped back out into artificial light.

When he stumbled and fell with exhaustion in the driveway of a movie palace, where music and dramatic voices rose from the air ducts, he found it felt good to lie there on a trampled patch of grass, but thought of returning to the Big Hospital and accepting the bed one of the guards had offered him.

"Any cot in block four. Take any cot in block four. Barrack seven, block four. They're all vacant there."

The doorman, a former miner from Leys, had handed Bering's safe-conduct papers through a sliding glass window to another man, had clapped him on the shoulder and rattled on about how he had fled Leys years before and signed up with the army. Then he had asked about Moor and a fisherman whose name

Bering didn't recognize, and wouldn't stop talking and asking questions and happened to mention that block four was intended for the evacuees from Moor, no doubt about it, that's where the people of Moor were to be quartered once the army took over the lake country for maneuvers. . . . A sergeant—he was sitting in the guard room at a desk behind the glass partition and had greeted Lily like an old acquaintance—stamped their papers and barked an order to the talkative fellow, which to Bering sounded like: "Shut up!"

Block four. No, no weariness, however great, could force him back to those empty barracks. Was he a vagrant who had to beg the army for soup and a blanket? Leftover schnapps in paper cups was keeping him warm. Punch was keeping him warm. He was the bodyguard for the Dog King. He was the protector of the most feared man in Moor—no, he was the *reason* for that fear.

"Be not afraid." He babbled a phrase from the blacksmith's wife's Bible and felt under his jacket for the pistol hidden there. *Be not afraid.* No, he would definitely not go back to the Big Hospital before morning. Block four. He was in the lowlands after all. In the heart of vast wealth. A hospital was no great loss—or an army base, either. He would rather sleep under the shadow of movie posters, on a damp patch of grass drenched with spilled beer and wine, and listen to voices from the black air shafts and let strange dogs sniff at him.

He closed his eyes and had to open them again at once because no sooner had the world vanished behind his eyelids than it began to spin around him. He was drunk. The speed with which the darkness whirled about him made him sick to his stomach. "Attention!" he said, mimicking a voice from one of the court-yards at the Big Hospital, and opened his eyes wide and concentrated so hard on his mouth to keep from slurring his words that it made his lips very narrow, turned his mouth into a beak: "Atteeention! Open! Eeeyes open!"

He giggled. He lay on the damp ground and was too exhausted to fall asleep. But when the spinning world and the nausea let go of him, he was suddenly seized again with a spasm of rage like the one that had overcome him in the hospital guard room and driven him back out into the night.

Block four! And did block four include those beautiful lowland hotels, maybe, the ones people in Moor gushed on about while they dug through the ruins of the Bellevue for glazed tiles and other still usable construction materials? With each step he took through this city of lights, new wonders leaped out at him about which the idiots in Moor and Haag had not the vaguest. Lily! Lily, sure. She knew all this. She had dropped off two half-blind fools at the Big Hospital and then retreated to one of these high-rises, to one of these shining towers, any one of which cast more light into the night than all of Moor together.

Lily. *She* wasn't sleeping in block four, was she? She had vanished from the guard room quick enough. "I'll be back tomorrow morning." Lily. She knew all this. Had always known that all the bullshit about penitence, about reflecting and remembering, was a giant hoax. *Never forget. Our fields grow the future.* One big hoax.

Cars, tracks, runways! High-tension lines, department stores! Garbage cans full of delicacies, whole kettles full of punch—and so much meat that even the stray mutts got fat on it. Was that the penitence, the punishment that the great Bringer of Peace had prescribed for the lowlands? Was that their punishment? Was it? Shit, goddamn bullshit.

Had there been no camps of barracks in the lowlands? No lime pits full of corpses? Brand and Hall and Greater Vienna and all those other so-called Reconstruction Zones on the map at the secretary's office in Moor—hadn't they also sent soldiers into war against Stellamour and his allies? Had a few windblown villages up in the mountains been the only source for the army of Stellamour's enemies, been the only towns that believed in a final victory—until that army had been stamped into the ground?

So, then, it was probably only fair that Moor and the lake

country were still doing penance now, two and a half decades after the war, still doing penance, while the lowlands got a fireworks show and had a row of limousines standing in every alley. Only fair, right?

All for monuments, all for shrines and memorial plaques—that had always been the slogan whenever the largest blocks of granite had been dragged off from Moor Quarry down to the lowlands, back when the granite had still been flawlessly thick, not brittle and banded with fragile streaks. All for peace. All for the grand memorial enterprise. . . . Bullshit.

So where were the plaques? The monuments? The inscriptions? There were fancy façades of highly polished primal stone, built as if to last for eternity, but these were certainly not temples of remembrance like the ones the secretary of Moor invoked in his holiday speeches—and there were no rows of candles and torches inside, either, no blocks of chiseled names and plaques with quotes by the Bringer of Peace like in lake country shrines, but . . . hell only knew what these palaces contained—bank safes, stockpiled goods, casinos, army cathouses, and who knew what all. . . .

There was a Peace Plaza here, too, with a monument to Stellamour in the middle, but at best it was a reminder that the high-court justice in his residence on the island of Manhattan was sinking deeper into senility every day. *Never forget!* The ancient geezer sat huddled in his wheelchair, read off two stumbling speeches a year, and probably couldn't even remember his own name.

"All a hoax!" Bering yelled at the wall of posters displaying a gigantically enlarged movie hero. "All a hoax!"

And if the penitents in Moor or Eisenau blackened their stupid faces with soot ten times a year just because some army lackey of a secretary would then treat them to a few coupons for coffee and tobacco or another sack of horsebeans, at least they still *held* their damned processions. And although the Grand Inscription at the quarry was vanishing among piles of gravel and overgrown moss and gradually falling into ruin, at least the Grand Hotel, the Bellevue, the Stella Polaris, and all the other villas and doghouses were falling into ruin along with it! Into ruin! And weren't rising up out of the rubble adorned with neon writing and clad in polished granite like the towers of Brand!

Some justice—the lowlands sparkled and shone like a huge amusement park, while up there, on the steamer dock in Moor and under the cliffs of the Blind Shore, black flags were raised on anniversaries, banners were unrolled: *Never forget. Thou shalt not kill.* Bravo! The idiots in the Societies of Penitence droned on for hours on end, rattling off commandments, dragging them over the fields on embroidered banners—while shining advertising slogans spilled across the façades of Brand. In Moor, there were ruins. In Brand, department stores. The great penitential spectacle of Stellamour, Bringer of Peace, was surely staged only where there wasn't much else to stage—and nothing to win. Long live High-Court Justice Stellamour.

"Beat it, you mangy mongrel!" Bering yelled, and banged his fist on the muzzle of a scruffy terrier that was trying to lick his face. The mutt bounded off yowling into the night.

Somewhere in the darkness, high above in the Stony Sea, lay Moor, cut off, mired in the past, while Brand basked in the electric glow of a lovely future.

And Moor's future? Moor would soon be spangled with light, too—from flashing gun barrels, bursting grenades, pillars of fire. . . . Block four. Target zone Moor. Deployment area Moor. Maneuver terrain Moor. *That* was the future. Artillery grenades for the ruins of the Grand Hotel. Rockets for the Bellevue. Bombs for the lakeside resort, for the weather tower, for the Villa Flora. . . . The future of Moor and of all the villages along the lake was exactly like the night of bombs that *he*, the servant in a house of dogs, listed as the date of birth on his safe-conduct papers. Moor's future was the past.

Never forget.

Forget it all.

Was he sleeping?

Was he merely dreaming his exhaustion? His rage?

Bering did not stir even when, sometime after the end of the movie palace's last show, laughing filmgoers walked right over him. He was dreaming about dogs. Dreamt that Ambras's pack was pouncing on the food he ladled into their bowls night after night. He lay on the damp ground and had just put the last spoonful into the bowls, when the terrier he had struck crept back out of the darkness, cowering, cautious, and slowly dragged away the plastic sack of food scraps that he was holding in his ladle hand.

The dog sensed its enemy's deep sleep and so did not flee with its prize, but ripped the sack apart while still close to the hand that had struck it earlier, and devoured sandwich halves, sausages, pretzels, and even the dried pears Bering had gathered up as he passed by the victors' banquet tables.

When the thief's victim was awakened at dawn by a vigorous shove, he saw black laced boots near his eyes—and then, far above the sheen of leather and dark against a brighter sky, two faces gazing down at him.

Military police.

"Your papers!" the first face ordered. "Where are you from?" the second asked.

"Where am I . . . from?" A stabbing headache restored the memory of where he was. He rolled over on his side, yawned loudly, and was stretching like a dog, when a boot kicked him in the back.

"Get up!"

His clothes were wet with dew. Angry, hunched, and sore from his uncomfortable night, he stood before the two soldiers, rubbed his back, and looked at his tattered sack of provisions. "Didn't you have enough to eat already?" He was hungry. The soldiers didn't understand him.

His safe-conduct papers were wet, too. The patrol just wanted to see his safe-conduct papers. They weren't interested in his letter of authorization from the Dog King.

Bering smoothed the letter out and stuck it back into his jacket and suddenly felt the cold weight of his pistol.

But all the soldiers wanted was a piece of paper. They didn't frisk bums.

Did they even know where somebody was from when "Moor" was written on his safe-conduct papers? *Place of birth: Moor.* They had no idea. In one move he could have pulled his pistol from his jacket and shot them dead. They had no idea.

"From Moor?"

"From Moor," Bering said.

The darker of the two nodded, returned the safe-conduct papers, tapped his forefinger to his helmet, and climbed back into the jeep—its antennas whipped like fly-fishermen's rods. Then the tires ground the tattered sack of food deep into the soft earth.

Bering walked stiffly over to the display cases of the movie palace, where in brief, irregular spurts a fountain was spitting little jets into a metal basin. He washed his face and neck and, unable to control his thirst, drank the water, in which black leaves floated. The boggy brew burned his throat, burned his eyes.

Burned his eyes.

He had to get back to the hospital. *Morrison.* Yesterday in the guard room Lily had asked about a Morrison. Doc Morrison, the doorman from Leys had said with a laugh, could make the blind see again. He had to find this Morrison.

He got lost on the way back. He kept ending up at the river, and in the hazy distance he saw the steel beams of the bridge across which Lily had ridden ahead of him yesterday. Had he wandered so far last night? Was the spot where he slept out of the wind under the wall of posters really so far from the hospital where he had left his father? Its lights extinguished, the city lay in the morning sun. The few wreaths of light bulbs still shimmering in treetops and on façades seemed dull and powerless against the dazzling light. And yet all of Brand—its streets, its squares—was still in an uproar.

Victory! Unconditional surrender! Cars, vehicles everywhere. People everywhere—staggering revelers from the night before next to early risers headed for work with impassive faces, delivery men, chauffeurs, clearing the way with curses and honks. And, above all, soldiers. Soldiers marching in formation or in full battle gear aboard open troop transporters, and soldiers strolling along in little groups, not marching anywhere—gesticulating, laughing warriors who had won the battle. . . . Some wore snapshots of women on their caps or on the camouflage nets of their helmets, and attached to the antenna of one armored car was a flag on which that mushroom cloud had been painted in signal red. The cloud of Nagoya. Like a comic-strip balloon, it surrounded a single demand printed in an almost childish hand:

TAKE US
HOME

The army wanted to go home. Stellamour's army, which for decades had fought alongside ever-changing allies on tangled fronts that crossed every longitude and latitude and had gained the victory and left behind a Peace of Oranienburg here, a Peace of Jerusalem there, a Peace of Mosul, of Nha-trang or Kwangju, of Denpasar, Havana, Lubango, Panama, Santiago, and Antananarivo, peaces, peaces everywhere . . . and in Japan this army had forced even an emperor to his knees and in token of its invincibility had branded a mushroom on the sky above Nagoya. And now, now the army wanted to go home at last. *Take us home.*

And however hellish the fire of that bomb—whose resplendence could be seen on television screens in a display window or in a newsreel at the movies and even pictured on sandwich boards carried by men struggling through the morning crowds—

for both Brand's inhabitants *and* its occupiers, the mushroom cloud above Nagoya had apparently been only a sign that the final enemy in the World War had now been defeated. And what, except a World Peace, could follow such a war?

A man dressed in white, who stood on a park bench in the pose of a preacher, was roaring through a megaphone at his audience as they hurried by, and he, too, kept proclaiming an endless, final peace that would make flowers bloom on every battlefield, in every occupied zone, and ultimately even from the ashes of Japan. Oranienburg! Jerusalem! Basra! Kwangju! Nha-trang! Mosul! . . . From his megaphone the names of all the many armistices and peace treaties sounded no different from the litanies of a penitential procession through the reeds of Moor. But the beacon of Nagoya! this preacher shouted, the beacon of Nagoya was the rising sun of World Peace. For if the time had come at last in which the destructive force of a single bomb was enough to make the most stubborn of enemies capitulate, then in the future the mere threat of nuclear fire, indeed the mere mention of Nagoya, would suffice to turn all fists into open hands and to nip every war in the bud.

"Hurrah! Sure will. Bravo. Long live Stellamour!" bawled a listener draped with paper roses, stuffed animals, and other shooting-gallery prizes from the previous night's festivities, and, stumbling in the crowd, he tried to keep his balance by flinging his arms around Bering's neck—who pushed him away angrily. Bering's head was booming. He turned away from the preacher's shouts, but for a long time he could still hear the names of those many peace treaties behind his back—until his own footsteps and the footsteps of the crowd grew louder than any voice. The litter of the previous night—broken bottles and glasses, smashed paper cups—crunched underfoot. The squares and streets were strewn with glass. Every step sounded like ice breaking.

When he finally found the red neon cross above the entrance to the Big Hospital again, the sun was standing high above the rooftops. Thunderclouds were massing over the mountains in the south. It was probably already storming in Moor; at the first rumble of thunder some of the dogs fled into the dark hallways of the Villa Flora.

The neon cross had been turned off and the sergeant who had been on such easy terms with Lily yesterday had vanished. Not a trace of Lily. Only the miner from Leys was still sitting behind the sliding glass window in the guard room. He raised a hand, saluted with a grin. "How was the festival?"

Bering did not return his greeting and wasted no words on last night, but asked about Lily. Then about Morrison.

"The girl from Moor? No idea," the guard said. And Morrison hadn't appeared for work today yet. He probably got lost last night, too. No wonder. Everybody had really been—

"When's he due in?" Bering interrupted.

"You can wait over there for him," the doorman said, pointing to a one-story building painted white and surrounded by blossoming broom. "In the Blind Clinic. Some others are waiting there already."

Late in the morning it began to rain. It was a warm summer downpour that washed the blossoms from the broom and the first yellow leaves from the crown of a maple tree shading the entrance to the Big Hospital. Bering sat on a wooden folding chair between patients who had bandaged heads, bandaged eyes, or wore dark glasses, and he stared through the Blind Clinic's barred windows out onto the same street down which he had escorted his father to block four just last evening. A city within the city. The Big Hospital was a city within the city, the doorman had said—the sick and wounded from three different zones, plus all the displaced persons, lots of misery, too many poor people. . . .

Was he the only civilian in the barrack? Some of the people waiting were talking, murmuring in the army's language, others in the dialect of the lowlands. They all wore the same smocks, the same shirts—institutional garb. No one spoke to him. He appeared to be the only one without a visible eye problem.

It would have been better to wait for Morrison in the guard room with the talkative guy from Leys rather than here with these people with eye diseases—or were those injuries? But the rain—falling in such sheets that even the nearby guard house had vanished—and a drowsy numbness prevented him from standing up and leaving. And where would he go? Without Lily. Would he be any better at finding his way alone on the mule tracks of the Stony Sea than alone in the streets of Brand? How long would he need to get to Moor on foot, alone? Moor lay in another time. Moor lay above the clouds.

"So you're from Moor."

Bering had nodded off. He had not noticed the door opening, had not noticed anything—the suddenly louder gushing downpour, the low voices that greeted the dripping-wet newcomer. Bering had been up there, way up there, alone in the Stony Sea.

In front of him stood a short, pudgy man in uniform, a white coat thrown over his shoulders.

"Morrison?" Bering got to his feet.

"Who else?" the man said. He hardly came up to Bering's chin.

"Dr. Morrison?"

"Medic Morrison. Only my blind dates here call me *Doc*. But at least they realize that Morrison does the work of a doctor. . . . Hey, Carthy," he called back over his shoulder, never taking his eyes off Bering, "tell the man from Moor who's treating those puppy-dog eyes of yours and has guaranteed you'll get a sharper look at your Miss America than ever before?"

"Sir, Doc Morrison, sir!" said a little man with a wide bandage across both eyes. He laughed.

"That woman from Moor is always bringing us surprises down from the mountains," Morrison said, and gazed so steadily into Bering's eyes that Bering had to lower them. "What do you say, Carthy, this time she's brought us a Moorman who's trying to go blind. The woman from Moor says this guy here is trying to go blind. . . ."

The man Morrison called Carthy said nothing. A few other patients started to laugh.

Dumbfounded, Bering stood frozen in place in front of the short man and was still incapable of moving even when the medic suddenly stepped up to him and with one quick, assured gesture spread Bering's eyes wide with thumb and forefinger, as if checking the pupils of someone unconscious or dead.

The sudden draft, the chill of evaporating tears was almost painful, but before Bering could collect himself, raise a hand in self-defense, even turn his head away, Morrison had already let go. "Is that right, what the woman from Moor tells me? Are you trying to go blind? . . . Well then, come with me."

The matter-of-factness with which the short, pudgy soldier touched him, and spoke of the most private things right out in public, made Bering blush. He stood there speechless among the patients, while every eye in the waiting room that was not bandaged or swollen shut was directed at him. And yet in these moments of utter confusion, he also felt a strange sense of relief. It was as if not only his most secret fears, but all his secrets, too, became little and insignificant in the presence of this little man, and he would not have been surprised if Morrison had also asked about a chicken thief buried in the rocks or about the dreams that tormented him when he lay beside sleeping dogs in the salons of the Villa Flora.

This medic knew about the fear of blindness. He also knew about conditions in Moor, and he spoke of Lily as an old friend. . . . But the only thing in which he had a passionate interest—as Bering would come to learn that morning in the Big Hospital—was the human eye.

"What are you waiting for? Come with me," Morrison said impatiently and took hold of Bering's arm and led him out into a narrow entrance hall glistening with wet footprints. Bering did not shake his arm free, but let himself be led like some distracted child down the hall and into another room—a room with so many glass cases, display stands, bookcases, mysterious instruments, and glass models of the eye in various sizes that there was hardly room left for a table and two chairs.

"Have a seat."

The table was a heavy plate of glass laid across two crates of books and piled high with magazines and bundled papers. The rain rattled against the panes of the only window. A multicolored glass model of a human head gleamed among the piles of paper—eyeballs lay like marbles in glassy sockets.

"Transparent," Morrison said, and rapped a knuckle on the brow of the glass head. "Everything should be transparent. What do we have eyes for. Eyes! The only thing about our body, you see, that lets us infer something like consciousness. Close your eyes, and you already look like a corpse, everything about you simply looks like meat for the slaughterhouse, to be sold by the pound. . . . Keep your seat, my boy. Look at this chart—no, not at that diagram, at this chart, *here*. . . . What do you see? Read aloud what you see."

And if in the waiting room and on the way down the hall, Morrison had asked questions and gone right on talking without waiting for answers, here amid this chaotic collection of medical gadgets, models, and books, he now transformed himself into an attentive listener who nodded at every word Bering read from the chart. The nodding medic led his patient line by line through the chart's trellis of ever-smaller symbols, led him to the end of a meaningless text that served only to test visual acuity.

Bering read. Smoothly at first, then ever more slowly. And as the shrinking letters blurred before his eyes or sank into the pitfalls of his vision, he instinctively switched from reading to explaining, described the darkened zones of his eyesight and, for the second time since departing from Moor, revealed the secret of his perforated world.

Morrison nodded. Nothing seemed to surprise him. He was familiar with such worlds. Whatever Bering described—the iridescent rim and the dark center of his flawed eyesight or the way parallel lines looked distorted against the white background on a chart—Morrison would nod, interrupt sometimes for greater detail, or supplement the description of a symptom if Bering got stuck. Morrison knew everything.

As if hypnotized by the confidence and assurance with which this little man approached his secret illness, Bering followed each instruction: laid his chin in a metal head-support and pressed his forehead against its cool bar; stared into the bundled light of an ophthalmoscope, then into the rays of a slit-lamp; held his head immobile and merely blinked when Morrison dropped an anesthetic into his eyes with a pipette to dilate the pupils and make the cornea insensitive to the discomfort of the examination. When Bering batted his eyelids, the narcotic drops bathed his eyes, leaving a veil over his iris through which he could see only phantoms. His pupils grew as large as those of a hunter in the night. He felt only the pressure, but none of the parching cold of the three-mirror lens when the medic gazed through its eyepiece into the dark wells of his eyes.

Morrison's eyes remained invisible behind the polished lenses, but his open mouth was so close that Bering could smell the strange breath.

"Foveal reflex weak . . . metamorphopsia . . . confluent edema of the retina . . . subretinal exudate . . ." While he let the bands of light from the slit-lamp glide across the back of his patient's eyes, Morrison took up an arcane conversation with himself, muttering the names of symptoms and reflexes as if building a mosaic of an illness word by word: "vesicles in the macula . . . central matrix right, paracentral matrix left . . . micropsia. Positive scotoma . . ."

Bering did not understand a word. He thought of the forge. That was the way he had talked to himself, too, when running a checklist on a defective engine. How tired he was. He stared sleepily into the light—phantoms behind opaque glass. Shadows under the ice. Distant, unreadable—this was probably how his father had learned to see the world as his eyes grew worse over the years and he cursed what he saw: *Read me what's on this damned flyer, I can't read it. What's on this box, on this poster, I can't see, damn it. Read it to me.*

"Retinopathy . . . chorioretinitis centralis serosa . . ." Morrison's murmurs sounded now like the Latin litanies in the prayer book of the blacksmith's wife.

"Hey, don't fall asleep. Do you sleep with your eyes open? The fellow sleeps with his eyes open. Roll up your sleeve, my boy. I need your arm."

Without changing position, hunched against the head-support and the three-mirror lens, bending toward the light, Bering pushed up his jacket sleeve. He barely felt the prick of the injection needle.

"It's only dye. A kind of coloring," he heard Morrison say as something icy or searing hot dissolved in his veins. "Just for contrast. It flows through your veins, heart, and carotid artery directly to the eyes and makes it easier to see the holes in the deepest layers of the retina. Harmless magic. You'll turn yellow for a few hours. Yellow. That's all. A few hours of circulation will disperse the dye. Your blood will rinse you white again. . . . Now lay your head back—way back, you hear . . ."

Bering obeyed. He leaned back. Closed his eyes. Holes in his retina. So there really were holes. He could feel sweat bead on his forehead.

For minutes nothing was audible except the breathing of the medic and the gushing rain in the background. Then Morrison ordered him back to the lens. Back to the light.

"So then," he said, and to Bering each word felt like a cold draft across his brow. "Red clouds. Reddish, unmistakable clouds. Don't move. Hold still."

"Clouds?" Bering spoke through clenched teeth. The weight of his head, the weight of his brain, his eyes, his cheekbones, pressed his chin against the support and forced his jaw closed. "What clouds?"

"Mushrooms. Mushroom clouds," Morrison said. "Or jellyfish. Have you ever seen a jellyfish floating through the twilight of the sea?"

"I've never seen the sea."

"Unmistakable. Wonderful," Morrison said, and there was something of the joy of discovery in his voice. "The smokestack phenomenon. The cloud of smoke . . . You've never been to the shore? But you've seen those pictures from Japan, haven't you? The mushroom over Nagoya. Jellyfish or mushroom cloud. Pick whichever comparison you like. The edema in your retina, the spots in your eyes, are the same shape as either one—jellyfish or mushroom. It's a typical symptom."

"Of what? What's wrong with my eyes? What sort of disease is it?" Bering automatically raised up and the medic did not force him back now into his hunched-over position, but moved away from his lenses, stood up, and switched out the light. Although the anesthetic was wearing off and the fog was lifting, Bering saw Morrison's face only as a bright oval, with a dark smudge for a mouth, dark smudges for eyes.

"You want to know what your problem is?" the foggy face said. "You ask me? You need to ask yourself, my boy. What does a man like you stare at? What is it you can't get out of your head? I've seen spots like that in the eyes of infantrymen and sharpshooters, of people who went half-crazy in their tank trenches or who spent weeks lying in ambush behind enemy lines, until they started seeing cross hairs in the shaving mirror, on their own face, you understand?

"All of them people who, whether out of fear or hate or iron vigilance, stared a hole in their own eyes, holes in their own retinas, leaky spots, *vesicles* through which tissue fluid seeps and forms blisters between the membranes of your eyeball and creates those shifting, mushroom-shaped clouds, the holes in your vision—call them what you like, murky spots that slowly merge and darken your eyesight.

"But you? . . . What have you been staring at? You're not a trench soldier or an AWOL sharpshooter. Are you? Up there in Moor you pelt people at best with beets or stones. Have you been

staring at a sugar beet? Or have you been keeping some enemy in
the notch of your slingshot? Or some girl? Don't drive yourself
crazy. Whatever it is, let it go. Look at something else."

"How dark can it get? What happens to these people?" Bering
tugged his jacket sleeve down over his arm and used it to wipe
the sweat from his brow. "Do they go blind?"

"Blind? Nonsense. No one goes blind. They all see a few spots,
creep out from their hiding places, out of the trenches, and come
running for fear of the dark. To me. Just like you did. Then they
sit there where you're sitting. And then they realize that they've
survived, that for now and temporarily and somehow they have
survived, you understand? And then they calm down. And what
happens? The clouds pass. Not right away. But in time. Over the
course of weeks, sometimes months. The clouds dissolve, their
vision grows brighter, and in the end no more than two or three
delicate traces of fear are left on the retina. That's all. I've seen it
happen. Over my thirty hospital years, I've seen it happen. And
it'll happen to you, too."

"And now? What should I do now?"

"Nothing," Morrison said. "Wait."

"But the spots . . . they've increased."

"They always increase. And then they disappear."

"And what if they don't?"

"Then you'd be one in a thousand," Morrison said. "Then I've
been mistaken. Then you'd be the exception. Then it would go
dark. Forever. For the rest of your life, then, you'll see the world
as if through blackened glass. But you are no exception, my boy.
You, too, are just one of many. I've never been mistaken yet with
eyes like yours. Do whatever you want. Lay hellebore on your
closed eyelids or swallow a fistful of pills every morning, run
around in circles at full moon or speak the name of your disease a
hundred times into a hole in the ground—it all does the same
good. What you need is time. You just have to wait. . . ."

"And the name? For the hole in the ground. Speak what name
a hundred times?"

"Mushroom or jellyfish. Latin or Japanese. Pick a name: *Chori-*

oretinitis centralis serosa, if you have a good memory. And if your memory has holes, too, then think of a Japanese eye doctor, his name was Kitahara. He described your kind of darkened vision long before you were born. Drink a glass to his health, relax, and just call your couple of spots Kitahara, my boy. *Morbus Kitahara.*"

CHAPTER 28

A BIRD IN FLAMES

BERING RAN THROUGH THE RAIN. HE
stormed down the street, past rows of barracks on the
grounds of the Big Hospital, past empty stretchers and
wheelchairs left out in the cloudburst, and sometimes he leapt
in mid-run, as if trying to fly away or reach up for a branch,
for a piece of fruit dangling above his head. But wherever he
reached there were no branches, no fruit. There was only the
dark, gushing sky.

Bering ran, and with every step, every throb of his pulse, his
heart pumped dyed blood through his veins and tiny bits of color
into his eyes, which were still numb from Morrison's anesthetic.
Yellow-skinned, stained to his fingertips with the contrast dye of
the exam, he ran along and his path had never looked more
blurred and fuzzy, and yet he could not hold back his laughter.
He laughed. He was happy.

Morbus Kitahara. This Japanese disease would not leave him
blind. Not blind! Doc Morrison had promised. The holes in his
world would disappear. He had only to wait. To have patience.
And the clouds above his field of vision would turn bright and

disappear, as if evaporated by the artificial sun above Nagoya.
Time. All he needed was time. The darkening of his sight was as
fleeting as this morning thunderstorm, whose sheets of water
soaked him to his yellow skin. Bright and brighter. It could take
weeks. At worst months. But he was no exception. He was one of
many. Doc Morrison had promised.

Bering ran. He did not realize he had run in the wrong direction until he had to slow down and finally stop to catch his
breath. He wanted out. Wanted Brand. Wanted to be in the
open. But what now emerged ahead of him out of sheets of rain
was not the gate of the Big Hospital, but a three-foot-high sign
on which stood just the number 4. Block four. Moor's future. In
his happiness he had got his directions switched. He had stormed
out of the Blind Clinic and run the same way he had walked with
his father the evening before, down the path that awaited everyone from Moor. The quarrymen, the saltworkers, the fishermen,
charcoal burners, and sugar-beet boilers of the lake country—all
of them, in the belief that they were on their way to freedom, to
the riches of the lowlands, would end up in block four of the Big
Hospital.

What stood there so black and menacing in the rain was the
barracks, wasn't it—where his father lay under army blankets at
the head of a long row of iron-frame beds? It had been cool in the
dark ward yesterday evening, cooler than outside under the
nighttime sky, and the dark had smelled of floor wax, of insect
powder and disinfectant. No, he didn't want to go back to that
ward. Not now, not ever. The warrior was in the army's care. But
Bering was on the move, in the open. Still breathing heavily, he
was about to turn around when he suddenly had to laugh again:
headed blindly in the wrong direction!

But as he slowly turned, there at the perimeters of his vision,
he thought he saw movement in one of the windows of the barracks, a shadow behind the sheets of rain. There behind a pane of
glass veined with tangled rivulets stood the old man. The warrior.
His father. Wrapped in blankets, he stood at the window. And
raised his arm now. And waved. He was holding a handkerchief,

some bright piece of cloth, in his hand and swinging it in great, slow arcs, as if standing at the railing of a ship and waving to land sinking away, left behind.

But no. There was no one there. It was only a torn blind, a curtain billowing in the draft. Bering wiped the water from his eyes. The window was dark and empty. He turned around. Began to run again. But he no longer leapt into the air or grabbed for invisible branches and fruit, but simply ran away.

"You can fly!"

Lily did not greet him or ask him about last night or even about Doc Morrison. The first thing that she called to him, when Bering obeyed the signal of a strange soldier behind the sliding glass window and entered the guard room at the hospital's front gate, was "You can fly!"

Lily was sitting alone with the soldiers. She had decked herself out with feathers and strings of freshwater pearls as if for a festival. The guard room was packed. The talkative mercenary from Leys was missing. The odor of wet clothes, cigarettes, schnapps, and coffee took Bering's breath away. More than a dozen soldiers were perched on or standing around the desk where the sergeant had stamped their safe-conduct papers yesterday evening. But no one was interested in the papers of a drenched civilian now. And the guy who had ordered him inside through the sliding glass window was also busy again, examining a fist-sized crystal, and did not even raise his head when Bering stepped in front of him. His signal had only been at Lily's request. It had been Lily who had ordered Bering inside. Lily had had him called.

Scattered over the desk were goods to be traded: a brightly polished bayonet, epaulets, belt buckles, a plummeting silver eagle, medals—all found in the topsoil of former battlegrounds. But there were other items, too: a beetle trapped in amber, rough emeralds, smoky topazes, mother-of-pearl, fossils from the Stony Sea. Deals were being made. Outside, by the tollgate at the entrance, a horse whinnied. Lily's animals were standing in the rain with their feedbags on. The packsaddles were empty.

"You've got half an hour," Lily said. "In half an hour a heli-

copter will be taking off for Moor. Your king is to get a visit from
the army. The army's taking you along. You can fly to the house
of dogs, or hike back alone on foot. I've got a couple of days'
business here yet and don't need somebody like you on the
return trip . . .

"He likes to shoot, you see," she said, suddenly turning to a
fair-haired man sitting beside her and pointing at Bering. "He
shoots at anything that moves."

Had Lily been drinking? A soldier kicked an empty bottle that
rolled across the floor and chinked as it struck the butt of an
assault rifle leaning against the wall.

"He shoots?" the fair-haired man asked. His bomber jacket
bore the black stripes of a captain. "What does he shoot with?"

"Stones," Lily said, and looked at Bering without smiling. "He
and his king have a whole lakeshore full of them."

Bering held firm under Lily's gaze. The vestiges of Morrison's
anesthetic that still blurred his vision also protected him from
her eyes.

"So, what will it be?" she said. "Fly or hike? The captain here
will take you to Moor."

Fly?

This wasn't flying.

What Bering felt barely an hour later, already high above the
airport at Brand, high above the first folds of the Stony Sea, was
not excitement at the first flight in his life, but disappointment.
This being lifted up, this crouching inside a dark shell pierced by
portholes and stinking of oil and sweat, this being rattled by the
lashing, roaring whirligig of rotor blades—it had a lot to do with
the limitations, the sluggishness, the disruptive engine noise of
every mechanism, but nothing to do with real flying, nothing to
do with the magic of a bird in flight, where the only sound was
the hissing sky under its pinions.

Wedged between soldiers in battle uniform, Bering crouched
in an armored helicopter and thought of the birds in the reeds at
Moor, of the bank swallows that each evening opened their beaks

wide to race through columns of swarming gnats—so swiftly that you could barely follow their flight with your eye.

Flying. On some other day and under different circumstances, he might have been excited by the mere sight of rows of military planes, standing wet and glistening with rain at the airport—fighter-bombers, their radar noses painted with predatory eyes and fangs. And outside the hangar—a good three times as large as that war ruin in Moor's Pilot Valley, with its bullet-riddled roof of corrugated tin—he had seen a whole squadron of helicopters, a swarm of dark gunships resting before battle, whose rotor blades, mounted gun-barrels, sponsons, and stabilizers made them look like monstrous insects. People in the lake country got to see such machines only if a retaliatory expedition was under way or if during maneuvers a formation of these bristling monsters made a low pass over the fields of reeds.

But what was the airport at Brand, what were jet engines, radio beacons, and flying machines, compared to Morrison's diagnosis, compared to Doc Morrison's promise that the blind spots in Bering's vision would heal over and at least in the deep layers of his retina everything would once again be as it had been before the shadows of a darkening world first appeared.

Now the portholes turned blue. As if the whirling of the rotor blades had rent the rainy sky, the portholes suddenly turned deep blue. Then dazzling sunlight burst into the cabin—in which Bering was not flying, but sat captive.

He staggered to his feet and in the jolting turbulence climbed over rifle butts and soldiers' boots, waiting for an order, for someone to forbid him to press his forehead to the glass of a side window and stare down into the depths. But not one of the more than thirty soldiers sent on this mission to Moor paid him any attention. No one spoke. No one tried to outbellow the rotors. No one forbade him to gaze into the depths.

Barren, sun-bathed, chalk-white, the wastelands and high plateaus of the mountains glided past below, streamed, rushed past deep below them, back toward Brand, which now lay behind

a distant reef of clouds. Of glass . . . if the helicopter floor had
been of glass or as transparent as Doc Morrison wanted the
whole world to be, then perhaps this disappointed, yellow-
skinned passenger would have discovered a hint of flight in the
grand panoramic view. But as it was, he simply left greasy traces
of his skin on the window, barely visible smudges, and stared
down into a treeless stone desert.

At times he thought he could recognize certain corries, cliffs,
snow fields. Down there, at the foot of a pillar, at the base of
a wall, down there, across that scree, he had walked, ridden
with Lily and his father, yesterday, back then, in another time
long ago.

But now! . . . He thought he was falling. They were crashing!
He grabbed for a hold, grasped empty air. A soldier sitting
behind him shouted something at him. He didn't understand a
word. The horizon cut across the window on a slant, tipped,
became a cliff. Bering could feel his own dead weight trying to
yank him away from the view. He cut his hand as he banged it
against some metal ribbing, but at the very last moment found a
handhold. The horizon sank back to horizontal. The plunge had
been only a pattern in their flight, a loop of descent. The helicopter's shadow scurried across fissured rocks, and suddenly the
soldiers, too, were crowding to the side windows.

Down below, at the edge of a wide field of firn, seven, eight,
nine panicked figures dived for cover, threw themselves into the
gravel, crept into crevices and holes, trying to escape the gunship
as it swooped down on them out of the sun.

Too large and massive for quick flight, only a cow was left
behind in the zone of fire—a brown-and-white spotted cow. No
less panicked than its herders and dragging its lead rope behind,
it galloped in ponderous bounds across the open snow, leapt into
the firn, and sank up to its neck. Its bellows were lost in the pennants of ice crystals whipped up by the helicopter.

The soldiers laughed—at the panic of the cowboys down
below, at the cow trapped in the snow . . . and a few of them

probably also laughed in relief that the captain had not given an order to attack. Laughing, they fell back into the blue of the sky. The pilot banked away. The army had more important things to do than worry about a few isolated cattle rustlers.

And then, although still distant and shimmering like a mirage, a stream seemed to flow toward them out of the mountains, a fjord set between steep slopes and meadows of reeds. The lake. Deep in the Stony Sea a moment before, the helicopter now raced along above green waves and the glistening tracks of gusts darted wildly before them. Now the Blind Shore swerved ahead of them, the quarry stairway—from this height it all looked serene and sleek, the decaying Grand Inscription like tissue paper. The rusty arms of conveyor belts beside the gravel stockpiles, then the lake promenade, the ruins of the Bellevue, it all came and went below them—lakeside resort, chestnut-lined road, Grand Hotel, walls white in a clear autumnal sun. Bright and light as a feather, as radiant as some long-promised land, the shore of Moor hovered ahead of the bodyguard returning home. But suddenly the depths revealed just one thing—that he had come too late.

A mushroom of tarry smoke was seething up from the steamer dock, and bedded in a nest of fumes and flaming tongues lay the Crow, lay the hallmark of the Dog King, lay Bering's most ingenious work, rolled over, its open hood a gaping beak. There below, surrounded by spectators—perhaps powerless to help, perhaps arsonists—so near to water and yet blazing with unquenchable fire, was the only luxury liner that had ever lurched through the potholes of Moor during the Peace of Oranienburg, and it burned the way only a machine drenched in gas and oil, replete with plastic, white rubber, and ethereal colors, could burn.

The landing, the gradual, clumsy process of being set down on the parade grounds outside the secretary's office, went unbearably slow for Bering. Even the gawkers, who came running now from the dock to the parade grounds for a new sensation, seemed faster than the helicopter. Bering saw them run and stop, then look up and run some more. When they should be shoveling sand on the fire, sand and soil! Put this thing down, fast! Why didn't the pilot let the machine plummet the way he had just now for those few wretched cattle thieves? The Crow was burning!

And the soldiers? Didn't they understand that now, at this very second, they were needed at the steamer dock? Bering tried to show them his burning creation, a bird in flames, and pointed down, pounded his fist on the glass of the side window, against the metal ribbing of cold armor. But these soldiers had seen far worse before this than a burning car and nodded and laughed, until one of them—it was just as they were touching down— finally realized that this yellow-skinned civilian was beside him- self with rage or fright. He grabbed the raving man by the sleeve, tried to pull him back to the bench of soldiers: "Hey, man! Cool it, man! Sit down, man!" and then bellowed an order in the lan- guage of the locals, a sound as scathing as its intent: *"Sitz!"*

But Bering was not to be held back and tore himself out of the soldier's grasp. At the jolt of touchdown he stumbled over an ammunition crate, banging his head against a helmet, falling between army boots, pulled himself up, and pushed and shoved his way to the now opened hatch—and was among the first to leap out into the dusty whirlpool of the parade grounds.

Moor's secretary stood there as if in a desert storm, waved a crutch in greeting and pressed his other hand to his temple in a salute—or maybe only to hold his green cap on. No locals from Moor could be seen in the mass of dust.

Eyes burning, Bering ran past the figure of the secretary, but as he crossed the grounds, making straight for the smoky mush- room by the shore, he heard an unmistakable voice in the dying uproar of the rotor. It was his master's voice.

He did not understand what Ambras called out. He under- stood only that this was not a cry for help, but an order, and that the order was meant for him, him alone. He stopped, looked around, searching.

By now the rotor blades were circling as lazily as the ceiling fan in the administrator's shed at the quarry on a summer day. The cloud of dust sank back onto the parade grounds, revealing the assembled residents of Moor standing off at a safe distance. And there, well apart from the gawking crowd, he at last discovered his master. With the mastiff, as if rooted in place by his side, Ambras was standing in the office door and waving him over.

"Come here!"

Bering obeyed. Ambras did not appear to be wounded.

"Move it! Faster!"

Bering reached the Dog King at almost exactly the same moment as the fair-haired captain, who, along with two military police and the gesticulating secretary, had reviewed the gawkers as if they were an honor guard. The soldiers were emptying out of the helicopter and dragging black crates, two machine guns, and a grenade launcher across the parade grounds.

Ambras's hand was extended to shake the captain's, but before greeting the officer in the language of the victors, he called to his bodyguard, "Stay here!"

"Stay here! There's nothing left to save. They want to kill us. They've set the Crow on fire."

CHAPTER 29

RAGE

Bravo. *The big boss would have to walk the lake promenade on foot now, too. He could race his mongrels now, from the house of dogs to the secretary's office or the steamer dock and back—or wherever. Hell was the only place he'd be driving in the Crow at any rate. That crate had burned like a can of gas. And no fire department for miles around. What a shame.*

Wouldn't that have been lovely. Carry water to put out a fire for an army spy and then get blistered with burns for your trouble. Get the hair singed off your head so the spy could go on driving through the villages in a luxury liner. It was his fire. And what had he *done? Not a damn thing. Stood there beside the burning jalopy, holding his mastiff on its chain so it didn't run off like his ferryman, like his blasting foreman and the others, just stood there, gaping stupidly at the flames and then slunk off to the secretary's office.*

But there's gonna be trouble. I'm telling you, there's gonna be trouble. Not a wise idea . . .

What *wasn't a wise idea?*

Setting his Crow on fire.

We didn't set it on fire. Did we *set it on fire?*

292

We stood there at any rate and watched while those drunk quarrymen rolled the crate over and stuck the fuse in the gas tank.

So what? Were we supposed to give them a lecture? No open fires allowed! Is it illegal now too, maybe, what with all the stuff that catches fire every day, to watch an old jalopy burn? Were we supposed to put on blindfolds? And was it wise of him do you suppose to nail that poster to the wall at the secretary's office and then slip off without a word? Was that wise, maybe? Nails up that goddamn poster and then walks away, climbs aboard his raft cool as can be so he can be ferried over to the quarry, as if he'd done nothing more than tack up just any old notice on the bulletin board, some invitation to some beach party—shit. Hits us over the head with an evacuation order and buzzes off to the quarry!

But it was the quarrymen who always kept saying up *and* away, *sooner today than tomorrow, off to the lowlands, to Brand, to the West Zones, to America, anywhere, just away from here. . . .*

Sure, off to the lowlands, off to Brand, sure, off to Brand without any papers even. But not like this! Clear out our homes inside of a month. The quarry closed, the lake country quarantined like there was a plague! And just because the army needs a new sandbox.

Shit. Troop *maneuver zone. What are they supposed to be training for now? It worked after all. Nagoi . . . right? What's the name of that place where they won? They won over there, after all. Blew half of Japan sky-high and say, that's it, they were the last, they're all taken care of, peace and quiet now—and the next day they turn the lake country, the mountains all around, into a shooting range, because they want to go on practicing. . . .*

And us? Us idiots can gather up our things, gather 'em up just like in war, and vamoose, one, two, three.

And who's their lackey again this time, huh? The spy. The dog-fucker. Nails Beat it! *and* Out of my sight! *on the wall and then is amazed when sparks start flying. Just walks off, sits there on the gravel barge, and on the way across is probably already calculating how much the next best Jew will give him for all the scrap iron at the quarry. . . .*

Well, he didn't have to calculate long. Had to head right back again full-steam ahead, because that light went on down by the dock. Up in flames. Grilled crow. And full-steam reverse.

He was just lucky the crate didn't explode under his ass. That would've made the prettiest fireworks if the miners had blown him and his mutts up along with the rest. Maybe now he'll get it through his doggy skull that he can't treat us like that. Tells us one day everything is going ahead as usual—the mining, the gravel mills, all in low gear, but still moving ahead, and a few days later he nails that shit on the wall. . . .

The order did come down from the High Command after all. And he is their administrator after all. They just used his hand to nail their orders to the wall. They just let him take the heat, just like he does with the blacksmith.

He's the administrator? Administrator of what? What's he in charge of? A pile of rubble, a bunch of stones, a kennel—that's what he's in charge of! Shit. Administrator. He's a mangy dog and should be treated like one. A kick, a stone bounced off his head, fire under his ass—end of story.

And what good would that do? The army is right behind. You kill one of them, and ten more show up. And it takes three blows to kill even the first. That's one tough dog, let me tell you. One tough dog. If the camp didn't do him in, nothing is gonna do him in easy. Knock him over the head and set his house on fire—he'll wipe the blood from his nose, brush the soot off, bark orders into his two-way radio, and here comes the army to clean up, brings him a new jalopy, gives him a new house. . . . The gentleman's house burned down? The gentleman is wounded? The gentleman has a victim's passport? Oh, and a camp tattoo on his arm as well? Here, please, your stipend, compensation for all your pain. And it starts all over again. We know all about it. Know it only too well.

And what happens when our houses burn? When the skins toss torches in at our windows, chase after our women, and drive off our livestock? Shit. Nothing happens. Then it's just: you're the ones who spawned 'em.

*How long did his crate burn? Ten minutes? Fifteen? It barely
caught fire and half a company comes flying in aboard one of their
hornets, even brings him his bodyguard back.*

*Bodyguard, don't make me laugh. The blacksmith's boy a body-
guard? He just needs his ears boxed good, and then it's march right
back to your anvil. Didn't you see him? He went scurrying off across
the parade grounds like a scared chicken, until his master whistled
him back. . . .*

*Scared, my ass. Watch out for him, I'm telling you. He carries his
pistol even when he's fishing. That boy's gone wild before this for a
lot less.*

*Him, wild? The blacksmith's wife raised him with candles and
pictures of the Virgin. He came floating down the hill on holy water.*

*Watch out for him. The Dog King has screwed him up. Has got
him on his side. Put who knows what in his grub.*

*Ha! Somebody's afraid it seems. Well, just go ahead and send him
some peppermint tea and cotton candy. Begging your pardon ever so
much, but it looks like the Crow flew a little too high. Must have got
too close to the sun. Suddenly caught fire. Burned like a can of gas,
that bird did. Like a can of gas. No harm meant. And bon voyage.*

*Go ahead and laugh. I'm telling you—watch out for him. Have
you ever looked him in the eye?*

*In the eye? Are you that taken with him? I don't give a shithead
like that a glance, not even if he sets out a crate of tobacco and coffee
just for me. I don't give a shithead like that a single glance.*

*Say what you want. I've looked him in the eye, and I'm telling
you he stares at you like some animal, he's got eyes like some kind of
animal. . . . He looks at you like a wolf.*

The first night after his return from the lowlands, Bering
found no sleep. He could no longer stand the doggy smell of his
bed (the pack had taken over his room while he was gone and
first had to be forced back within their old bounds). He could no
longer stand the creaking of the parquet floor and the stifling air
in the Villa Flora's hallways, could stand nothing about the
sleeping house and fled outdoors.

As silently as an animal stalking prey, he roamed the park, walked beneath the black arms of the giant pines, patrolled the tangle of barbed wire, which had become a metallic-organic palisade overgrown with wild roses, ivy, and thistle; he leaned against the wall of the turbine shed by the brook and listened to the bass song of the paddle wheel coming from inside, climbed down the long stairway to the dilapidated boathouse, and hurried back at the first suspicious sound he thought he heard coming from the impenetrable darkness near the drive's grillwork gate.

He would have thrown himself like a madman at any intruder, any attacker, and would even have battled the dogs for the right to be the first to plunge his weapons into the fat, the muscles, the flesh of a foe. While Ambras had sat at the kitchen table, drinking and studying the construction plans of the gravel mill, Bering had spent yesterday evening at his workbench in the empty garage—had transformed a telescope spring from one of the quarry's power sieves into a steel rod and screwed one of the forged bird talons from the Crow's grille to the handle. He had sawed the talon off the hot wreck and once it had cooled, had filed and polished it until it was as sharp as the blade of his jackknife. He did not need a pistol for an arsonist from Moor— with this claw he could knock, could hack, the torch right out of his hand!

But when Bering, gasping, reached the driveway and the giant pines towering blacker than night into the starless sky, there was nothing to be heard. Beside the lily pond, beneath the pines, in the wilderness around the sleeping house—everything was still. Even the pack made not a sound.

He let a few of the dogs accompany him on patrol. He knew each of them even in the dark, but he whispered no commands, not even the nicknames Ambras sometimes used. He did not encourage his companions; he did not pet or praise them, and did not order them back into the house, either, but allowed them to stay at his side, panting—and with each step he sank deeper into his consuming hate. Doc Morrison had promised him that the holes in his vision would grow brighter and finally disappear. And so he could promise these arsonists that he would find them in their houses, in any hideaway, any refuge. He swore to them he would find them. He talked to himself.

The dogs accompanying him pricked up their ears. What did he want? They did not understand this muttering. They ran alongside, paused repeatedly, panting, staring at him, and one of the short-haired mongrels, in whose wiry, spotted body all the traits of the pack—the power and the viciousness, the tracking nose, the love of the hunt—seemed to merge, began to bark now in confusion. And immediately, in both the nearest and most distant darkness, there arose a yelping and yowling that lasted for minutes. Bering paid no attention. It was as if he were deaf. He was remembering. He saw welding seams creep across the metal of the Studebaker, watched the transformation of a wreck into the image of his fantasy, saw the fiery traces of his labor glow hot again, and die out. The handle of the steel rod in his fist felt like the handle of the welding apparatus during the weeks of major repairs, and he rewelded every seam and hammered the car doors into the form of bird wings folded to dive and forged the beak and talons of the grille over and over, forged dozens, hundreds of talons and dug them all into the mocking faces of Moor, into the temples, the cheeks, the eyes of those smirking mugs that had appeared in the dusty whirlpool of the landing helicopter—he ripped and hacked at everything that the memory of the hour of his return could grab hold of. He mourned for his machine.

As he walked past the veranda's wooden columns and the weathered fauns on the staircase—after completing his ninth, tenth, eleventh round—he banged his steel rod on the edge of an empty basin circled by dancing stone nymphs, beat out a quick, unmelodic signal of his vigilance on the rust-eaten waterspouts and gutters, or on a faun's mossy skull. The shutters of the music room stood open. If the Dog King was lying awake in his kennel, this drumming was meant to tell him that his bodyguard was not

asleep, either, and was eager to confront his foes and defeat them
and put out every spark that leapt from Moor into his collapsing
empire. . . . And even though the army was advancing and there
was no staying on here by the lake and they all would have
to disappear—all of them: not only quarrymen, saltworkers, and
trappers, but secretaries and agents as well—he, Bering, the Dog
King's bodyguard, who now sensed his old powers of vision
returning even in this darkness, would defend the Villa Flora
against Moor until the day and hour of departure, and at every
chance would pay back those arsonists for destroying the
Crow.

The only bit of light that found its way across the lake promenade and the ruins of the hotel and up the hill to the Villa Flora
was the flickering watch fire by the Bellevue. Sometimes the distant rumble of a diesel generator could be heard, rising and
fading with each change in wind direction. But even through his
binoculars, Bering could detect no other visible sign of the army's
presence than the shifting red reflection in the crowns of the
plane trees beside the Bellevue's washhouse. Like so many retaliatory expeditions before them, the soldiers of the fair-haired captain had set up their tents under the blackened balconies and
dead windows of what had once been the most fashionable hotel
on the lake. But this time, having set up camp, they did not
swarm out to chase killers and skinheads. This time, damn it,
when they would not have had to take a single step into the
mountains and wilderness, but had only to reach out their hands
to capture the arsonists in their houses or even right out on
Moor's parade grounds—this time they didn't give a shit about
the enemies of the Dog King, though they were their enemies
as well.

As the helicopter rose again out of the dust, shrank to a black,
singing dot, and disappeared over the snow fields of the Stony
Sea, these soldiers, like a troop of weary sappers, had simply
begun makeshift repair on the piles of the steamer dock and
to lay trench plate across its planks. And as the Crow's embers

died out and the black pennant of smoke drifted out over the lake, the captain spent the rest of the afternoon with the Dog King in the secretary's office, bending over a military map, scribbling wavy lines and circles over the lake country in red pencil, and drinking the secretary's home-brewed schnapps. Bering had waited mutely at the open door and listened to the two of them converse—and laugh—in the language of the victors. But he had understood only that Ambras himself did not want to bother any further with the fire by the steamer dock and was casually ignoring the gawkers and arsonists on the parade ground, ignoring his foes.

"We don't need the Bird anymore," Ambras had told him—told *him*, who had returned from the lowlands to protect the Bird and everything that belonged to the house of dogs from Moor's destructive rage and envy and greed. "We don't need the Bird anymore. We'll be riding in tractor-trailers, in armored cars, in jeeps . . . you can take your pick tomorrow. The army's on the march. You came back with the advance party, you understand—that was just the advance party."

Tomorrow. The army. We don't need the Bird anymore. The army was on the march. It would not be arriving next month or next year, as the Dog King himself had said only a few days before. It was arriving *tomorrow*, and laying claim to land conquered decades ago. For now that the last armed enemies had been burned or blasted in the fire of Nagoya, now that there was no longer any power capable of attacking the army of the Bringer of Peace or of merely resisting it, now Stellamour's warriors needed an entire mountain range, needed the lake, the hill country, the Stony Sea for perpetual maneuvers on artificial battlefields to ready themselves for the hour when some new but still nameless enemy would emerge from the rubble of burned-out cities, would arise from the future.

"Let them come. Just let them come right ahead," Bering muttered, and the dogs listened and were at a loss. Just let them come, these bringers of peace, let them plow the land under with their maneuvers clear up to the timberline, up into the region of glaciers. That was fine by him. That way the people of Moor and everyone who lived with them by this damned shore, all the arsonists and sons of arsonists, would no longer be able to tell their fields and pastures from the wilderness or their last, antiquated machines from the burned-out wreck that now lay cold on the steamer dock, a monument to rage.

The next morning, night having passed in chilly silence, Bering sat sleeping on the veranda in Ambras's wicker chair, sleeping despite the cold that sent his breath drifting off in little white flags. The meadows by the shore shimmered with frost. Autumn was here.

When a distant rumbling awakened the bodyguard, at the first moment of waking he thought he heard the Crow and started up so abruptly that he stepped on the talon of his steel rod, which had slipped from his hand as he slept. He stumbled and fell among the dogs dozing at his feet. The rumbling swelled, but even before he got to his feet again, he was awake enough to recognize that this was not the sound of a single motor, but of many motors in unison. Only the army sounded like that. In a cavalcade of bulldozers, Caterpillars, trucks, tanks, and jeeps, the victors of Oranienburg and Kwangju, the conquerors of Santiago and Nagoya were rolling past fields of reeds toward Moor. . . . And Moor, whose inhabitants gathered on the parade grounds where this great column came to a halt bit by bit— Moor remembered: this tumult, this din, these dust-coated soldiers staring straight ahead as if deaf to every call and certainly to every plea—it was all just like the last days of the war; no, this *was* the war.

"The army giveth, the army taketh away," the voice of the captain boomed from the parade-ground loudspeakers this morning. In vain, Bering had searched the rooms and hallways of the house of dogs, even searched the park, for his master and had then run in pursuit of the column, had run and run all the way to the parade grounds, to the secretary's office. There, at last, he had found the Dog King at the captain's side. They were both standing on a tank! But only the captain held a microphone in his hand and shouted into the rumble of the column. *The army giveth, the army taketh away.* "Blessed be the army!"

Moor stood facing its occupiers in unorganized, muttering groups. No order had been issued to assemble at the parade grounds, but more and more people emerged from their houses, crowding the streets to the square. Those who had been most curious now had to push back against the newcomers to keep from being shoved out into the moving tracks and wheels—and especially into a cordon of infantrymen holding their assault rifles chest-high at the ready.

Like a commandant in the first years of occupation, the captain stood on the gun turret of the tank and occasionally interrupted his own shouts to direct the driver of a troop transporter or bulldozer to its parking place. Before the eyes of Moor, the column deployed itself as if for battle. Diesel fumes obscured the view. Then the rumbling died down. Then the only sound was the voice from the loudspeakers. But most of what it babbled at the people of Moor could also be read in the flyers that two soldiers were throwing from the bed of a truck.

The army was laying claim to the spoils. Decades after victories in the Stony Sea and the lowlands, the army was at last laying claim to land it had fought so hard to win. It needed the lake, the meadows, the upland moors. The whole mountain range. But it had come not only to put these wastelands to use as terrain for troop maneuvers in the cause of peace, but it also now demanded back all the items so generously left in loan at the Blind Shore till now—all the tools and machines for splitting and processing granite, the chain saws, crushers, conveyor belts, windlasses, tipcarts . . . everything. The army knew as well as the inhabitants of the lakeshore that the granite of Moor Quarry was exhausted, that in all directions lay loose stone, waste rock, slip faces. . . .

These tools and machines, the captain shouted, would therefore be more useful elsewhere, at places more productive for Stellamour's grand memorial enterprise, more beneficial for world peace, than here at Moor Quarry, which by the will of the Bringer of Peace and his generals was to be transformed into a shooting range. And it truly was not asking too much, the captain shouted, for the army to require—upon completion of the loan and in token of gratitude, so to speak—that those who had previously benefited from this industrial site should help in its dismantling and transport and in the construction of a military camp, a training camp, a barracks camp at the quarry. "And in payment the High Command intends to provide each of you free passage to the lowlands. A job, housing, and a new life in the lowlands for each of you! The army is giving each one of you more, far more, than all of you together deserve! . . ."

Forced labor. Many of those assembled, whose view of the captain was blocked by an army vehicle or simply by the crowd, thought they heard Major Elliot's voice coming from the loudspeakers, and asked, "Is he back?" "Is that madman here again?"

The madman? Him or some other guy. Whoever was shouting, bellowing up there, was an enemy at any rate. An enemy like the Dog King. Like the secretary. Like the blacksmith and all those turncoats, all those traitors.

The people of Moor bent down for the flyers and yet did not dare crumple them up. Did not dare any sign of protest, any word of outrage. The enemy had its cannons and gun barrels pointed at them. They would have been strong enough yesterday to defeat the Dog King with fire and stones. But today. Today that king was enthroned beside a fair-haired captain in the midst of a hostile army.

Bering was standing so close to the soldiers that he thought he could smell the oil of their weapons, and yet he did not see his master all that differently from the way the other people of Moor did at this moment—a mute man up beside the gun turret of a tank, menacing, distant, unassailable, invincible. Whoever was

defended by such an excess of power did not need a bodyguard anymore. And whatever the captain of such excessive
power might shout into his microphone and order Moor to do—
build a camp, work the quarry, or simply vanish—it was as good
as done.

CHAPTER 30

DOG, ROOSTER, OVERSEER

T HE AGE OF PARTIES WAS OVER. WHAT
occurred in Moor and on the Blind Shore in the days
and weeks after the army arrived in Stellamour's name
and under the fair-haired captain's command was no longer some
penitential rite, no mere reconstruction of forced labor as in the
days of Major Elliot, but work itself, reality. Both the gyratory
and hammer crushers at the gravel works had to be dismantled,
and eccentric shafts and crushing jaws made of manganese alloy
steel and weighing several tons had to be dragged from the mills
to the loading ramp. Every burden now weighed what it weighed
and was not just a dummy like the hewn stones of a Stellamour
Party in Elliot's day, and there was no regimental photographer
standing alongside every drudgery to capture bent backs and
gray, dusty faces for an album of cruelty. . . . Nothing was *past*,
nothing a mere memorial anymore, it was all the present now. If
someone sank to his knees under a burden at the foot of the
Grand Inscription, it was from exhaustion and not because a
photographer or master of ceremonies ordered him to strike a
pose. And if on his free day a saltworker or sheep breeder began

emptying out his house in Moor or in Haag, the bare rooms, cracked walls, and bundles piled in the entryway no longer reminded him of flights and expulsions of the past, but now only of the future. And the future meant leaving Moor.

You . . . and you! Yes you, that guy and you! Hey, I mean you, over here! You too, come here! Move it, let's go, faster!

If on a given morning not enough volunteers were standing at the dock ready to board the *Sleeping Greek Maid* for the dismantling work on the Blind Shore, two trucks of a conscription squad would rattle through the villages and collect able-bodied men. Each evening, the captain had the quota of workers required for the next day posted in large numbers on the secretary's bulletin board, and he did not care if a backwater village got its volunteers to appear at the dock the next morning by drawing lots, by simple persuasion, or by threat. But if the required number was short only two men, the squad would drive off—and then there was no more counting, the trucks were filled, and every hour of delay caused by this search had to be made good at the quarry. Work shifts sometimes lasted until late into the night. There was no pay. Brawls were frequent in Moor after such exhausting days, for whoever tried to escape the quarry and thereby increased the burden on the others would be pursued by his own neighbors and given a thrashing.

There was a great deal to be destroyed on the Blind Shore. The tracks of the light railway that branched off from the loading ramp to seven different working faces had to be ripped from the rocky ground just as the switches and tracks at the Cross of Moor had been demolished back then. But this time the work was not done as punishment by a company of tattooed soldiers. Day after day, the pontoon ferry heaved across the lake so overladen with metal that water sloshed over its deck at even the simplest maneuver. After only a week of dismantling, an ever-growing monster of rusty cargo lay ready for transport to the lowlands: rotating sieves, trolleys, tension weights, and sheet-steel slides; box riddles, drill mountings, cables, chain saws, and flywheels; grates, rabbet ledges, damper plates, and even the corrugated tin roof from the gravel works, through which over the years had rattled every grade of filler for the streets and embankments of the lowlands—it all piled up now at the steamer dock as if in gargantuan imitation of the blacksmith's sunken iron garden.

The days turned cold. Some mornings the Dog King and his bodyguard stood wrapped in military coats at the dock while a sergeant called roll by having the laborers count off. Whenever anything needed doing now, at the quarry or on the way to it, there were always soldiers nearby—within gunshot—guarantors that every directive of the Dog King or his bodyguard would be obeyed as an order. The captain himself rarely came to the Blind Shore. He remained in Moor, played poker with the secretary and a few army agents, and referred all village petitioners seeking a reduction in workload or other favors to the Dog King—who was as deaf to all requests and complaints as the army, and let his bodyguard speak for him. Bering refused petitions. Bering issued orders. Bering threatened. In the shadow of the army, Bering took his revenge for the burning of the Crow. And his master gave him a free hand. His master sat in the administrator's shed and wrote lists.

As the dismantling and the evacuation of houses in backwater villages proceeded, as the quarry was transformed into an army shooting range, control of the Blind Shore appeared gradually to shift from the Dog King to his bodyguard. *He* was the one who had always serviced the chain saws, conveyor equipment, and generators, kept them in constant repair, and was as familiar with the mechanism of the gyratory crusher as with the gears of one of his own creations. And with agonizing meticulousness he now saw to it that every flywheel and every connection was carefully dismounted, numbered, loaded, transported across the lake, and stored under a corrugated tin roof by the steamer dock. A laborer needed only to drop a tension weight, a crude piece of iron, and Bering would fly into a rage. The volunteers began to fear him.

Protected and backed by the army—as unassailable, in fact, as his master—he and his outbursts of rage grew more unpredictable from day to day.

Dog, that was what the volunteers called him now among themselves, dog and rooster and sometimes just overseer. And he did indeed harry them like a watchdog unleashed from its chain. From the rock faces to the gravel works, from the gravel works to the loading ramp and back again, he was forever goading them and pounding his steel rod angrily against railings and rusty plates, and could look very much like a rooster, too, when in a breaking voice he shouted instructions across the open slopes and menacingly raised that steel rod with the talon screwed to its handle.

But, then again, for minutes on end this rooster, this overseer, this dog might just stand there, as if turned to stone—in front of the weathered slip face at the foot of the Grand Inscription or beside the loading ramp or the white-dusted walls of the gravel works—and stare off into space. He let his perforated gaze glide across boulders and cracked cliffs and gray water, was obsessed with each movement of his eyes, with those rising and falling blind spots, in which he thought he recognized the first signs of the fulfillment of Morrison's prognosis: the spots were losing their blackness, were growing translucent at the edges. Was that really the return of light? The spots were shrinking. Doc Morrison had not been mistaken. Morrison would be proved right. His eyesight was coming back.

But when Bering awakened from his stony state and saw piles of gravel, the loading ramp, and the volunteers—the arsonists—his rage was reawakened as well. On a cold, sunny fall day, when puddles shaded by the ramp lay under a fine crust of ice till noon, Bering struck and wounded an obstinate laborer with his steel rod—a teamster from Haag, who was not going to take orders from a snot-nose, from some whore's bastard, from a spy's lap dog. Bering struck the man on the chest, head, and shoulders so suddenly that the fellow barely had time to raise his arms and staggered and sank to his knees under the fury of the blows and lay there writhing and bleeding as they continued—until Ambras stepped out of the administrator's shed and shouted, "Stop!"

The soldiers on guard, who were eating canned meat beside a fire near the shed, grabbed their rifles and stood up—and then sat back down on the stones when all there was to see was two laborers helping the beaten man to his feet and the overseer obeying the administrator's signal to join him inside the shed.

"What's going to become of us?" Bering asked that day after a long silence. "Where are we going?" He was sitting at the table in the shed, looking his master in the eye. On the stained wooden tabletop between them lay the steel rod, the talon. Ambras pushed the weapon—the teamster's drying blood was almost indistinguishable from rust—back across the table, propelled it off the table and into Bering's lap, and repeated what any one of the volunteers outside could have said: "We're going wherever the army wants us."

"To Brand . . . ?"

". . . and beyond. Always following the stone. Someplace where there still is stone—*stone*, you understand, and not just slip faces, rubble, and debris."

"When are we leaving?"

"When we're done here. Now get out. Give that guy out there the first-aid kit and tell the others not to overload the barge like yesterday. Move, get out."

Always following the stone. That was all? The Dog King did not know anything more about the army's plans or his own route? But he saw the captain almost every day. He had to know more. Yet whenever Bering asked, Ambras only hinted at an answer or said nothing, as if it were a secret or as if wherever this life might lead had become unimportant to him. "Someplace. Maybe. Could be. What do I know. Let me alone. Scram. Out of my sight."

Twice now, Bering had overcome his reluctance, had worked out the sentences in the language of the army and asked the cap-

tain's driver, as well as the guards at the quarry, about the High
Command's plans, about the future. But the soldiers shrugged
and shook their heads and pretended not to understand him.
And Lily, who could obtain or learn anything she wanted from
the army, Lily was nowhere to be seen these days. And otherwise . . . otherwise there was no one else left on speaking terms
with the bodyguard, the overseer.

Ever since Bering had returned from the lowlands without
Lily, scarcely a word was spoken in the house of dogs. Ambras,
tormented by the pain in his shoulders and arms, was sullen,
strange, removed—or was it because his bodyguard had been so
transformed by the lowlands that there was nothing left to be said
between him and his master?

In the evening, the two of them would often sit silently in the
main salon of the Villa Flora, the one working on his lists, the
other hunched over blueprints of machines. At such times, they
did not even speak to the dogs. Each did his job at the quarry,
and at the end of a shift they stood mutely at the railing of the
ferry, walked mutely back to the house of dogs from the dock,
strode mutely between the rows of pines, down the drive that
once again now bore only the tracks of dogs and men. Sometimes
the captain would be waiting in a jeep at the dock. But then they
rode directly to the secretary's office and after discussing Moor's
situation would be driven nowhere but to the wrought-iron gate
at the border of the Villa Flora's park. The captain was afraid of
the dogs.

As he had done before, Bering sometimes had to brush the
dust from his master's hair now, and once he even performed
Lily's chore of bathing his scars and shoulders with soothing
lotion, but he never again got as close to Ambras as he had been
before the trip to Brand. They missed Lily. Without her presence
many attempts at conversation died with the first sentence.

And yet Bering felt neither relief nor joy when on the morning
of the first snowfall (which melted again under a cold sun), he
saw Lily's mule grazing in the lakeside resort's meadows, soggy

now with melting snow. That morning, Bering was walking behind Ambras along the footpath to the shore road. Ambras's head was lowered and he did not appear to notice the animal grazing under the linden trees by the shoremaster's house. They walked in silence past the soot-blackened ruins, an unroofed gallery, rows of empty windows from which shrubbery grew—the weather tower lay some distance off. There was no sound coming from the tower. Its shutters stood open. Ambras's mastiff suddenly came to a stop, as if picking up a familiar scent—but then leapt to catch up with its master, who had moved steadfastly ahead. Bering shivered. The mule was not saddled, but its legs were fettered. No doubt of it, Lily had returned. But with her there also returned the memory of feathers and down falling like snow on a fatally wounded chicken thief, memories of a corpse that was still warm as it slapped against projecting rocks and black ledges, falling deeper and deeper into a gorge of the Stony Sea; and above all there returned the memory of the hate in Lily's eyes, of the pain when she grabbed *him*—the man she had once embraced and kissed—by the hair and pulled him back from the riflescope and into the awareness of a love now extinguished. *Stop it, you asshole, stop it now.*

But when Lily met with the Dog King and his bodyguard in the office of Moor's secretary that same evening, she said not a word about the trip to Brand and the shots fired in the field of sinkholes. The captain had called a meeting there. Lily was sitting with him and several agents from the villages along the shore (the one from Eisenau was there, too) in the television room and seemed in no less a good mood than she had been among the soldiers in the guard room at the gate of the Big Hospital. This time there were no goods to be traded on the table, but only newspapers, magazines—and a deck of cards. Had Lily brought nothing but newspapers back from the lowlands?

"I won! The captain brings me luck." She held a crinkled fan of bills out to Ambras when, leading his chained mastiff and followed by Bering, he entered the bare, unheated room where

Moor still gazed at a television screen every Wednesday evening. The television, now draped with a cloth that bore Stellamour's picture, stood on a crude wooden column. "Won it all. . . . How about you? Lost the Crow, did you? How are you?"

"Tired," Ambras said, and dropped into a chair. "Tired."

"Coffee or schnapps? Or both?" Lily shoved a tray across the table—a bottle, clinking glasses, a coffeepot.

"Water," Ambras said.

"No dogs," the captain said.

Ambras turned around to Bering and, with a nonchalant motion, wrapped the dog chain around the bodyguard's wrist. "Wait outside."

Lily's vacant gaze brushed Bering as he left the meeting. Pulling the mastiff behind him, he passed the table and was about to pick up a magazine, on whose cover he saw the sun of Nagoya exploding in a garish cloud. But one of the agents was quicker and snatched up the magazine and paged through it with fleet fingers until he finally found the photograph he wanted to show the man being excluded from the meeting: a dark double-page spread, a tangle of charred limbs and heads burned bald, and in the foreground, among glassy rubble, a hand held open, a talon. "Pocket change," the agent said, "coins . . . the heat was so intense that coins melted in their hands."

Nagoya, a bursting sky at the far end of the world, a hail of incandescent stones and a boiling sea. What were the reports from a capitulating empire, accounts that had flitted across the screen and gone out again ages ago now, even in the television rooms of backwater villages, what were they on an evening like this in comparison to the evacuation and organized disappearance of the lake country—and especially in comparison to the big news Lily had brought with her from the lowlands?

Lily?

None of the agents could say later whether Lily had actually brought the news to Moor, or if it had perhaps crackled over the secretary's radio or been mentioned by the captain—and only then spoken at the table for the first time in loud triumph by Lily. There was no doubt, however, that this news certainly suited no one in Moor or all along the lakeshore better than it suited the Brazilian. In a loud debate with the volunteers aboard the *Sleeping Greek Maid*, the helmsman even went so far as to conjecture that the Brazilian had not merely brought the news, but had triggered it herself, that through her friends in the army and her good connections all the way up to the High Command she had contributed decisively to the realization of this order, which, in the days following the agents' meeting, the population of the lake country often greeted with disbelief and interpreted as Stellamour's final act of retribution, as revenge for the burning of the Crow, or simply as a business deal between the Dog King and his lady smuggler. That order read: The High Command in the lowlands had decided that all conveying equipment and machines from Moor Quarry, every damn piece of metal ever put to use on the Blind Shore and now rusting away at the dock under a corrugated roof, would be shipped to Brazil. Every piece of iron in the Stony Sea shipped overseas to Brazil!

To Brazil? Nonsense, impossible—or so the townsfolk said— *send a load of junk overseas?*

Impossible? Why impossible? What about before the war? What about during the war? Ships, nothing but ships to America, to New York, and Buenos Aires, to Montevideo, Santos, and Rio de Janeiro, ships filled to bursting with expelled and hunted emigrants who didn't want to be herded onto battlefields or into camps, to their death. And then what about afterward, when everything had fallen apart, in the chaos after the war and during the first years of peace? Ships again! Ships full of people bombed out, expelled, and homeless, and right beside them a lot of the instigators and hunters and pursuers from before, generals and camp commandants in civvies, leaders who had shit their pants, who had first sent the dumb foot-sloggers into the line of fire and then left them to the mercy of the tattooed victors. Impossible? It had all seemed impossible, absurd at one time or other—but it had happened. And as for the machinery and equipment at the Blind Shore, everyone who had heard the news on the secretary's radio or could read between the lines of those bulletin-board notices knew that this shipload of scrap iron was part of the spoils, a belated payment to a Brazilian general whose twenty thousand soldiers had fought on the side of the allies against Moor and won. That general—or was it his brother?—had invested in stone after the war and now ran a granite quarry on Brazil's Atlantic coast, from which blocks were being cut that were as flawless, as free of the finest crack, and of the same deep green as those quarried on the Blind Shore in Moor's greatest days, now lost forever.

And! Here came the best part! The loudmouths on board the *Sleeping Greek Maid,* among the volunteers at the quarry, or at the Dock Inn often did not mention the most remarkable part of the iron shipment until the end of their speeches, as a sure-fire punch line that was always received with applause or laughter. *The best part was: the quarry administrator and his overseer, that dog . . . and of course the Brazilian, the outsider, the army chippy, all three of them would be accompanying this junk to Brazil; the population of the lakeshore was being driven out by the army, to perish in the lowlands—but this scum, this trio, would be sailing overseas with a ship full of junk.*

CHAPTER 31

UP AND AWAY

A ND HER?"
"Who?"
"Lily."
"What about her?"

"Is she coming along?"

"Do you think she's been hanging around Brand all this time, chewing the fat with a dozen officers, just so she can watch us take off to Brazil all by ourselves?"

"So she's coming along?"

"Her passport and all the papers have been in her pocket for weeks. She even knows the name of the ship. She's started buying, *buying*, stuff. With *money*. She's not trading anymore. Of course she's coming along."

"Where is this quarry?"

"On the ocean."

"But the town . . . what's the name of the town?"

"What do you know about Brazil? Ask Lily. The burg is somewhere on the road between Rio de Janeiro and Santos."

"And how long will we stay? . . . Will we be coming back?"

"Back to what? To a shooting range? We're going to deliver our machines to Brazil and reassemble them at a quarry that still deserves the name—you understand, that's our job, and then, who knows. . . . Maybe the army will reassign us to the Brand Zone or some mountain of rubble. . . ."

It was the first time in days that the Dog King and his bodyguard had spoken. They were driving through the night in the captain's jeep.

"No one's forcing you to leave," Ambras said. "You can stay at the lake and guard army supplies or become an orderly in the Big Hospital. Or a chauffeur, like our friend here." He clapped the jeep driver on the shoulder. The fellow, a former stonepolisher in Brand, was driving them back to the Villa Flora on the captain's orders. He looked into the rearview mirror, with a grin, and saluted. Bering held his impatience in check and said nothing. The idiot didn't avoid a single pothole or puddle, seemed to enjoy spraying fountains of muck. This wasn't driving, this wasn't like gliding and swaying in the Crow. They lumbered past the black, rustling fields of reeds. In the headlights, the mixture of falling snow and rain looked like horizontal hatch marks across the darkness.

"Stay?" Bering said. "Stay here? Never." His feet, his hands were cold. He had waited for Ambras for more than three hours in the stairwell at the secretary's office, and had almost fallen asleep leaning against the motionless mastiff waiting for that damn meeting to end, when one of the agents—it was the guy from Eisenau—had suddenly staggered out of the light of the doorway into the black of the stairwell and, with a laugh, had said, "You're going overseas, going to Brazil," and then, more to himself than to the blinded bodyguard, he added: "Going to Brazil . . . the dogs, and for us it's the lowlands." Bering had to hold the mastiff back and had understood no more than that the guy from Eisenau was drunk.

It was only as they were sitting in the jeep with rain and snow pelting the windshield and the few lights of Moor vanishing behind them, only when the driver, too, suddenly said something about Brazil, about final victory in Japan and the New Order for the conquered territories and the disbursement of all the spoils— only then did Bering grasp that Brazil was not just a word on the map in Lily's tower, not just the name of a longing, the name of a country beyond reach, but a goal, and that the trip there was also just a journey from one place to the next, no different from the trip across the lake to the Blind Shore, no different from the trip to Brand.

The departure for Brazil, which took place five days after the agents' meeting, resembled those images of caravans of tanks and heavy vehicles that had hovered so often before Bering's eyes when his father told about the war. Camouflaged in army colors and creaking under their burden of steel and rusted iron beams, a convoy of trucks moved out early that morning, leaving be- hind a cold oasis in the desert, cold houses, a cordon of freezing gawkers, an inert cold lake, where far out in tattered fog the *Sleeping Greek Maid* lay as still as if at anchor. The glaciers and peaks of the Stony Sea were invisible in an iron-gray sky— invisible as well, the quarry's distant stairway, the Blind Shore.

While the convoy slowly picked up speed, soldiers with batons ran alongside the heavy vehicles to keep the vagabonds among the spectators from jumping aboard the rigs as stowaways. Until all buildings had been emptied and a final check had been run on all evacuees, the old zone borders and restrictions on travel were still in force. The backwater villages would have to wait another week or two for their evacuation, for their departure.

In the truck beds and on the running boards were more armed guards as well, who only gradually turned away from the gawkers to watch the road ahead. The black walls of the Bellevue, the last buildings of Moor, were left behind in diesel fumes. Not one stone, not one fist, not one refugee disrupted the departure. Only some of the dogs from the pack at the Villa Flora, freed now from their chains and collars and with the gray mastiff out in front, followed the convoy in search of their king, leaped at the crawler-tracks and wheels, barking, struggling in the deep, mired ruts. But their king was only a shadow—mute, barely visible behind dirty glass, on an unreachable throne high above the giant wheels—and he gave no sign. Bering sat beside his master in the cabin of the tractor-trailer that carried the large gyratory crusher and could not keep his eyes off the panting, yelping dogs. In time they exhausted themselves, slowed down, fell back, were left behind.

"What's to become of the dogs?" he had asked Ambras the previous evening. They had been sitting at the kitchen table, not saying a word, as if the coming night would be followed by just another day and not by departure, by their farewell to Moor. Neither had taken more than a half hour to pack. What did they have to pack? The covered grand piano in the music room, the record player, a cabinet decorated with birds? A man who wasn't going on a trip, but was leaving for good had no need for a lot of luggage. Photographs of a laughing woman and of lost brothers slipped among some clothes, a leather bag full of gemstones taken from the cotton-ball nests of the bird cabinet—emeralds, pink quartz, iridescent opals—a pistol, the steel rod, binoculars, Ambras's duffel bag, Bering's cardboard suitcase bound with twine: that was everything. Books, utensils, the record collection, and whatever else had been of value for life in the Villa Flora now lay in the darkness behind the bolted iron shutters of the music room.

"What about the dogs? What's to become of the dogs?"

"They're staying here. They were here long before us," Ambras had said. "The dogs don't need us. Take off their collars."

At the Cross of Moor the convoy left the muddy road that ran alongside the overgrown railroad embankment, turned onto the old Pass Road, and crept up the first incline toward the tunnels, whose curtains of ivy and vines had already been ripped down weeks before by the army's evacuation vehicles. Partridges flew up out of a thicket that hid the remains of a switch. Now the last dogs from the pack gave up on the caravan and bounded off into the wilderness. Only the gray mastiff stood there in the mired road, did not follow any farther up into the mountains, but did not pursue the prey either—it stayed behind, panting and watching vehicle after vehicle disappear into a black maw.

Lily was sitting with the fair-haired captain and four of his soldiers in a wheeled tank, the first vehicle in the column, and the sudden darkness evoked her laughing protest. She was holding her portable radio on her knees and had been searching in vain for a station with no interference, for music. Here, inside the mountain, the distorted tones from her radio, vaguely reminiscent of cries of triumph and electric guitars, now dissolved into a placid murmur. Music! In Brand or at some other stop along their journey to the sea she would try to buy a new radio—a new radio from the money she had made from selling her horse and mule to the evacuee who now owned her white Labrador as well.

A new radio. Maybe one of those little featherweight gadgets like the ones soldiers in Brand hung from their belts or carried in their jacket pockets, so that they could be up and away and still deep in their music. Rock 'n' roll from dainty earphones, as loud and overpowering as up in Pilot Valley. No more crackling box hung around the neck of a mule, no interference! No tinny band music from the parade-ground loudspeakers, no skinheads, no burned ruins. That was over.

"Hey!" Lily nudged the captain, as if only now in the dark had she become aware that with each passing second she was farther and farther from Moor. "Hey, we're moving. Brazil! We're on our way." Water seeped in black veins down over the tunnel walls, rough rock whose bits of mica schist and splinters of crystal flashed and then went out in the headlights.

Bright.

The column dived into the gray light of a ravine and vanished into the next tunnel.

Dark.

Bering pushed his master gently away. Ambras was fighting off sleep, but his head kept sinking down against Bering's shoulder.

The driver of the tractor-trailer rig, a soldier, who was as uncon-
cerned about his two passengers as he was about the occasional
rumble and clatter of the freight at his back, whistled an
inaudible melody into the din of the journey. This second tunnel
seemed to have no end. Bering thought that just on the other side
of the warmth of Ambras's nearness, he could feel the pressure of
the mountain, the chill of a huge mass towering hundreds, thousands of feet above them. Somewhere in the depths of this layer
of mountain—trapped within it forever like a million-year-old
lacewing in amber or like the pyrite crystals and bubbles of gas
inside the emeralds Ambras was now carrying with him in a
leather bag—there lay, there *floated* the corpse of a chicken thief.
Perhaps at this very moment they were driving deep beneath the
bottom of the field of sinkholes, deep beneath a floating limestone cemetery that preserved the frozen bodies of a column of
refugees and Lily's rifle and a thug whose bald head was covered
with the snow of bloody feathers.

Snowlight. The mountain spat them out of each tunnel—into
a ravine filled with droplets as fine as dust, into deserted valleys
sloping gently toward the lowlands. Without stopping once, the
column moved past the ruins of stalls and dairies, past stone walls
barely distinguishable from moss-covered rocks and bordering
meadows now run to seed. Fields of scree tumbled from the
white heights. The peaks and ridges already lay under snow. Two
or three times Bering thought he saw the smoke of distant campfires near the timberline, the delicate, drifting shapes of distant
columns of smoke. His perforated vision no longer hid the world
from him. Pale and translucent, his blind spots floated through
this wasteland. Cloud shadows glided above corries and rocky
bluffs.

Although the short days of winter had already begun, the
convoy reached the loading docks and sidings of the railroad station in Brand before nightfall. The city remained invisible
behind grimy warehouses and sheds, was no more than a dome of
light expanding in the dusk. In a gap between two poorly illumi-

nated trains surrounded by crowds of people, Bering also spotted the wrecks of train cars that had shrubs and spare birches growing from their bullet-riddled or simply rust-eaten roofs.

Pulling onto a gravel approach lined with crookneck lamps, the convoy slowed to a crawl. Soldiers in marching gear and civilians lugging bundles, crates, suitcases, and poultry cages were pressing toward train platforms and loading ramps, making any tempo other than their own pace impossible.

"Refugees?" Bering asked.

"Evacuees for resettlement," Ambras said. He had been awakened by the honks of their rig. "The army has promised them uncultivated land."

The North Sea Express was standing at a bumping-post on a siding and looked like a mad collection of every railroad car ever requisitioned, junked, or left as prey to rust, plunderers, and scrap-iron dealers in the bombed-out terminals of the Peace of Oranienburg. Open and closed freight and cattle cars stood behind first-class cars with broken windows, tank and dump cars behind Pullman and club cars—all coupled together as if by random design and overloaded with freight, cows, and people.

Bering, however, saw in this hundreds-of-yards-long Express, with its two monstrous tank locomotives, a hazy image of the Freedom Train, whose remains were still rotting in the overgrown ruins of Moor's station. His powers of memory did not reach deep enough into his own history to let him recall how, on a cold day of his childhood, that train had come gasping toward him under a cloud of soot, bringing him a father out of the desert, a stranger with a fiery red scar on his forehead. But as he boarded a waiting train for the first time in his life, climbed into the club car right behind Lily and Ambras and under the escort of the captain and two military police, he felt rise up within him a hint of the same panicked cackling that had convulsed him that day when the strange man lifted him skyward— and dropped him.

The Pullman—a relic of an almost forgotten age, when the

wealthiest guests of the Grand Hotel and the Bellevue had traveled in rolling parlors through the Stony Sea to the fresh summer air of Moor's lake—was coupled to a flatcar with a load of unmilled tree trunks and jammed with soldiers returning home to America, who were sitting in rickety leather armchairs screwed to the floor, sleeping on ragged plush benches, or playing cards at one of the mahogany tables. Several of them hooted when Lily appeared.

The captain chased two sleepers from their benches and cleared a space for his civilians in this club car reserved for marines. Lily pulled a bottle of cognac from her baggage, set it on the largest table, and asked—in the language of the army and with a smile—if she could close the window. Or were the marines on a survival-training mission in this cold? Four soldiers stood up simultaneously to assist the captain's girlfriend.

"Him and his girlfriend?" one of the cardplayers whispered. "That blond pygmy and a hot chick like that?" Why didn't he kiss her, then, when he said good-bye to her and those two peasants and disappeared with his gorillas? Blue, moth-eaten velvet curtains billowed in the draft. The car door banged shut behind the captain and his guards. The night was turning stormy.

As Moor's iron freight dangled from the arms of cranes, from chains and steel cables above the loading dock, the dust of the Blind Shore drifted from flywheels and rotating sieves out over the siding tracks. Hour after hour, the jolt and racket of loading penetrated metal struts, cushions, mahogany, bones, and muscles and precluded any sleep for passengers attempting—on plush benches, cold plank floors, or cattle-car straw—to doze away the time until departure. Departure? At train stations like this, a traveler found his train, battled for a seat, and then waited for hours and sometimes in vain for the town that he wanted to leave to vanish at last from his compartment windows.

It was long after midnight when the train started to move—with such an abrupt jerk that one returning soldier, who had just stood up from the card table and was reaching for the baggage netting, lost his footing and fell with a curse into the arms of a fellow cardplayer.

The trip from the edge of the Stony Sea to the alluvial shores of the Atlantic Ocean lasted the rest of the night and two more cold nights and three cold days. The very first day, Bering assembled a stove out of an empty oil canister and two tin pails that were found in the club car's cleaning closet—although windows and doors were the only flue for the smoke. Open fires were lit in the cars full of evacuees. Winter had come early this year.

The train plowed through fog, rain, and driving snow and was sometimes held at zone borders and checkpoints for hours—and sometimes stood for hours in open fields for no obvious reason. Peddlers with strapped-on trays, baskets, or two-wheeled carts would suddenly appear as if out of nowhere and run shouting alongside the cars, but all they had to offer was sheep cheese, bread, herbs, cider, or hard candy on strings.

A new radio? Where was Lily supposed to buy a new radio in this wasteland? The North Sea Express crossed windblown steppes, and in the course of the journey the lights of high-rises were spotted only twice—oases, towers of shining glass, much like the palaces of Brand. But for the most part it was only low, rolling fallow land, sometimes under a skiff of snow, that passed before their compartment windows—or the ruins of deserted villages and overgrown, mossy meadows, where hundreds of panicked wild rabbits would bound away as the train approached. *Nuremberg*, Bering read on a signal tower overgrown with black vines, behind which, however, lay no train station, no city, only more steppe.

Out there in the no-man's-land between zones, said a brakeman Bering happened to run into on a platform while on one of his expeditions, out there nature had pretty much recovered from the human race; there were birds out there again that had long been thought extinct—sakers, imperial eagles, merlins, willow grouse. And then the flowers! Lady's slipper and other orchids with names no one knew anymore—a paradise. Hamburg? Hard to say, the brakeman replied before Bering scrambled across bumper and coupling to the next car, maybe another twenty, maybe even thirty hours.

Only a few of the cars on the North Sea Express were joined by gangways. Anyone who wanted to get from the tank locomotives to the end of the train had to take advantage of slow stretches and scramble between cars, like Bering, or jump off if the train stopped and look for metal stairs and ladders two or three cars farther along, but with no assurance that the Express would not start moving again while he was changing cars.

Sometimes, after hours of standing in open country, in the fog and rain, it seemed as if the journey would end in nowhere, but the undertow that had taken hold of the passengers on this train and was pulling them toward the coast was stronger than any obstacle. They rode along, rode farther and farther, and even when they stopped they kept on riding in conversations and dreams, and each of them was excited about a different goal: the men returning home about nightclubs, about barbecues in their own backyards, about hunting and fishing for salmon in the forests of America; the evacuees about the pastures and marshes promised them for resettlement in the north, about abandoned farms they would get running again, about lost islands just offshore inhabited only by birds, about a better life under a sky that wasn't trapped between mountains. . . . But only the captain's girlfriend was excited about Brazil. *That* paradise belonged exclusively to the three civilians from Moor.

While the land rolled back in the direction of Brand, toward the past, grew flatter and flatter, melting into snow and sheets of falling rain, Lily spread her ragged, mildewed map (from whose folds whitewash from the weather tower still trickled) latitude by latitude over the table and showed several of the returning soldiers—and Bering, too—just where along the coast of Brazil this quarry, this backwater village, this Pantano, was. The name was not to be found on the map. But Lily had made a circle with her pencil in a deep-green coastline that bore no trace of highways or railroads. There, somewhere. But Pantano was not *her* goal. The quarry, in which even the granite was the color of the rain forest, was on the road to Santos. As Lily's mother had sat before her easel, painting her husband's portrait or scenes of sailboats and glowing sunsets, she had dreamt of Santos, of a coastal mountain range rising into the clouds above a sweeping bay. The emigrants who long ago had watched one of their number swing from the diving tower on Moor's beach had moved on to Santos. *Santos.* Now, at last, Lily was continuing a journey that had been interrupted on the meadows by the shore at Moor.

When she sat at one of the tables in the club car speaking with Ambras about Brazil and reading him vocabulary words from a well-thumbed dictionary, Bering sometimes asked short, spontaneous questions, and then she did not keep silent or look right past him the way she always did when he sat alone across from her, but told him the Portuguese words for bread, thirst, or sleep, and the bodyguard had no trouble repeating them after her.

"Pantano," Lily read one afternoon, when the train stood hour after hour just before a steel bridge at a zone crossing, and she handed Ambras the book. " *'Pantano.'* It's right here. It means 'marsh, swampy wilderness, wetlands.' "

Ambras took the open book from her hands but without glancing at the lines she was trying to show him, looked past Lily and out into the winter landscape, and said, "Moor."

CHAPTER 32

MUYRA, OR, HOMECOMING

THE SEA? THE ATLANTIC OCEAN? THE ONLY
sea Bering knew was one of limestone and granite,
whose highest waves and petrified breakers were capped
with glaciers and snow. The nineteen days aboard the *Monte
Neblina*, a Brazilian general cargo ship sailing between Hamburg
and Rio de Janeiro, were not a voyage but a flight from the icy
fog of Europe into the summer sky aglow above the Bay of
Guanabara—a floating and gliding across submarine mountains,
deserts, plateaus, and inky-blue hills.

And although Bering could observe these peaks, which rose
from the depths of the sea and yet never broke the ocean surface,
only as hairlines drawn on the ship's sonar map or merely sur-
mise them in the tumbling shadows beneath a swell, he nevertheless felt each wave like a gust of wind, like a thermal current
lifting him high above the mountains at the bottom of the sea.
From the breakers and cross seas of the Bay of Biscay to
the Guinea and other southern equatorial currents, their waves
smoothed by trade winds—every motion of the ship was for him
a figure of flight. The *Monte Neblina* steamed along, listed and

rolled, but Bering took off, rose in spirals, let himself plummet again, circled and sailed above the blue abyss. Slipping away far below him were the valleys of the Iberian Abyssal Plain and the Cape Verde Basin, the coral-covered bluffs of the Azores Plateau, the barren cliffs of the Mid-Atlantic Ridge, and finally the sludge fields and clay deserts of the Brazilian Basin, into which a plumb line, a knife cast over the railing into the water, could sink and sink and sink twenty thousand feet and more.

Bering flew. He often sat for hours on an iron stairway that led down into the engine room, into a thudding space where the temperature could reach over 120° Fahrenheit, sat lost in gazing at the most colossal machine of his life—a diesel engine as big as a house, a two-cycle engine with nine cylinders and twelve thousand horsepower, that used forty tons of oil a day, a black house. He sat on the stairway landing, leaning back, and yet he flew and sailed—floated with his eyes closed as he had long ago in the darkness of his first years, dangled there in warm security—until the propeller screw, which sometimes rose with a howl above its own wake in heavy seas, tore him from his dream. During the only storm on the trip, early one morning at the latitude of Madeira, Bering automatically joined in the howl of the screw and felt a breaker, felt the gale lift him from his swaying cradle and hurl him into the blackish blue of the sky, into the blackish blue of the depths, and bear him away in flight.

On many nights at sea, as he lay awake in the stifling cabin he had to share with Ambras, Bering heard the Dog King moaning and did not know whether he was merely dreaming of pain or actually in pain. But he did not ask him in the darkness; he lay there in his bunk, silent, motionless, angry, and could not help thinking of the pack at the Villa Flora, kept picturing the dogs in a thicket of thorns and barbed wire, until he could no longer bear the moaning and the dogs and the nearness of his master. Then he got up as softly as he could and fled to the engine room.

Among the machinists on the *Monte Neblina*, it was a kindly engineer from Belém who, long after midnight and above the booming din, would shout the Portuguese words for valve, cylinder head, and diesel generator to the sleepless passenger and clap him approvingly on the shoulder if he could shout the words back without making a mistake.

During quiet night watches, the machinist took the passenger along on his inspection tours of the shaft tunnel, led him beside the rotating steel column of the drive shaft, as far as the thunder of the propeller and back again into the blazing heat, up to the cylinder-head station, showed him where the temperature of the shaft bearings was measured, how water and oil levels were gauged, how air intake was regulated and the pressure in the exhaust boiler relieved—and spoke and shouted everything he did, while Bering, dripping with sweat, spoke and shouted it back.

After one such night, he came up on deck to catch his breath under the dazzling morning sun. As the blinding effect eased, not only the pale-green and reddish-orange spots left his vision, drifting away like phantoms, but so, too, did darker things, shadows, black balls. The blue of the sky turned flawless.

In the caves, corridors, and tunnels of the engine room, the smudges in his vision could easily be lost, camouflaged as shadows among many shadows, and he would never notice. But here? In this blue? In this light? Morrison had been proved right! Bering raised his head and in the cloudless sky saw only floating glassy scars, thin as wisps, but nothing else that could resist this great light and darken his vision.

As always when Bering returned to his cabin early in the morning, Ambras was already somewhere else—at the anchor station in the bow (where he often sat alone for hours in the lee of the bulwark), in the dining room, or perhaps deep below in the hold with his iron from Moor. The smell of the sea wafted through the open portal. On this occasion, too, Bering crept back into his bunk undisturbed by his master's presence and pain and fell asleep—and did not awaken as usual later that morning, but only hours afterward, when the tropical dusk was descending so rapidly that as he stretched with a yawn and brushed the tangled hair from his brow, he saw stars appearing in the portal.

Lily.

Bering's first thought after his dreamless day was Lily. *She* had led him to Morrison. She had pushed him away and cursed him and perhaps even hated him just as he had hated her, up there in the field of sinkholes. But she had led him to Morrison. And Morrison had been proved right. One sign, if she would have given him one little sign now, *Come here*, he would have gone to her. He would have risked any path to her one more time.

But Lily was not in her cabin. And in the dining room an accordion player was singing some wild song to which two couples were dancing, tumbling out of synch at times in the rolling seas. And a merchant from Pôrto Alegre, who was sitting at a table with Ambras, said, "Beautiful as a Brazilian woman . . ." He did not mean Lily, however, but rather a life-size Madonna lying in a bed of excelsior and paper in the hold. Forty-seven crates, the merchant said, forty-seven crates full of statues of angels and saints, princes, martyrs, generals, and crucified redeemers from the ruins of Central Europe, all purchased cheap and being delivered to rich *fazandeiros*, collectors, and industrialists, from Rio Grande do Sul to Minas Gerais, and up north, too, to Bahia and Pernambuco. The business of the future. The only aid these heroes and saints provided the zones and no-man's-lands along the Danube and Rhine was what they sold for on the market. Emigrate, the merchant said, emigrate . . . wasn't much else left for a man to do there. In his family, for example, only the emigrants had amounted to anything.

Lily?

Neither Ambras nor the merchant had seen Lily since morning. Some days she did not even appear for meals, but ate in her cabin or wherever, and when she did come to the dining or smoking room, she seldom sat at a table with the men from Moor, but usually with Brazilian passengers, tourists on their way home after adventures in the ruins of Europe's war—or with businessmen and headhunters, who had been looking for workers in the zones, looking for new markets and usable debris. With her dictionary and map of Brazil in hand, Lily had spent time at almost all the tables of the small band of passengers aboard the *Monte Neblina*, and had long since begun speaking Portuguese, even with the merchant from Pôrto Alegre, although he would have understood the dialect of Moor.

But when Bering finally found her on the sounding deck and was about to tell her that the holes in his vision had closed, closed, just as *her* Doc Morrison had predicted, she looked so serene and distracted, gazing right through him to the white, dying track of the wake, that he could not utter a word. He saw the features of Lily's face before him, distinct and yet deep in shadow, as if the darkness that had left his eyes were now smoke rising up from inside him and darkening not only the face of a lost love but also the sea, the sky, the world.

He turned around and left without greeting her and climbed down into the engine room and sat there on the iron stairway for hours, and wanted to hear only the pounding of the pistons— and the machinist from Belém understood that he had best not talk with his passenger tonight. Bering sat listening to the symphonic rumbling and could differentiate within it the deepest and shrillest metallic voices, and yet not a single tone hurt his ears. And as the ship began to roll in the first waves of a tropical thunderstorm, he did not hold fast, but separated the thunderclaps, which occasionally found their way down to him, from the stroke of the engine's pistons, and swayed between the stair railing and the steel exit door like a pendulum, like a man who had fallen asleep. But he was not sleeping. He sat there with eyes open until the sea grew calm again. Up top it had to be shortly before sunrise.

Only now, as if he had finally heard his name in the engine's tumult, did he get up and climb out of the heat of the cylinder-head station into a morning that was only a wisp cooler. He stood at the bulwark, in the light, taking deep breaths, and yet felt as if he were falling into a dream—a mountain range! A line of black mountains rose up out of the ocean, out of the smoke of mother-of-pearl fog banks: granite towers, cliffs as dark and mighty as the precipices of the Stony Sea. Domes polished smooth by erosion, floating above the clouds like jellyfish, were transformed by swathes of fog into the backs of monstrous beasts that gradually grew hairy with trees, their blossoming pelts thick with cloudy vegetation and palms and fettered by lianas and creeping vines.

As near and yet as distant as only a dream can be, the mountains rose against the assaulting surf and hurled jungle-covered islands, floating gardens, back at the dreamer and his ship, and then the mountains turned lazily in the wind to reveal bays and capes, the sickles of bright beaches. And between water, rocks, and sky, along the hem of mountains and sea, there were now shining façades, high-rises, promenades, and over the peninsulas, slopes, and bays were strewn villas, churches, a white fort whose gun turrets and flagpoles sank back into the fog twice and re-emerged twice, as radiant as if covered with mirrors or flashing with cannon fire. And somewhere high above this swirl of clouds, surf, walls, and stone, the passenger dreamt a towering figure atop one of the peaks. It spread its arms wide—and he was flying toward it, when suddenly a fist landed on his shoulder and thrust him into the deep. Then he heard laughter. The sun had risen. Now he would have to awaken. The machinist was standing behind him. Clapped him on the shoulder. Laughed.

But the mountains, the bays, the outspread arms did not disappear. The vegetation on the domes, the jungle, began to glow a deep green. The rocks remained black. And the machinist remained where he was, too, and kept crying out a single name in triumph, again and again, until Bering finally understood that this city, these promenades and beaches and everything toward which he was flying, was not part of his dream, but of the voice of the machinist, who cried out *Rio!* over and over, and laughed and drummed the syllables on his shoulder: *Rio de Janeiro!*

No soldiers, no general was waiting at the docks at Rio de Janeiro, only a dark-skinned woman, and standing beside her on the gangway were two servants or porters in red livery. The woman was named Muyra, and when she said her name Bering thought it was a greeting in the local language.

Muyra?

A word of the Tupi, she said. It meant Beautiful Tree.

"The Tupi?" Lily asked.

"Jungle people," Muyra said. "At one time they lived on this coast."

"At one time?" Lily asked. "And now?"

"Now we still bear only their names," Muyra said.

Everything about Muyra was dark: her skin, her eyes, her hair, even the sound of her voice. She was hardly older than Bering, and he forgot to let go of her hand and kept holding it in his own until Muyra pulled it away so that she could apportion the baggage between her liveried escorts.

"I welcome you also in the name of Senhor Plínio de Nacar," she said. The *patrão* had business in Belo Horizonte and would not return to Pantano for a week or two. He had also promised to bring a new machine, a bulldozer. Everything had stood abandoned and rotting for years at the largest quarry on the Fazenda Auricana, and the road to it was always impassable when it rained.

Muyra understood the newcomers' language, but without knowing anything more about the zone where Moor was than that someone in her family had come from someplace there— from Brandenburg, wasn't that close by? He had built bridges, had built viaducts in Salvador and had never returned to Europe. And what she knew about Europe was that it was small, too small, and that wars broke out there more quickly, one after the other, than in a country that, despite cities with millions of people and skyscrapers, receded into the wilderness, into the rain forests of the Amazon, into the swamps of Mato Grosso.

"Monte Neblina," Muyra said as they drove off from the docks.

"*My* ship. You came on my ship. . . ." The new arrivals from Moor sat squeezed between baggage in a jeep driven by one of the men in livery, and they watched the ship sink into a forest of cranes, derricks, loading tackle, drawbridges, and radio towers. The iron of Moor would not be unloaded till the end of the week, after the Christmas holidays, and would follow them to Pantano on flatbed trucks.

Brazil was so large, Muyra said, that the country's highest mountain had been discovered and measured only in the last few years, a mountain in the jungle on the border with Venezuela, the Pico da Neblina, almost ten thousand feet high. And not just peaks of such height could remain hidden in Brazil until the present day, but also whole peoples. Even now, certain tribes in Amazonas, for example, were known only by columns of smoke from their campfires, vanishing signs of life in the aerial photographs of surveyors. "Pico da Neblina!" Muyra cried, "that's *my* mountain." She would go there one day, to Manaus and up the Rio Negro and then ever farther into the wilderness, following those columns of smoke to the end of Brazil, to the end of the world.

The coastline of Rio de Janeiro rolled lazily by under tires that sang on the hot asphalt. "Slow down!" Muyra laid a calming hand on the driver's arm. Each time some new sickle of beach, some new glittering promenade, opened before them, Muyra turned around to the newcomers and told them the names of these beaches and bays, and sometimes Bering soundlessly formed his lips in the shape of the Brazilian woman's beautiful mouth: Praia do Flamengo, Enseada de Botafogo, Praia de Copacabana . . . de Ipanema . . . Leblon . . . São Conrado, Barra da Tijuca. . . . They left the city behind. After passing an expansive, practically deserted bay, which Muyra announced as Grumari and whose roaring surf made the engine and tires almost inaudible, the rumbling car dived into the shimmer and silence of a mangrove forest, out of which a flock of heron took flight.

Senhor Plínio a general? The *patrão*, the boss, a general? Muyra laughed and shook her head, when Ambras asked her about the new owner of Moor's iron. The *patrão* had always been proud of having fought as a *tenente* in the corps of Marechal Mascarenhas de Moraes, Muyra said, in the corps of Brazil's great hero, who had won battles alongside America and its allies in the World War. . . . Even now the boss would still get excited remembering the victory parade through the streets of Rio, the triumphant carnival . . . but Senhor Plínio de Nacar a general?

The drive to Pantano followed the coastline, traced the deep cuts of rocky bays, the gentle loops of sandy bays, the edge of a jungle that fell in dark cascades from the clouds to the sea and sometimes opened to reveal a surprising view of a waterfall, of roaring veils whose plunging flight toward the breaking surf resembled the foam and whitecaps far below. . . . And as coastal villages—frame shacks hung with bundles of bananas, gas stations shaded by blossom-covered rocks, mud huts lost in undergrowth—rumbled past the newcomers, Muyra told about the boss's geometrically planted eucalyptus forests, about the sugarcane plantations, cassava fields, cattle ranges, and quarries that were part of the Fazenda Auricana, the *patrão*'s great estate; told about Senhor Plínio's love for America, about his deep regard for Marechal Mascarenhas and his plan to erect a monument to Brazil's hero on a cliff near Pantano—an obelisk made of the quarry's green granite that would be a permanent reminder of the joy of Brazil's triumph and of her sorrow for her fallen soldiers. . . .

Ambras nodded at times in response to Muyra's tales. Had he heard the story of the boss once before? Bering saw only that his master was in pain and attempting, to no avail, to stave off the jolts of the drive. Ambras sat there with his arms crossed over his chest, pressing his palms against his shoulder joints as if hugging himself. No, he had not been listening for a good while now; he was far away. And Lily, rapt in the vision of the coast, in the crests of oncoming breakers—she was on her way to Santos. The convoy that would bring Moor's iron to Pantano and then proceed down the coast farther south, that was *her* convoy. She had arrived. She was almost in Santos.

Only Bering, he alone, as weary and exhausted as he was, did not miss a word this Brazilian woman said, and sometimes he bent forward very tense, very alert, plunged deep into her eyes, and felt her dark hair brush his forehead as it whipped in the wind—he was all alone with this woman. What she said, she said to *him*. And among all these new names and words, he now likewise heard the names of European battlefields, which she sang as if they were a counting rhyme, and laughed afterward and told him how the boss had demanded that the children in the schoolhouse at Fazenda Auricana be required to memorize and recite them, in chorus and solo: Monte Castello, Montese, Fornovo, Zocca, Collecchio, Castelnuovo, Camaiore, Monte Prano. . . .

Whoever could recite those eight *vitórias* by heart in one breath had been awarded coins or caramel-covered peanuts by the *patrão*, for on all those battlefields, which lay somewhere in Italy, Brazil, under the serpent banner of Marechal João Baptista Mascarenhas de Moraes, had triumphed over the world's enemies.

CHAPTER 33

AURICANA

T HE MAIN HOUSE OF FAZENDA AURICANA
stood on one of the many terraces that the *patrão*, Plínio
de Nacar, had ordered dug, blasted, burned, and
pounded out of the jungle by the Bay of Pantano after his happy
return home from Europe and war.

Like a grand stairway overgrown with fields, pastures, and
hanging gardens, the steps of his estate descended from the slopes
of the Serra do Mar to wide beaches that sent the soothing
thunder of surf rising to the verandas of the fazenda. Herdsmen
might be busy lassoing animals chosen for slaughter out of a herd
of panicked zebus or pressing the grubs of gadflies from the open
boils on a breeding bull's back and smearing the sore with a
smelly salve—but if they looked up from their work and gazed
down across the tops of termite hills, they saw the sea.

At America's side and under the banner of his beloved
marechal, Senhor Plínio de Nacar had defeated the European
barbarians and, later, the wilderness itself. Decorated with
Brazil's most coveted war medals, he had inherited the estate in
the same year he returned home to the Bay of Pantano and with

an army of peons had cleared the land, planted cassava, coffee, and bananas, and had opened quarries—and finally he built the aviaries and cages that now lay scattered about the main house in the shade of aurelias, fan palms, and bougainvillea, and in them he placed all the creatures he had hunted and trapped on arduous journeys through the jungle regions of his homeland: maned wolves from Salvador, black jaguars from the Serra do Jatapu, alligators from the Amazon, sloths, a tapir, king vultures and toucans, more than a dozen different kinds of monkeys and parrots, vermilion coral snakes, and an anaconda as long as a tree trunk.

Over the years, the rusting iron bars and bamboo lattices of many cages and aviaries had become so overgrown with the ever-advancing bush that a visitor to the fazenda would no longer have been able to say where the boss's zoo ended and the wilderness began. Were those jaguar's eyes staring out between bars wrapped in green tendrils or simply out of the supple, wind-blown underbrush? And that Bahia macaw with its sky-blue and garish red tail feathers as long as reeds—was it sitting in an invisible aviary or in open, dense vegetation? But however unquenchable the boss's thirst to collect, the number of wild animals freely prowling his empire far outnumbered the captives in his zoo. At dusk, Muyra would point out the armadillos and iguanas to Bering—this odd European who could amuse and sometimes confound her with his ability to mimic birdcalls—and she also showed him a row of jars in which, on the boss's orders, any coral snakes killed by the stableboys in the calf barn were preserved in spirits.

Within the first few days after his arrival at the fazenda, Bering could identify seven different kinds of hummingbirds. He swayed through the hot, humid afternoon air in a hammock on the veranda of the guest house while the tiny birds hovered about glass flutes filled with sugar water and dangling from the beams. Sometimes the hummingbirds stopped still in the air like dragonflies, made a circle of themselves, became hovering feather crowns, dipped their curved beaks and threadlike tongues into the artificial flowers decorating the flutes, and seemed to merge with the columns of water sparkling inside the glass and form enigmatic symbols—totems of iridescent feathers, beaks, plastic flowers, water, and light.

But the ruler whose omnipresence these bird totems declared remained invisible. For the cloudbursts that had drenched the coast in the days between Christmas and New Year's Day, and sent mudslides and rockslides thundering down across the beaches of many bays and into the sea, now held the mighty *patrão* himself, Plínio de Nacar, prisoner in a tiny village no more than sixty miles north of his fazenda.

There was no comparison between the storms of Pantano and any summer thunderstorm the newcomers from Moor had ever known. These frenzied cloudbursts with their chain-reaction explosions of lightning and thunder would sometimes drift along under a low sky, disguised as simple curtains of rain, and only when very close would they then congeal into a wall of water, broken branches, blinding light, and foliage. These storms could rage for minutes or hours, obscuring the day, illuminating the night. Mud roads and trails were transformed into bottomless, savage torrents, and the uncovered driveways and stairways linking the fazenda's terraces and gardens became roiling cataracts.

The mountain roads of the Serra and many connecting roads along the coast, a voice on the radio said, were blocked at several points by landslides, and another voice, very similar to the one on the radio, cursed from the loudspeaker of the fazenda's transmitter, but then laughed a short, fierce laugh—and Muyra translated: "This could go on for days yet. We're stuck." It was the voice of her *patrão*.

The big shipment. The convoy of iron from Rio? There could be no thought of that for now.

When the sun broke through the blockade of clouds—a piercing white sun that made every task difficult and exhausting—fog rose in shining, steaming swathes from the coastal

forests, and with it rose such a screech of cicadas that it was as
if not just rainwater but the earth itself were evaporating in air
scented with flowers and rotting foliage. And at the far end of the
bay the village of Pantano vanished in the fog: houses and mud
huts flung across a steep slope, the bell tower of the Adventist
church, the tin roof of the village movie house, the cold-storage
shed patterned with black mildew, where fish and the semen for
impregnating the boss's finest cows were kept on ice.

"Down *this* road?" Bering asked on the last day of the year,
when after riding in a mud-encrusted jeep with Ambras, Muyra,
and one of the boss's miners, they had been forced to leave the
vehicle and continue on foot to reach the remotest of Fazenda
Auricana's three quarries. "Semis are supposed to drive this? How
can it be done?"

"I don't know," Ambras said.

The rutted track, down which they proceeded very slowly even
on foot, was more like the bed of a waterless brook, repeatedly
blocked with gravel and driftwood, than a road for heavy rigs. It
led between granite boulders the size of houses and, beneath an
interwoven cover of trees overhead, to a wide bowl where the
heat and mosquitoes were almost unbearable. The miner
laughed. "He says the *patrão* will build a road," Muyra translated.
"He says, the *patrão* has built many roads before this."

The quarry, Santa Fé da Pedra Dura, lay at the end of a valley
where the fountainheads of Pantano's springs were located. Here
the rush of water could be heard from every gorge and gully in
the rocks—but no sound of surf. Preceding the boss's guests, the
miner forded a brook in which debris from a collapsed bridge lay
like bristled islands surrounded by swarms of insects. Bering
noticed brightly painted figurines in the lemongrass of these
islands—and dozens of burning candles! Clay and porcelain
statues of the Virgin and Christ, their heads knocked off and
candles stuck in the necks, were surrounded by bottles full of
whisky, plates of overripe fruit, corn, and grain—they stood like
maimed candlesticks in the grass. At the feet of some of the

decapitated Madonnas were bridal veils, rotting dresses, bloody bandages.

"New Year's gifts for the spirits," Muyra said. "Sacrifices." The miner crossed himself.

A quarry? Nothing in this rockbound bowl looked like the working terraces and dusty diligence of the Blind Shore. There were no terraces in this quarry, no heaps of stone, no gravel works, but only one huge cone of granite that towered so high into the sky, higher than the edge of the bowl itself, that Bering shivered despite waves of heat that brushed his face with each breeze. The monolith was overgrown with lichen and vines, and only where it looked as if it had been gnawed at—far below, at the foot, where a filigree of bamboo scaffolding was propped against the rock beside a tumbledown frame shed—was the wonderful green of this stone visible.

In no quarry of Fazenda Auricana, Muyra said, was the granite as flawless and beautifully marked as here. That the boss had delayed making use of these riches was due to his many businesses in São Paulo, to the difficulty of access—and probably also due to macumba devotees, who wanted to continue invoking their spirits in this valley undisturbed. But the *patrão*'s patience was exhausted. The tallest skyscrapers in São Paulo were being wrapped in cloaks of primal stone like this.

On the way back to the sea, the Bay of Pantano with its cloud-draped heights shimmered below them as beautifully as the lake of Moor, and Bering told Muyra about the snow that surely lay deep over Moor now. By the time they reached the coast, it was dark. Fires sprang up along the beach—and the first bouquet of tracer rockets. The year was ending.

In the hours before midnight, everywhere in Pantano people dressed in white left their houses and verandas. The people at the main house on the fazenda also dressed in white. They rose from the banquet table and walked down toward the shore, carrying torches and candles, and waded with the other white-clad villagers out into the dark sea. Standing in water up to their hips, up to their breasts, they waited for the oncoming waves and launched white floral wreaths, white garlands of petals, and torches set in buoys of wood or cork, they wished one another good luck, they embraced.

Seven waves, Muyra shouted to Bering above the roar of the surf, each person had to plunge into seven waves tonight to wash away the year past and to be free and light for everything new. And Bering, who was wearing the white shirt of one of the fazenda's secretaries and already deep in the foaming water, felt the first wave pull the soft, sandy bottom out from under his feet. And then Muyra was beside him and would not let his feet find the bottom again. She held her arms out to him, held him in the warm flood, held him suspended there—and then pulled him to her and embraced him and, laughing, kissed him on both cheeks, kissed him while the second wave rushed toward them, a mighty breaker that bore the reflection of drifting torches on its crest.

In the first days of the new year, the ferocity of the thunderstorms abated, but the heat and humidity increased, and could be eased only by ventilators, fans—and idleness. The iron and all the machines from Moor stayed where they were, and the boss took the first cleared road back to Rio de Janeiro, gave instructions now from a garden on the beach at Leblon, and sent his guests greetings from there as well. He would be coming soon.

In Santa Fé da Pedra Dura everything was quiet.

Bering awoke sweat-drenched every morning, rose sweat-drenched from his bed, lay sweat-drenched in hammocks on the verandas, and sat sweat-drenched at the table. A woolen shirt from Moor, all the extra clothing he had brought along but that now lay unused in his room, began to mildew in the damp. Even the shoes he had long since traded for sandals and the photograph showing him with his vanished brothers bore dainty colonies of mold. For the first time since Ambras had armed him, he no longer carried his pistol. After a walk along the beach by Pantano, his sweat-drenched skin was so sunburned that the weapon had rubbed it raw. In any case, the man the weapon was meant to protect stayed hidden. He spent entire afternoons lying in his darkened room, tortured by the pain in his shoulder joints. Fazenda Auricana was a safe place. And so Bering wrapped his pistol in oilcloth and put it with his talon in the mildewing cardboard suitcase—and the very next morning, well before sunrise, he grabbed it from its hiding place and ran along the veranda to his master's room.

Someone there was calling out. Someone was groaning as if locked in fierce struggle. Someone there had called out. And for a few strides, a few seconds, the bodyguard, still dazed with sleep and entangled in a dream, was back where he came from, heard the skinhead panting in pursuit, heard the pained cries of some woman being dragged by the hair from her house in the early morning.

When he reached Ambras's room, the door to the veranda was standing open, and he ripped a curtain aside. In the soft light that fell over the mosquito net glistening like a silky tent above a bamboo bed, he saw Lily. She was sitting upright inside the flimsy tent, and Ambras, covered with a sheet or a white shirt, lay in her shadow.

Strange how, now that he finally saw Lily sitting before him naked in an eddy of white cloth—as beautiful as he had dreamed her to be in so many, often agonizing, fantasies—it was the brilliance of her eyes he noticed above all. Ambras and Lily. The Dog King and the Brazilian. He saw only her eyes. For in his dreams he had already exchanged her pale skin, the mark of her navel, that pale, slender body . . . for something darker, more mysterious, for Muyra's softness and warmth, which he had felt in the spindrift of New Year's Eve. Except that those eyes, those brilliant eyes were also looking at him again now, staring out of this new vision. Lily shouldn't look at him! She shouldn't stare at him! She should get out of his sight! But she remained. She sat mute, erect, naked in the glistening tent. He lowered his pistol and turned away, turned from her and his master, and without pulling the curtain to behind him, stepped out on the veranda, into the open.

Dead tired. Was there such a term, dead tired? The raging pain in his shoulders and the stupor caused sometimes by sugar-cane schnapps had made Ambras forget so many words. And amid the flood of new words and names that entered his darkened room from the fazenda's courtyards and gardens of an afternoon, his own language sometimes seemed unintelligible and strange. *Dead tired.* Even in the camp he had never been as exhausted as during these first days of the new year.

"Go," he said to Lily when at some point she entered the darkness of his room to tell him about the open roads and the news from Rio and to ask about his pain. He knew that she had begun to say her good-byes. She would be in Santos in a few days. "Go now, I'm dead tired."

But she laid her hands on his searing shoulders. And what happened then only revealed to him how long ago he had ceased to be among the living. It was not her lips that he felt on his forehead, on his cheeks, on his mouth. It was not her hair that flowed through his hands in the darkness. And words, which found their way into his mind but could not be spoken, formed the same sentences over and over all on their own, kept repeating themselves inside him this night—monotonously and mechanically and a hundred times over—without his ever uttering a single one: *I am healthy. I am doing fine. Where were you, my dear. Don't forget me.*

Did the lakeshore buried under snow still exist, the place where tomorrow, a Sunday in January, was called the Feast of Three Kings? Moor's fields of reeds, glassy and tinkling with ice, and snowdrifts towering high above the ruins of the camp by the gravel works—was that memory or illusion?

In the Bay of Pantano, it turned so hot on the Feast of Three Kings that a column of smoke rose above one of the many islands lying like the heads of a swimming herd in the distance, in the farthest distance, of the blue sea. Muyra stood with the *patrão's* guests in front of one of the fazenda's jaguar cages and pointed beyond its rusty bars to the smoke drifting far out over the ocean. "Brushfire," she said, and tossed the Black Jaguar of the Amazon a scrap of meat. Under the January sun, even wet, moldering foliage, deadwood, and branches broken off in the storm became rotted tinder within a few hours.

The distraught jaguar paced relentlessly back and forth across the shadows of the bars, across the diagonal ladder on the clay floor of its dungeon. Blotched with scabs and open sores, it paid no attention to the flies following it, or to the meat. "It has mange," Muyra said. "Senhor Plínio will shoot it."

But the boss's guests suddenly seemed less fascinated by the disfigured animal than by the thin column of smoke drifting off into the blue. What had she said? What was the name of that island out there? And Muyra, surprised by this sudden change of interest, repeated the name that was so familiar to her that its translation sounded like a vulgar curse word: *Ilha do Cão*. Dog Island.

CHAPTER 34

THE FIRE IN
THE OCEAN

RUSHFIRES IN JANUARY WERE LAZY AND tough, and because they were constantly driven back by thunderstorms and cloudbursts, they sometimes strayed through the wilderness for days, hid in nests of embers, crept out of their lairs for new attacks, until finally, exhausted by rain and invincible damp, they died out in the green dusk of uncharted forests. For a hunter or ranger, the menace of panicked animals in flight was greater than any danger of dying in one of these muddled fires—poisonous snakes that struck at any enemy who stood unsuspecting in their path of escape or, on the Ilha do Cão, the wild dogs from which the island took its name.

Muyra could not tell the boss's guests how many years Dog Island had been a prison, off-limits, guarded by bloodhounds. The dogs, so it was said in Pantano, would have pounced on intruders or fleeing prisoners with equal fury. Muyra had still been learning the Brazilian army's *vitórias* by heart in the fazenda schoolhouse, when a senate in São Paulo decided to enlarge the prison and move it to the mainland. Four rows of barred stone buildings, a lighthouse, the jetty, and a shored-up beach then reverted to wilderness. The prisoners and their guards had long since vanished aboard ships rattling with the sound of chains, when fishermen noticed the sound of barking dogs still coming from the island. A few of the beasts from the pack must have stayed behind—been abandoned, chased off, or simply forgotten. Who could say nowadays? The fact remained that with each new generation of increasingly savage offspring, these bloodhounds were now as wary of men as their prey was. They loved shadows, hid in the underbrush by day, rarely came down to the beach, and were hunted with shotguns or harpoons by fishermen and bird catchers who sometimes spent the night in the prison ruins.

Dangerous? Was it dangerous to take the Fazenda Auricana's cabin cruiser to the smoking Ilha do Cão, to go ashore, always with the assurance of knowing you could return to the boat anchored in a sheltered bay? Muyra couldn't say what wild dogs might do out of fear of fire, but anyone coming from Europe was surely used to worse. "There are probably some harpooner fishermen there, too." The loveliest fish took refuge in the undersea grottoes of the Ilha do Cão. No danger.

In the stifling noonday heat of the Feast of Three Kings, the kitchen staff in the main house gathered up equipment, canisters of diesel oil, and two or three days' worth of provisions for a trip of at least a hundred nautical miles aboard the cabin cruiser. Early that afternoon and in a light wind, Muyra put to sea with the boss's guests. The fazenda's boatman had to carry the flag today for a procession to Santa Fé da Pedra Dura, but Muyra did not need a man to handle the boat. And she did not want to hand over the helm of the *Rainha do Mar* to this bird man, either. Even if he did know a lot about diesel engines—the reefs in this labyrinth of islands were deceptive. Not all the shoals sent fountains of spray into the air. And in the smoothest, bluest waters, the peaks of sunken mountains were still a menace.

In Muyra's hands the wheel spins as if this were a game. A chart? She doesn't need a chart to find a safe channel. Shaded by an awning, she follows a baffling course toward the fire in the ocean. The pennant of smoke is now floating so close to the horizon that it sometimes disappears behind the swells. Perhaps the fire is already dying out.

As if it took only the name and history of an island to call him out of his darkened room and back into the world, the Dog King is sitting on a deck chair in the same position in which Bering has seen him spend so many hours on the veranda of the Villa Flora—arms crossed at his chest, head tipped to one side, gaze directed out over the water. Does he hear what Lily says to him? She searches the archipelago, beach by beach, with the binoculars, but only rarely does she spot houses, mud huts, roofs floating on the flickering light beyond the surf. Most of these islands are uninhabited. Uninhabited, like the one that gradually emerges, steep and as large as a mountain, out of the sea ahead. There is no smoke to be seen now.

Bering would love to be alone with Muyra out on this ocean, beneath these garish white towers of clouds. The mute nearness of his master and Lily's looking and searching and talking and all the other things that prevent him from being alone with Muyra have made him restless. Have made him angry. At one point he stands staring back at the mountainous coast beyond the dinghy dancing in their wake; then he stands up in the bow again as if spellbound by the island as it grows taller and taller, and long before the water of a pale-green, mirror-smooth bay bursts under the anchor of the *Rainha do Mar*, he goes belowdecks where the equipment lies piled. There are tarps, hammocks, and a carefully coiled rope, mosquito nets, hand-forged axes, and—lying across a tin chest filled with bottles and chipped ice—a carbine from the *patrão*'s arsenal. Muyra has thought of everything, even of mad dogs. Presumably, however, there will be nothing more to be seen of the pack on Dog Island this time than she has seen or heard on earlier visits—tracks, scat, maybe a distant yelp in the night or a woeful howl like that of a jackal.

"Who'll take the gun?" Muyra asks as they get ready to load

the dinghy to go ashore. The jetty has been worn away by breakers and cracked by roots as thick as a man's arm—no boats have tied up there in a long time.

"The gun? Give it to him," Lily says, like someone who is in charge. But *she* has no say in this. Not anymore and not here. All the same, Bering takes the gun from Muyra's hands.

Ambras stands up to his knees in water, arms hanging at his sides, and watches the women and his bodyguard pull the dinghy through a breach in the ruined shorings and onto the sand. He cannot help them. They haven't decided yet how long they want to stay. Maybe until evening. Maybe for a night. Maybe they'll sail farther, as far as Cabo do Bom Jesus, even beyond. Muyra points to the only one of the prison buildings hidden in the thicket that still has its roof. That was where the fishermen built their fires. They could set up camp there, too.

But then, there in the shade of a cliff that encircles the extensive ruins like a huge cupped hand, each of them is suddenly alone. Dazed as if by the first sight of a newly discovered land, the newcomers scramble over rubble and what remains of walls, bend down here for a shard, there for a rust-eaten chain that has grown into a tree trunk, break through the thicket, get lost in a wilderness that grabs hold of deserted places with less caution, less hesitance than in Moor, and instead swoops down on everything left behind, leaps through windows and cracks into the inside of buildings, storms out again over rotting floors, collapsed stairs, and through shattered roofs—a wilderness that entwines, seizes, rends, devours anything in its path, before it can itself be devoured by rot or a brushfire gone astray.

The fire. They can smell it everywhere. Even through the fragrance of flowers and the odor of rotting tree trunks and beams, the newcomers can smell the brushfire. It is as hidden as each of them is from the others now. But it is there. It is devouring something somewhere. It is waiting. But they see not a single tongue of flame. And no smoke.

Ambras cuts his hands on a spiral of barbed wire overgrown by hibiscus. He can smell the ovens. The corpses. This almost impenetrable thicket here, this must have been the drill field. Along the road through the camp, between the stony watch-towers, inside the barracks—the fire is present everywhere and yet soundless and invisible. Anyone who does not shout his number loud enough at roll call can be burning by evening—can be smoke dispersed into the night and trickling back down over the camp in the cold of the next morning, falling as soot, black dust, onto columns of workers moving toward the quarry, filling their noses with stench, creeping into their lungs, their eyes, ears, and dreams.

Where is the gate? The fence? The gate to the camp must be somewhere here, between these two caved-in barracks. And to the left and right, the embankment, and atop the embankment the electric fence. The cliff ahead of him towers into the sky, is hung with a mesh of blossoming lianas, dangling wiry roots, ferns. The wires pass through white blossoms, insulators of white porcelain. Those are the stairs, too, that lead up the embankment to the watchtower, where each night light falls in rotating cud-gels. Whoever makes it to these stairs has been moving in the firing zone for a good while. Ambras climbs, step-by-step. He is so exhausted. He must be close to the crest of the embankment. Muted by curtains of lianas, the sea shimmers far below. Now a beam of light grabs hold of him. He has to stop, catch his breath. *I am healthy. I am doing fine.* Are they shooting yet? The shot he hears—is that shot meant for him? He is not afraid. For he is searching for his love, for everything he has missed for so long now—searching where so many lost things get caught. He walks into the fence.

To think that iron can be so brittle. With his bare hands, Bering breaks bars that rust has peeled thin, layer after layer. And the iron railing of stairs that lead down into a cellar likewise snaps in his hand. Down below, in the debris and wet foliage that has fallen through light shafts and holes in the floor, he finds iron bolts and hoops, the remains of iron bed frames, and iron grids whose purpose he does not know, finds iron rings that were bolted in the cell walls but that he can pull out of the masonry with no effort. A bayonet's wooden handle lying in the muck on the floor of a vaulted chamber is only a handful of decay strewn across a rust-eaten blade.

No file, no oil bath, no forge will help this iron garden. And the brushfire, whose odor has found its way even into this cellar, has nothing to do with the bright-red coals of the forge, which could be brought to a blaze with a single puff of the bellows. It is quiet here. As quiet as in the cellar of the fort at Frost Pass, and just as he did then, Bering hears the blood tolling inside his head. But beyond the tolling is something else—a gentle, steady murmur. That's not his blood. That's rain. How long has he been wandering through this suite of subterranean cells?

Bering climbs a steep ramp of rubble back up into the underbrush, and watches long, narrow ribbons of rain drift in from the ocean, whose surface is a jostling crowd of cloud shadows and lambent specks of sun, restive glittering islands of light.

Rain! Now it is Lily who is angry. Where have they dragged her off to? What is this here? The lakeside resort at Moor? She is standing in the middle of prison ruins, in the rain, in the ruins of the lakeside resort, in the rubble of the Bellevue. She wants to go to Santos, and is standing in the middle of Moor! The coastal highway has been cleared for a good while now, but she is standing in Moor, in a dripping wilderness that stinks of cold ashes. Where are the others? She has to get out of here. Has to get back. She's not going to wait any longer for that convoy from Rio, either. Her good-byes have lasted for days. Every morning, Muyra said, there is a bus for Santos. Every morning.

A strange boat is rocking in the light green of the bay. Fishermen from Pantano. Harpoon fishermen. Muyra is standing in the water, holding fast to the side of the boat with one hand, and with the other she accepts two fish tied together at the gills, holds them up, and laughs as Lily wades out to her. "I've bought some fish! Garopas."

"I want to go back," Lily says. Are you going to Pantano? Will you take me with you? is what she wants to ask the two fishermen in her new language, but Muyra has to help her ask. The men in the boat are already reaching out their arms for this foreign woman, who is a guest of the *patrão*—but she has to return to the beach again. The *Rainha do Mar*'s dinghy is there, and she fetches a knapsack, her things. And as she hurries back to them, she searches and rummages in this army pack for a gift. The best item she finds is a raincoat, American army issue, a loosely cut poncho with a hood and spotted with the camouflage of the marines. Lily has worn this poncho on many trips through the Stony Sea. It was always dry and warm under this raincoat.

One of the fishermen claps his hands—he would love to have the raincoat. But Lily embraces Muyra, pulls the poncho over her shoulders, and pushes her hair into the raised hood as she would with a child who isn't supposed to get wet. Then she points back to the beach, to the ruins into which the Dog King and his body-guard have vanished, and says, "I can't stay. Tell them that I can't stay any longer. Tell them I've gone to Santos."

Muyra stays behind. The hem of the poncho dances in the rise and fall of smaller waves. She swings the glistening fish, waves to the boat as it quickly grows smaller. Santos. She wants to go there sometime herself, not to end a journey but to begin the greatest journey of her life—from the harbor at Santos to Salvador, Fortaleza, and São Luís, to Belém and Manaus and then on, and on forever.

Muyra runs through the rain, across the warm sand, up the beach as far as a barrier of smoothly worn boulders, between which a freshwater rivulet flows to the sea. There, under dangling roots and swaying fronds, she kneels beside the water, which is cooler, much cooler than the ocean, and slits opens the guts of the fish with a knife, scrapes off scales as large as mother-of-pearl coins, and is rinsing out the empty bellies when a cracking blow strikes her in the back and rips open her new raincoat, her skin, her heart. Already bent forward, she falls into the water. Nothing has happened. But as she tries to get up, she sees blood bubbling up from her chest as if from a well and flowing over one of the fish. No, she no longer sees that now. The fish, bathed in blood, lies there in the sandy bed of the rivulet for a while, until a burst of water that had been dammed up by the corpse rinses it a second time and flushes it back out to sea.

Muyra. Bering wants to call her. The beach is deserted. There is no sign, no sound of her in the ruins. He would have to shout, cry out above the noise of the rain, and then the Dog King and Lily would also hear that he was looking for the Brazilian. He doesn't want that.

And why has Muyra left the dinghy, their equipment, lying open to the rain—the hammocks, the rope, the rifle? They have tarps, after all. Has Muyra got lost in the ruins like the others? No, Lily is back now. She's crouching up ahead there, wrapped in her army poncho, beside a brook. The spotty camouflage on the poncho makes her almost invisible among the dangling branches. She has her back to him, is scooping up water. Or is she looking for stones? Muyra has shown him people washing for gold at the mouth of a river near Pantano. But if he cries out Muyra's name now, calls to the ruins, Lily will be the first to hear him and turn around. She is always there where Muyra should be. Why hasn't she left for Santos yet? Why is she still waiting for an iron convoy, for trucks, when all she needs to do is book a seat on the overland bus? She should vanish, get out of his sight, now.

Leaning against the side of the dinghy, Bering is sitting in the sand, waiting for Muyra. This rifle here, is it lighter or heavier than the one Lily threw into the sinkhole? He weighs the carbine in his hands, estimates the distance to that figure crouching there. Fifty yards? Not even fifty yards. Not that he is *aiming* at the camouflaged figure. He is simply guessing the distance in the sight. Sees the poncho's spots of camouflage dance in the notch of the rear sight. Spots. Where Lily is, there are always spots. Camouflage spots, blind spots, there is always something to remind him of Moor, of what he has survived. Fifty yards. He could never shoot at anybody so defenseless. Yes, he could. Up there in the field of sinkholes it had been very easy. And *she* had been there, too, and had pulled him up by his hair. No, he is not aiming at Lily. He is just looking at those damned spots in the sight. And when the carbine suddenly recoils in his hands, yes, really kicks against him . . . and when the loud crack that has deafened him before, over and over, now echoes off the ruins and the cliff . . . none of that is part of him. It has nothing to do with him. He didn't pull the trigger. The rifle kicked at him and bruised his forehead. He doesn't even have to drop the weapon. It leaps from his hands. He didn't do anything.

But the spotted figure there, not fifty yards away, has grown even smaller. Something has fallen down out of the branches and bent the figure way over and made it smaller. Totally still, a camouflaged bundle, it lies now in the shallow, restless water.

He does not say: *Holy Mary. Mother of God. Help me. I have killed her.* Nor does he say: *Thou Comforter of the Afflicted. Thou Healer of the Sick. Thou Refuge of Sinners*—it all says itself inside him. A whole litany has to recite itself inside him before he finally does what he failed to do only just now: "Muyra!" he cries. "Muyra!" He bellows her name so loud and in such terror that a flock of herons, which has only just come to rest in the treetops after being frightened by the shot, takes off again.

What has he done? He has killed Lily. He has killed Lily. What should he do now?

Muyra has to help him. She is the only one who can help him now. He doesn't dare go to that bundle there. He doesn't dare go there. He is cold. Muyra has to go with him and has to tell him that he hasn't done anything.

The beach is deserted. The ruins, deserted. The boat lies untouched in the sand. There is only one path left, the path to the cliff. Muyra must have gone through that wall. From up there, in clear weather, she said, there was no more beautiful view of the mainland, of the coastal mountains. We'll need the rope, she said. He only does what she said. He throws the rope over his shoulder.

The iron ladders that lead through the wall and up to the lighthouse, which lost its light and roof long ago, are rusted, the steps broken. Gasping, sobbing, Bering climbs higher. He has always done what he is asked. And if Muyra were to tell him she is off to Monte Neblina, through the jungle, up the river, following the columns of smoke farther and farther, all the way to a world without people—then he would go with her, then he would do that, too. But first, just this once, Muyra has to accompany *him*. She needs to come with him, just to that brook down below, to that bundle you can no longer even see under the branches.

Help me. The litany recites itself again. Be quiet, he gasps, be quiet for once—*quiet, quiet,* over and over—until he sees the Dog King ahead of him. He forgot about him. Now he is suddenly standing in the way. Ambras has to get out of the way. He has to find Muyra. "Go away!" he shouts at him, "out of my sight!" He is ready to kill anyone who is blocking the path to Muyra. "Out of my sight!"

And then he realizes that the Dog King can no longer hear or understand him. Ambras stares at him so drunk—no, so deaf, so helpless, from so far away—that Bering awakens out of his own helplessness, his own terror. The Dog King is not just standing there—he can't go on. This part of the path, a stairway cut into the rocks, must have fallen into the depths a long time ago. All that is left is a narrow ribbon of steps and the bolts of a rust-eaten iron railing.

We'll need the rope. Bering only does what Muyra said. He takes the rope from his shoulder and ties one end around his hips to keep his hands free for the ribbon of rock. Muyra must have come this way without a rope. He wants to give her something to hold on to when she returns to the sea.

Can Ambras understand him? Bering presses past the mute man. Ambras does not have to steady him or hold him—Bering has often walked such paths alone in the Stony Sea before. All Ambras has to do is let the rope run through his hands and make sure the loops don't knot while his bodyguard proceeds step-by-step up the ribbon of rock and strings a new hold, a new railing, across the rocks. The Dog King takes the rope. Stares at him. Says not a word.

Bering is very calm now and has begun to forget his master again. He is already halfway to the next firm footing, when he sees what he thinks is Muyra's footprint in several crushed seashells brought up here by gulls. Then suddenly something tugs at him, tugs with such force that he is already falling before he can even think of holding on. A handful of leaves and white blossoms is all that he can grab in flight, and as the curtain of lianas is torn open, birds flee. Are those gulls? Wings, feathers brush past him. And that deep blue—is that the sky or the sea? The crests of the waves are very near. Or are those clouds? Right, right, those are clouds. Those must be clouds. And so he falls, a flier among birds, toward a whirling sky.

Lily is far out at sea when she hears a shot from the island. So the dogs come down to the shore after all, do they? The two fishermen nod and laugh. Dogs, sure. Dogs. Then it is quiet for a long time. Lily sits between baskets and tin chests full of fish and watches the island shrink, grow as small as a distant ship. A steamer. And the smoke is rising again now, too. A black flag above a stony funnel. There goes the *Sleeping Greek Maid*, the excursion steamer, on a cloudy, almost serene summer afternoon.

The pennant of smoke. Ambras finally sees the fire that for so long lay hidden and burning. He has turned around to his pursuer, who has followed him up the steep path to the top of the embankment. Ah, it's only one of those who beat people with steel rods in the quarry. He's not afraid of him anymore. But in the abyss that yawns behind his pursuer, in the depths, rather gray and insignificant now, he can see the camp—and there, between the barracks, the fire. Slowly but doggedly it creeps toward the drill field. It has burned all this time in its hiding place, in the ovens behind the infirmary. Now it is free. His pursuer cannot see the fire, but sees only him, yells at him. He has a rope. Does he want to bring him back to the camp? Does he want to tie him up again and string him up so that everyone can see him dangling again?

And then his pursuer has reached him. Strange, he doesn't hit him. Doesn't shoot. Doesn't tie him up. He presses past so close that Ambras can feel the breath on his face—and the man hands him the rope. Then he goes on, simply walks on by. Leaves Ambras behind. Lets him do as he wishes, spares his life.

And now at last Ambras is standing at the fence, at the barbed wire with white porcelain insulators for the high voltage. And yet with that first step he now takes, he feels no shock, no pain. And there is no rain of sparks, either. He simply steps into emptiness.

How light everything is in this emptiness. Wonderfully light. His searing shoulders, his arms—so light that now at last he can lift them over his head again, high over his head. And while the cord, the rope, the string makes circles, loops, spirals in the air, everything that burdened and tormented him loses weight. A cliff floats past. And then, freed of all its slabs and stones, the whole world grows light and lighter, begins to climb, ever higher, pulls the string gently from his hand and drifts away with the clouds of smoke.

Printed in the United States
by Baker & Taylor Publisher Services